GODIVA

THE VIKING SAGAS

WHITAKER
HOUSE
+
CastleRose

GODIVA

A Novel

DAVID ROSE

GODIVA: The Viking Sagas

ISBN: 0-88368-028-9
Printed in the United States of America
© 2004 by David Rose

Whitaker House
30 Hunt Valley Circle
New Kensington, PA 15068
website: www.whitakerhouse.com

Jacket Design, Illustration, and Book Design:
Koechel Peterson and Associates, Inc., Minneapolis, MN

Library of Congress Cataloging-in-Publication Data

Rose, David, 1949–
Godiva / David Rose.
p. cm.
ISBN 0-88368-028-9 (hardcover : alk. paper)
1. Godiva, Lady, fl. 1040–1080—Fiction.
2. Great Britain—History—Canute, 1017–1035—Fiction.
3. Coventry (England)—Fiction. I. Title.
PS3618.O7835G63 2004
813'.54—dc22
2004017750

1 2 3 4 5 6 7 8 9 10 11 12 **WH** 11 10 09 08 07 06 05 04

DEDICATION

This place we call earth with all its magnificence is also a place filled with endless reasons for cynicism. My own life has seldom been a stranger to what was a myriad of difficulties and sufferings that would have broken me, if it were not for meeting two amazing people.

The first is my wife, Toni. She truly is my heart, my soul, and my true inspiration. After thirty-four years of marriage, she is still the reason I continue to believe in that so-called antiquated notion of "true love." I cannot doubt its existence since I see it every day in the eyes of this beautiful and gracious creature. It is to her that I dedicate this book. She is my Godiva in the flesh.

I also dedicate this book to the second person, the one who looked down upon my years of utter distress and gave me life, love, and hope to see all the goodness that could still exist. He is the one who is truly loving and good, who continues to love us though we too often make Him look like a fool.

P.S. Lastly, I dedicate this book to the other great women in my life, my daughters, Rebekah and Esther, my son's wife, Rachel, and my four granddaughters, Hannah, Elizabeth, Isabella, and Skylar.

Acknowledgments

In any project like this there are many people who play a part in its success. I want to thank you all for your contribution. You know who you are.

I take my hat off to Bob Whitaker Jr. and all his amazing staff at Whitaker House. I thank you all for your hard work, dedication, and love for this project.

I say bravo to Dave Koechel and John Peterson for your generous support and artistic brilliance in designing a cover that conveys what I could only attempt with a thousand words.

I also want to thank two people in particular who contributed to the story of Godiva, Marina Muhlfriedel and David Michael O'Neill. What seems now ages ago, as I began writing I shared my excitement and enthusiasm with Marina, who worked with me writing and developing other screenplays. Both of us were excited to bring this story to the silver screen, and to that end David Michael O'Neill, a screenwriter whose work we loved, was brought on board to help us with the first Godiva screenplay. Thank you both for your great contribution to the story of Godiva.

Special Acknowledgments

More than any other person, my editor Marina Muhlfriedel contributed to this project. Her generous husband, Mick, with whom I share a birthday, must have had the patience of a saint. Marina's intelligence, sense of story, and creative genius, as well as her giant heart, made it possible for Godiva to be presented to the world. Marina, you are a jewel ready to be discovered, a priceless gem. I thank you from the bottom of my heart.

PREFACE

s extraordinary as it may sound, I can still remember that sunny spring day when my mother first told me of my family's relationship to Lady Godiva. It had been a long, cold winter and the warm sunshine was a great excuse for me to liberate myself from my winter clothes. Apparently I had gotten a little carried away. My mother found me naked as a jaybird running around in the yard.

That little encounter lead to what turned out to be one of the few sweet memories I had of my mother. She began to tell me the story of the Lady who had ridden naked on a horse through the town of Coventry; at five years old I thought that was about the funniest thing I had ever heard. My mother wasn't laughing, though, and after nearly fifty years, I can still recall the look on her face as she told the story.

What I saw was the first rare glimpse of the tenderhearted side of a woman I had only known to be harsh and mean. At that age I had no way of understanding the suffering and difficulties my mother endured, being the primary breadwinner for eleven children. All I knew was, for that moment, I saw the beast transform into a radiant beauty as she spoke of Godiva, permanently etching the images on my mind.

It wasn't the first time I had heard stories of my family tree that contained notable characters, both royal and common, but at that age I couldn't have cared less. My grandmother, who had died only a couple of years before, had been an avid genealogist with countless books and charts dating back numerous generations.

Was it the hand of fate that stepped in that day? Or perhaps what captivated me was the way in which my mother spoke with such reverence and admiration about a woman that she had never known. Regardless, I know this novel never would have come into being if not for the events of that spring day. What I do know is this: that my mother believed, as did my grandmother and great-grandmother, that they had been given a sacred trust to keep alive the true story of this beautiful, virtuous woman. After I saw the effect Godiva had on my mother, I began to believe it, too.

You can understand why the telling of Godiva's story has become so important to me. I have spent almost ten years researching both history and genealogy, traveling to libraries and countries and castles in the pursuit of the truest story of her life. Though, no doubt, some will disagree with my interpretation of the facts, I believe that I have found—with the aid of devoted friends—the true spirit of this remarkable person. Though she was a woman of extraordinary beauty, her inner beauty exceeded her outer.

—DAVID ROSE

FOREWORD
TIM LaHAYE

✦✦✦✦✦✦✦

Most of us have heard of Lady Godiva. "Didn't she ride naked on a horse?" is the common response. Some people may even be able to recite some additional facts: She lived in England in the 11th century, and she took the ride to protest unfair taxation. But unless they are medieval scholars, most people can't tell you more than that, which is a shame. For the real story of Lady Godiva tells of an epic battle between good and evil, between freedom and bondage, and between Christianity and paganism. It is a dramatic tale, rich in heroism, strength, forgiveness, love, honor, and most of all, faith.

In *Godiva,* author David Rose convincingly transports us a thousand years back in time. I have known David for some time, and the passion he has for Godiva's story has always been evident. As descendents of Godiva, David's family passed down her amazing life story from generation to generation. The tale of her courage and character has been an inspiration in David's own life journey and now, in his debut book, *Godiva,* he skillfully shares that legacy with the world.

Lady Godiva was a woman of extraordinary beauty, but it was her uncompromising faith in God that was her most valuable asset. She was a true hero for men and women alike, the type of role model we would all do well to acknowledge, a godly example in troubling times.

What I find most exciting about the story of Godiva is watching the characters' hearts change as a result of being in the presence of a woman who truly lived by the wisdom of the Gospel. A millennium later, the same thing is happening... the hearts of people are being changed today by Jesus Christ and by the hearing of His Word. Despite all our advances in modern technology—computers that can process billions of bits of information in the blink of an eye, or vehicles that can travel to the outer reaches of space—some things, such as our need for a Savior, never change. In that respect, *Godiva* is truly a timeless story, as relevant today as it was back in the town of Coventry a thousand years ago.

—TIM LAHAYE

PART ONE

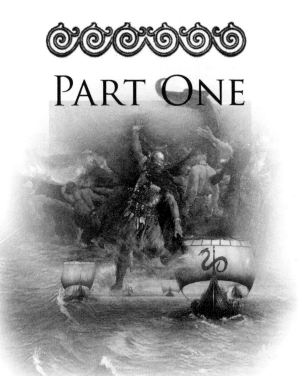

ONE

Spring 1016

T hreatening clouds blew in from the east, partially obscuring the light of the full moon. The wind began to stir, and a thick fog permeated the jagged English shoreline. The sheer cliffs and jutting rock formations, so rugged and regal by daylight, took on the eerie appearance of giants emerging from the moonlit mist.

The cold, damp weather was torment to the flesh of those on watch. Three burly night sentries of the Mercian guard peered into the choppy seas along the coast of the fledgling country of England. The soldiers had spent a boisterous night, full of wine and jesting, in celebration of a young sentry's recent engagement. Their eyelids grew heavy as the tedium of the dense fog and silent winds lulled them to sleep. The last embers of their campfire dwindled to gray ash and the world waited for the sun to rise. All was quiet.

Several hours passed. One of the men had begun to nod his head sleepily. His companions nudged each other. Suddenly, the man's head flopped downward, jarring him awake. He shook his head and peered out at the succession of crashing waves that had begun to pound the shore metrically.

"A storm is upon us," he muttered to the other guards, squinting into the fog. They laughed at his attempt at alertness after falling asleep on duty.

Then, in the distance, he saw something else, something ominous—a thousand glowing eyes advancing toward shore. Puzzled and frightened by the devilish sight, he rubbed his eyes vigorously and peered out again.

"Look! What is this vision that hell has conjured up?" he cried.

Out at sea, fire could be seen burning through the thick fog. Then they heard it. From deep within the gray, the terrifying bellows of a thousand shrieking voices washed up on the shore. The sentries scrambled to extinguish the scant remains of their fire and find cover as the veiled beasts moved toward them.

"Good God, have mercy!" one of the sentries screamed.

As the first rays of morning light splintered through the darkness, a dragon's head emerged from the mist, followed by another and then another, until as far as the eye could see, hundreds of Viking ships filled the horizon.

The dreaded monsters from the sea had arrived. Thousands of Danish warriors and their horses began to stream onto the shore, carrying torches and shouting battle cries. Viking scouts, most wearing tightly fitting iron helmets and chain mail, quickly found their way through the maze of stony spires while their comrades fell into line on the sand.

To the sentries above, it appeared that the cauldrons of hell had burst forth out of the fiery depths and spilt their venomous cargo on England's fair shore.

⚬⚬⚬⚬⚬⚬

The sentries raced off to warn their army of the onslaught. If they had remained just a few minutes longer, they would have seen a single ship, grander and more terrifying than all the rest, enter the harbor. At its helm was the most ornate of the dragonheads—a massive red and gold snout, wild black and green eyes, and jewel-encrusted pointed teeth. The sides of the ship were overlaid with thirteen distinct shades of gold and a huge royal Danish insignia. By its sheer magnificence, there could be no doubt; the gilded behemoth carried the warriors' leader.

Indeed, King Canute the Merciless, the fearsome ruler of Denmark, Norway, and Sweden, stood at the helm of the enormous ship as it ventured forth into the harbor. His hair and beard were thicker and darker than most of his troops, and his eyes were a distinctive brown with splinters of gold that seemed to glisten as brightly as his vessel. He too wore an iron Viking battle helmet, but his was carefully etched with a border of pagan symbols. Canute deeply inhaled the scent of wet earth and stayed attentive to even the most minute shifts of the wind.

The Viking warriors kept their eyes on the pagan king as he and his great ship drew closer. At Canute's signal, a mere flick of his wrist, thousands more of the warrior-soldiers, looking more beastlike than human in their heavy Viking armor and fur, thundered with their horses onto the shore.

Battle drums pounded rhythmically, reinforcing and exaggerating the crash of the waves. King Canute peered out at the shore, pleased. England, the fragrant fruit of Northern Europe, would soon be his. He cast his eyes to the red sky of dawn and called to his men.

"Look up, our future is before us. Surely you all can see that we alone are held in Odin's favor!"

A roar went up from the men. Canute's heart beat faster as he thought of the victory at his fingertips. He strode boldly off the ship, sinking his boot heels into the wet, gritty sand.

After weeks at sea, he was prepared for battle. He relished the awesome sight of his armada of ships. Thinking of the puny English army fighting against his mighty legions, he couldn't help but laugh. His commanders gathered before him. He gestured to some of the closest men.

"Bring that royal wench to me. Now!"

The men rushed to obey. Soon the sounds of a scuffle reached his ears. Several warriors appeared, dragging a frightened woman to the king. Her hair was tangled, her frock shredded into rags. She struggled to break the strong hold of the two Vikings gripping her upper arms.

"Though I hate to give her up, here she is, Your Majesty," leered Prince Harold as the men shoved the woman to the sand in front of Canute.

"Thank you, brother." The king regarded the woman for a moment with a smile that didn't quite reach his eyes.

"Ah, lovely Princess Élan, let it never be said that the king does not keep his word." He reached out his hand to help her to her feet in a kindly manner. As she found her footing, he softly stroked her tearstained cheek. She pulled away with a look of disgust.

"Have I not brought you back alive to your beloved England?" the king softly asked. He looked up into the sky. A brilliant flash of lightning streaked across the sky, followed by a low rumble of thunder.

Fear and awe spread among the warriors as they witnessed firsthand their king's legendary ability to command the weather. Such affirmation of the gods' goodwill swelled Canute's heart with pride. With a flash of power in his eyes, he turned and thrust his sword into the woman's stomach. Her eyes opened wide in horror. She grabbed hold of the sword then fell to the ground, stretching out her bloodstained hands.

"That, Saxon quail, was all I promised!" the king hissed coldly, chuckling as he yanked his sword from her flesh.

He lifted his bloodstained blade to the sky and called out, "We pledge to you, Thor, great god of thunder and war, that this will be the fate of all who oppose our rule!" With that, the king mounted his steed and rode through the ranks of his assembled warriors. His men let out a deafening roar—a battle cry.

The roar traveled up the hill to the waiting English army. Their leader looked out at his cavalry and unflinchingly raised his sword.

"Ride men," he cried. "For today we fulfill our destiny! Let us boldly ride to meet Canute and his warriors!"

Earl Edric Streona, the ruler of the northern portion of Mercia, England's fairest region, was renowned for his iron fist and bravery in battle. He was a striking figure, tall with a finely chiseled nose and chin that evidenced his Roman heritage. He was shrewd, aggressive, and well suited for both battle and civic duties. He knew quite well that England's fate hung in the balance with only him and his Mercian forces to fight for her survival.

From the back of the ranks, the Duke's wiry nephew appeared. Norman was sniveling and sly and could usually be found riding beside his uncle, groveling for favor.

"Uncle, wait for me! My Lord Edric! Let us ride, as you say! Let history write your name with blood and honor." He lowered his head in an obsequious gesture. "And may it humbly record my place, as well, right by your side!"

Edric rolled his eyes but had to grin. He was amused by his nephew's enthusiasm as long as it was convenient. Without replying, he raised his sword and rode off. His army deftly followed, kicking up grass and mud as they raced down the mountainside toward the Viking horde.

⚬⚬⚬⚬⚬⚬

"They come!" King Canute proclaimed, watching from horseback. He and his younger sibling, Prince Harold, watched the approaching English army descend from the high cliffs.

"Who leads them, my king?" asked Harold.

"I'm sure that it is Edric, Earl of Northern Mercia."

"King Edmund Ironside's brother-in-law? He rides to meet us?"

King Canute turned to Harold and the other commanders. They drew in, encircling him. Canute rode back and forth inside the enclosure. "Since Edric Streona has come to meet us, let us begin by demonstrating to him how the gods have chosen us to rule!"

With a mighty howl, he turned his horse, pushed through the circle of commanders and galloped directly toward Streona and his men. He didn't take his eyes off them as they assembled on the beach. Canute's forces followed him, struggling to match his breakneck pace. The two groups raced toward each other.

Edric yelled to his mount, pulling the reigns back sharply and signaling his army to halt. Canute followed his example. His massive white stallion shook its head violently. The two armies fell in line behind their commanders and faced off, with only the length of a jousting field between them. Neither leader drew his sword.

"Careful, my lord," one of Canute's soldiers whispered. Canute did not turn around. His eyes bored through Edric.

The earl and the king stayed utterly still for a moment. Weighing. Watching. Finally, Edric dismounted and walked slowly toward the Danish king. Canute's army gripped their weapons, prepared to strike at the slightest sign of treachery.

The king kept his gaze fixed upon Edric. He remained atop his splendid horse as the Englishman drew near. Neither spoke.

Then, Streona did the unthinkable. He drew his sword and slowly laid it on the ground before Canute. He bowed. Canute sat stone-faced.

"I don't understand, Your Highness," Harold muttered.

Canute didn't respond. He kept his eyes fixed on the Englishman before him. He would not be tricked by any duplicitous Saxon ploy. Suddenly, a knight came up behind Edric, handing him a large lumpy burlap sack.

"King Canute, I believe I have brought precisely what you requested," said Edric. He opened the bag to reveal the severed heads of two loyal English earls. "The heads of your enemies, sire. Shall I now be closer to you than a brother, as you vowed?"

King Canute snapped his fingers and a commander rushed forward to take the bag. Canute still did not break his probing gaze on Streona. He smiled slightly, showing his favor to the English earl before him. He reached out his hand, displaying a gold and ruby ring inscribed with the legendary hammer of Thor.

"The ring of power," the king said.

"My lord." Edric bowed again. Without hesitation, he knelt and kissed it.

Canute roared, raising his sword in triumph to his fellow warriors.

"You see how my words have power? Soon all of England will be ours! With Earl Edric on our side, their pitiful King Edmund and his puny army will be scattered like dust in the wind."

His men raised their fists to the sky, shouting and chanting victoriously.

"Arise, Edric, great Saxon betrayer," Canute ordered to the earl, kneeling in the sand before him.

Edric rose to his feet, pounding his chest and crying, "Long live the great King Canute!"

"Let us drink the cup of wrath and together conquer this land, for there is no power in heaven or earth that can stop us now!" Canute cried.

TWO

Morning sunlight broke through the clouds, bringing warmth to the farming town of Coventry, deep in the heart of Mercia. It would be hard to imagine a quainter or lovelier place. Even in those difficult times, the deeply rooted Anglo-Saxon community lived in relative harmony with those of the old pagan ways. The peaceful villagers went about their business, unaware of the events unfolding less than sixty miles away—events that would drastically impact their lives.

In a home, perched on the hillside above Coventry, the radiant face of a beautiful young girl reflected off a finely tooled mirror in a polished wooden frame. At thirteen years of age, Godiva was already a stunning beauty with shimmering fair hair, a rosy complexion, sparkling green eyes, and a brilliant smile. She thrust a sword at her reflection, pretending to stab at an enemy. She giggled merrily as she fought a mock battle until her play was interrupted by a voice calling her name.

"Godiva, what have you done with my sword?" her frantic older brother, Thorold, demanded from a neighboring room. "Not being allowed to come with me is no excuse for stealing my things."

"I won't give it back until you apologize," Godiva said, watching herself dramatically sweep the blade through the air.

"Apologize? For what?"

"Don't you even dare pretend not to know."

At that moment, Thorold burst through the doorway of her room, immediately spotting the sword in her grasp. "Aha! There it is!"

"You still haven't said that you're sorry," she taunted, playfully swirling the sword's point in the air before him.

"Godiva, give it to me! I have to go. It is my honor as the son of the Sheriff of Coventry to be there. And I still need to prepare my horse and pack!"

"Alright then, Thorold, if you really don't know, I'll give you a small hint. If you ever dare call me that again, I'll have your head."

"Oh, so *that's* what this is about."

"Apologize."

"Okay. I'm very sorry for..."

"Go on!" she said, placing her free hand firmly on her left hip.

"For the millionth time! I am desperately sorry for calling you a little girl. Now, dear sister, give me my sword!"

"Say please."

"Godiva, PLEASE give it to me! I have to go."

Godiva beamed widely as she handed it to her adoring brother, having gained the victory she wanted.

❀❀❀❀❀❀❀

Nearly two hours by horse, south of Godiva and Thorold's home, stood the venerable castle of Lord Leofwine, the elderly earl of Southern Mercia. With its double walls and four square towers, the stone edifice was one of the oldest and most elegant in all of Mercia. On that beautiful morning, a small band of the earl's guards was patrolling the periphery of the castle when a gawky young guard noticed something unusual in the distance. He ran to his superior, calling out, "Sir, an army approaches!"

The captain of the guard sped to the youth to see what the commotion was.

"Is it King Edmund?" the captain asked as two more guards joined them. "I was told that he is still in Ashingdon, assembling an army of those still sworn to England. Perhaps he is coming to visit the Earl."

"I think not, sir," replied the young guard anxiously. "I believe those are the Danish banners of King Canute. Look at all the men flanked aside him!"

Panic erupted as they surveyed the scope of Canute's approaching army. The captain quickly leapt onto the back of his chestnut horse and rode off as fast as he could toward the castle gatehouse.

"I must see Lord Leofwine immediately," the captain cried to the gatekeeper. "It's urgent!"

"He's not well, but I'm sure his son will see you."

The captain leapt from his horse, tossing the reins to the gatekeeper, and ran with all his might to the castle doors. He burst through, calling to a guard as he sped past. "I must find Lord Leofric!"

The guard yelled his answer to the captain's back. "He's upstairs in the library."

The captain found Leofric crossing the long upstairs hall. The tall twenty year old wore a somber expression on his handsome face.

"What is the matter, captain?" he asked.

"Lord Leofric," the captain panted, "it's King Canute! His armies approach, sir. We've seen it from the hill."

Leofric's face grew grave. "Canute? Here? What is his position?"

"He grows closer by the minute, heading straight for us along the road from the coast."

"And my brother?" Leofric hesitated. "Could you see my brother Norman or my Uncle Edric?"

The messenger cleared his throat. "I am not entirely sure, sir. They were still quite a distance, but I'm afraid, my lord, that it appeared they rode as well, along with Earl Edric's army."

"Did they seem to be prisoners of the Danes?" Leofric pressed.

"No, my lord. If my eyes did not deceive me, it appeared they rode freely on either side of Canute. They bore the king's banners."

Leofric smashed his fist down on the table, "Are you sure of this?"

"I am truly sorry to bring this news, my lord. What shall I tell your army's commander?" the captain asked.

"Tell him that I will meet with my father presently and to ready the army to fight."

Leofric turned and walked briskly toward the stone staircase that led to his father's chambers. The torches on the walls cast deep shadows on his face, exaggerating his frown. He stopped outside the earl's bedroom, took a deep breath, and knocked.

An elderly servant came to the door. Martha, his father's caretaker, was bent over with age, but she always had a kindly smile for Leofric. "Come in, dear Leofric. Your father is awake now." Martha had been with the earl's family throughout Leofric and Norman's lives and had cared for them since the death of their mother several years earlier.

"Thank you, Martha," Leofric said. He patted her on the shoulder as he passed.

His father, Earl Leofwine, lay in a large canopy bed that dwarfed his frail body. A pot of herbs and flowers was boiling over the fire, filling the room with the fragrances of foxglove and rosehips. It pained Leofric to see his father lying there, the shriveled shell of a once-great warrior. Leofric had the utmost respect for his father—even in his sickness, the old earl still had the capacity to govern Southern Mercia.

The old man moved slowly, grunting with the effort. He propped himself up on one arm and beckoned Leofric to his side. The effort made him cough, and his chest rattled as he fought to regain his breath. Leofric flinched at the sound.

He leaned in close, his eyes full of love for the man before him.

"Father, how are you today?" he asked, lifting the old man's hand. He hated to break the vile news, which his father might not be able to handle in his weakened condition.

His father coughed heavily before answering. "The same. Still the same, my son. What is it that brings you here? A visit for an old man or business of the house?"

"Father," Leofric began. "I do not wish to worry you. You need to rest and mend."

Leofwine looked up sharply. "What is it, son? You must speak plainly to me."

"I have some news, bad news. Norman had spoken to me about such matters, but I didn't believe it possible."

"What is it, son?" his father asked again. His intelligent eyes were snapping, as if he already knew the situation and was just waiting to have it confirmed.

"Norman, it seems, has allied himself with Uncle Edric. They've taken their armies and joined with King Canute. Father, they have betrayed England. The guard has just informed me that they are on their way here. They will arrive shortly." Thinking of all they had to do, Leofric jumped to his feet. "We have to act quickly! With your permission, I shall assemble the men to defend the castle."

"Sit down, son," Leofwine sighed.

"But we must be ready to meet them," Leofric argued. "I have heard that in these past weeks, Canute has already laid siege to four other Mercian towns between the coast and Hereford—with the help of my uncle and brother, I now realize!" Leofric's face flushed red as he continued. He had unconsciously balled his hands into fists. "They have killed their women and children, burned their homes, and pillaged their livestock."

"Calm yourself, Leofric!" his father commanded. "Sit down!" Leofric reluctantly complied. His father noted the anguish on his son's face and softened his tone. "How many men ride with Canute?"

"They are said to be as numerous as the sands of the sea. With Edric's forces, they will surely outnumber us more than twenty to one."

"As I thought," Leofwine nodded. "How far away are King Edmund's armies?"

"They are gathering at Ashingdon. Too far away to be any help to us now," Leofric answered.

Leofwine looked deeply into the face of his son.

"Leofric, I know what is in your heart. Even through these dimming eyes, I can see it clearly. You must realize that a courageous death in defense of this castle will never do England a toad's tail of good. I have apparently lost one son to King Canute. Although I love him, Norman is no longer a part of this family. I will not lose you as well! We must find a way to buy time and counter this unconscionable turn of events."

Leofric paced the room, rubbing his temples to soothe the pounding in his head. "But, Father...my own brother has betrayed us."

"Yes," Leofwine answered somberly. "My *son* has betrayed us, but there is no time for hysterical outbursts that do no good. We must be practical. Reasonable." Color began to return to Leofwine's pallid cheeks. His voice grew strong, losing the weak tremble. "Leofric, you must not agonize so—it will keep you from your senses. I have spent much of my life dealing with men like Edric Streona and King Canute. Trust me when I say that Canute will first come to our gate seeking not our blood, but our concurrence and support."

Leofric fretted. "How can you be so sure that he will not attack us instead?"

"Canute learned much from his father, Swein Forkbeard—perhaps the most ruthless of them all. Canute is a Viking. He will first try to force our loyalty, with the threat of a siege. That way, we suffer without the loss of even one of his soldiers—not that he holds any concern for their lives. He acts simply to conserve his resources. Our wisest course of action is to make him believe that we will not oppose him. For the moment, Edric and Norman's betrayals will serve as a cover for us. Canute knows as well as we do that his army is too large for us to resist. Now that Edric and his men have joined him, I fear that no one, not even King Edmund, would be able to stand against them."

"What if I were to take my best soldiers and join with King Edmund at Ashingdon?" Leofric offered. "Maybe then we could stop Canute's advances. We must protect the rest of England from falling into his hands! Please, Father, give me your blessing."

"Leofric, you look at me and see an old man and think I have no passion for what is courageous and ultimately right.

But sometimes, son, following your heart without scrutinizing the consequences is wrong."

"Are you saying that I would be wrong to join forces with King Edmund?"

Leofwine sat up as straight as he could in his bed. "When there was hope of defeating Canute, that would have been the most strategic thing to do. But now that Edric and your brother have jeopardized England's sovereignty with their treachery, we no longer control our destiny. We must put our trust in God and the wisdom He blesses us with."

"Are we to do nothing? Simply put our trust in the unseen?"

Leofwine smiled knowingly. "My son, you are young, you are strong, and your desire to fight is like that of a caged lion, but you put too much faith in the sword. Your courage must now be found elsewhere."

"But it is you who has always taught me not to surrender to evil."

"You are a man now, Leofric, and you must realize that a fight can unfold in many ways. This one is to be a battle of cunning and wit. Since our beloved King Edward died, many of the members of the Witan Council, representatives from every corner of England, have lost their will to fight. One by one, they have relinquished their support to Canute. King Edmund seems brave enough, but he is young, and we do not yet know if he will ever be able to raise an army powerful enough to defeat Canute."

Leofric stopped pacing and sat down in a large chair to listen to his father.

"King Canute has made a brilliant tactical move. By turning Edric, he now controls all of Northern Mercia. We in the South are surrounded and have been cut off from joining King Edmund. Your brother sides with Edric, so even our own forces are divided. We must comply while keeping our true allegiances secret," he explained.

"Yes, Father," Leofric replied gravely. "I understand." Then, after a moment, he added, "Father, I pray to God that some-day I will have your degree of confidence. But, you lie here weak before me, and while I believe you can and will regain your strength, I fear that, too soon, all this will fall upon my shoulders."

"As I appear before you, Leofric, I promise to stay alive long enough to counsel you in these matters. My sickness is not life threatening. Someday I will die, of course, but not this time. I give you my word. You must trust that God is still with us. Take courage. I need you to work discreetly with me for the day when the true England shall rise again.

"Now listen carefully. When Canute and his army arrive, you will be expected to ride with them on their siege of the towns between here and Ashingdon. I will try to get word to King Edmund of the subterfuge, but you must not let anyone know of that. As you go with Canute and Edric, you may find opportunity to help our cause. Do so, but carefully. There may be a trap. If he suspects, your brother will seek to expose your true loyalties in order to inflate his own importance. Be care-ful not to let them know your heart. If Edric Streona could so easily betray King Edmund, he and your brother will not hesitate to betray us as well."

"I understand, Father. I will do my best."

Leofwine reached for his son's hand, pulled him close, and kissed him lovingly on the forehead before bidding him good-bye, with his blessing.

☙☙☙☙☙☙

On a wide hilltop outside Coventry's gates, in view of Thor-old and Godiva's family home, stood a simple wood and stone church in the middle of a large grassy field. Beside the church was a small stone abbey. The abbey was surrounded on three sides by well-tended herb and flower gardens. A tall aviary, full of a variety of birds, filled the space between the two structures.

The abbess was a highly revered and kindly woman. To people for miles around, Sister Osburga was more than just a spiritual mentor; she was a mother, friend, and servant to all who knew her.

"There," Sister Osburga said as she proudly tended her garden. "Two more rows of petunias. The pink ones will grow nicely here in this sun." The nun's cheeks glowed apple red as she bent her ample bulk to dislodge a pennyroyal seedling that had taken root between the petunias. "Now, how did you find your way all the way over here? Wanderlust?" she asked the flower jovially, then called to a younger nun who often helped her in the garden. "Sister Agnes, would you mind bringing this wayward shoot over to the creek bed where the rest of his kind grow?"

"Not at all, Sister," replied Agnes. Osburga handed her the stem, brushed the dirt from her hands, and reached for her watering can. Agnes walked a few feet to where a spring fed a small stream. "Sister Osburga," Agnes began, hesitating because she liked to hear the story often and Osburga didn't like to discuss it and risk the sin of pride. "I just have to ask once more."

"What's that, dear?" the abbess asked, watering the blossoms with a gentle stream from her can.

"When you sang to the pope..."

"Yes? It was a most uplifting experience."

"Were you afraid?" Agnes asked, using her finger to wiggle out a small hole in the damp soil.

"Afraid? When I sang to his magnificence? Hmm..." Osburga considered the question, sitting down on a round boulder near the flowerbeds for a moment's rest. "One should never be fearful in the presence of those who are close to God."

"But it was the pope," Sister Agnes protested, patting the ground around the pennyroyal and rising up. "You mean you weren't afraid of the pope, not even a little?"

"To be completely honest, yes, I was a little afraid."

Sister Agnes grinned and scooted next to Osburga on the rock. "What was he like?"

"As I have told you before, he was old—old enough to be a grandfather. When he spoke, he was kindly but as wispy as a wheat stalk and nearly as frail."

Sister Agnes' face broke into a broad smile. Her eyes gleamed as she imagined the scene. With a twinkle in her eye, she asked, "Did you touch him?"

"Touch him? The pope? Agnes, sometimes I think I have been far too forthright with you."

"Go ahead; say it just one last time," she laughed. "I want to hear it again."

"Alright, Agnes. He put out his hand for me to kiss...and it smelled of garlic!"

Agnes burst out laughing at the thought of the pope being human enough to reek of his lunch.

Sister Osburga smiled, looking away to resist her own giggles. She knew she shouldn't humor the younger nun, but she loved to hear her laugh.

<hr/>

The elder Thorold, Sheriff of Coventry, was a gracious man who loved his family—including his children, Thorold and Godiva—and cared deeply for his neighbors. As Osburga weeded, he walked through his own gardens, waving to one of the workers in the field.

Although he was a wealthy landowner, Thorold was truly a man of the people. As sheriff, he was fair, judicious, and endlessly devoted to England and the young king, Edmund Ironsides. He was a spiritual man who believed in the work of Sister Osburga and generously supported her and the school and choir that she ran. He had sent Godiva to be taught by the abbess, and for many years, he and his family had provided the abbey with funds for land and maintenance.

"Leave enough peat for Sister Osburga," he called to the men putting in a row of young plum trees at the bottom of the hill. "She'll be tending her garden right about now, and it seems she can never have enough good peat moss." The men waved and nodded that they'd heard. They began to load a cart for her.

"Be sure to find out what else she needs," Thorold added, walking past a fountain where some small robins were bathing. He glanced at his son emerging from the nearby stables. "Thorold, come out here before you leave," he called. "I want to speak with you."

"Yes, Father? I was just checking my saddle, but I'm nearly ready to go," Thorold's namesake said excitedly. "Thank you again for the sword, Father. I'm so proud to be carrying the same one that you used in battle." He grinned, sliding the blade out of its sheath at his side and admiring its glint in the sunshine.

"Your mother doesn't want you to leave, you know," the sheriff said as they walked toward the house.

"She never wants any of us to go anywhere."

"How well I know that, son," Thorold laughed, reaching a hand out to stroke his son's hair. "Maybe we should wait for

Lord Edric and his soldiers. The king will need all of us if he is to stand against Canute."

"Father, the call was urgent. King Edmund must know that our loyalties are with him. I know that mother is worried, but I will be careful. I promise. I am a man now, you know."

Thorold paused with his hand on the door and looked at his son intently.

"I know you are capable of fighting, son, but this is a different kind of battle. You're going to need to be wise, as well," he implored. They stepped inside and Thorold called out to his wife. "Anna, come. Your son is ready to leave."

Thorold and Godiva's mother came into the front room. She looked like an older version of Godiva, though she wore her long locks coiled on either side of her head.

"Oh, Thorold, are you sure that you should really be doing this?" Anna asked, putting her arm around her eighteen year old's waist.

"Yes, Mother. I am absolutely sure. Someone has to take word to the king. Would you send a servant instead of me?"

Anna tried to repress her concern. "I have packed some pastries, ale, and bread for your journey. Please promise me that you will be back by next Sunday."

"Mother, please don't fill your heart with concern! I will be back on Sunday. There shouldn't be any danger. I will simply deliver our message of loyalty to the king and bring back his instructions. Now, where is Godiva? I want to say goodbye to my little...I mean...charming sister."

Godiva appeared instantly in the doorway. "Did I hear my name?" she teased. "You do know that it means 'God's Gift,' don't you, good brother?"

"Yes, we have all heard that many times," he replied, but his thoughts were not with the conversation. Looking at her as she stood beside their mother, he realized that she was indeed blossoming into a confident and attractive young woman. Even as her brother, he could see how striking she was. He would have to watch over her carefully—before long, there would be suitors to worry about.

"Godiva, come say goodbye. I have to leave." Thorold put his hand out and she playfully skipped to reach it. She was his little sister again. He hugged her tightly and she wriggled away.

"Father, I offered to ride along with him, but he and Mother think I should stay here. Can't I go, too? Please?" she begged.

"Godiva, we all know how anxious you are for an adventure. Certainly Thorold would appreciate the company, but I need you here. With your brother gone, who else will help me take care of Coventry?"

Godiva beckoned her father aside.

"Papa, I know what you're trying to do. But I am no longer a naïve little girl."

"You never cease to amaze me, young lady!" he laughed. "But you are a young lady, and riding to bring a message to an army is no task for you."

"Don't forget, Thorold," Godiva admonished him, invoking a long-running joke, "if you run into any dragons, be sure to save one or two for me!"

Thorold laughed, shook his head, and bid his family one final goodbye. He mounted his horse with the excitement of a young man anticipating his first taste of battle.

"Until Sunday!" he cried. "Pray for England!"

THREE

T he trumpets sounded, announcing the arrival of King Canute and his armies. Leofric slowly descended the castle's stone steps to greet the Danish king and his entourage at the lower gate. Beside Canute stood Prince Harold and Leofric's Uncle Edric, wearing a smug expression on his face. Edric boldly took the lead, rudely pushing past Leofric and entering the castle grounds, followed by Canute, Harold, and then Leofric's older brother, Norman.

As they stood inside the gate, a glimmer of nervousness crossed Edric's face. He gave Leofric a quick, covert wink, indicating that everything was okay.

"Leofric, greet your new king," Edric said grandly. "For in a short while, we will defeat Edmund Ironsides, and Canute shall be king of all England, unifying us with the noble northern lands of Denmark and beyond."

Leofric stared, waiting to see what his uncle would say next.

"Our new king has affirmed to me that your father and I shall continue to rule in Mercia as a reward for our loyalty."

Leofric bowed to King Canute and, as difficult as it was, cordially welcomed him to his father's castle. Norman would not meet his brother's gaze as he entered his home as a traitorous stranger.

Canute had been watching Leofric and, before he had a chance to say anything else, he wanted to put him to the test.

"You are Edric's nephew and Norman's brother, is that right?"

"Yes, Your Highness," replied Leofric, unsure of where the conversation was heading.

"You are reputed to be one of the finest young swordsmen in all of England. Do you think you are more skillful than I?" Canute asked calmly, but with a deadly seriousness beneath his words. Leofric sensed it, and chose his response carefully.

"I have always heard that it was you, Your Highness, who is *the* best swordsman in all the world," Leofric countered.

Canute laughed. A fortnight of victories and English plunder had left him jovial.

"Perhaps we will have a chance to test your skill," Canute mused.

"Any skill that I have is yours to command," Leofric answered.

"I like this man. I can see in his eyes that he is not afraid of me and that he knows the right thing to say, a man of both strength and intellect. Maybe we shall find some real men in this country after all!" he laughed. The company laughed along with him.

Canute paused for a moment to address Leofric again as they entered the castle.

"I have been informed that your father is ill. We have no wish to disturb him. But I would like very much to know if your hospitality includes any good ale because, young Leofric, we have traveled far, and I would like to celebrate with our newest allies."

"We have some of the best ale in the world. I think we can find something suitable." Leofric turned to alert the staff to prepare a feast.

Norman was fuming as he watched his brother play the adept host. Being upstaged made his blood boil. As the older brother, he should have had the distinction of welcoming Canute into his father's house.

Edric saw Norman's anger and whispered softy in his ear, "Don't fret. Your time will come." The two men walked in together, silently.

⊚⊚⊚⊚⊚⊚⊚

The next few days were a time of rest for the Viking army. The troops set up their tents in the lands surrounding Leofwine's castle while the officers were quartered within, as honored guests. The servants stayed busy preparing food and drink for Canute and his advisors around the clock.

Leofric was frustrated and woeful but followed his father's wishes and revealed not an inkling of his true feelings nor spared any expense or effort in providing for the army's every need.

In the meantime, Leofric hoped that he was buying King Edmund time to amass his men at Ashingdon. He only hoped that Edmund could recruit enough soldiers and weapons to have a fighting chance against Canute.

After a few days, Canute gave the order to move out, and his troops headed for Ashingdon by way of Coventry, pillaging along the way. Leofric reluctantly rode along beside his brother and uncle.

"We make camp at sundown!" a commander yelled out. "Pass it down the line!"

"Camp at sundown," echoed the call down the rows of men.

As they settled in that night, a page came into Edric's tent with a request that the king wished to see him immediately. Edric put down his goblet, nodded to the men gathered in his tent, and followed the page out.

The interior of Canute's traveling tent was as lush as a palace, with thick carpets, a dozen lanterns, and a heavy suite of furniture.

"Come in, Lord Edric," the king motioned to a chair.

Edric sat at the table beside him.

"Thank you, my king."

"What do you think of Leofric and Leofwine? Are they truly with us?"

"Out of fear or obligation, they will make motion of being our allies. Only time will tell if they can be trusted. We should be careful, though. I have my doubts."

The king nodded at Edric's evaluation.

"After Coventry, I want you to take your troops on ahead and join with Edmund Ironsides."

"Join Edmund, Your Highness?" Edric asked, puzzled by the king's order.

"Yes. Make sure he believes that you would support him to the death. Position your men in back."

Edric nodded, already anticipating the rest of the plan.

"Then," the king's eyes lit up, "when the battle is in full force, you are to turn on Edmund and strike his army as aggressively as you can from the rear. Do you understand?"

"Gladly, Your Highness," Edric bowed.

FOUR

E arl Leofwine lay in bed, his chest rattling as Martha applied an herbal poultice to soothe him. He had finally fallen asleep when Prior Albans, his trusted priest, arrived.

"Come in," Martha said quietly. "He was calling for you over and over. But now, oh, Father, I'm afraid it may be too late," she sobbed.

Prior Albans knelt by the edge of the bed, looking grimly at Leofwine. He reached over and gently folded the earl's hands across his chest, preparing to administer last rites.

Suddenly, Leofwine bolted awake. "What on this soggy earth are you doing, Father? I may be aging, but I'm not dead yet!" he exclaimed, pulling his hands away irritably.

Martha backed out of the room.

"But...but, I was told that you needed last rites!" Albans stammered.

"I sent for you as a cover," the earl said, calming down. "I must get word to King Edmund at Ashingdon, and there is no one but you who I can trust with such a task. King Edmund must receive this letter with my seal as soon as possible," he explained solemnly. "You should understand that its contents, if anyone were to know them, would surely mean both of our deaths. If it did not concern the very survival of England, I would not ask you. Will you do this, Father Albans?"

"Yes, sir. I will do anything you bid."

"I have decided not to tell you what the letter says because I know it is not in you to lie. I only ask that you find a way to keep the letter safe and deliver it to King Edmund. I have been informed that spies have been assigned to watch me," Leofwine added. "Therefore, you must avoid suspicion. Wait until Mass is over on Sunday to start your journey; otherwise, your absence will be noticed. I suggest you take the back roads and stop for the night to make sure you're not being followed." Prior Albans nodded as Leofwine explained exactly what he would have to do. "And Prior Albans, my dear friend, may God be with you."

"May God be with you, as well, my son," Albans said, placing the sign of the cross on Leofwine's forehead.

Early the following Sunday, the large oak door of Sheriff Thorold's manor house suddenly swung open. Godiva emerged, shouting cheerfully behind her, "I'm sorry, Mother, but I'm late. Sister Osburga is going to be upset if I'm not on time. She told me she would show me the falcon chicks before Mass. One hatched yesterday and there may be more now. I must go. I promised."

"Godiva, you must also eat your breakfast," her mother said, wiping her hands on her apron. "Furthermore, I don't want you climbing around in the aviary with your new gown. And those birds. If they soil you..."

Godiva interrupted. "Mother, was it not Jesus who said, 'Man shall not live by bread alone, but by every word that proceeds out of the mouth of God'?"

"My child, the holy Scriptures also say that you must honor your father and mother," Anna admonished gently.

"Oh, Mother. I do honor you and Father, with every beat of my heart," Godiva answered. She planted her heel and bowed low, removing an imaginary hat.

"Godiva," her mother sighed, exasperated, "If I've told you once, I've told you a hundred times. You are not a boy, and you are not to bow to me. You are thirteen, almost a woman! You need to learn to act like one. You must curtsy as a young lady should!"

"Yes, Mother," Godiva said as respectfully as she could, with an exaggerated curtsy. "From now on, I shall look only for female dragons, and instead of slaying them, I will curtsy and discuss the finer points of embroidery."

"Oh, Godiva," her mother laughed. "Your father and brother are to blame for this, exciting you with those stories of King Arthur and Boadicea. Run along, Godiva, and see your chicks. But after Mass, you and I and Abbess Osburga are going to have a serious conversation about the appropriateness of your behavior."

Anna couldn't help but smile as she watched Godiva hurry off. "Enjoy yourself, dear," she called out. "I will see you at the church."

Godiva raced toward the abbey. The gardens were in bloom and a sweet fusion of scents perfumed the air. She could hardly wait to see the newborn falcon chick in the aviary.

Outside the abbey, Sister Osburga absentmindedly pulled a handful of weeds from the herb beds as she waited patiently for her young protégé to arrive. She decided to go into the aviary on her own to check on one of the nests. Supported on an outstretched limb, Sister Osburga cautiously climbed up the tree to the nest that seemed to be in peril. She moved slowly, unsure of how high she could hoist herself up.

The tiny branch was bending under the weight of the nest. Osburga finally climbed high enough to peek inside and was rewarded with the miraculous sight of not only the falcon that had come out the afternoon before, but two newly hatched babies, and one that was pecking through its last bit of shell as she watched. She gazed in amazement as it found its way out into the big world. "How surprising it must be to see the light and feel the breeze for the very first time," she thought. "I never tire of witnessing the wonder of God's creation."

She contemplated the sagging branch and decided it would be best to move the nest. She reached out carefully toward the little chicks crying inside. Thinking that her hand was food, they cheeped and suckled her fingers.

Just then, Sister Osburga noticed Godiva enter the aviary. "Shhh," she whispered, putting a finger to her mouth and then motioning that Godiva should join her.

"Come look at this miraculous sight," she breathed. "Life appearing before our eyes! We must be very gentle, for some are still not hatched."

Godiva brushed aside her long thick hair. "How exciting! Oh, Sister, let me help you," she whispered, her eyes full of wonder.

"The limb is weak and the weight of the nest might be too much," the Sister explained. "We mustn't let them fall. We'd best find another support."

"Will the mother falcon know where you're moving them to?" Godiva asked.

"Oh, yes," Sister Osburga assured her. "We won't move them far. She'll recognize their cries." Osburga reached down, carefully handing the nest to Godiva.

"Move very slowly and quietly," she implored.

Godiva was captivated by the freshly hatched occupants of the nest.

"They're so little and perfect—trying so hard to figure out how to move. Look how skinny and fragile," she gushed.

Osburga glanced down at her young friend. "Fragile, perhaps, but one day they will be the most regal of birds, soaring through the skies, their majestic wings carrying them across God's great kingdom."

Godiva smiled down at the hatchlings. It was nearly impossible to imagine the vulnerable creatures becoming full-grown falcons. Osburga's simple words often gave Godiva a completely different view of life. Godiva thought about how Osburga was always a teacher, not only when they were sitting and studying lessons in a schoolroom. She looked up at her mentor lovingly, just as a sudden gust of wind ballooned the Sister's habit out.

Godiva tried her hardest not to laugh. She didn't want to jiggle the nest.

"Sister, I can see that as perfect as you are, you still have one...bad habit."

Sister Osburga stopped for a moment, unsure of the insinuation until Godiva's pun hit her. She looked down and laughed at the sight of her inflated lower half. She smiled mischievously at Godiva.

"Alas, sweet child, after we settle the falcons, I must try to fix the robin's platform. Run quickly to the work shed and get me Prior Albans' one and only vice."

Godiva almost took off, still holding the nest, when she realized that Sister Osburga had been kidding. "Tit for tat. That's a good one, Sister." Godiva returned to where Osburga was testing the strength of different branches.

One of the tiny chicks started chirping. Godiva stuck her finger out, and it attempted to feed. "Ooh! That tickles!" she shrieked before remembering that she was supposed to be quiet.

"And look, this one looks like a bony old man with a big nose. Sort of like...Prior Albans," she laughed. "Don't you think so, Sister?"

"You shouldn't say such things, Godiva," she scolded. "Even if they are true." Osburga chuckled, stretching out her neck to see. She found a perfect place and looked back at Godiva.

"Now, Godiva, very carefully hand the nest back to me." Godiva slowly passed her the nest. Sister Osburga checked a final time to make sure the nest was secure, then dropped to the ground as gently as she could.

"Well done, dear. They will be safe now."

Godiva eyed a ragged leather ball with thick flax stitching on the ground. She ran to it and began to kick it skillfully around, cautious not to let it hit any of the trees or disturb any of the birds.

"Playing with that ball again?" Osburga asked, smiling.

"It's fun," Godiva replied, passing it back and forth between her feet as gracefully as one dancing a jig. "I'm better than my brother at it, you know."

"I'm sure that you are," Osburga grinned. The church bells began to ring.

"Come, leave it. We must not be late to Mass! I'll race you to the church," she said. Godiva couldn't help but laugh. Osburga was older than her mother, but her zest for life was never short of exhilarating. Godiva loved her dearly.

"Impossible, you can't beat me!" Godiva shouted as she grabbed the ball and dashed to catch up with the nun, who was already yards ahead of her. Much to Godiva's dismay, Sister Osburga beat her to the church door, panting and breathless.

"I won!" Osburga said, hanging on to the doorpost, grinning from ear to ear.

"That's not fair!"

Osburga corralled her through the open door into the church as the last summons of the bells chimed. "Shhh. Straighten your gown. Mass is starting," Osburga whispered, suddenly the picture of grace and reverence. She glanced down. "Why did you bring the ball?"

Godiva shrugged her shoulders as an altar boy lit the candles. Smoke from the incense wafted through the high vaulted ceilings and within the rays of light filtering through the tall, leaded glass windows. The Christian families from nearby Coventry attended Mass there, and most were already settled in their pews. Prior Albans stepped up to the altar, ready to lead the Latin celebration.

Godiva walked toward her seat, whispering to Osburga, "See what I mean about Prior Albans?"

Sister Osburga had to stifle the laugh in her throat, but she gave Godiva a stern look. Such comments were inappropriate during the solemnity of Mass. She hated to discourage Godiva's exuberance, but the young girl had much to learn. Still, Osburga had to admit that the prior's resemblance to a newborn falcon was undeniable.

Godiva squeezed into a pew beside her family as Sister Osburga found her kneeling position next to Sister Agnes.

"Why do you grimace so?" Agnes whispered, looking straight ahead, her hands folded for prayer.

"I will tell you later. It's time to pray now, dear Sister," Osburga replied out of the corner of her mouth. She was already ashamed of her impious behavior in church. She made an effort to find a mind-set of worship and refused to look in Godiva's direction.

After the Mass had concluded, Agnes found the abbess in the churchyard.

"Tell me now! What was so very funny?" she demanded.

Osburga felt her pent-up laughter resurfacing. Again, she tried her hardest to silence the laugh, but it was vibrating inside her belly. She could feel the churchgoers glance in their direction.

"It must be the spring weather. It just tickles me," she blurted.

"That can't be all, Sister! Tell me, please," Agnes implored.

"All right," Osburga gave in. "Godiva pointed out that Prior Albans looks uncannily like one of our bald baby birds with its prominent beak. I can't get the image out of my mind," she confided, unable to restrain her laughter any longer.

Sister Agnes' eyes flew open, and she looked over at the scrawny monk who was conversing with some members of his flock. She burst out laughing and giggled into the long sleeves of her habit. Prior Albans cast a stern look in their direction. They quickly stopped laughing and looked away, knowing they shouldn't be poking fun at him.

Interrupted by the laughter, Prior Albans remembered that he needed to leave right away for Ashingdon. He ambled behind the church, where his wagon was already packed and, following Leofwine's instructions, left alone on the back road from Coventry.

◎◌◎◌◎◌◎

The open field in front of the church and abbey was quickly filling up with parishioners, as dozens of merchants appeared, some with carts, some with trays, selling a wide variety of foods and trinkets.

The children leaving church wasted no time launching into their games. "Look, there goes Godiva," Agnes said. "She is so lighthearted, a blessing in all our lives, is she not?" They watched Godiva weave her way in and out of the people gathering in front of the church, kicking the ball in front of her.

"Yes, she keeps me young," Sister Osburga responded with a benevolent smile at her pupil.

"It is the hardest thing for them to come to the church on such a sunny day. Do you remember how it was? How long Mass seemed when the weather was bright?" Sister Agnes asked.

"Ah, the precious impatience of youth!" Osburga leaned over to touch her head against Agnes'. "Why, when I was a child, I could hardly sit still. All I could think about was playing and running through the hills!"

"Do you know, Sister, I still think about playing...nearly as much as praying!" Agnes confessed in a childlike voice, gazing at Godiva wistfully.

Osburga had to hug her. "Me too, Sister. Me too."

Sheriff Thorold left his conversation and made his way over to his wife.

"Do you really think it's a good idea to let her compete in the game today?" Anna asked her husband. "I am told that it's to be mostly boys again. Sometimes I have to wonder..."

"She has plenty of time to learn to be a lady," he assured her. "And as I recall, you weren't much different when you were her age," he said, patting his wife's hand reassuringly. Anna sighed, smiling up at him.

The sun was high in the sky, with hardly a cloud visible anywhere. The children loved the time after church when they could all play together. Godiva's parents watched as she ran over to her friend Shannon.

"Follow me," Godiva said.

"Are we going to play with the boys?" Shannon asked.

Godiva looked to see if anyone was listening. She leaned closer and whispered, "No, we're going to beat them!"

She picked up the ball, and they ran to the center of the field with more children running loudly behind. Anna followed the crowd, calling out to her daughter, "Godiva, remember I want to have a talk with you and Sister Osburga!"

Godiva stopped and began to bow like a gentleman. Then suddenly, she remembered her earlier scolding and dropped into a perfect curtsy. "Can't it please be later, Mother. I promise I won't forget," she said as her mother caught up with her.

"Don't forget, your brother returns home today. I have a wonderful dinner planned, so hurry back as soon as you are finished with the game." She hugged Godiva tightly again.

"I will, Mother."

"And keep your gown straight! If you're going to play ball, you have to play like a lady, Godiva. I don't want you falling down and your skirt twisting up over the top of your head."

"Oh no! That would be improper," Godiva laughed, teasing a little. She waved her arms, pretending to lose her balance. Her mother shook her head, unamused.

"Please don't mind me, Mother," Godiva said, steadying herself and straightening her skirt. "You know I want to grow up and be exactly like you someday."

Anna's heart swelled.

"Go and play," she said. She had to admit she was proud of her daughter's words.

"Now, I don't want you to make a ruckus about it," Sheriff Thorold said, catching up to his daughter and wife, "but give them all you've got and win this match!"

"Just watch, Papa. I'll make you proud!" Godiva lifted the edges of her skirt off the ground and ran toward the field where her friends had gathered.

FIVE

T he children had adapted their game of kickball from
sports that the knights played, and they took it very
seriously. In the boys' minds, losing to the girls would
be the ultimate humiliation. To the girls, victory meant a coup
for their gender.

The captain of the boys' team was named Wulfstan. He and
Godiva had grown up together as friends and had both been
in Sister Osburga's choir since they were six years old. Besides
being a good ballplayer, Wulfstan showed promise in becoming one of the finest singers and musicians in Coventry.

"Wulfy, you had better watch for us!" Godiva taunted.

"Watch you what? Lose?"

"Wulfstan! There's not a chance you're going to win!" Shannon called, following Godiva's example.

"There's no chance I could lose, playing against you!" he
snipped back.

Sometimes Wulfstan and his friends seemed to enjoy teasing Godiva and her friends more than the actual ballgame.
Any of the young girls in Coventry would be pleased to have
Wulfstan's attention. He was one of the most popular lads in
town, coming from a good family and having such musical

talent. But not Godiva. She was more interested in competition than affection.

Godiva called out to Sister Osburga and Sister Agnes. "Watch me! Watch!"

"We are watching," they answered together as they settled into the soft grass. Godiva threw the ball to Shannon, who began to kick it quickly up the field. One of the boys, Rayal, raced over and shot the ball from between Shannon's legs. As the ball flew off, his feet became tangled in hers, and they both fell to the ground.

"Rayal! I can't believe you would do that!" Shannon ranted as she struggled to get up and straighten her dress.

During the commotion, Godiva ran over and rescued the ball, then drove it fluidly up the field. She deftly moved it along, enjoying the breeze rushing past. Wulfstan headed toward Godiva, intent on stealing the ball.

"Godiva, you should be back at the abbey learning to sew and tend herbs," he taunted. "You run like a silly, knock-kneed, little girl!"

"Wrong choice of words. Watch this," Sister Osburga said to Agnes.

"Little girl, huh? Not today, Wulfstan," Godiva yelled back. "Not when there is a battle to be won!"

Wulfstan tried to sound manly. "That's right, by me!" But his voice cracked mid-sentence, and Godiva laughed with delight as she gained speed. Now he was even more determined. He moved into his best defensive position while Godiva expertly maneuvered the ball beneath the long folds of her gown.

"You don't have a chance!" Wulfstan said.

"We'll see about that," she responded calmly. Godiva suddenly weaved right and fired hard. Wulfstan dived forward, but the ball flew over his outstretched fingers and into the trees. Godiva scored! Wulfstan shook his head in disbelief. The girls' supporters cheered, and Shannon ran to Godiva. They jumped up and down excitedly.

"Godiva, that was amazing!" she exclaimed.

Godiva looked for Sister Osburga. "Sister, did you see?" she called out.

"Yes, I saw!" the Sister replied as she ran out to the middle of the field to congratulate the two girls.

Godiva was so excited, she couldn't stop talking about her goal. "But I started all the way back there. Way back there!" she gushed.

"Yes, it was very impressive," Sister Osburga assured her.

Wulfstan just shook his head in disbelief. "Lucky shot, that's what it was! It will never happen again," he vowed. Godiva smiled and took a very exaggerated bow.

"Get the ball!" Rayal yelled, eager to get back to the game. He gestured toward the thick woods where the ball had rolled.

"Come on, Sister Osburga! Let's go get it! Race you!"

Godiva and Osburga ran happily into the trees to retrieve the stray ball from where it was lodged in the tall grass. Osburga bent down to pick up the ball when she thought she heard something—a low, rhythmic pounding. She looked up to see if it might be thunder rolling in, but the skies were clear.

Godiva heard it too and looked up questioningly at Sister Osburga. The low rumble quickly grew and, in moments, a multitude of horses was upon them. Godiva and Osburga peered out from the trees. They watched in horror as Canute's entire army raced toward the field.

"Oh, good God, no!" Osburga cried in fear. Her face went white as she grabbed Godiva's hand, pulling her deeper into the forest. They hid under the brush and prayed that no one had seen them. The horses thundered past, just a few feet from their faces. Osburga tried her best to cover Godiva's eyes and ears, but there was no blocking the cries of terror that had begun. Godiva pushed Osburga's hands away and strained to see.

"What's happening?" she cried.

"Be silent, Godiva. They must not hear us," Sister Osburga said, trying not to shake.

"Sister Osburga, who is it?"

"Shhh, don't speak," Osburga said, holding her as close as possible.

"Our Father, who art in heaven, hallowed be Thy name," Osburga whispered as fast as she could, putting extra emphasis on "Deliver us from evil."

Canute's assault cut right through the field. The riders crashed upon the middle of the crowd, wildly swinging their swords, not sparing anyone, regardless of age or class. Nuns, monks, townspeople, children, and even babies were slain without thought or hesitation. Wulfstan grabbed Shannon's hand and took off running, dragging her behind until a rearing horse struck him in the face with its hoof, knocking him to the ground where he lay unconscious and bleeding. Shannon froze, unsure what to do, then ran into the screams and confusion.

A huge Viking saw her as an easy target. She screamed, but he rode up behind her and struck her down with his sword—putting no more thought into it than a man reaping a shaft of grain with a sickle. She fell to the ground as her killer rode on without a single glance back. The people scattered like ants, defenseless against the great onslaught.

Godiva sobbed and trembled in the underbrush, her voice unheard over the cries of terror, Viking shouts, and horses' hooves. She squeezed her eyes tight as Osburga held on to her, praying.

The soldiers systematically doubled back across the fields and began combing the woods for anyone who had escaped.

"Check every tree and every bush! There have to be more people hiding," a commander yelled. Screams could be heard as cowering men and women were pulled from their hiding places. Even worse than the screams was the moment when they were abruptly cut off.

The slaughter grew closer and closer to Osburga and Godiva's spot in the thicket. The armies slashed through the undergrowth with their swords with no regard for the victims of their brutal destruction.

"They're coming," Osburga whispered, realizing there was no escape. She quickly lifted a wooden cross on a string from its place around her neck and put it over Godiva's head.

"I love you, my dear child," she cried, embracing her tightly. "Stay alive, stay true. Do not let what you see here today poison you with bitterness. I will always love you. And remember that all things work together for the good of those who love God. You must trust Him above all else. You may not understand this now, but someday you will." Godiva stared at her in shock, not realizing what her friend and mentor was about to do.

"Dear God, protect this child," Osburga prayed as she cupped Godiva's face for a final moment. "Watch over her life, and keep her safe." Tears were streaming down both their faces. Sister Osburga held Godiva's chin as she spoke so Godiva would have to look at her. "Godiva, be absolutely silent, and stay tight to the ground. No matter what happens, do not make a sound. Do you hear me? Not a sound!"

Before Godiva could answer, Sister Osburga leapt from the woods and ran until she was in the direct path of the soldiers.

Godiva tried to muffle her cries but the words rang out just the same. "Sister Osburga! Sister Osburga!" she screamed as Osburga did all she could to distract the soldiers from discovering Godiva's hiding place.

Osburga was only focused on distracting the soldiers to give Godiva a chance. She paid no heed to the carnage around her. She may have lost her nerve if she had realized that the Vikings had moved on from readily slaughtering all in their path in favor of raping any women who were left.

Osburga ran around them, yelling, not knowing what else to do. Then she saw something that stopped her in her tracks. Ahead of her, she saw a Viking rip off Sister Agnes' head cover and throw her to the ground. An anguished scream ripped through her throat as she watched Sister Agnes kick against the man's attempts to pull her habit up.

"My Sister! Agnes! O God, help us!" Osburga cried, wanting to sink to the ground in defeat. She knew she had to do all she could to protect Godiva. With all the strength she could muster she made her way as fast as she could away from the forest where Godiva crouched.

Osburga glanced back over her shoulder to check on Godiva and saw a Viking closing in on her. She waved frantically. "Run, Godiva! Run deep into the forest! Get up and run! Stay away from Coventry and hide yourself, for hell has surely come!" Godiva desperately tried to make out the words, but all she could make out was, "Run." As she took off running, she saw a horseman jump off his steed and wrestle Osburga to the ground.

As she fell, Osburga's arm hit a sharp rock, tearing her sleeve and gashing her arm. "Get up, wench!" the horseman yelled at her. Sister Osburga struggled to stand. She grasped her wounded arm and pulled her fingers away when she touched something wet. She was surprised to see them covered in blood.

⊚⊚⊚⊚⊚⊚

Leofric rode slowly, following the path of carnage. The stench of blood assaulted his nostrils. The sounds of battle rang in his ears. His stomach clenched and he fought the urge to be sick. He had accompanied the party as his father insisted, but he struggled with his decision. How could he be part of such destruction and hatred? He was alone with his thoughts. Norman and Edric had ridden on ahead, determined to prove their loyalty to Canute.

The field was filled with the dead and dying. Canute's army had effectively delivered their warning to King Edmund. No one had been spared in the ruthless slaughter. This would show the king of England that he should not expect a mere siege, but ruthless, bloody, carnal warfare.

Dozens of the churchgoers had been lined up in front of King Canute. He rode down the line, questioning them, "Does your religion not say an eye for an eye? Then learn well from your own teachings," he lashed. "This is your punishment for taking the lives of my countrymen!" The people cowered before him, terrified. Canute relished their terror-stricken faces. They knew that their lives were in his hands. He could kill them or let them live on a whim. Their God could not protect them against him and his gods.

"Bring me your most pious so that I might prove to you the foolishness of your beliefs!"

A monk was roughly dragged forward from the back of the crowd.

"Would you like to live? Or perhaps you would choose to die for your faith?" Canute taunted him. "Let your God save you now!" he yelled as adrenaline coursed through his veins.

He raised his sword and with a barbaric yell sliced through the monk's collared neck. The monk collapsed to the ground, blood spurting from his wound. The crowd wailed in horror. There was no way to tell what this madman would do next.

"Bring me a torch!" Edric Streona called out from the entrance of the abbey.

"Here!" one of his men yelled back, passing the fire through the crowd of soldiers. With a great heave, Edric threw it onto the roof of the church. His men followed his lead, rushing around the sides of the building, burning and smashing in the shutters and tossing their torches inside. The dry oak of the benches quickly burst into flames, which then spread to the altar. The candles melted into pools that dripped to the floor. The large crucifix crashed to the ground and was consumed by fire. More flames licked the floor until the entire altar was consumed.

※※※※※※

Three miles down the road, Prior Albans sniffed the air and turned to see a plume of dark smoke rise into the sky behind him. He stopped for a moment and held his heart. He closed his eyes and after crossing himself, continued onward, knowing he couldn't let Lord Leofwine down for anything.

※※※※※※

The wall of the church that supported the aviary suddenly caved in. The rush of air blowing from the outside fueled the fire and the flames roared, igniting the netting and sending trapped birds squawking and panicking in all directions. A small turtledove plummeted to the ground, while her partner hurled himself against the burning netting in confusion. From her hiding place, Godiva could see her beloved aviary in flames.

"No!" she screamed. It was too much to bear. She edged along the trees, keeping close to the ground. When she thought that no one was watching, she darted toward the aviary. She had to save Osburga's precious birds. She ran with all her might, not taking her eyes off the aviary for a second.

At that moment, Leofric arrived at the burning church and could barely believe his eyes. He was stunned at the sight of a beautiful young girl boldly running toward the burning aviary. She was completely unaware of a soldier chasing her. Leofric spurred his horse, cutting off the leering, young swordsman from his uncle Edric's army. "This one is mine," Leofric snapped, grimacing at the man's pockmarked face. The soldier shrugged and rode off in search of another target.

Godiva ran fearlessly into the blaze, and Leofric trailed closely behind. Birds were caught in the flaming net, and a falcon frantically flew above, screeching for her young chicks. Godiva made her way to the heavy support beam and began to climb. Curtains of fire rippled on every side of her. Leofric looked up as Godiva hung thirty feet above the ground, struggling to unfasten the netting. He knew she wouldn't be able to untie all the knots in time, so he raced forward and slashed through several of the ropes with his sword, releasing the birds to freedom.

Godiva dropped to the ground, avoiding the hot embers at her feet. She raced toward the falcon nest, not acknowledging Leofric's presence. She climbed out on the limb, stretched as far as she could, and lifted the nest, hiding it within the folds of her tattered gown. She ran out of the aviary and toward the woods without looking back to see if anyone was chasing her. She just ran.

⚬⚬⚬⚬⚬⚬

"This one is their leader," Edric Streona said gruffly. He pushed Sister Osburga forward, holding his sword at her back, forcing her to stand in front of Canute. Osburga looked sorrowfully at Edric. She had known him for many years and was at a loss to explain his sudden cruelty toward her. Canute was surprised that a woman—a nun—would be the leader. He yanked off her wimple to reveal lovely crimson hair that spilled down around her round face. Her blue eyes were opened wide with fear, but the result was a startling beauty.

"Such a comely woman," he mused. "I thought women became nuns because they couldn't find men who would have them," he taunted. "Maybe some of my men would enjoy making sport of you before I kill you," he said wickedly.

"Dear God, give me strength," she prayed, closing her eyes.

Edric Streona cracked the flat of his sword against her back. "Silence! Your prayers are an affront to our king!"

Osburga writhed in pain as Edric grabbed her by the hair and pulled her face up toward Canute. "Apologize to our king, for he wears the ring of power!" Osburga said nothing, but struggled to compose herself even as Edric yanked her hair again. "Now honor him and kiss it, wench," Edric demanded.

Canute held out his hand to Osburga. A sudden crack of thunder caused his horse to rear up. Canute looked up at the rapidly darkening sky. An unusual formation of storm clouds threatened to shut out the sun. The wind increased, but there was no other hint of thunder or lightning, just an ominous, encroaching darkness. Canute looked away from the sky and held out the ring to Osburga.

"I will not kiss it, for I have only one King, and that is Jesus, my Lord and Savior," she said, the strength in her voice hitting Canute like a slap.

"You are a brave but extraordinarily stupid woman," Canute chided. "Do you not realize that I hold absolute power over your life? I am the one who will decide whether you live or die!" he growled.

"You would have no power unless it was granted to you by heaven," Osburga replied calmly. A sense of peace flooded her heart. She felt the presence of God and all fear was gone.

"Are you saying that I need heaven's permission to kill you?" He was bemused. The power of her God could not compare to the power of Odin, king of the gods. "Where does this persuasion of strength come from? How did you learn to be so brazen? I thought nuns were meek."

Sister Osburga gazed at him steadily. Her brilliant blue eyes bored through him. Her red hair blew freely in the sharp breeze for the first time in many years. "If only you understood, for power does not come from rings or in omens from the sky."

"Do you dare mock the gods?" He stared at her, waiting for a response, but she was silent. His anger grew. "Answer me!" He slapped her. Her head snapped back, but she merely turned to face him again.

"There is no power in that ring of yours," she said softly. "I will not say otherwise, though you may slap my other cheek."

The crowd gasped at her insolence. Canute's soldiers could not believe she would challenge him. None of the people watching thought she would be allowed to live much longer.

"Stubborn woman, I have heard enough from you!" He turned to his men. "Gather wood and tinder. She shall be burned immediately!" he roared.

Sister Osburga's face remained clear. "So be it," she said quietly.

"I call out to my gods, and they give me calm seas and fair skies by their power. You call out to your God, and He does nothing!"

Canute's men rapidly gathered a pile of wood. Osburga's hands were tightly bound together with rough lengths of rope.

"Bigger!" Canute screamed, as the men scurried to finish the pyre. "I want the fire to be seen in every direction!"

"We shall see just how brave the nun remains, once she is in the flames," Canute told himself.

Moments later, the wood and tinder were set in place and Sister Osburga was tied to a post in the center. Edric lit the pile in three different spots with his torch. The flames instantly caught and began to consume the tinder. The fire licked at Osburga's feet and singed the bottom of her habit. Her face remained calm, and she called to Canute.

"You say that my God does nothing? Then why do your fair skies abandon you in your moment of victory? Answer me that, King!"

The king looked up at the mass of dark clouds. Since they had embarked on this quest, the weather had obeyed his whims. Try as he might, he could not rebuke the clouds. He fell silent, for once in his life, utterly speechless at the loss of his power.

Sister Osburga gazed steadily at Canute through the fire. Her expression was not one of fear, hate, or anger, but of compassion and forgiveness—even love. It tortured Canute. He watched her close her eyes, but at the end, she began, not to scream, but to sing.

Her voice was soft and clear, never faltering, echoing above the crackling of the flames. Her song was a simple repetitive melody of devotion and faith.

Let us praise, this day, the Maker of the heavenly kingdom,
Author of all miracles.
How He gave earth's children heaven for a roof,
And a world with lands such as these to live on.
Almighty Lord, we praise you.

Soldiers and townspeople, the powerful and the prisoners—all who saw her were stunned by the hymn that emanated from the fire. Those who knew her wept in wonder at her faith and bravery. Many of the English soldiers could not contain themselves. They began to wail prayers and scream for mercy. Canute could not avert his gaze, much as he wanted to block the sight from view. In all his years he had never seen such a thing. Sister Osburga was engulfed by the inferno. Her habit was in flames, her red hair burning so brightly that the people could not distinguish the hair from the flame. But still she did not stop singing....

Let us praise, this day, the Maker of the heavenly kingdom,
Author of all miracles.

Everyone stood motionless, frozen by her song.

Finally, Edric could no longer stand it. He thrust his sword into the fire. It was less an act of mercy than a way to end the torture of the awful beauty of the Christian woman's song. Sister Osburga was at last free from the agony of the fire, and safe in the arms of her Lord.

SIX

Sister Osburga's ordeal distracted Agnes' attacker and he left her, shaking and bruised, on the ground. As he headed curiously toward the commotion of the fire, she managed to escape into the forest. Agnes felt the complete numbness of deep shock and wandered aimlessly, unseeing of her surroundings.

"Osburga, we have to get back now," she called out as she stumbled along, eyes glazed over.

A short distance away, Godiva carefully placed the falcon nest on an obscured branch of a secluded tree. Having completed her task, she looked around to make sure no one was nearby. Suddenly, she thought she heard someone approaching and quickly crouched down amid some brambly blackberry bushes.

"Someone's moving through the brush here!" she heard a man call out. She could hear his boots tramping closer. Suddenly, he lifted a branch and was face to face with a huddled Godiva. Realizing that she had been found, she rolled to her left, leaped to her feet, and ran frantically through the forest. She jumped over several fallen trees, dodging limbs as she desperately tried to lose her pursuer.

The traitorous English raider raced ahead to cut her off. He was the same one who had pursued her earlier when she was running to the aviary. She could not evade him, and as she tore past, he reached out and tackled her to the ground. "Now I finally got you!"

Godiva screamed. Her pursuer was the most wretched looking man she had ever seen. He had a long wooly beard, blackened teeth, stubby fingers, and a crooked nose that had obviously been broken on more than one occasion.

"Such a pretty little girl," he drooled. "You look frightened. Don't worry. I think you'll live for a little while longer. I don't even want to hurt you. See? Here, I'll give you a nice kiss," he jeered.

He pinned her arms with one hand while pulling her head toward him. Godiva struggled against him, stretching her neck and shaking her head vigorously.

"Please, let me go!" Godiva pleaded. A twig snapped loudly behind the soldier. He turned, keeping a tight hold on Godiva's arms. A broadsword whistled through the air and struck the middle of the man's chest. The astonished raider looked up in horror to see the hurler before collapsing to the ground.

"I told you this one is mine!" Leofric scolded. Godiva recoiled in horror as Leofric yanked his sword out of the body.

"He won't be bothering you anymore," he said softly, trying not to frighten the trembling girl any more. He lifted Godiva onto his horse and swung up behind her. "You were the one setting the birds free, weren't you?" he asked kindly.

Godiva looked up at him with wide eyes. "Aren't you going to kill me?"

"No, of course not. I saw you before and didn't want you to get hurt. You were saving the birds..."

"Yes, that was me. I just put the nest over there." She motioned back to where she had hidden in the woods.

"That was very brave of you," Leofric said. "What is your name, child?"

"I am Godiva. My father is Thorold, the sheriff."

"Thorold of Coventry? I know of him. My name is Leofric. I am the son of Earl Leofwine." He paused to listen. The sound of horses was drawing uncomfortably close.

"We must be very quiet or they'll find us, Godiva," he said in her ear. "Hold on tightly!" He quickly guided the horse deeper into the forest, further from the other soldiers. Godiva's knuckles were white as she gripped the edge of the saddle.

As they rode, Godiva noticed a familiar figure teetering at the edge of a small abutment ahead. Water was gushing from a spring in front of the woman and bubbling over the rocks to the stream below.

"Agnes! It's Sister Agnes!" Godiva said, pointing. "She's alive!"

Leofric assessed the situation and quickly rode up to the nun. He helped Godiva dismount beside the shivering, disheveled woman. "Both of you must jump down into the stream. The soldiers will not be able to find you in the water. Hide beneath those rocks, and I will lead them in another direction. Now go, as fast as you can, and stay far away from Coventry!"

Godiva hesitated at the edge of the drop. She contemplated the icy water and then the noise of the horses, which suddenly seemed to grow much louder. Leofric saw the determination in her eyes as she grabbed Sister Agnes' hand and pulled her over the edge, splashing into the water below.

Leofric watched the two women dragging themselves against the current to hide beneath a rocky overhang. They were safe, at least for the moment. He was riding back toward the soldiers when Edric and several other man intercepted him.

"What have you been doing, Leofric? We heard voices."

"It was nothing. I thought I saw someone trying to get away," he said, brushing aside their questions.

"Let me see your sword," Edric ordered.

"What?" Leofric asked, startled.

"Your sword. Hold it up," Edric repeated.

Slowly, Leofric unsheathed his weapon and displayed it for his uncle. The blood of the soldier still stained the blade. Edric reached for his nephew's wrist, raising the sword into the air.

"Look, Norman, you were wrong. Maybe there is hope for your brother after all." He returned the sword and heartily patted Leofric on the back. Leofric gratefully pondered the soldier's blood that may have saved his life. Edric gave the signal for the solders to continue their search, but Leofric lingered for a moment.

As the raiders crested the hill, Leofric looked back toward where Godiva and her friend had hidden. He bowed his head and whispered a prayer. "Dear God, take care of this girl, Godiva, and I pray Thee, give me strength to do what is right."

SEVEN

T he news of the attacks on the abbey had barely reached Coventry before the first warriors entered the town gates. Like a wave of locusts, the initial surge of raiders, led by Prince Harold, swarmed in, indiscriminately destroying everything and everyone in their path. The citizens of Coventry had no time to react. Some tried to hide while others ran terrified through the narrow lanes and across open fields, hoping to get away—only to be struck down effortlessly by Vikings on horseback.

The raiders were everywhere, murdering, looting, and raping, just as they had at the abbey. None were spared. The soldiers confiscated livestock and food stores then torched the barns and silos that had held them.

As Harold and his men destroyed the town, King Canute headed past the main gates with a smaller group of soldiers—straight for the sheriff of Coventry's house.

❦❦❦❦❦❦

Sheriff Thorold and his wife were busy with preparations for their son's homecoming when the bad news came. Thorold was writing a letter in his study when he was disturbed by his wife's screams.

"Thorold! Oh, no! Thorold!"

He jumped up, overturning the ink stand as he tried to replace the quill and ran downstairs to find his wife wringing her hands and crying hysterically.

"The abbey! They've attacked the abbey, Thorold," Anna screamed.

"What happened? What's going on?" he asked fearfully.

"We have to get back there! The Vikings, they've arrived and they're killing everyone! The neighbor's son escaped. We have to find Godiva, Thorold! O God, don't take my daughter! My daughter!" Anna's words were lost in her weeping. She stumbled blindly toward the front door, followed closely by her husband. When she opened the door, she found herself face to face with King Canute, Earl Edric Streona, and their men.

"Oh, my lord," she gasped.

"Where is the sheriff?" Edric questioned sternly.

"Here I am," Thorold said, stepping out behind his wife. "What do you want?" He recognized Earl Edric and Norman, and took in the rest of the soldiers. They were holding bloody swords, and many wore clothes that were certainly not English. He knew that it had to be none other than the legendary King Canute who now stood directly before him. He protectively clasped his wife's arm, moving in front of her so he could shield her with his body. Anna was frozen in fear, staring at the blood that dripped from Edric's gloves.

"Edric, I didn't realize..." Thorold began and then faltered. By his sycophantic position next to the Viking king, it was obvious that the earl would be no help. The last bit of hope drained from Thorold's heart. He turned to Canute. "Please, sir, I need to find my daughter."

Canute cut him off impatiently. "Thorold, Sheriff of Coventry, it is your duty to ride with us. Prepare yourself and your men."

"But, Your Majesty..."

Edric cut in. "Thorold, I have gone to great lengths to intercede on your behalf to the king, asking him to spare your life and that of your wife. Do not make me look like a fool. Mercia is in service to King Canute. You have only one choice: Either you are with us or you are dead. You must decide now."

Thorold opened his mouth to speak, but before he could, he was stopped by the sound of screaming.

"Stop it! Let go of us!"

Several Viking soldiers were dragging two young girls and their parents across the yard. The mother was crying and screaming, "Please don't hurt us!" The children clung to their mother, wailing in fright.

"Thorold, I think that's it time you make a choice," Canute said. "These people are traitors to the crown. You must do your duty and kill them."

"These are my neighbors. They are not traitors," Thorold pleaded. "Please, they've done nothing to deserve death. Spare them, and I will ride with you."

"Are your loyalties with us or not?" Canute challenged. "You will draw your sword and kill them to show me that you can be trusted or you will watch them die and then face the sword yourself."

Thorold looked to his wife and then to his neighbors, his friends, whose eyes pleaded for help. Save us, they seemed to be saying. He searched his conscience for what he should do or say, trying to find a way out.

"Please, sir, have mercy," the woman begged.

Thorold looked across the valley to the smoke still rising from the smoldering abbey. Then he turned to the town and saw the soldiers wreaking havoc. He thought of Godiva, and his heart pounded with fear and anger. She could be lying somewhere dead, or hiding in fear, or struggling with a soldier like the two little girls before him now. He could take no more. The only solution was to kill Canute right then and there. He grabbed the sword that Edric was holding out to him and pointed it at the king.

"Thorold!" Anna cried out, as the king laughed at her husband, daring him to act.

Thorold closed his eyes for a moment, holding the sword high in the air. He lunged toward the king, but was stopped almost immediately by two huge Vikings. They held his arms to the side as he struggled in helpless rage. Finally, with a cry of frustrated rage, he let the sword drop from his fingers. It hit the ground with a thud.

"I refuse to harm these innocent people!" he yelled out, hanging limply from the Vikings' grasp. "Kill me if you must."

Canute nodded at Edric, and he bent to pick up his sword.

In the sudden quiet, Thorold began to pray, lifting his hands to the heavens. "Our Father, who art in heaven, hallowed be Thy name."

"Shut up!" Canute cried, covering his ears. "I said shut up!" He could stand it no longer.

Defiantly, Anna and the others began to pray with him. "Thy kingdom come, Thy..."

"Kill them all! Destroy everything!" Canute screamed. With all of his rage, he drew his sword and ran it through Thorold. The warriors took the signal and attacked. Anna fell as a sword was pulled out of her back. The cries of the neighbor's children were quickly silenced and, in a matter of seconds, the life of every Saxon on the grounds had been taken and the manor had been set ablaze. Rain began to fall, and the clouds, smoke, and thunder engulfed Coventry and its surroundings, swallowing them up.

EIGHT

Godiva and Sister Agnes huddled together beneath the rocks in a hollow barely big enough for them both. Godiva hadn't realized that she had suffered burns but now they were throbbing, and she did her best to ease the pain by splashing them with the cool water. More than an hour had passed and the light had grown dim. They were both hungry and shivering. The rain fell in curtains and showed no sign of relenting.

"We need to find a better hiding place than this," Godiva said, summoning her courage and looking out. "Without food and shelter, and in this rain, we'll soon become ill. Come on, Sister Agnes. Let's go."

"No, no, no!" Agnes moaned. "The soldiers are still out there. I can hear them. We have to stay here." The wind howled and drove the stinging rain into them.

"They're gone, Sister Agnes. We're alone. We can't just stay here, and I have to find my parents." Godiva assumed that the raiders had moved on from their patch of woods. They hadn't heard anything in quite a while. She left Agnes for a moment and ventured slowly out, listening for the slightest indication that the enemy raiders were still nearby.

The rain pounded on Godiva, and all she could hear was the thunder and the roiling waters around her.

"Sister, we're going to find a better shelter. Come with me," she said, ducking back in to stoop beside her. Sister Agnes didn't respond. She stared blankly ahead as if she hadn't heard a word Godiva had said.

"Agnes?" Godiva said, shaking her gently to get her to respond. She sighed in frustration and turned to go. "I'll come back for you soon."

Sister Agnes looked up in alarm.

"Where are you going, Godiva?"

"To find us someplace safe."

"Don't leave me alone! We're safe here."

"Come on, Agnes. We must go very quietly. No one will hear us. There's a path we can follow," said Godiva. Agnes allowed herself to be led out from under the rocks and water and into the open. She looked around with wide eyes, like a scared rabbit. Godiva took her hand, and they moved cautiously into the woods.

The rain slowed as they followed the overgrown trail. Godiva didn't know where they were heading, and she couldn't ask Sister Agnes. The nun was talking softly to herself and didn't seem to be aware of what was happening. Godiva just continued to trudge forward, telling herself that every step was taking them further from danger. She squinted into the trees ahead.

"Agnes, what's that?"

"Hmm."

"Agnes, that building. Do you know what it is? Maybe we can hide there."

Agnes' eyes cleared. "Hermitage," she murmured. "The monks, they go there for solitude and silence."

"Come on, we can at least get out of the rain," Godiva said, relieved. She ran the last few steps and lifted the wooden latch.

The small shack was dilapidated and dusty but dry. Godiva wiped her soaking face with her dress, squeezed water from her gown, and shook the rain from her long hair before stepping inside.

⚬⚬⚬⚬⚬⚬

The hermitage was sparsely furnished. A rough-hewn table and chair and a straw mattress were the only furnishings, but there were two thick blankets folded neatly on the bed.

Sister Agnes was trembling miserably. Godiva helped her wring the water out of her torn habit, noticing the awful bruises and scratches along her arms and legs. Godiva took her hand and looked her in the eye.

"You'll be alright. They will heal," she promised. Godiva glanced around and saw enough dry wood to make a fire. "Look, we'll soon be warm."

As Godiva bent down to arrange the logs, Sister Agnes lay trembling on the mattress and began to cry. She wept bitterly, sore in body, mind, and soul from the way the soldier had touched her. She could never tell anyone of her awful shame. Godiva tried to comfort her but didn't know what to do. She knew that Agnes was scared, but she couldn't see anything physically wrong, and she was too young to suspect what the soldier had done. Agnes sobbed until she at last drifted into a restless sleep. Godiva stirred the fire with a stick and sighed, listening to the gentle crackling of the logs. She closed her weary eyes, wrapped herself in a blanket, and lay down to rest in the firelight.

"Sister Osburga! Sister Osburga! Where have you gone?" Agnes cried out, jarring Godiva awake. Godiva moved to the nun's side, put her arms around her, and held her for a moment.

"Wake up, Agnes. It's just a dream." Godiva began crying and couldn't stop the tears. She could take no more.

"I have to go, Sister Agnes. I have to look for my parents. I hate to leave you alone, but I must find them."

"No! We can't go out there," whimpered Agnes.

"You stay here, Sister," said Godiva. "No one will find you here. I'm going home. I'll come back for you later, after I find my family."

Godiva left before Agnes could object again. Agnes turned her face to the ground and sobbed.

Returning from his journey to the king, Thorold had almost reached Coventry. When he crested the next hill, he'd be able to see his family's home. He came bearing good news. He was greatly reassured by the vast number of soldiers that King Edmund had managed to recruit. His father would rejoice at the news. But something was wrong. As he turned onto the south road, Thorold saw grey gusts rising in the distance from where the abbey should have been. Acrid smoke filled his nostrils.

"My God! What has happened? Faster," he screamed, spurring his horse and galloping toward the smoke. His heart pounded. Had there been a fire at the abbey? Was it an accident? He tried not to dwell on his worst fears.

As he approached the abbey, he couldn't believe his eyes. Nothing of the buildings remained. Motionless bodies lay in various positions on the ground. Children lay facedown on the grassy field in puddles of their own blood. He spotted a girl with blond hair. Fearful that it was his sister, Thorold slowly dismounted, walked over, and gently turned her over.

It was Godiva's friend Shannon. Thorold turned his head and retched into the grass.

"Godiva! Godiva!" he screamed. He left his horse and raced across the field, examining each broken body, praying that he wouldn't find his sister. His eyes swept the gruesome scene. "Help me, God!" he wailed. In the midst of the horror, he could just make out the burnt remains of Sister Osburga's funeral pyre. It was incomprehensible. He shook himself vigorously, wanting to awake from the terrifying nightmare.

"Father? Mother? Godiva?" he screamed as he rode through the area in a panic. There was no answer. He had heard for many years about the brutality of the Vikings, but never thought he would see it with his own eyes. In the time he was gone, the Vikings had taken everything he held dear. His friends, his church—if only he could find his family safe. The optimism he had felt about King Edmund had disintegrated, leaving only gnawing despair.

Thorold searched madly for any sign of his loved ones. He turned his horse and galloped toward home, praying for a miracle the whole way.

⊗⊗⊗⊗⊗⊗

Godiva made her way from the hermitage in the woods up the hilltop path. She recognized her surroundings and stood for a moment, contemplating the best way to her home. She was still cold and wet, and the sun was dipping low in the west, when she reached the hill across from her house. She stopped, shocked, trying to match the sight before her with the picture she had in her mind. There, smoldering in the distance, were the remains of the home she had been born in—the home she had slept in every night of her life.

Her footsteps became heavy and deliberate. She started slowly up the path to the manor house and saw a dead boy in the front garden. It was the eleven-year-old son of one of the workers. She froze, afraid to go on. It was deathly quiet. Would the tragedy of this awful day never end?

"Where is everyone else?" she whispered.

She took a few more steps and noticed some shredded pieces of fabric. It was part of the blue and white smock that her mother had worn to Mass that morning. Her mother was lying facedown in the gravel, her arm outstretched before her.

"Mother!" Godiva screamed. "No, no, no!" She fell to the ground and cradled her mother's body. Her face was burned and discolored by blood and dirt. Godiva wrapped her hand around a golden locket that adorned her mother's neck. She remembered admiring it just that morning. It seemed like a lifetime ago. She couldn't believe that the vibrant woman who had scolded her and hugged her was the heavy, lifeless body that she now rocked in her arms.

Then Godiva noticed her father a few feet away. She reached for his large, limp hand and clutched it tightly. She let out an anguished wail.

Thorold found her this way when he arrived a few moments later. He had raced toward the sound, relieved to hear someone else alive.

"Godiva?" He ran to her, threw his arms around her, and tried to pull her away. She refused to move, pushing away his hands.

"Godiva, it's okay. I'm here, it's okay," he said, trying desperately to console her and harness his own devastation at the same time. He wrapped his arms around Godiva's shoulders, and they wept together. The rain started again, and the entire earth seemed to wail with them.

NINE

K ing Canute sat before a roaring fire with Prince Harold, Earl Edric, Norman, and his commanders. The Cofa Tree, a massive ancient oak considered the most sacred site in all of Mercia by the pagans, towered above them. The tree itself was an object of worship—a symbol of life and fertility. The imposing oak glowed in the flickering light. Buildings still burned close by. The dead of Coventry lay everywhere. Canute and his men feasted upon stolen livestock and everyone indulged in vast amounts of ale and communion wine taken from the church.

Canute leaned over to his brother. "It's been raining ever since we put the nun to the stake. Do you think the gods still favor us, Harold?"

"Of course, brother," Harold replied, shoving a tender chunk of lamb into his mouth and downing it with ale. "Our victory is a sign of their favor. It may rain, but the fires still burn."

The king brooded, staring into the fire. Even drunkenness had not improved his spirits. Instead, he was more morose than before. Usually the picture of control, he sloppily slurred his words.

"The weather, it changed. You saw it, Harold. Do you think the nun made it rain?"

Harold wished Canute would stop dwelling on the subject and enjoy the victory celebration. What was one life? Out of the hundreds they had killed, why did Canute suddenly care so much about this individual woman?

"Did you notice the nun didn't cry out even once? She was singing. Singing!" Canute exclaimed.

"Don't trouble yourself with this woman," Harold said, reaching for a hunk of bread.

"I'm not troubling myself!" Canute said, poking Harold in the chest. "I've just never seen such bravery, even in our own warriors. I don't understand how she did it. Why didn't she cry out?

"When I was only thirteen, I saw them put Uncle Bjorn, the bravest of warriors, to the torch at the battle of Jutland. He cried out over and over again when the Swedes set him ablaze. He was screaming, tormented with pain. It was a horrible, horrible thing to see." The king leaned over to one of his commanders. "Rand, did I tell you he was screaming? I still hear it, like a sword piercing my ears." He clasped his hands over his ears.

Edric leaned over to join the discussion. "This is nothing to be upset about, my king. It is merely a trick of their strange religion, not great bravery that gave her this 'strength.'"

"She was a ridiculously stubborn woman," Canute continued. "She would rather die than give honor to the ring. She challenged me with her eyes. She defied me to my face! I couldn't let a nun get away with that." He sighed. "Why didn't she break down once the fire began to burn her?"

Canute's men exchanged looks. They were growing tired of his rantings. But he was king, and they had no choice but to listen—or at least pretend to do so.

"I wanted to see her face as she met her fate. I looked right at her as the fire grew hotter. I peered right into it, and do you know what she did?" Canute looked to Harold, who was smirking across the fire at Edric. "I said, Do you know what she did?!"

"No, I do not know what she did," Harold answered impatiently.

"She looked at me through the fire, more defiant than ever, with a look of impossible serenity," he stammered. "She looked right into my eyes. It was as if she knew a secret, and then she smiled. Her face showed not one hint of fear or pain. Nothing! Did you hear me, Edric? I said, Nothing!" He took a gulp of ale and wiped his mouth before continuing.

"I gave her body to the fire to be consumed. I burned her flesh, yet she mocked me to the very end. Where did she get this power, Harold?"

Norman was growing bored with the discussion. He was anxious to change the subject. He wanted to talk about the thrill of battle, not some dead nun. When Canute paused for Harold's answer, Norman broke in.

"King Canute, this is a day to rejoice. We celebrate your great victory, and soon you shall possess all of England. Here, here!" Norman gushed, raising his goblet.

"Stop patronizing me, you foolish idiot," Canute yelled. "I am not a dolt who can be distracted with such obsequious babble. I want to talk about that nun!"

Norman was fuming, but managed to keep his tongue in his head. He would get into the good graces of the king later, when he was more rational.

Canute turned his attention to Leofric, noticing that he was not celebrating with the others.

"Leofric, son of Leofwine, why do you not drink with us?" Norman glanced cautiously toward his brother, glad the focus was off him.

Leofric chose his words carefully.

"I have no wish to disturb you, sire."

"Then why do you not celebrate our victory?"

Leofric stood. Fearful that his own heart would betray him, he turned and walked away.

"You do not answer? The king asked you a question," Canute called drunkenly after him.

Leofric stopped and turned. "King Canute, you are a great warrior, and I mean you no disrespect. But today, I saw no battlefield, no soldiers, no army to defeat! We conquered innocent women and children. Tell me then, what was this great victory that I must celebrate?"

Canute became very still. Leofric took a deep breath, sure that he would pay for his outburst. Then Canute started to laugh. Everyone breathed a sigh of relief, except Norman, who watched the king, hoping he would punish Leofric for his words.

"Do you see what I mean?" Canute burst out. "He's not afraid of me like the rest of you goats!"

Edric was furious. He jumped to his feet and threw his ale into the fire.

"How dare you?" he yelled at Leofric, starting after him.

King Canute stood up, stepped in front of Edric, and put his hands on Edric's shoulders.

"Stop, Edric. The fighting is over! Let him go. He made his point. He's right. They were only women and children, easily replaced. Come, have some more ale."

Leofric rode off into the smoke and darkness.

꧁꧂꧁꧂꧁꧂

Thorold threw down his shovel and brushed the dirt from his hands. He stood over the fresh graves and numbly tried to pray. Lowering his head, he quietly said, "Into Thy hands we commend their spirits."

He had worked hard digging two graves. A rectangular one for his mother and father, and a larger mass grave in which he had laid the other bodies side by side, carefully folding the victims' hands across their chests. He had made an effort to place the children next to their mothers and keep each family together. It was all he could do.

Godiva had fallen asleep and awoke to find her brother loading a small cart with whatever food, clothing, and possessions he could salvage from the ruins.

"Here, you should keep this," he said softly, looping the cord of their mother's locket over Godiva's head to hang beside Osburga's cross. "We have to go now. It's not safe to linger here."

"What are we going to do, Thorold?" Godiva asked.

Thorold didn't know what to answer. "Come, I have some bread for you to eat."

He led her over to the cart. Godiva climbed in next to her brother. The two sat silently, looking at the fresh grave of their beloved parents. Godiva reached for Thorold's arm. He patted her hand and signaled the horse to move, guiding the cart away from the ashes and stone—all that was left of their home. They rolled along the bumpy road in exhausted silence toward the hut in the woods where Sister Agnes rested.

"These woods are thick. It's too hard to see," Thorold spoke up after a few miles. "I think I know where we're headed, but I'm not sure in the dark. We'd be better off camping here for the night, rather than getting lost. We'll start again at first light."

"What about Agnes?"

"She'll be alright at the hermitage. We'll fetch her in the morning."

Thorold lifted his sister from the cart, carried blankets to a flat patch under a tree, and began to build a fire. Late into the night, they stared wordlessly into the flames, grieving. Finally,

Godiva spoke, "They're dead, Thorold. What will become of us?"

Thorold stirred the embers with a stick and sighed deeply, not having the words to answer.

"What will we do?" she asked again.

"We will continue to be a family," he said after a moment. "We will honor their memory. In time, I will find a wife, you a husband, and we will teach our children who their grandparents were."

Godiva was grateful that she still had her brother. At least they had each other. At the same time, she felt a hole in her heart so wide that she was sure it could never be filled again. She thought of her parents and Sister Osburga and had to cover her mouth to quell her sobs.

"They're gone forever, Thorold."

"Yes, Godiva, but they are forever at peace in heaven where we will see them again one day." It was hard for Godiva to remember the promise of heaven in her present pain on earth.

TEN

L eofric made his way from the fire at the Cofa Tree to the woods where he had left the terrified young girl. He couldn't shake his concern for her and wanted to make sure that she wasn't still hiding with her nun friend. As he rode into the night, he was tormented by the images of the day. The destruction, death, and misery haunted him.

He forced his thoughts back to Godiva and her bravery. If there was one shining light in the midst of such a bleak day, it was meeting her.

He finally reached the stream. By now, the woods were nearly black around him, and he could see nothing but shadows below. He peered into the inkiness.

"Godiva," he called, but there was no response and no sign of her or the nun. He hoped they had reached safety and hadn't been lost in the woods or met up with a party of raiders.

He rode on through the forest, looking for a sign that would point to them. He felt so alone. Exhaustion began to overtake him. He knew he would be able to search more easily and thoroughly in the morning, so he decided to camp for the night. The only thing that brought him any peace was the fact that he had, at the very least, prolonged the life of the beautiful girl and a young nun.

He lay on the ground, looking up at the stars, wondering how he would ever calm down from the anxiety that had taken root in every bone of his body. Hours passed and he finally fell asleep, vowing that he would do anything and everything in his power to find the girl in the morning.

Leofric awoke at dawn and looked up into a clear sky. The rain had stopped and through the trees he could see the strands of pink and orange announcing sunrise. Suddenly, he heard a twig snap. He froze, alert and listening closely.

Thorold had started out on the road at first light, and he led the cart along a small path through the dense trees while Godiva slept soundly in the back of the wagon. He thought he saw wisps of smoke coming from a campfire. He carefully continued on, keeping himself in the trees, hidden from view. He moved closer, until he could see what looked like the remains of someone's camp. There was a smoldering campfire, a pair of boots, and a blanket wrapped around the sleeping body of a...

"Raider," Thorold hissed.

Thorold looked around. Obviously the man had been separated from his group and had camped here for the night. Thorold had the opportunity to avenge the many victims—at least by one person. He left Godiva in the cart, hidden carefully behind a thick clump of bushes, and crept closer until he stood directly over Leofric's sleeping body. He soundlessly drew his sword and steeled himself. He brought his blade down with all his might, groaning as he thrust it into the center of the sleeping man's chest.

But the contents of the blanket were softer than they should have been. Instead of the thick resistance of flesh, Thorold felt only a dry crack. Thorold flung away the blanket and saw nothing but twigs and leaves. He gasped. His eyes darting around, wildly looking for the missing raider.

Leofric jumped out from behind the trees where he had hidden himself when he heard the cart approaching. He lunged toward his attacker with his sword. Thorold spun around in time to deflect the blow with his sword, and the two men faced off, ready to fight to the death.

"Murderer!" Thorold screamed, thrusting with all his strength.

Leofric was taken aback. "I am no murderer," he yelled back, just managing to keep Thorold at bay. He parried the blows. His opponent wasn't fighting wisely in his rage, but the strength behind his blows made up for his lack of skill. "Why do you wish to kill me, sir? I've done nothing to you."

"Nothing more than slay the innocent of Coventry. I will kill you for your crimes!"

"My crimes? You are wrong, I swear," Leofric panted. "It's not what you think!" He dodged and darted from Thorold's sword.

Thorold was deadly in his fury and drove his opponent further and further back, until Leofric tripped over a loose stone and fell hard to the ground. Thorold drew his sword high, poised to finish him off.

"No, Thorold!" Godiva screamed, running out of the woods. She had awoken in the cart and panicked because her brother wasn't there.

"Godiva, get back! What are you doing?"

"This is the man who saved my life, Thorold. Don't kill him! He's not one of them."

"Listen to her," Leofric pleaded from the ground. "I mean you no harm."

Thorold took a ragged breath. He looked closer at Leofric's face. There was something familiar about him.

"Who are you?" he demanded, stepping back but still holding his sword menacingly.

"My name is Leofric, son of Leofwine, Earl of Southern Mercia," he said, sitting up.

"A nobleman? I should have known," barked Thorold. "You expect me to trust you? If you're still alive, you must be a traitor. My father was a loyal man, and what did it get him? Death!" he screamed. "He was murdered by those Viking monsters. And for what reason? Tell me!"

"These men do not need reasons," Leofric sighed. "They are animals. They act out of evil. Trust me, I hate these men as much as you do."

"Do you?" Thorold stared down at him, weighing the facts against his rage. He wanted a reason to kill him.

"Thorold, listen to him," Godiva begged. "You have to believe him."

"Why should I?"

"Thorold, my brother, please. Put down your blade. Listen to me. He's not one of them. He saved my life, I swear to you."

Thorold lowered his blade and leaned up against a tree, chest heaving. He closed his eyes and tried to collect his thoughts.

"I came looking for you, Godiva," Leofric said quietly. "I wanted to make sure you were safe. I'm so glad to find you—and your brother—alive. And I'm so sorry for all you've lost. There must be some way that I can help you both." Leofric struggled to stand up. He brushed himself off, wincing more with the pain of a bruised ego than anything else. Godiva reached to help him, but Leofric put up his hand.

"I'm fine."

"We're going to meet Sister Agnes, the nun who was with me at the river." Leofric could see Godiva's face fall as she thought about the Sister. Tears welled in her eyes, but Godiva held them back.

"They burned down our house, and we have no place to live. I went looking for my family and found Thorold. We're going to go back for Sister Agnes and then find a way to survive," she said with determination, managing a weak smile. Leofric caught her gaze and warmly returned the smile.

"Come on, Godiva. Let's go." Thorold said as he returned with the cart.

Leofric approached him. "Please, let me help you. You're exhausted. I'll tie my horse to your team, and you can sit in the back with your sister."

Thorold searched his face, trying to read Leofric's intentions. He decided to trust the man before him and gratefully handed him the reins. He had not slept the entire night, but he had been trying to be strong for his sister. Godiva exhaled deeply, finally beginning to feel safe with these two men looking out for her. Thorold leaned up to the front of the cart.

"Someone must get word to Edmund. He has to be told of Edric's treachery. We have to warn him."

"I should not say anything, but I shall trust you as I asked you to trust me," Leofric said, glancing over his shoulder at Thorold. "You must not tell a soul, but my father has sent someone to forewarn him."

Thorold sat back, closed his eyes, and put his head back. There was nothing else he could do.

ELEVEN

King Canute sat high in the saddle. The questions and despair of last night had given way to optimism in the bright sunshine of the morning. The gods' favor was upon Canute. He sensed that a great victory was at hand in Ashingdon. His mount was decorated in its finest battle wear. Golden chains looped gracefully across the stallion's long mane. Prince Harold rode alongside his brother, relieved that Earl Edric had gone ahead to feign loyalty to King Edmund and that he could resume his rightful position alongside his brother.

"Canute, do you think that we can trust these English?" he asked. "I have heard some of their soldiers questioning your command. While they performed somewhat satisfactorily at Coventry, it seems that many of them shied away from the old men and women and the children and hunted down only the men and the fittest of women."

"Don't worry," Canute assured him. "Soon they will see the superiority of this kind of warfare. Their hunger for power and lands will ease their consciences. They will lose sight of their moral protests and compete to be in my good graces."

"Are you sure?"

"Harold, when I first fought alongside Father, I was appalled by his orders to kill women, children, and babies. But he was Swein Forkbeard, and he understood the power of the gods. He knew that you must first demoralize and terrify the enemy. You must destroy all that they hold precious. You must kill their women and children as viciously as you can. You must devastate their towns and burn their holy places—then you become all they have. Show the slightest glimmer of weakness or compassion before that point, and you lose everything."

"And it was he who devised this method of battle?"

"Yes, of course. Our father was younger than you when he began to win battle after battle. He was strong and feared by all. His tactics disgusted our grandfather Bluetooth. But that was because he himself was no longer a warrior. The fight had left his heart. He had become weak—soft and weak. Father believed that it was wrong for Denmark to be ruled by such a limp fist, so he killed him."

"Killed our grandfather? But I was told he died from a fever."

"They lied to you Harold. Our father was dauntless. If anyone ever dared to get in his way, he would threaten, 'If I can murder my own father, I can and will kill anyone.'"

"But to kill one's own father?"

"Listen closely, little brother, for these are lessons that you too must learn. The object of war is to win and nothing else. The more ruthless you are, the better; and the quicker you will succeed. The enemy must never doubt your willingness to annihilate them. They must not think of us as men, but as monsters—undefeatable monsters."

"Yet, it was not with the sword that you turned the heart of Edric Streona and got him to betray his own family," Harold argued.

"I didn't need it. The heart of betrayal was already in his nature. I only saw it for what it was and used it to my advantage. Edric has been a betrayer since the day he was born. It is not me he serves, but himself."

"Do you think he and his troops will follow through at Ashingdon?"

"You must also understand, Harold, that I never trust anyone entirely. I suggest you do the same. That, more than anything, is what differentiates me from this English king, Edmund Ironsides. I will never trust a man, especially one who has betrayed for me. One never knows when he will turn again. Edric's forces will be placed on the back side of Edmund's, far away from us. Therefore, if he decides to betray me, we will realize it long before he reaches us. It is better than if he and his men were among us when they revolted. Meanwhile, King Edmund knows nothing of Edric's heart. At worst, he has heard and doesn't believe. He still thinks of Edric as his loyal brother-in-law. Can you imagine? If he does come through, this should come as quite as shock, don't you think, Harold?"

Harold looked at his brother, not sure if he was meant to answer.

"Edric is passionate," Canute continued. "He is like a scorpion, compelled by his own instincts to strike, always aiming to sting. He is drunk with the notion of power. He knows that he will achieve it by being on the winning side."

"But will his men be able to kill their own people?" asked Harold. "These will not be peasants and monks. They'll be facing soldiers like themselves. It is said that Edmund has managed to gather quite a collection of credible warriors."

"To Edric's credit, he has groomed a remarkably loyal band of snakes. They are like thieves who use the cover of darkness to steal what they want. They will swallow up their

English brothers without a second thought. And don't worry about Edmund's warriors. The clever ones will quickly come to the realization that it is better to submit to Danish rule than to die."

⚇⚇⚇⚇⚇⚇

Mercia was overcast with uncertain whispers of rain and distant rumbles of thunder when Prior Albans again untied his small horse-drawn cart. He had spent the night in the wagon with his simple provisions, although he had hardly slept at all. He was terrified by what fate may have befallen Coventry and his church but knew that the most important thing he could do is continue on and reach King Edmund, at any cost. He had never before been entrusted to deliver such an important message. He went over and over in his mind how he might hide Leofwine's message from any inquisitive soldiers.

"Dear God," he prayed, "I am only a simple man, with a near-impossible task, it seems. Please give strength to my heart and speed to my feet. Help me to do all in my power to save England."

"Good boy," Albans kindly said to his horse. "I've got a nice bit of hay here for you when we arrive, and a special treat."

He reached the outskirts of Ashingdon with his horse pulling him along at a casual pace. At the top of the hill, a guard stood alone, watching him approach. Albans continued on, knowing he was being watched, and tried to appear at ease, merely a servant of the Lord. The guard stood in the middle of the road, blocking the path and waiting to meet him. Albans recognized him as one of Earl Edric's commanders.

"Stop, please, and get out. We will have to search this wagon."

"Please do, sir," said the prior confidently. "I certainly have nothing to hide, Elbert."

The guard squinted, trying to place the familiar face. "Prior Albans! What are you doing all the way down here in Ashingdon?"

The Prior gave the alibi he had worked out with Earl Leofwine. "I'm on my way to see an old friend. He's near death, I sadly say. I would like to be the one to administer his last rites, if possible."

"I'm afraid, Father, that I've been given strict orders not to let anyone pass. If you attempt to go, I'll have no choice but to kill you. Orders, you know. Please, save us both a lot of nasty trouble, and find another way." He paused to spit on the ground.

"I understand," responded Prior Albans, not wanting to make trouble.

Two of Elbert's men stepped up and began searching the cart. After several minutes, they had found nothing suspicious, and Elbert waved the prior on.

"You're free to go. Sorry about the delay. I hope your friend recovers," Elbert called.

Prior Albans veered his cart around to take a different path.

"Bless you, my friend," he said with rehearsed warmth as he waved cordially to the guard. He proceeded slowly back the way he had come, wondering what to do.

"I am sorry for the lie, heavenly Father," he spoke quietly in prayer. "But Lord Leofwine did say it was a matter of life and death, so perhaps it's all a matter of perspective." A small roll of thunder rumbled through the sky. Prior Albans shrugged. "Then again, I could be wrong."

ʘʘʘʘʘʘ

Lord Edric's army arrived at the outskirts of Ashingdon, not far from a large military outpost that had been strategically placed on a hilltop outside of town. Elbert mounted his horse and rode up to meet the earl as soon as the party came into sight.

"Here to report, sir."

"Anything come this way?" Edric asked.

"Nothing important."

"I'll be the one who decides what's of importance, captain. Speak up."

"Earlier this morning, Prior Albans did come this way, but it was nothing. He was on his way to visit a sick friend. I made him turn around and go in another direction."

"You idiot!" Edric howled.

"But, sir, he's just an old priest. My men searched him thoroughly. He had nothing with him, sir, no weapons or documents."

"Nothing? Prior Albans is an old priest who just may be a messenger to the king. Visiting a sick friend? What sick friend? Did you even ask?" He looked at the soldier's ashamed face. "How could you be so daft?"

"I didn't realize," Elbert stammered.

"I need a brigade of men to find that monk," Edric barked, turning his horse to face his men. "We have to get him immediately." Edric scowled at Elbert. "We must make sure that Prior Albans doesn't get through to Edmund." Edric turned to Norman. "You know this monk, do you not, nephew?"

"He's my father's priest."

"Good, take a dozen men and make sure he is eliminated. I will meet up with you at the camp."

TWELVE

Leofric stopped the cart in front of a large, sturdy hunting lodge, isolated in the woods nearly an hour's ride out of Coventry.

"We'll be safe here," he said, walking to the back of the cart to assist Godiva and Thorold as they got out and unloaded their belongings. "I think you'll be quite comfortable. There's plenty of room inside."

Godiva glanced up at the stone-faced building.

"It's huge," she said. "There would have been plenty of room for Agnes to stay with us. I wish she hadn't been so stubborn."

"We'll go see her in a week or two," Thorold promised. "She wanted to stay at the hermitage where she felt safe. I think she needs to heal in her own way right now. Maybe we will convince her next time."

"I hope so. This is a fine-looking home, Leofric. Whose is it?"

"It belongs to my family," Leofric replied as he carried Godiva's things to the door. "My father inherited the surrounding land from Alfred the Great."

"Alfred the Great?" Godiva probed, smiling at him. "Wasn't he a king?"

"Godiva, you mustn't pry," instructed Thorold, although he was glad to hear some of her old personality in her voice.

Leofric didn't mind, though. He smiled at her wide-eyed innocence. It was the first time he had smiled in what seemed like a long, long time. She would bounce back with the resilience of youth. She had seen enough good in her life not to think that humankind was doomed because of one senseless episode.

Leofric had never felt such a connection as he had with this young girl. He opened the heavy door, which led to a stone-walled keep with an ingeniously designed, massive hearth in the middle. A staircase to the left led to the second and third floors where six sleeping rooms and their adjoining parlors wrapped around the central chimney, which spread heat to each room.

"Yes, Alfred was the king of England, and I am his descendant. My father shares a bloodline with many remarkable men."

"What about the women?" Godiva asked.

"Godiva!" Thorold chastened.

"It's fine, Thorold. What do you mean, Godiva?"

"Were none of the women remarkable?" she explained innocently.

Leofric laughed. "Godiva, you amaze me with the things you say. Where do you get all these questions?

"I believe that if you were a woman, you wouldn't need to ask."

"Point well taken. I'm sure there were many remarkable women in my father's bloodline, as well. After all, they raised the men who went on to earn great names for themselves with their courageous deeds."

Godiva smiled, accepting the compromise. Her eyes drifted to a large wooden plaque hanging along one side of the room.

Thorold saw her open her mouth for another round of questions and quickly spoke up.

"It's damp in here. Shall I build a fire, Leofric?"

"That would be fine," Leofric replied. "I'll prepare some food for us."

"This wallpiece is so beautiful. What are these carvings?" Godiva interjected.

"They represent my family's royal line," Leofric explained.

She stared at the intricate figures, tracing one with her finger. "Does this mean that someday you'll be represented up here as a prince or a duke or..."

Leofric laughed. "My father is the Earl of Mercia. Someday, I too will be an earl."

"Really? Does it frighten you to be so important?"

Thorold was embarrassed by Godiva's unrelenting questions but gave up trying to censor her and focused on the fire. He knew she was unstoppable.

"Sometimes I feel the weight of it. When I was younger, I felt like the boy who was expected to fill his father's too-large boots. But now I know that being an earl is my destiny. I will use the lessons my father has taught me and rule to the best of my ability. What else can I do?"

Leofric gazed down at Godiva's angelic face, thinking about how courageous she was. Out of questions, Godiva stared back. He was different than anyone she had ever met. Godiva was still too young to be thinking about marriage, but as she stared at this handsome man who had saved her life only the day before, she began to feel something churn inside her. For the first time in her life, she felt the flutter of attraction. Leofric was her hero—strong, brave, and so handsome.

"Shall I put my things upstairs, Leofric?" Godiva asked, ending what seemed like an eternal silence, though it had lasted only a second or two.

"Of course, please choose any room you like."

Godiva ran upstairs as her brother finished building up the wood in the hearth.

"I hope she'll be alright," he mused. "Even at my age, the loss of my parents is almost more than I can bear. She's so young."

"But a strong, young woman," Leofric assured him. "In time, with your help, she'll be fine."

"She's always had an enormous sense of daring and independence."

Leofric waited until Thorold looked at him before he spoke. Meeting his eyes, he said, "From the first time I saw your sister, she seemed completely fearless. She raced out of the woods, chased by a soldier, and all she could think of was saving the birds in the aviary." He looked off into the distance for a moment, picturing the events of the day before. "I saw her hang above the ground in the middle of an inferno, risking her own life to save those birds. Frankly, I don't know any grown men who would have had the courage to do that, Thorold. She's a remarkable person."

"That sounds like Godiva, willing to stake everything for what she loves. She's always been like that. She can't stand to see anything or anyone suffer. All her life, she has cared for even the smallest of creatures. One day, we found her weeping over a dead mole in the garden," he said, starting to chuckle. "Then our family and the neighbors who lived on our property were made to attend the funeral!" He burst out laughing. Leofric smiled, too, pleased to find some common ground with Thorold, far preferring it to being threatened by his sword.

"My mother was always worried about her," Thorold added. "Now it will be my job." They both fell silent at the weight of his words.

"I know this is very hard for you and for her. But you must trust that, with time, you will heal and adjust. When I was a little younger than Godiva, I lost my mother. She was everything in the world to me, and I was heartbroken. Eventually, though, I accepted the fact that she was gone. I found peace. So will you."

"I'm sorry for your loss."

"One good thing came out of it. My father, in his awkward manner, reached out to me in a way that he never would have if my mother had still been alive. We became closer than I ever could have imagined. I've learned so much from him. I don't know if I would be the same person today if he had not starting teaching me in order to keep my mind off my grief. If you show Godiva that she still has someone who loves her and will be there for her, you will have nothing to worry about. If anything, with her strong character, she may end up looking after you!" he smiled.

Thorold took comfort in Leofric's words. "I'm not going to let her down. We're going to go through this together. You can be sure I'll be there for her."

"She is fortunate to have you."

Thorold turned his attention back to the fire. He struck a flint and the tinder caught. Soon the room took on a warm glow. Heat started to radiate through the house, and with it, a sense that life would go on.

Leofric picked up the remaining two sacks of Thorold and Godiva's possessions and started toward the stairs.

"Let me put these away for you."

"No, it's fine. I'll take them," Thorold said, reaching out his hand. He was thankful for Leofric's generosity, but he didn't need anyone to wait on him and his little sister.

Thorold turned on the stairs and gruffly cleared his throat. "Thank you for your hospitality, Leofric. I don't know where we would've gone. You've been a godsend to us."

While Thorold put away his belongings, Leofric laid out a meal of some dried meat, fruit, and ale he found in the larder, plus some bread he had in his pack.

Godiva had taken it upon herself to explore upstairs and discovered a sitting room filled with etchings and woven rugs. The cozy room welcomed her like an old friend—a friend she desperately needed right then.

She distracted herself looking at the drawings. There were sketches of dozens of plants, each with its Latin name written beneath it. For a few moments, she was able to escape into a world where everything was as it should be.

A few minutes later, Thorold came back downstairs. "I hope you don't mind, but my ever-curious sister is entertaining herself exploring upstairs."

"If it lifts her spirits, she's welcome to look at whatever she likes. Sit down, please, my friend" Leofric said, motioning to a large table where he had set out the food. The benches squeaked as they moved along the stone floor. "Have something to eat," he urged.

"I don't really feel like I can right now, but perhaps I could have something to drink."

Leofric poured him a goblet of ale.

Thorold looked deep into the dark liquid, running the stem of the vessel between his fingers. He couldn't stop thinking of his parents and the way they looked when he found them.

"I must do something to avenge their death," he muttered.

"You must be careful. Avenging their death would be an easy way to get yourself killed."

"I don't care. What kind of man would I be not to avenge a man as good as my father?"

"I hate the evil that Canute and Edric have spread as much as you do, but forgive me when I say that perhaps you should not be thinking that way."

"What other way can a man think when his family has been brutally murdered?" Thorold slammed his ale down on the table. "I will have my revenge! I will kill Canute myself!" he said, standing and shoving the bench back.

"I understand how you feel, Thorold. I really do," said Leofric, raising his voice to match Thorold's. "But, you must also take into account the fact that Godiva's well-being needs to be your first priority. You must not do anything foolish. For her to lose you now, to be left all alone in the world, would be a cruel fate." Leofric could see the torment that Thorold was going through. Leofric combed his fingers through his thick blonde hair, struggling for words. "When I saw your sister yesterday, I realized I had a purpose for being there in that hell," he said, his voice quieting. "I was meant to be there. I had to rescue her!

"There is something more important, Thorold. If you give your life for revenge, then Godiva would truly be an orphan. Let us make a pact, right now, as brothers in a cause, to fight the Danes in a way that will mean freedom for all our people, so that there will be no more orphans.

"Canute has not only killed our families. He wants to kill our way of life. He will take everything from us—our faith, our homes, our country. We must live in such a way that we give hope to others that we can reclaim these things. What is most important in this world? Love and family. Godiva is all the family you have left. You must take care of her so that Canute will not be able to steal your most precious treasure from you."

Thorold looked at him for a long moment. He knew it was the right thing to do but rued being unable to hunt down his family's killers. Slowly, painfully, he sat down and extended his hand. "Alright then, the pact, as you say, is ours." They firmly clenched each other's hand.

As he let go of Leofric, he stood up, strode across the room, and launched himself into the night, while Godiva sat in the darkness on the staircase, silently looking down at Leofric.

THIRTEEN

I t was gray and cold, but King Edmund Ironsides burned with the heat of confidence. Mentally, physically, strategically, and spiritually he was prepared—eager in fact—to face Canute of Denmark. At not quite thirty years old, Edmund boldly held the reigns of power. He was filled with passion for his people and his country. He had forced Canute back from his land before, but not in a fight of this scope. This time it would be a matter of pushing Canute out of England forever.

The young king had vigorously rallied the free men of England, and they had been training at Ashingdon for more than three months. Each and every soldier was prepared to defend his wife, his mother, his children, and above all, his precious country. King Edmund looked down at them from Ashingdon Hill, each man like a brother, ready to face death for the good of the family.

They knew that the brutal Vikings regarded warfare as a barbaric art at which they excelled. Many English soldiers had wondered—as Canute hoped—whether the Danes were indeed men or if these creatures, with their insatiable thirst for blood, had actually escaped the sulfurous pits of hell. Even so, Edmund's army exuded conviction and determination. They could not fail.

Weapons were sharpened and stockpiled. There was not a man there who didn't stand ready to fight to the death. They would face this master of dragons from the north and, if necessary, give their lives to defeat him.

In the valley below, the distant flames of Canute's Viking butchers could be seen flickering against the horizon. There were hundreds of bonfires burning, sending a warning to anyone who would dare to challenge them. The fires were meant to instill fear in the English army, to intimidate them— but they had just the opposite effect. The fires ignited the urgency of victory in each English heart.

King Edmund sat on his favorite horse and looked off into the distance, watching for any change in the fires. Two knights waited beside him, eager to fulfill any request he might have. The wind blew against Edmund's face, and he shook away the thought that an ill wind brings no good. He tightened his fist against his saddle and fidgeted with the reins. His horse seemed to share his anticipation of the brewing battle. Edmund pursed his lips, knowing the time to fulfill his destiny was near.

"We shall fight them with all we have, with all we are worth," he vowed.

"All of us, Your Highness. Not one is afraid to give his all for this fight," contributed one of the knights. "I do believe, Your Majesty, that the Viking's season of easy slaughter in England is over."

"Come, join me," King Edmund beckoned the two knights. "Let us ride to the open field; I have something to show you. Let us greet those who have recently come to fight by our side.

Let us give them confidence to inspire them to victory." They rode to the far reach of the hill and looked out on the mass of congregating soldiers.

"It's amazing, sire," the knight declared. "Look to the west, to the far horizon. Do you see them? Our numbers have doubled, and there are even more arriving!" His voice quaked with optimism.

King Edmund surveyed the line of soldiers snaking over the hill. For as far as the eye could see, an endless procession of troops was making their way toward them.

A senior respected advisor to King Edmund rode up to them, his long gray beard flying behind him.

"Yes, Marsdin. What have you to report?"

"Good news, Your Highness. There are many thousands coming to support us. They carry every sort of weapon...from finely smithed swords and expertly strung bows to hammers and rocks. They come from all over our great land—Devon and Cornwall, even Scotland and the mountains of Wales, sire! They all treasure freedom. I think they would fight with their bare hands if they had to!"

"Canute has no idea what is before him, Marsdin. He underestimates us, which offers a valuable advantage," Edmund said fervently.

"We will give him the greatest battle he has ever seen," the king continued. "Who would have believed this, Marsdin? After my father's death, the whole country fell into disarray. But now, at last, our fortunes have turned."

Marsdin smiled confidently. "The day is ours, sire!"

Edmund's voice grew quieter. "You know, Marsdin, after the Witan council voted for Canute, I feared that we might never be able to raise an army capable of resisting him. But now, seeing this, I am more than hopeful. I thank God for the courage of the people of England, that they fight for us. This zeal, this passion, is proof that the vision will not die.

"We may still indeed have an England worthy of our dreams."

"Yes, Your Majesty," Marsdin agreed. "And when Edric's troops arrive, we shall surely have the power we need to drive these Viking monsters back into the sea."

Edmund smiled. His beloved England would not be lost.

Prior Albans' crucial news of Edric's betrayal had never arrived. Norman and his men intercepted the gentle priest along the road and searched him, but found nothing in his cart except the sparse provisions he had packed. He carried no message, nothing that could tie him to Leofwine or suggest that he was bound for King Edmund.

Nonetheless, they dragged him from his cart, hung him from a tree, and brutally beat him to death, leaving King Edmund with no advance warning of the treachery brewing.

Upon his return to Ashingdon, Edric took Norman aside and grilled him on the encounter. "Are you absolutely certain that Prior Albans had no message? I do not believe he was really visiting a sick friend."

"I searched him thoroughly," Norman gleefully recounted. "Stripped him of his clothes and hung him upside down. I do believe we extracted the naked truth from him, sir!" He guffawed, quite pleased with himself.

Edric was not at all amused. He scowled. It would have been one thing if the monk had been found with a message. But now, there was no way to prove that he had been carrying any information. Edric feared the prior would quickly become a martyr, a symbol for England's armies to avenge. On top of that, a stunt such as this would seem petty and excessive to some of his men, who would find no political justification for the cruel act.

Norman cleared his throat and attempted to redeem himself. "Though I am sure that no one got through, we must be prepared for an ambush." He attempted to sound assured and authoritative but knew that he had failed miserably and now looked all the more foolish.

Edric cut him off with a wave of his hand. He was unable to bear any more of Norman's prattle.

"When we reach King Edmund, do exactly as I have instructed," he said curtly, mounting his horse, and moving back toward his assembled men. "There will be no room for your idiocies when we greet him."

Edric led his men to the top of Ashingdon Hill. They moved as soldiers on a mission, adrenaline beginning to surge with the anticipation of the upcoming battle. The first soldiers of King Edmund's army stood waiting to meet them.

"Greetings in the name of King Edmund," they called out, lifting the banner of their king. "The king awaits your arrival."

Edric hesitated for a split second, but no one noticed. He responded with the ease of an skilled actor.

"How does my kinsman fare? Have the armies been assembled?"

"Beyond any expectation," responded the commander proudly. "God has been gracious, and King Edmund has gathered a great and loyal army. Come see for yourself, sir." They rode up to the top of the ridge and looked out at the massive army. It stretched across the entire length of the valley. Edric felt the blood drain from his face. He did his best to conceal his shock as he assessed the huge military force before him. He had no idea that such numbers of loyal fighting men still lived in the nation. He wondered how it could be that so many men would risk their lives for this young king.

"Look, Norman," Edric pointed out. "A fine show of troops, wouldn't you say?"

Norman glanced at Edmund with a worried look, before taking his cue.

"Yes, Lord Edric. Most impressive indeed." He did his best to disguise his alarm, but a thin sheen of sweat appeared on his face. Perhaps they had bet on the wrong side of the conflict. He looked again at Edric, wondering how he could be so calm. Edric glared at him with a sharp scowl, insinuating that he should contain himself.

"Apparently the spirits of our countrymen have been revived," Edric said smoothly, carefully picking his words. "Do they await our arrival?"

"The soldiers will take great courage from the support of the great warrior Edric Streona with the armies of Mercia," one of the commanding knights answered. "Come, sir, the council awaits."

Edric was led into the council chamber, a long wooden structure erected explicitly for the planning and execution of this battle. The many earls, knights, and noblemen who were determined to fight for England used it to meet with King Edmund. The tables on the floor and the galleries along the sides were filled with those who would counsel the king and help to guide the coming battle.

King Edmund had just taken his seat on a dais at the end of the room and was about to speak when Edric and Norman were shown in. The tension and anticipation in the room were palpable, threatening to erupt into chaos. None of the men present had yet heard of Edric's betrayal. He was respected for the power he wielded, although he was never particularly well liked.

"I see that my brother-in-law, Edric Streona, has at last arrived. Please greet him," King Edmund said, walking over to embrace him. The entire room gave an obligatory cheer.

"Edric, welcome," said Earl Elfric.

"My lord, greetings," bowed Bishop Ednoth.

"We greet you, Lord Edric," Marsdin said heartily, motioning to a seat at the table in the center of the room. "You are just in time. Please, join us as we prepare for the battle." Edric slowly sat down. He felt a sliver of fear. Perhaps they had heard of his treachery and were waiting for the right moment to confront him. King Edmund nodded to Edric then returned to the dais.

The king stood up straighter and addressed the assembly.

"Men of England, we enter this battle with the future of our country at stake. Will history record that we found the valor to give our lives to save what is noble and true? Or will it find that the sacrifice and dreams of our forefathers have been in vain? We hold destiny in our hands. Let us fight the good fight! Let us win, that the story passed down to children in all ages will call us men of courage!"

The tent exploded with cheers and clapping. The men yelled as loudly as they could, some banging their shields against the ground. The sound was so loud that those outside began to join in. In one spontaneous wave, the roar spread to the far horizons as each man embraced his destiny. With one heart, one vision, one purpose, each man looked to his companions and knew that they would not fail. The taste of victory was at hand.

The council was adjourned and Edric motioned to Norman to meet him outside.

"Over here," Edric hissed as Norman walked past him. He led him to the edge of the field, behind a large tent.

"As I have always said, you can never predict the outcome of any battle," Edric began intently. "Isn't it exhilarating, Norman? Don't you see? We...I...now hold all the power! If I choose to fight for Canute, he will be king. And if I choose to fight for Edmund, it is he who will be king. Either way, we alone will determine the future of England. We must be patient, wait and see how the battle goes—then we shall know how to act."

"I see your point exactly," Norman grinned.

Edric's eyes gleamed wickedly, revealing the sickness in his heart.

FOURTEEN

T he early morning light broke across the valley and shone through the crowns of the trees. The day of battle had arrived. The air was crisp and dry, and each side felt that victory was within its grasp. King Edmund was astride his horse, dressed in full battle regalia. His horse was adorned with a blanket of his royal colors. His sword was sharp and ready. He felt a swell of pride in his countrymen as he valiantly rode up to Edric.

"Are you ready?" the king asked the man he believed to be one of his closest comrades.

Edric smiled and nodded. "The eyes of the world are upon us, sire. We must show them that these ruthless creatures are just men. Flesh and bone that can and will be defeated!" Edric patted the king heartily on the back.

"It's good to have you here with us, Edric." To keep his mind off the coming battle, he turned to small talk. "I hear my sister is with child again?"

"I hear the same of your wife, my king. With the frequency by which you seem to have children, I have often wondered how you have time for the affairs of state."

They both laughed heartily, clearly needing to break the tension and stress of the morning. The two men looked out upon the battlefield, each with his own thoughts. Edric used the moment to his advantage.

"If I might suggest something, my king, I think it may be wise for me to take my soldiers to the rear, for this Canute cannot be trusted. You will need someone to lead if he should attack from behind."

Edmund considered the proposal for a moment, carefully weighing the possible consequences. "Yes, Edric, I believe you are right. I will take the lead at the fortified hill. Once it becomes clear how he is going to array his forces, take your soldiers and ride from the rear."

"Yes, sire. I shall do as you say," Edric answered, bowing his head in feigned respect. He and the king moved apart.

The forces under Edric's command began moving to the back while King Edmund's men positioned themselves along the front lines. A powerful force, they were now ready for battle, with each man looking to his compatriots for support. The time of reckoning was at hand.

"All men in position, Your Majesty," King Edmund's commander called out.

"Tell them to wait for my command. They are not to move until they hear it," the king ordered. He was keenly aware of the importance of waiting until just the right moment to unleash his warriors and did not want anyone charging into battle until then.

❦❦❦❦❦❦

The Viking horde moved forward with Canute leading the charge. The wind began to intensify. The horses galloped on, fiercely ascending the hill at breakneck speed, and flowed over the top of it like wild creatures going in for the kill.

Upon seeing the multitude waiting for them, Canute was stunned. He blinked to make sure it was not an illusion.

"Where did all of these men come from?" he said, slowing his army's pace as he absorbed the mammoth scope of the forces assembled against him. It dawned on him that this would not be the quick and easy battle that he had envisioned. The uncontested victory he had imagined was being snatched away from his grasp. For a moment or two, the great Canute felt a sharp pang of helpless despair.

"Wait for it!" Edmund's commander yelled out, holding back an eager knight who had stepped ahead of the line, his sword drawn and ready to charge into battle. Like the rest of the soldiers, he was anxious to start the fight and put the horrors of the Danish oppression behind them.

"Hold!" the king cried, calculating his timing, his sword held high in the air.

The sun was beginning to warm the air, and he could feel the sweat flowing under the weight of his armor. Only his great resolve to do all he could to gain victory gave him the strength to wait to give the order of attack.

As the two great armies waited for the battle, each man could do nothing but commit himself to fight for all he was worth. Many of the soldiers said silent prayers to various gods, asking to be allowed to see another day.

King Canute paused for a moment, looking up into a clump of passing clouds to see what he could determine. A thousand thoughts raced through his mind.

"What do you see?" Harold asked as he rode up alongside.

"Don't bother me!" Canute snapped. He himself was puzzled, not knowing quite how to interpret the signs. He was beginning to grow impatient. The clouds worried him. He looked across the horizon and then back at the clouds. Finally, unable to wait any longer, he slashed his sword through the air and shouted the order to attack.

The entire Danish army took off at full speed, spurred on by the sounds of trumpets, native Viking instruments, and ferocious cries. The monster had been unleashed.

"Now!" King Edmund bellowed, bringing his sword down and releasing his men. The soldiers rushed toward the Vikings. Their horses' hooves barely seemed to touch the earth as they charged.

As they drew close to the Vikings, Edmund's soldiers hesitated ever so slightly and were initially driven back by the brute force of the Viking warriors. Soon though, the more courageous of the English commanders embraced the advantage of fighting downhill. Within seconds, the first Viking victims began falling to the ground, limbs severed by the swords of the gallant English soldiers.

As men saw their comrades fall, they fought with an increased sense of urgency. The stench of death began to fill the air and, despite the fact that the sun was shining brightly, it became hard to see as the battlefield filled with dust, blood, and chaos. Yelling men and screaming horses moved through the chaos, always looking for the next victim.

English spirits were high with the initial surge forward. As they pushed the Danes back, the army became energized. Shouting "victory or death!" they drew strength from one another.

"My lord! Behind you," a Welsh soldier yelled out to King Edmund. He ducked, barely avoiding a dagger aimed at his neck. It had come so close that he felt the whoosh of air rush across his skin. He turned and rushed, cutting the enemy soldier down in an instant. He twisted the cold steel of his blade deep. He felt a sense of relief as his attacker fell from his horse, dead.

"Thank you!" he yelled to his comrade-in-arms as he galloped forward, brandishing his bloody sword.

The battle raged on. Countless Viking and English soldiers fell beneath the arrow and the sword. The sound of swords clashing and clanging was deafening. The wounded and dying fought as long as they could before collapsing onto the battlefield. Before long, bodies were strewn everywhere and horses tramped upon them, making footing treacherous. The ground became muddy and slippery as blood soaked into the dirt.

King Edmund's forces held strong, repeatedly repelling the Vikings.

"My king! The victory is ours," Earl Elfric shouted, his sword held high in the air.

"Not until the last Viking is dead," the king yelled back. "We must destroy these creatures of darkness." He was determined not to rest until every single one of his enemies was crushed into the dirt of the battlefield.

⊙⊙⊙⊙⊙⊙

Canute had had enough. The battle was not going nearly as well as he had expected.

"Get out of my way," he bellowed at Harold. He lifted his hand, and a soldier raised his banner to signal Edric to release his army as planned. It was now or never, and he was counting on the deception to shift the balance in his favor.

"It's time to turn on this English king," he growled.

"Now!" he yelled, repeating the signal to Edric. A Viking brigade under Canute's trusted captain Thorkel had made its way around the hill to the upper side where Edric had placed his forces. Hundreds of soldiers headed for the rear of Edric's army, ready to join him in the surprise ambush. Edric saw their approach and had to make his choice.

"Now is the time!" Thorkel screamed out. "Did you not see the signal? Attack!"

Edric basked in the split second of decision and power. The moment was his, power beyond either king. He stalled, weighing his options and evaluating which scenario would ultimately afford him more power. He smirked, lifted his hand and signaled his forces.

All at once, they raised their swords and began to overtake the troops ahead of them, slaying the shocked English from the rear. Frightened and dazed, soldier after soldier fell in the ambush. Chaos and panic spread through the English army, and immediately, the balance began to shift.

To further frighten and demoralize the English army, Edric sliced off the head of a dead English solder who happened to resemble King Edmund. He stuck the head on the end of a spear and paraded it up and down the battle line.

"King Edmund is dead," he shouted wildly. "It's over. Can you not see that this is his cowardly head. Surrender or die!"

The men were devastated. Hysteria began to consume the ranks, as they tried to figure out what to do.

"My God, the head of our king," a boyish soldier cried out in fear.

"It's over! What do we do?" cried another.

"Retreat! Retreat! The king is dead!"

Word quickly spread about their defeat. Within minutes, the English were panic-stricken, unsure who was in charge.

Marsdin barreled his way to King Edmund, who was still very much alive and fighting valiantly up at the front.

"Edmund, King Edmund!" the advisor shouted, racing so quickly toward the king that he feared his horse would collapse.

"Edric Streona has joined forces with the Vikings," he panted. "He attacked from the rear and many of our soldiers have already been slain. He has taken the head of Afton of Northumberland and parades it about, taunting our soldiers with the news that you are dead! You must show your face or all will be lost!"

King Edmund was stunned. "Come with me," he said, without hesitating. They raced up the hill, screaming to the retreating men.

"Turn back, turn back! The battle is not over!"

"The king! Our king lives!" one of the men yelled to those around him, sending the word rippling across the battlefield. With that, he rallied his strength and sliced through a Viking's neck, sending him to the ground in a heap.

The king quickly gathered some of his strongest soldiers to repel Edric's advances. They momentarily regained their momentum. The king continued to cry out with no regard to his own safety. "Raise your sword and fight!" He kept swinging his sword without pause, and within moments, he had cut down several more of his enemies, inspiring and encouraging his men.

❦❦❦❦❦❦

"You know what needs to be done. Now do it!" Thorkel screamed at Edric.

Edric had strategically placed his finest archer in a tall tree. He was highly skilled and could hit a moving target from thirty-five yards.

"Now!" Edric signaled.

The archer took careful aim and released an arrow. Then another and another. The king had nearly turned back the tide when the first arrow found its mark in his left side, just below his rib cage.

"I've been hit!" Edmund grimaced, hunching over in the saddle and grabbing the arrow. Blood leaked through his fingers, and no sooner had he gotten the words out of his mouth than he was hit again, higher on the same side.

"O God, no!" He could not believe this was happening. Never in his wildest dreams had he imagined that he would be betrayed this way. For a brief second, he hoped that he was only dreaming, but as the pain began to intensify, he knew that his wounds were real.

"My king!" screamed Marsdin. "The king is wounded. Help!" Then, to the soldiers around him, he called, "Look in the trees—there is an archer. Hurry!"

King Edmund's men barraged the trees with their own arrows, hoping to hit the culprit. With the help of another soldier, Marsdin pulled the wounded king from his horse and led him off the field on his own mount.

"There he is!" yelled a soldier. The archer was trapped on a high branch, unobstructed from the soldier's clear view. He knew he was exposed, but he had completed his task. Three arrows found their mark in his chest, and he crashed to the ground, dead.

At the same time, Marsdin and the king were escorted off the battlefield by two of their men, who stuffed cloths over Edmund's bleeding wounds as the king struggled even to talk. They lifted him from the horse and laid him on the ground, unsure of how badly he was injured.

With Edric now slaughtering his own countrymen from the rear and Edmund wounded, Canute's army quickly gained the upper hand. His warriors drove the English into the valley where they were forced to fight in two directions at once. Swords and spears cut through the air and found their targets. So much blood was shed that the ground became saturated and turned a harsh, soggy shade of red. The remaining English commanders fought valiantly, despite the high number of casualties.

The battle raged until nightfall when both armies could no longer see if it was friend or foe they were fighting. Utterly exhausted, they pulled back to rest and regroup. Though both sides had suffered substantial losses, Canute had by far made greater progress.

King Edmund's wounds were serious. His physicians were not sure if he would live through the night. They each silently prayed for a miracle that their king would somehow survive. Blood had soaked through the king's garments and he drifted in and out of consciousness. The arrows were carefully removed, and he was bandaged with thick cloth pressed against the wounds to stem the bleeding. But King Edmund's wounds went deeper than the arrows. He was devastated by the betrayal of his own brother-in-law, Edric. Although he was not fully conscious, he was aware of what had taken place. His heart ached with the thought that he had been brought down by someone he wholly trusted.

"Drink something, my king," urged a soldier.

"Edric, Edric," he mumbled in his fever.

"My lord, drink this," the soldier coaxed, offering him some tea.

"He won't drink anything," the soldier said, looking worriedly at Marsdin.

"Then just let him rest," replied Marsdin.

As the English soldiers regrouped in camp, the mood was somber. They sat by campfires and tended to the wounded. Their hearts and minds were heavy and weary as they contemplated what had transpired. They were discouraged and disillusioned. It was a day of massive loss. Some of the country's finest men, those who had forged valiantly ahead with a steadfast vision of a unified and free England, had been killed.

Edmund's army was not the only one to feel discouraged that evening. Neither Canute nor his warriors had anticipated such loss in their ranks. Though they now held the upper hand, they had been prepared for an easy defeat. Nonetheless, while the twenty-seven-year-old king of England fought desperately for his life, they were already strategizing for their victory.

FIFTEEN

T hat evening, by torchlight, each army took stock, counting and identifying the dead, tending to the wounded,
and honing battle plans for the next day. King Edmund
stared into the fire, clutching his side, and, in lucid moments,
tried to devise a strategy of his own.

On the fringes of Canute's camp, a carriage suddenly
appeared in the moonlight. Earl Leofwine sat weakly within
its cab, surrounded by a mass of blankets and pillows. His son
Leofric walked alongside, looking for Viking guards.

As they approached the perimeter, Leofric saw two patrolling soldiers and asked them to immediately notify King
Canute of his father's arrival.

Tired and contemplative, Canute personally came out of
his tent to greet Leofwine and Leofric and escort them into
his compound. The day had turned out as difficult as his first
look at the massive loyal English force had portended. Edric
had thankfully lived up to his promise, but without his help,
Canute knew he would have suffered defeat at the hands of
Edmund Ironsides, and that made him terribly uncomfort-
able.

"Earl Leofwine, Leofric," Canute said, extending his hand.
"Leofwine, I can hardly believe that you've traveled all the way
here, to a battlefield, in your condition."

"It seems I had to. Representatives from the Witan came to my door, requesting that I leave without delay to see you, Your Highness," Leofwine said. "Some things cannot wait."

"Come; rest yourself in my quarters where we can talk," Canute said, then called out to an aid. "Bring us some ale, bread, and cheese!" Canute helped Leofwine into his tent, supporting his weight. Leofric trailed a few steps behind them.

"Here, rest here," Canute said, easing Leofwine into a chair. Leofric quietly sat down against a wall. He knew he was privileged to be admitted into Canute's tent with his father and wanted to be as inconspicuous as possible so he could hear his father deliver his message.

"King Canute," Leofwine began, "I have already heard news of the outcome of today's battle and the staggering losses suffered, both by Edmund's army and your own. By all accounts, you are favored to win. I have also been made aware of the means by which you secured victory. The Witan has asked me to deliver an official message on their behalf, and I would humbly like to offer you some additional advice of my own." Leofwine shook with a deep, rattling cough. As he recovered, Canute answered.

"Of course, I welcome any word from the Council of Elders, those who have most graciously embraced my bid to be king. Beyond that, Lord Leofwine, I respect any advice offered by men of age and wisdom, so please say your piece."

Leofwine coughed again, then began. "King Canute, it is most clear that you *will* be king of England. This is not in question. What is in question is what you will actually be king of. You are still young and have many years ahead of you in which to rule. Someday, not long from now, you will no longer worry about the tactics of war but about how you should reign over your kingdom. What you do now will greatly influence your future as a ruler."

"Go on," Canute urged.

"Your Majesty, may I bring in the food and drink?" an aid asked, entering with a wooden tray.

"Very good. Leave it here," the king motioned to a low table.

Leofwine patiently waited for the aid to leave before he continued.

"First of all, I must give you the official words of the Witan. They are proposing that you stop this battle immediately."

"What?" Canute barked, incredulously.

"They recommend that you release your men and allow this dispute to be settled privately between yourself and King Edmund in a contest of personal combat."

"Personal combat? What are they thinking? After all, they invited me to assume the rule of England!"

Leofwine reached for a flagon of ale and took a slow sip. "This is the message that I was sent to deliver. After much debate, the Witan proffered the idea of personal combat, in the hope of saving lives."

"Personal combat?" Canute said again, as he began pacing, rolling the idea around in his head. "But Edmund is injured, weak, even delirious, I heard."

"This is what they have proposed," Leofwine calmly repeated, gnawing on a piece of bread.

"You know both of us, Earl Leofwine. What do you think of this idea? Who do you think would win such a contest?"

Leofric listened in the corner.

"Allowing that Edmund recovers, and I believe he will," Leofwine began, "I think that whoever would win this fight would be left the loser, for he will not have gained the loyalty of the whole country. Even if you kill Edmund, many of the English will refuse to accept the rule of a Dane. There will be fighting for years to come. You will always need to look over your shoulder, never knowing whom you can trust. I believe that I have a better proposal for you, King Canute."

Leofwine leaned forward and pinched off another small chunk of bread. "Everyone knows that you have already defeated Edmund. You have clearly established your superiority as a warrior. I suggest that you now show yourself as a great politician. There are many who will stay loyal to Edmund, no matter what. If you were to make peace with him, give him a chance to save face, it would show the people that King Canute is clearly not a barbarian. Let Edmund have Wessex, a place you will not easily rule, a place where you will need to keep many soldiers and spend a great deal of energy—not to mention gold—keeping the peace. The people will then see Canute as a wise ruler, a man who is cunning and adept enough to earn the loyalty and respect of all the people. At the moment, the English see you—forgive me, sire—as Canute the vile, Canute the murderer," he said, pausing.

"Do this and they will soon regard you as Canute the Great!"

Canute struggled with Leofwine's proposal. "You must know that I came to these shores to become king of all England."

"I know you did. Soon enough, you shall be. But for now, let it be an England that is strong enough to endure and prosper. You know that there are many other nations that would love to plunder our fair isle. If you weaken these provinces too much, you will invite the invasion of others."

Canute paced up and down, weighing the possibilities before him. He wondered how the Danish council would react to a truce. They were warriors at heart and would expect brute force and strength to finish this conflict. The Danish council was not weak, like the English Witan representatives. They had been against Canute's voyage to England from the beginning. Although they indulged him, they saw England only as a potential territory of Denmark and not a treasure on its own. He looked at Leofwine.

"Your words are provocative, yet there is much for me to consider. I will think about what you have said, Earl Leofwine. I trust that there is more to your visit here?"

"I want to urge you to be magnanimous," Leofwine said, leaning forward. "Give Wessex over to Edmund with the provision that whoever outlives the other shall rule the whole of England."

Canute rubbed his chin as he paced, mulling over the proposal. "Edmund was very courageous in battle. He fought well. Perhaps an honorable peace is the best solution." Canute walked forward, extending his hand to Leofwine.

"I appreciate the wisdom of your counsel. Stay with me, Earl Leofwine. Be my advisor. I am surrounded by buffoons who know about making war but nothing of state and society. Help me to understand this nation of yours."

Leofwine was pleased. He had been sincere in his counsel to the king and knew that his plan to save King Edmund had worked.

"I must return to my home and mend, sire," Leofwine told Canute. "But, please, call for me any time. I am in your service."

Leofric admired his father's brilliance and finesse. And, as much as he hated to admit it, he was impressed by Canute's humility and the respect that he had shown his father.

SIXTEEN

L eofric rode beside his father, who was propped up on a makeshift bed in the back of the carriage. They sat quietly for a long time, bouncing along the road as their trusted driver negotiated its twists and turns by the bright glow of the moonlit night.

Finally, Leofric spoke. "King Edmund was deeply grateful for your intervention, Father. His page said that he would have liked to have told you so himself, but his injuries prevented him from traveling to the perimeter to meet you. He sends his apologies."

"There are no apologies needed," Leofwine said wearily. "Let him know, when you can, that I understand and wish him good health."

Leofric looked at his father and took a deep breath. The closeness he once felt for him had been rekindled, brighter than ever, that night. For several years, Leofric had watched his father weaken in illness. He had, at times, mistakenly thought that his father's intelligence and will had weakened as well. But in that moment, he fought the urge to embrace his father and tell him how awed he was by the old man's strength.

Instead, he simply placed his hand on his father's. "You saved many lives tonight, Father," he started.

Leofwine breathed arduously, not even opening his eyes. He nodded slightly to show he had heard, but didn't answer. He was appreciative of his son's words, but he knew he had acted not as a hero but as a piece in a greater puzzle, just a pawn in history.

"You did, Father. I'd say that you not only saved lives but perhaps the future of our nation," Leofric tried again.

Leofwine cleared his throat and blinked. "Leofric, you give me too much credit. I just spoke the words that I hoped would bring peace. That's all."

"That's a lot. I've learned something about you these last few days, Father. I thought you were too tired and ill to pay attention to the events that have been unfolding. Yet you have been aware of precisely what has been going on. In fact, I was trying to keep foul news from you. I'm sorry. I underestimated you. I have been inexcusably foolish."

Leofwine chuckled and suppressed a cough.

"Now I realize that it takes great strength to be patient, that it is courageous to wait and use wise counsel."

His father smiled faintly at his son's attempts to speak about his feelings.

"Your wisdom has kindled the hope of England's survival. I thought battle was the only way. I couldn't have imagined what you proposed." Leofric's voice trailed off. The cart rolled over a large rock, and they both bounced off their seats for a moment. Leofwine adjusted himself and tried to get comfortable again.

Leofric began again softy. "I'm proud to have you as my father, to be your son."

Leofwine smiled and sighed peacefully. His coughing had ceased. Neither of them said anything for a long while.

"My son," he finally began in a comforting voice. "I am also proud of you. I am at peace. I have longed for these moments of understanding."

Leofwine pulled his son close and hugged him. Leofric felt such love for his father. He closed his eyes and beseeched God to keep Leofwine alive until he would be mature and astute enough to fill his father's place in the world.

"You rest now," Leofric whispered as he gently pulled away from the embrace. At the crossroads, he moved up front to sit with the driver. He looked up into the night sky with renewed hope. He was sure he would not forget that moment for as long as he would live.

There was stillness again, and peace. He thought of the hope he had for the future and for rebuilding England, for those who had lost and suffered so much. Then he remembered Godiva and the pact he had made with her brother.

"It's a nice clear night, my lord," the driver said pleasantly.

"It certainly is," Leofric answered, taking in the vast swath of stars above him. "Clearer than I ever remember seeing it before."

⊙⊙⊙⊙⊙⊙

At the crossroads of the small village of Ipswich, not far from Ashingdon, sat the Blue Boar's Head Inn. Nearly two months after the negotiated resolution of the battle, a pair of rough-looking men entered the tavern, squinting to see in the dimly lit room. They walked over to a table where a man wearing a hood that hid his face sat sipping ale.

"Sir, we travel to London, and our cart is broken down," one of them said carefully. He was a stringy-haired man with several missing teeth. "Perhaps you would find the generosity in your heart to aid some poor travelers with the purchase of a drink," he asked, as if he had rehearsed the request many times.

"It's me, you stupid troll!" the hooded man hissed, putting up his hand. "You don't have to speak in code anymore." He reached down and pulled a small leather pouch from his left boot. The weight of coins was evident as he flopped it on the table. The second man whipped it away and tucked it in his belt.

"Now get out of here," the hooded man ordered. "Do as you have been told, or I will track you down and kill you."

"You don't need to worry about us, sir," the stringy-haired man snapped back.

"Consider it done," the other remarked, revealing a mouth of chipped, blackened teeth in a wicked grin.

The strangers disappeared into the night and Edric Streona, still beneath his hood, slipped out the back, unnoticed.

Early the next morning, the first flurry of winter settled upon King Edmund's castle. The fire had gone out in his chamber and the room was chilled by the wind. The king lay in his bed, mulling over the state of affairs in Wessex.

His wounds had threatened his life for more than a week, but then his fever had subsided. While he still suffered pain, the arrow punctures had finally closed up.

He shivered as he carefully climbed out of his bed. He had taught himself to move in a way that would least stretch his skin and irritate the wounds. He walked toward the small stone room that contained the toilet hole. He grimaced for a moment, holding his side. The small room had open windows allowing the cold November air to blow away the stale air. He cringed as he sat down on the frigid seat.

Suddenly, his expression of irritation gave way to confusion and then, horror. He fell forward, and the last inch of a bloodied sword retracted from a small opening in the wall behind the toilet. Blood flowed onto the floor. Edmund was dead. King Canute would now be the sole ruler of all England.

PART TWO

SEVENTEEN

May 1027
King Canute's Castle
Winchester

T he king studied a sequence of rune stones laid out on the table before him, desperately trying to glean their cryptic message. Suddenly, a page burst into his private chamber. "My lord, the trumpet blasts. They approach the gates."

Canute stood, gathered the stones from the gold inlaid table, and without a word in response to the page, hurried out of the room, through the corridor, and toward the Hall of Kings.

More than ten years had passed since he seized the throne of England. In that time, he had conquered every one of his enemies and had grown an empire larger than any other Viking ruler before him. His power and might were the greatest in Europe. He had not been able to take the time to visit his homeland for some time, and he restlessly awaited the arrival of a delegation from the Danish War Council.

Canute had long since laid aside the hammered iron and layered hides of a rugged Viking warrior, preferring the more refined costume of a dignified Englishman. The soft sleeve of his shirt had an ivory button that he quickly fastened as he regally entered the room.

"Your Majesty, the emissaries from the Danish Council have arrived," the page informed him.

Canute walked out onto the enormous upper balcony that opened from the Hall of Kings over the courtyard of his castle. He was a different man in his English clothes, more polished and aristocratic. He watched the Danish councilmen enter beneath him. They were led by Gunnor Thorson, who had been a good friend of Canute's father. The man looked old, worn, and weary. Canute considered him for a moment then appraised the other Danes, recognizing in them a reflection of himself in his earlier years.

"Tough Viking leather," he said, shaking his head. "It's always the young ones who feel compelled to put on appearances." The members of the council disappeared beneath the balcony.

Canute moved purposefully. The council had governed for too long by its own standards. It was time for Canute to assert his rule. He knew it would be a battle, imposing himself upon the powerful position they had carved for themselves.

Canute proudly placed the gold and jeweled crown of Alfred the Great on his head, feeling the heavy weight of rule. He stood there a moment, glancing at a tiny carved Viking ship on his table. He was ready. He took his seat on the throne and motioned for the page to open the doors.

"Your Majesty, the Danish Council," the page pronounced as he ushered them in.

"Gunnor Thorson, my father's oldest living ally," Canute warmly received the large, slightly hunched man, sporting thick fur boots that bunched up below his knees.

"King Canute," Gunnor said, bowing briefly. "We bring greetings from the council. They have been most anxious for us to meet with you. Your absence these last three years has been the cause of great concern. I have told them, of course, that the son of Swein Forkbeard has not forgotten them and must have a great deal of business to attend to."

"Gunnor, friend of my father. May you live long, for you continue to be honored in my eyes," Canute answered, but he was rudely interrupted by a sharp voice.

"King Canute, my name is Elsorn, son of Eyolf. This is General Bjork, and we have been sent here by the council to deliver the demand that you return to face them and bring the Danegeld that is long overdue," the younger man, flanked by a stone-faced warrior, declared as he stepped forward. They both wore Viking leather from head to toe. "Unlike the fossilized warrior who stands beside me," he brayed, "neither General Bjork nor myself have any desire to observe custom and form. We are not here to flatter and kowtow to you. You are lacking as a king. Do you intend to return to the ways of Denmark, or to become soft, here in the weak climate of England?"

Canute was livid. His eyes blazed fiercely, the only sign that the ruler's wrath had been ignited. He would allow the man to finish his searing tirade before responding.

"It is an insult to the Danish people that you have allocated no time for the core of your empire," Elsorn continued. "You have ignored our need for reparations from the English, yet we have patiently—and perhaps foolishly—waited these three years since your last visit, three whole years, for you to come with it!" His voice rose. "You have grown lenient and no longer have the courage to rule as you should. We are told that you now treat the English and Danes as equals. At first, I refused to accept that the great Canute would betray his own people." He glared contemptuously at the king. "As I look at you in those delicate English clothes, I can't help but believe it. Maybe you have also swapped your Viking heart for a delicate English imitation!"

Canute still did not move. He gazed down at the impudent delegate, and a strange smile crept across his face.

"I'm sorry. What did you say your name is? Elswick? Elton? Elder?"

"Elsorn!" he repeated irritably.

"Ah, yes. Forgive me, Elsorn," Canute said, his voice dripping with sarcasm. "Let me see now. I believe I have heard of you. You are the one who subdued the Swedish uprising with such cunning and finesse. Am I correct?"

"You are indeed," he replied with feigned humility. "I fought for my country as..."

"Silence," Canute ordered, rising from the throne dramatically. His gaze bored into Elsorn as he slowly circled him.

"You see, Elsorn, some news of my empire does reach me. In fact, I have heard that you have the loyalty of many members of the council. I have even heard that you are reputed to be quite a talented chess player. Have I heard correctly?"

"Yes, I do play chess. It helps to keep my mind sharp," Elsorn said, unnerved by Canute's pacing and the twist in conversation. He had expected Canute to react to his insults with a physical challenge, not talk of chess.

Canute calmly removed his outer robe and laid it across his throne. He walked over to the far wall of the room, where a collection of English weapons was displayed. He reached for the sword of Alfred the Great and tested its weight. He removed his crown and placed it nonchalantly on a table.

"You wish to challenge my authority," he said, looking straight into Elsorn's eyes. "You think that with your victory over the Swedes, you can now dominate my council. I must admit that it is a courageous move. Stupid, but most courageous."

Canute kept his voice calm and controlled. "Don't think I can't see your plan. You mean to provoke me into a fight so that you can kill me with your sword. Your fighting prowess would be legendary, and perhaps you would even become ruler in my place. Am I correct, Elsorn?"

Elsorn waited. He shifted his weight from foot to foot. Canute's responses were not what he had predicted. He eyed the sword that Canute held nervously.

"What do you think, Elsorn? Are these thoughts of yours the inspiration of a great leader? Or merely the vain fantasies of a cocky young bull?" Canute walked toward him until he was only a few inches away. "I have a better plan. Let us see just how great your tactical skills are. We shall play a game of chess to determine who is the better man. Let the winner be king."

Everyone gasped in amazement.

"Bring me a scribe. We will put this in writing," Canute said.

"Yes, sire," the page replied. "I shall fetch him at once."

To Elsorn's utter amazement, a scribe was brought in and a document attesting to the terms was signed and sealed with the royal crest.

"Now, let us meet at the chess board," Canute said calmly. Inside, he was furious, but no one would be able to tell by his outward behavior. He had learned that disguising his emotions often gave him a tremendous advantage.

Elsorn cautiously sat down at the table. He was sure there must be more to Canute's offer, but there was no trick that he could discern. He knew it would be weak to question the terms now, so he focused his energy on the game. Frowning, he shifted forward in his seat, trying to look imposing. He made two well-calculated opening moves.

"You're very good, Elsorn," Canute said, picking up his knight. They continued to play, Elsorn moving quickly, confidently, and Canute taking more time as he deliberately chose his moves.

"If you spent more time in Denmark, you would be aware of how often I win at chess," Elsorn looked up grinning smugly. "In fact, any man here will attest to the fact that I never, ever lose."

"Really?" Canute asked, moving his bishop. "That's odd, because I believe I have already outmaneuvered you."

Elsorn looked down at the board in shock.

"Checkmate. I'm afraid you won't be king after all, Elsorn," Canute said with a pity that almost sounded sincere. Elsorn was mortified. Canute stood and took up the sword of Alfred.

"Perhaps I should give the young man another chance?" Canute asked, looking at Gunnor and the other men for their reactions. "Tell me, Elsorn, do they still teach the lineage of kings? I hope they do. I must assume that you would know some of mine." Canute enjoyed playing with Elsorn. He was like a cat pawing a mouse before the final bite.

"My father was Swein Forkbeard, son of Harold Bluetooth, who was the son of Gorm the Old. This, Elsorn, is what makes me king of all Scandinavia." Elsorn looked up at him fearfully.

"But this—this is what makes me the king of England!" Canute shouted, waving the sword of Alfred the Great. "How is it that a puny Englishman, Alfred, beat our Viking ancestors in battle?" he asked, perusing the room with disgust. "He used his head. He was smart and strategic. He was educated and studied the vulnerabilities in our approach.

"Draw your sword, Elsorn. I will give you another chance," Canute ordered, allowing his rage to show. Elsorn jumped out of his chair, knocking it over. He unsheathed his sword, eager to fight. The two men met face-to-face in the middle of the room, swords of steel clashed and clanged as the others in the great hall stepped back to give them room. Elsorn fought daringly. He was lithe for such a big man and able to swiftly beat Canute back.

"My father, Swein, was a great warrior," Canute said in between jabs. "He taught me how to fight."

"Good for you," Elsorn answered mockingly.

"There is one thing you may have already forgotten, though."

"What's that?" Elsorn asked, as he thrust, just missing Canute.

"That this is the sword of my English ancestor, Alfred. He was the one who taught me how to think!" Elsorn's eyes flew open in horror as Canute's sword pierced his heart.

"And that," Canute said, withdrawing his sword from Elsorn's chest, "is why I am king."

The other Danes were shocked. Canute walked toward them, holding the bloodied sword away from his soft English silk.

"Report this to the council and tell them I shall be making a trip to Denmark shortly," he said, calm once more. His eyes met General Bjork's steely gaze and then Gunnor's. Elsorn collapsed in a heap, and one of Canute's aids leaned over him.

"He's dead, sire."

Bjork stormed out, but Gunnor stayed behind and whispered into Canute's ear.

Eighteen

May 1, 1027

Coventry

After years of hardship and grief, Coventry gradually rebuilt from the siege that stole Godiva's parents and her beloved friend Sister Osburga from her. After many painful and lean seasons, the town she so loved once again prospered.

Godiva had grown into a woman, and her closeness to Leofric had also grown. In the ten years since they had met, the pair had fallen deeply and profoundly in love. Only a few months earlier, they were married at a three-day feast at Earl Leofwine's castle. The Archbishop honored them by presiding over the ceremony, and Earl Leofwine announced that he had built them a home near Coventry as a wedding present.

The plentiful spring rains had raised the level of the nearby Sherbourne River, and the fields and hillsides were bright with seedlings, sprouts, and flowers. Rabbits, lambs, and goats frolicked in the fields. Children again ran through the village lanes, and life and optimism flowed through the veins of the hamlet.

Although ruled by the pagan King Canute, the pagans and Christians of the community were, for the most part, united in civic matters. They had suffered equally in the siege and banded together in its aftermath to revitalize their cherished town. They worked hard not to let their differences separate them. While their beliefs were very different, they would graciously step aside—at least in public—and allow each other to worship and celebrate in peace.

The first of May, however, was one of the few days of the year when the clash of the two cultures became obvious and the citizens of Coventry felt strictly divided. May Day marked the annual pagan fertility festival in front of the celebrated Cofa Tree. For as long as anyone could remember, Coventry was the traditional place for pagans to come from all over the region to perform rites meant to influence and encourage the replenishment of life—plant, animal, and human.

On that glorious spring day, Godiva stepped outside onto one of the large balconies of their new home. She was stunning. The pretty child of thirteen had grown into a graceful woman of twenty-three. Her flowing hair, sparkling eyes, and vitality were noticed by everyone. She had spent a perfect morning gathering herbs with her dear friend, Sister Agnes, who had made the hermitage in the woods into a quiet home. Godiva loved to visit her and bring her preserved fruit and bread from Ross, the baker. They rarely spoke of the past but spent their time together tending to the garden and observing the beauty of nature.

It was nearly noon, and Godiva's dark-eyed handmaiden, Cresha, stood beside her, folding the last of the laundry. Godiva brushed back her shiny, blonde hair.

"My lady, your hair has grown so long and beautiful," remarked Cresha.

"My dear husband loves it. I haven't trimmed off an inch since I met him ten years ago."

"I understand," Cresha said. "It might be bad luck for you to cut it."

Godiva laughed. "Silly girl, I'm sure I would cut it if I ever found myself treading on it."

Cresha noted Godiva's good mood and cleared her throat.

"My lady, as you may know, our May Day celebration is today, and I was hoping you might allow me to go with my family."

"Of course you may, Cresha. I won't even be here this afternoon. Leofric and I shall be going to town as well. You may leave as soon as you finish up the clothes. That won't be too long, will it?"

"No, not long at all. Thank you! I'm so excited to be able to go. They've made more costumes this year than last. I've heard that there will be a whole group of dancers dressed as Thor and the goddess Ester. There will be fortune-tellers and, of course, the fertility rite! It's so exciting. You should come see, my lady."

Godiva smiled, but she was not particularly eager to go to the festival. She had been before and knew how bawdy and wild the May Day celebration could be. Pagans from the surrounding towns would descend upon Coventry, costumed and bent on unrestrained festivity. For the non-Christians of Mercia, it was Norse mythology, Roman debauchery, and drunken revelry all merged into one. She had told Leofric that she would meet him, though, since he had never been and thought that it might be diverting. And so, a short time after Cresha left the castle, Godiva fetched her horse from the stable and rode into Coventry.

Before she even reached the open area in front of the Cofa Tree, Godiva could hear the hoots, howls, and laughter of the revelers. She tied up her horse and walked toward the festivities. Large numbers of people, in flamboyant May Day attire, strolled alongside her. The women wore brightly colored flower garlands on their heads. Some people waved branches and long bird feathers in the air. As she drew closer, Godiva watched pagans drinking and dancing through the streets in the bright sun.

Many of the Christian townsfolk wanted nothing to do with the boisterous activities and stayed as far away from them as possible. Others, particularly the young boys, dared to watch from the sidelines, intrigued by the costumes and events. Godiva knew that some of the Christians saw nothing wrong with the festival. They too enjoyed the outfits, the many visitors, and the excitement. But Godiva hated the noise, the intoxication, and the immorality. As she arrived at the festival area, she watched a robed Druid invite his followers into a ceremonial circle. Several alarmed Christian mothers pulled their curious children away.

A tall Maypole—itself a symbol of fertility—had been erected in front of the Cofa Tree and Godiva watched as the peasants gathered around the pole. The dancers sang as they weaved in and out, braiding colorful ribbons around the pole.

Godiva looked around, hoping Leofric would arrive soon. She didn't see him anywhere in the large crowd, but she did recognize another familiar face. She walked up to a handsome blind man and put her hand on his arm.

"I don't know where all these people come from. It's even more crowded and clamorous than last year," she said.

"It sounds like quite a romp," he replied.

"How many of these festivals have we come to, Wulfstan, always tucked in a safe corner like this? I'm so happy that we have been able to enjoy it together all these years."

"Your friendship has meant so much to me. I only wish I could still see your beautiful face. Well, at least I get to hear your lovely voice."

Wulfstan had been blind since he was knocked down by the kick of a horse on the day of the siege. His sense of hearing had grown very keen to compensate, and he could hear Godiva's faint sigh.

"What is it?" he asked.

"Was I that obvious?" Godiva asked as she watched a rather inebriated young woman awkwardly struggle to climb onto her horse.

"Something is troubling you, is it not?"

"A most unflattering and unladylike display. It's getting crowded and most of the people are drinking more than they should."

"How many people are here?" Wulfstan wanted to know.

"I'm not very good at estimating, but the streets are quite full. I would say at least several hundred, perhaps a thousand," she answered, tightly clutching his arm.

"At times like this, I really wish that I could see what's going on. It must be quite a sight."

"I'm actually glad you can't, Wulfstan," Godiva said. "An advantage of being blind is that you're protected from seeing the fouler things of the world. The flowers and the dancing are lovely, but at least you are saved from more disturbing sights."

Wulfstan reached his hand out to Godiva, steadying himself against the shoving crowd. "But it sounds so exciting."

"Perhaps for some people, but it is far too lewd an exhibition for me."

"Whew, what is that smell?" Wulfstan suddenly said, pinching his nose.

"It's awful, isn't it?" laughed Godiva. "I think they call it gorsh. It looks as strange as it smells—all bumpy and squiggly. I swear, I think I can see something moving in the bowls of it that people are walking by with. Would you like me to get you some?" Godiva teased.

"After you, my lady," he chortled. Wulfstan smiled at the shrieks of laughter around them and then pulled out the lute that he always carried strapped to his back. He strummed and softly sang in his glorious tenor voice, his blind eyes calmly closed. Two old women standing nearby picked up the tune and began clapping along, elbowing each other with approval. Others around them joined in.

꙳꙳꙳꙳꙳꙳

Exotic mummers paraded in bird masks, thrilling the crowd but frightening the smallest children with their pantomime dances. Men and women sashayed by, waving long green branches in the air as they whirled around the mummers.

Thurman, the town blacksmith, arrived with his young son Alin on his shoulders and protectively holding his older daughter Galia's hand.

"Papa, I want to see the bird people! Hurry," Thurman's daughter squealed, trying to break from his grasp.

Years of pounding red-hot iron in his blacksmith shop had endowed Thurman with arms the size of tree trunks. His massive hands were the size of sunflowers, yet he gently held on to his daughter.

"Wait, Galia. Papa has to hold your hand. We must be careful here."

"Hurry, Papa, hurry," she cried, pulling him along.

The trio made their way into the crowd. Just then, some children running in and out of the mummers bumped into

Galia. They tumbled together and fell into the skirts of the ladies along the side.

"Get off me, you filthy child!" a rather startled woman yelled at the toothless boy grinning up at her.

"Look, Papa! I can dance, too," Thurman's daughter shrieked, fleeing from her father to join the frolicking children. "Look, I'm a bird!" she laughed, dancing in and out of the parade behind the toothless boy.

Suddenly, one of Canute's men broke from his patrol along the edge. He jumped off his horse and marched angrily up to Galia, his large boots splashing carelessly through the mud. He grabbed the little girl roughly by the shoulders.

"Here, you! Get out!" He shoved her toward her father.

"Out, Saxon dog! We keep our wild hounds tied up," he shouted angrily at Thurman, wanting to exercise his power. "I advise you to do the same. Now get out of here." The crowd stared at them.

Thurman pulled his daughter close. He glared icily at the Viking.

"Is it the king's mandate to bar us from our own town, or yours?" he demanded.

"Go home! You don't belong here!"

"Not in my own town square?"

"You're a miserable Christian, Thurman. This is not your festival. Why don't you go pray somewhere? I thought you were forbidden to have such fun anyway," the guard quipped with an ugly smirk.

Thurman felt his daughter's hand reaching to him.

"Papa, let's go," she whispered, frightened. Thurman was seething, but he suppressed his anger to protect his children.

Godiva watched the exchange between Thurman and the Viking in puzzled concern, but she couldn't hear what they were saying over the sounds of the crowd. People were cheering loudly as they watched the inebriated woman finally succeed in mounting her horse.

"What has distracted you?" Wulfstan asked, noticing that Godiva had stopped singing.

"Oh, nothing important," she answered, compulsively brushing back her hair. Two men had begun to paw at the drunken woman's skirt.

"Come on, pretty. Don't be so bashful," one of them taunted.

The woman looked around, bleary-eyed, as they pulled her to the ground. She wavered for a moment and then began trying once again to climb on the horse.

"Why don't you just stumble over here in my direction?" the other man slurred.

"Good heavens," whispered Godiva to Wulfstan. "The woman is completely drunk, and they're all laughing at her. Let's leave, Wulfstan. I can't bear to witness this."

"You go," he said. "For all of the poor sights, this is a feast of sound for me."

"Will you be alright?" she asked him, holding onto his arm for a moment.

Wulfstan adjusted the strap of his lute and slipped it onto his back.

"I'll be fine," he smiled. "I find my way every other day. There's no reason I won't today."

Godiva pushed her way through the crowd and down the street, terribly upset. Suddenly, two arms grabbed her from behind, wrapping around her and pulling her close. All she could think of was the two drunken men pulling on the woman's skirt.

"And how shall we celebrate spring, my flower?" whispered the man behind her.

Godiva spun around.

"Leofric," she cried, throwing her arms around him. "Hold me," she said, burying her head in his chest.

"I will hold you in my heart, as well as in my arms," he laughed. "What a pleasant greeting! Now, give me an answer: how shall we celebrate spring?"

"Perhaps with a kiss," she said, recovering from her surprise.

"Kiss you? Here?" he teased, looking around at all the revelers, many of whom were sharing more than a kiss. "Well, you've been to more May Day celebrations than I. If you think it's appropriate..." His voice trailed off as he gazed into her sparkling green eyes.

"I am now your wife. You must kiss me whenever I want, whether it's appropriate or not!" Godiva playfully insisted. He ran his hands through her hair, leaned in, and kissed her passionately.

❃❃❃❃❃❃

As the festival raged on, several men watched from the forest, hidden within the dense trees. They held rolled banners of the king's emblem, just waiting for the chance to exercise their power in Canute's name. They were members of his elite guard, the Huscarles.

"Do you think we'll have any trouble here today?" one asked.

"I should hope so!" another answered.

❃❃❃❃❃❃

The drunken woman finally balanced herself again on the back of her large stallion. She began calling to the men in the crowd as she rode around the Maypole and on to the Cofa Tree.

The men roared with glee. Hysterically, she cackled with laughter, barely getting out the words, "Hail to the goddess Ester, who makes us fertile with child!" Fulfilling the tradition of the fertility rite, the woman then awkwardly unfastened the pieces of her outfit and let them drop to the ground to ride naked.

Leofric shielded Godiva's eyes, disgusted by the sight.

"Let's go, my love. Who knows what vulgar display might be next." He put his arm around her and escorted her away. Suddenly, they noticed the king's men at the fringe of the forest.

"Leofric," Godiva asked nervously, "What are they doing here?" At that moment, the king's men emerged from the trees and rode toward them.

"We're looking for Leofric, son of Earl Leofwine," the first Huscarle said.

"I am Leofric. How may I be of service?"

The Huscarle looked dryly at him.

"By order of the king, you are to ride along with your sheriff to Winchester for a reception tonight.

"Tonight? Very well," Leofric said matter-of-factly. "I'll meet you at the gatehouse. I shall make the necessary arrangements and prepare my horse."

The Huscarles retreated from Coventry's gates, leaving Leofric and Godiva alone.

Godiva's brother, Thorold, sauntered up from the festival, wanting to hear what the Huscarles had come for. He had followed in the footsteps of their father and was now the sheriff of Coventry. He tried to be as fair as his father, but as much as he tried to hide it, he never lost his fury toward Canute and the Danes.

"I've been watching those jackals all day. I guess they finally decided to show themselves," Thorold commented. "What is their business here?"

"The king requested to see us, Thorold," Leofric explained. "We must ride to Winchester immediately."

"For what reason?" Thorold asked.

"A reception of some sort."

Thorold paused. "I'll ready my horse and meet you at the castle," he said, resigned.

Godiva and Leofric rode toward their home, cantering through the lazy fields. The smell of spring was all around them, and tiny white blossoms floated through the dappled sunlight. Suddenly, Godiva broke off the trail.

"Godiva! Wait!" Leofric called after her.

She raced furiously through the woodlands, leaning into the wind and clutching the saddle as her hair streamed behind her.

"Godiva! What are you doing? Have you forgotten that the king has summoned me?" Leofric called, racing after her.

"No," she yelled over her shoulder at him. "But now I have summoned you as well." She spurred her horse to go even faster. Leofric followed.

Finally she slowed. "Whoa boy," she said to the horse, pulling in his reins.

"My gentle wife, the king is waiting," Leofric reminded her, trying to reach over and grab her horse's bridle.

"A woman always has a rightful claim to keep one waiting. Even if it is a king who waits."

"How could I have forgotten?" Leofric responded, succumbing to her charm.

Leofric dismounted next to a stream, while Godiva gracefully leapt from her horse onto a nearby grassy bluff. She turned to take in the view.

"Isn't it amazing?" Godiva beamed, looking at their castle in the distance and slipping into her husband's arms.

"It's you who are amazing," Leofric laughed. "Being back in Coventry and married to you these last few months has been the best time of my life," he smiled, toying with her long, silky tresses. "It is hard for me to leave you, even if it is for only a day or two."

"Why do you say you must go for a day or two?" Godiva pouted.

"Because that's how long it takes, my impatient wife," he said.

"Then you must take me with you."

"I would like nothing more, Godiva, but I can't."

He impulsively picked her up, swung her into his arms, and spun her around.

Godiva exploded with laughter as he turned faster and faster. "Leofric, stop!"

"Why?" he asked breathlessly.

"Because I can't kiss you when you do that."

"So, it's another kiss you want. I already kissed you once today. And I really must be leaving," he teased, setting her down.

"No, not yet."

They tumbled to the ground, waiting for the earth to stop spinning around them. Godiva propped herself up on one elbow. She ran her fingers through his hair.

"Leofric?"

"Yes, my darling? Why do you seem so serious all of a sudden?"

"I know that many people have come to feel differently about King Canute, but what he did to my family still haunts me, day and night. I am fearful for you to go see him. I worry that he might do something terrible to you."

"I understand; my concerns are the same. I will never be able to trust him entirely. No matter what good I hear that he has done, a part of me is always wondering what wretched thing he might do next."

"Do you think it's possible that he has actually changed?"

"In many ways, he is certainly different. I have been surprised on many occasions these last ten years. My father has had a moderating influence on him, but just how deeply he has truly changed, I cannot tell."

"Leofric, you know that your father won't be around forever. What will happen when he is no longer with us? Do you think Canute will listen to you when you become earl?"

"Who can say? I suppose that King Canute cares little for my thoughts," he said, picking a blade of grass and twisting it around his finger. "But I will speak openly to him if he asks."

Thoughts of her parents were vivid in Godiva's mind. She missed them terribly. How she wished her mother could have been at her wedding and that her father could have given her away.

"Before we go, my love, I must ask you something else," Godiva said softly, a smile breaking across her face.

"What, my fairest lady?"

"Leofric, have you ever given much thought to...children?"

"To children?" he responded with surprise. "Is there a particular reason to be entertaining such thoughts?" He waited for her answer, suddenly forgetting all about being summoned by the king and the festivities of the day.

"No, not yet. I was thinking about family, my parents and how much I still love them. Besides, it's only natural that thoughts of children occur to me. They must have crossed your mind."

Leofric leaned into her, gently rubbing his hand across her stomach. It was flat and tight, but he could easily picture a growing baby reshaping it. "My remarkable wife never stops thinking," he said moving closer. "We could have a child some-day. A son?" he asked, with sudden inspiration on his face.

"Or a daughter," Godiva added.

"Well, yes. Of course, of course."

"A girl can be as important as a man, if God's destiny is upon her," Godiva said straightforwardly.

"How well I know that. After all, you are God's gift, Godiva," Leofric concurred, referring to the meaning of her name.

They both fell quiet as the breeze blew through the grass around them, engulfing them in an ocean of green. He leaned in and kissed her.

"I love you so very much, Leofric," she whispered. "Forget about the king."

"I already have," he sighed, placing his lips on hers once more.

It was a perfect moment. They would always remember the honeysuckle on the wind and the sun on their faces on that one spring afternoon when their dreams still seemed so clear.

"We will have children," Leofric said, gently touching her face. "And they will carry on our memory long after these times have taken us."

NINETEEN

Along the road to Winchester, Leofric, Thorold, and the Huscarles turned up a well-worn path and rode through the woods to Leofwine's castle. Thick branches brushed against them as they made their way up to the huge stone entryway and staircase. Smoke rose from the upstairs chimney where Earl Leofwine lay on a couch, attended by Martha, his very elderly nurse.

As they secured their horses outside, Leofric asked his brother-in-law and the guards to go to the kitchen and have some supper while he took a few minutes with his father.

Leofric opened a small side door where a narrow, private staircase led him upstairs. He hurried across the huge marble hallway, through the side passageway, and straight through the door of his father's chamber.

"Oh! You startled me, my lord!" Martha said, further opening the door while awkwardly steadying her pan of water and rags.

"How is he?"

"Well, dear Leofric, your father seems a wee bit restless today," she confided, lowering her voice so that Leofwine wouldn't hear. "I've given him a little wine. It helps him to sleep," she said in her thick country accent. "His mind is as young as a spring chicken, but his body is as old as...well as old as mine," Martha laughed.

"Thank you, Martha. I'll look in on him now." Leofric walked slowly into his father's chamber.

Leofwine lay there on the couch, a mischievous grin on his face.

"Hello, Father," Leofric said, drawing near.

"Leofric," his father answered, clearing his throat and opening his eyes. "You're here. What brings you this way today, son?"

"I wanted to see how you were."

Leofwine leaned over. "Aren't you supposed to be in Winchester? I heard that the King had summoned you, and I would imagine that you have more pressing things to do than make a social call to an old man."

Leofric sighed. "Father, do you know why I've been called to his castle?"

"Canute is a very clever man. He may have something up his sleeve." Leofwine smiled. "But then, Leofric, you and I both know that my days of rule are nearly over. I believe that the king's intention may simply be to introduce you to the ways of his court."

"But the earldom is not yet mine, Father. You are the earl of Mercia. You will regain your strength and continue to rule for many years to come."

"The Lord has given me these long years, and most of them have been healthy. But I have had enough. If it is time to pass my duties on, then..."

"Please, Father, I have confidence..."

"Son, listen to me," Leofwine interrupted impatiently, holding up his hand. "It may be today and it may be a year from now, but when the moment becomes yours, I expect you to seize upon it with strength and grace. It is your duty and destiny to lead and my greatest honor to know that you are ready."

"Father, thank you. But, I..."

Leofwine leaned in toward his son. His eyes became focused and intent. "I've been in your shoes, son. I know what they feel like. Be proud, but be shrewd." He spoke with fresh power welling up in him. His face brightened as he offered his deepest and most heartfelt wisdom to his son. "Pay careful attention to power. Respect it. Court it. Let it speak to you before you attempt to regard it as your own."

His father gazed at him, and they both fell silent. Leofwine took in the young man before him. His youngest son, the one whom he had been a sole parent to for much of his life. What a fine man he had grown into! Kind and intelligent, fearless and calm. Leofwine's eyes filled with fire. His musings gave way to the urgency of time and the reality of his own mortality.

"Leofric, it is up to you. You must lift our family from the shame Edric and Norman have brought upon us."

Leofric said nothing. He glanced out the window and then simply turned around knowing it was time to go.

"May you travel safely, my son."

"Thank you, Father."

✾✾✾✾✾✾

The Winchester castle of King Canute stood high on a hill, surrounded by stately oaks and cedars. Large glacial boulders clung tightly to the hillside path as if they had been commanded not to roll down.

As Leofric and Thorold drew closer, the Huscarles broke away and a patrol of King Canute's men was dispatched to escort them into the castle. It was the first time that Leofric

or Thorold had been invited to visit, and they looked appre-
hensively up at the foreboding and heavily fortified edifice.
Bowmen could be seen standing guard along the walls. The
castle's towers loomed ominously against the sky, casting eerie
shadows as night began to fall. In the dying light, Leofric saw
Godwin, Canute's brother-in-law, arriving as well. He was one
of England's most powerful earls, and no friend to Leofric or
his father.

"Leofric! The earl's pup makes his rise to the king's banquet table, eh?" Godwin commented in a patronizing tone.

"Earl Godwin. I'm sure my father would send his regards,"
replied Leofric.

The two of them stepped together through the pair of
massive castle doors that Canute had brought from Denmark.
Thorold followed close behind them. Inside, dozens of lit
torches lined the great stone walls of the lavish hall, reflecting
off the polished silver set at each place on the rows of tables.
Nearly a hundred people milled around the room, dressed in
their finest.

"Let the music begin," the majordomo called out. The
sounds of bone whistles, harps, and drums filled the great hall
as musicians paraded in, followed by a troop of brightly costumed dancers. The celebration had begun.

King Canute appeared on a wide balcony. He stood with
his arms folded, observing the crowd. His carefully choreo-
graphed evening had started without a hitch. A constant flow
of people was now pouring into the hall, and they were being
directed to their places at various tables.

Servers carried heaping platters of pheasant, lamb, and
turkey and placed them amid the plates of bread and fruit,
tureens of soup, and pitchers of ale. As he was being seated
at a central table below the balcony where Canute stood, Earl

Godwin grabbed a turkey leg and held it up in the air, waving at Canute's brother, Prince Harold, who had just sauntered in.

Leofric's brother, Norman, sat down beside Earl Edric, who was already far gone with drink. They were not pleased about the banquet. Canute had not told them the reason for the celebration, and they didn't like surprises. Especially after learning that Leofric had been invited. With Leofwine growing too old and weak to travel, Edric was hoping to be granted the earldom over all of Mercia. But if Leofric was to be invited into Canute's inner circle, it did not bode well for him. He and Norman had been drinking since they heard the news that afternoon. Norman shoved his hand into a bowl of grapes and stuffed them sloppily into his mouth.

"Long life to you, brother," Leofric said formally as he walked over to greet him. "You seem like you're enjoying yourself."

"I work for King Canute now, dear brother," Norman slurred. "I have the finest of everything. If you had half a mind, you would stop this absurd resistance to the ways of the world and partake of the bounty before you. But you always were the self-righteous one, weren't you?" Norman squinted up with bleary eyes.

"You're drunk," Leofric answered, walking away in disgust.

"Edric Streona, my uncle!" Norman said loudly. "Have a grape or two."

He tossed a bunch of grapes into the air and laughed as they scattered on the table and bounced onto the floor. He drunkenly grabbed another handful as the trumpets blasted a fanfare.

"King Canute," a page announced. The people stood and cheered.

"Please, take your seats," the king said, grandly moving to his place at the main table.

Prince Harold slumped in his seat at the far end of the king's table. He was bored and restless. The only redeeming quality of the evening so far had been a troupe of scantily clad dancers.

Canute's English queen, Emma, poised herself beside her husband. She stared ahead, expressionless. Hers was the anguished face of a woman whose marriage had been unhappily arranged. As it often happened, a marriage made in diplomacy and alliance had not transformed into one of love and affection. Her bloodline had been of great importance to Canute. She was the second wife of his former enemy, King Ethelred, the father of Edmund Ironsides and of Edric Streona's wife.

Strategically, Emma was the perfect choice, a Norman and sister to the powerful Richard II, Duke of Normandy. She ensured peace with Normandy and provided royal blood for Canute's sons, as well. Canute magnanimously put up with the fact that Emma was a Christian. Sadly, she had long since given up on happiness. She gazed blankly across the room, her mind a million miles away. At one time she had been rather attractive, but many bitter years had stolen the softness that her face had once had.

King Canute sat in an ornate ceremonial chair that was carved from mahogany and inlaid with gold and jewels. The head of his Viking ship had been richly embroidered in the purple upholstery. He leaned over to his wife, squeezing her hand until it hurt.

"Look amused," he enjoined, gritting his teeth through his smile while almost crushing her fingers. "After all, you are their queen."

Queen Emma angrily withdrew her hand and rubbed it under the table.

"As you wish, my lord," she said. She forced a smile.

"A most lavish banquet, my king," Godwin simpered, leaning over to Canute.

"And the evening's revelries are just beginning," Canute observed.

Canute turned to Edric Streona, who was shoveling meat into his mouth.

"We have earned this night, my friend, Edric," the king remarked, raising his golden goblet. Streona raised his in return.

"To your empire, may it forever flourish above all others, Your Majesty!" Edric toasted proudly. Canute looked around, measuring, considering each of those chosen guests who shared his table. He beckoned Edric forward and spoke quietly to him.

"You know, Edric, many demons arrive as invited guests. They become impossible to recognize. They stay close and offer gifts. They're patient and wait for the perfect moment to strike." King Canute raised an eyebrow at Edric and waited for his response.

"My king, if I may," Edric began after a moment's thought, "the advice I might offer is to strike first and strike last," he nodded firmly, obviously proud of his insightful reply.

"Ah, strike first and strike last?" Canute savored the phrase. "Sound advice from sound council," he added, taking a delicate bite of lamb.

Canute's gaze kept sliding back to Leofric, who sat quietly beside Thorold at a far table. Queen Emma noticed his interest and wondered what scheme was hatching in her tyrant husband's mind. Edric turned to the servant girl who was clearing his plate and asked for more ale. He was oblivious to the king's interest in his nephew, Queen Emma, or anyone else for that matter.

✪✪✪✪✪✪

"He's staring at you again," Thorold said to Leofric, who was spreading honey on a chunk of bread.

"Who?" Leofric asked.

"The king," Thorold mumbled, not looking up from his soup. Leofric followed suit and concentrated on his food.

"You noticed as well? He's been doing so all night. What do you supposed he wants from me?"

A crash of cymbals suddenly signaled the start of the entertainment, and the royal players filed out. They each knelt to kiss Canute's ring as stage torches were lit. All eyes were on the empty platform as the first three players began their performance. The three men stepped out in front of the crowd to the applause of King Canute, who seemed excited, as if he knew what was to come. One man began leading the other two in a dance.

The leader bore a remarkable resemblance to Edric. Edric noticed this and paused a moment before motioning to one of the servants for another pitcher of ale. On stage, the two men were given cups from which to drink. They drank and then wildly flailed about in a pretended frenzy of poison and sickness. They soon fell in mock death, gaining a roar of applause from the onlookers.

"What's all the clapping for?" Edric mumbled to himself. "Who is that supposed to be?" he asked, watching the character who was so markedly a caricature of himself.

King Canute sipped from his heavy goblet. The music quieted. The one man remaining on stage paused. He appeared to be gazing heavenward, waiting for something to appear—a heavenly sign, perhaps. Just then, a bear-like creature waddled in from stage left. The third performer was dressed in an oversized bearskin and a Viking helmet—representing an ancient Viking king. The man fell to his knees before the helmeted bear king and overacting, in a most obsequious fashion, worshiped him.

"Yes! That's it!" cried one of the guests with great approval.

"Perfection," blurted another.

The guests burst into a roar, for the tale of Danish conquest was nearly complete.

"Long live the Vikings!" another guest screamed out from the audience, followed by spontaneous hoots and applause from all.

A troop of costumed dancers with large headdresses entered and scurried around, herding the guests outside.

"Come one, come all, those who would know the rest of the play and the end of the show!" one of the actors invited as he gestured his hand toward the door leading the audience out into the night.

"My Lord? What is this?" Edric Streona asked the king nervously. He quickly sobered, unsure of what would happen outside.

"Let us follow the procession," Canute answered reassuringly, placing his hand on Edric's back. "Come, Edric. Norman," he said brightly. Then he motioned for Emma to join them. "You may find this of particular interest, my dear."

"Then I would be delighted, Your Highness," she said, following him.

The entire household of guests and performers, nearly three hundred people, was now standing outside on the wide field in front of the castle. The wind was blowing, bending the black feathers of the dancer's headdresses. The group stopped near the bridge. Torch-bearing guards provided light, illuminating the babbling river.

King Canute still held his jeweled goblet and drank merrily from it as he walked between Edric and Norman, while the queen followed, lifting her skirts in the mud.

"There she is," cried Canute. "The river Thames. My precious river." He pushed his way to the front of the line, while pantomiming dancers pranced out of the way, theatrically shamefaced. Canute ran up to the bridge. He halted in the middle of it and put his hand up. On cue, the musicians began to play. They struck up the song they had begun earlier inside.

Leofric and Thorold were at the front of the crowd. They exchanged looks, wondering what in the world was going on. Prince Harold had also found his way to the front. He looked somewhat lost. Canute whirled dramatically, raising his goblet in the night air.

"A most spectacular presentation tonight," he shouted.

The crowd howled in agreement. The wind began to pick up, and one of the dancers had to steady his elaborate headdress to keep it from falling off. The crowd waited breathlessly for Canute's next move.

"A grand display," Canute bellowed. "Wouldn't you say, Edric?" he asked, studying his reaction.

Edric was ushered to the front of the crowd by the guards. He stood there, shifting nervously from one foot to the other.

"The ending, I'm afraid, has left me baffled," he said, chuckling nervously.

"You find the ending baffling, my friend?" Canute asked, growing even louder. "That is because the end is not yet here!"

Edric's eyes widened as the guard escorted him to stand beside Canute.

The actors and dancers at the front of the crowd nervously took a few steps back. Some folded their arms in front of themselves protectively. The king paused, staring long and hard into Edric's eyes. Queen Emma began nervously twisting the jeweled necklace at her throat. The wind rustled the trees along the banks of the shore.

"My king?" Edric asked with fear.

"Do you not fancy tragedies, Edric?"

"Whose?" Edric answered, his voice squeaking.

"Whose indeed, Edric?" the king smirked. "The very question at hand. You see, the king in the play, having conquered the enemy, must now rule his people, administer new laws, and apply justice fairly. Those close to him may feel they have been cheated out of their reward for their loyalty. These are the ones to look out for..." he trailed off as his Huscarles rode to block off both ends of the bridge.

"Your Majesty?" Edric responded, his lip quivering.

"Everyone around me must now be considered," the king continued as he paced in front of Edric. "I'm trying to recall what you said earlier this evening. Something about 'striking first and striking last'?"

Shocked understanding filled Edric's face.

"I've risked my life for you," he yelled, as the guards at the ends of the bridge drew their swords.

"Most clever, Edric. What runs in your veins, perhaps the cold blood of a snake?" the king screamed back. Canute flung his jeweled goblet wildly across the bridge and into the water.

"I killed Edmund, my own brother-in-law, to make you king! What more could I have done to prove my loyalty?" Edric pleaded.

"You prove only that you can't be trusted. What you did, you did to save yourself. I know you would gladly kill anyone that gets in your way.

"I allowed you to remain the earl of Northern Mercia, but that wasn't enough. You wanted more and more and still more! Your greed will never be satisfied until you make yourself king. I know of your secret treachery with Elsorn. Did you really think I would not find out? How dare you, you ungrateful curse!" Canute unleashed the fury that had been brewing within him for a week.

Edric lashed out.

"You hypocrite!" he yelled. The crowd gasped.

"Me? A hypocrite? How long did you think I would allow you to remain in my court? You fawn over me like a reckless jester, thinking I am flattered, and then plot treason behind my back. You are lucky I allowed you to live this long. You are, indeed, the vilest stench in my kingdom." Canute leaned close to Edric's face. The cloudy night sky darkened as he raged.

"I despise you," he said quietly.

A soldier stepped forward, bringing Norman to the front to stand beside Edric.

"Ah, Edric's protégé," the king observed, turning to Norman. "You have become twice the son of hell that your uncle is. Your betrayal disgusts me!"

"My king?" Norman questioned weakly.

Leofric stepped forward, but Thorold pulled him back.

"He's going to kill my brother," Leofric cried desperately. He jerked his arm away from Thorold and raced forward, drawing his sword.

"No!" Leofric yelled.

Canute's soldiers grabbed him before he could reach him.

"The loyal brother comes to save his sniveling sibling. How admirable and yet how foolish of you, Leofric. Did you really think you could save him?" the king chided.

"Let him go," Canute told his Huscarles. "Let him have his anger. I want to see it." The Huscarles released Leofric as Canute laughed.

As Leofric bolted forward, Canute pushed him back with startling force.

"Let us hear what you have to say," Canute taunted.

"My brother has been loyal to you," Leofric said. His knuckles were white around the hilt of his sword.

"He's been loyal to no one. Least of all the throne," Canute hissed back at him. "You do not know what you're talking about. You're naïve. You and your father were to be killed this very night by your so-called loyal brother, and this slimy toad, Edric Streona!"

Leofric looked at Norman, who would not return his gaze. He turned back to the king, brow furrowed in confusion.

"No, that can't be true!"

King Canute laughed. "Not true?" he answered quietly. "Do you want to know the truth, Leofric? Shall I enlighten him, Edric?" the king fixed his steely glare on Edric. There was silence.

"The truth is that, according to Edric's plan, your family lands were to be put under his authority. Norman was to take your place as earl." He spoke smoothly.

"How can this be true?" Leofric shuddered.

"I grow weary of your doubt. Bring me the scroll," Canute ordered. A Huscarle passed a piece of parchment to Canute.

"You'll find this enlightening," Canute told Leofric, handing him a single rolled sheet.

Leofric unfurled the document and began to read.

"Does this lie?" Canute asked. "Well, does it?" he shouted into Leofric's face.

"In their arrogance, they assumed I would embrace their devious plan. You see, Leofric, the truth of the matter is, I have saved your life and that of your father."

"Norman, how could you do this?" Leofric asked, pleading for an explanation.

Norman stared at him icily.

"Leofric, I would rather be dead than have to compete with you any longer. I am sickened by the sight of you."

Canute glared at Norman and shook his head in disgust.

Norman saw the rage in Canute's eyes. He knew that he would soon be dead. He helplessly looked around but saw no way out.

At that, Canute lifted his hand to signal his men.

"Huscarles, make it so," he cried.

"No, wait!" Norman begged.

In a moment, Edric and Norman's hands were bound tightly behind their backs. Canute cast his eyes deliberately in Leofric's direction as he ordered, "Rid me of this putrid sickness."

Before anyone had time to think or protest, the sharp knives of the Huscarles sliced across Edric and Norman's soft throats. They slumped to the ground, life spilling from their gullets.

"Their ambition toward my throne was disgraceful," Canute said, stepping over the lifeless bodies.

"Let it be known: These men are not to have burials," Canute decreed. Turning to his men, he coldly ordered, "Rid me of them!"

The bound, limp, and bleeding corpses were tossed over the bridge into the river. Their bodies floated in the dark water below. The crowd was shocked into a terrified silence. The breeze blew over the water, and all stared straight ahead, not daring to react.

"Norman," Leofric whispered. Whatever evil his brother had done, Leofric still loved him.

Canute looked up at his horrified wife. More than anyone, she knew the brutal side of this Dane. She and she alone fully understood the depth of his secrets. Canute had learned very well from his father that mercy was weakness. He despised weakness above all else. Canute's message had been sent and made clear to everyone: He was the law.

Then, Canute seemed to change. He turned and put his arm around Leofric, comforting him.

"You know in your heart, Leofric, that these men were deserving of death. In time you will understand, like your father, what it takes to rule."

In shock, Leofric didn't know what to say.

"From the first day that I met you, I liked you. I could see that by nature, you were a man of integrity," Canute said warmly.

"I know that some think I am a cruel man—a murderer. What I am, what I will be, that is for history to decide. You must know, though, that I was born to exact vengeance on those who killed my family. It was none other than King Ethelred, the first husband of my wife, who set the tragic events that now rule our lives in motion. The death and destruction he forced on the Danes who lived peacefully in this land has come back upon his people fourfold. He murdered my father's sister, Gunhilda. My beloved aunt! She was like a mother to me. My father and I came to this land to seek vengeance, and we got it. When he died, I vowed to conquer, and that I have done.

"Whether you recognize it or not, what was done here tonight was done for justice. What you, Leofric, must now know is that I want to make peace between our two peoples. I want to build a new and greater England, with the laws of your brilliant King Alfred as a foundation."

Leofric was shocked by this revelation. His head was spinning. He tried to absorb Canute's words but could hardly hear them over the sound of his pounding heart.

Canute walked him off to the side with his arm around him. No one said a word.

"This is a new era, Leofric," he said quietly. "Men of treachery no longer have a position in my kingdom. Danes and Saxons must no longer be regarded as adversaries but as fellow citizens. If we are to build a great nation, I must be served by men of honor. Men who understand real loyalty. Men like yourself. What is your decision, Leofric? Will you waste your honor defending dogs, or will you keep it for the people of a new, greater England?"

Canute looked into Leofric's eyes but saw no answer.

"Leofric, I understand your reticence, but you must understand that I am not the man that I was. I have spent these years listening to the wise council of your father. I have studied night and day the writings of Alfred and others. I desire to build a powerful nation that can endure a hundred generations," Canute's voice filled with passion.

"I know that a great England, where justice reigns, is also what you want. Your father and I have spent many hours talking of these things."

"Your Majesty, I did not know." Leofric began to see Canute in a new light.

"Leofric, you were not called here tonight merely to witness these events, but because I have decided to grant you the earldom of all Mercia."

Leofric surveyed the people surrounding him before speaking.

"Earl? But my father has the rightful claim."

"Your father is a good man—a great man, in fact—one who has become my friend, but both you and I know he no longer has the vigor to rule. I have watched you and have gained great confidence in your ability and...discretion."

Leofric glanced at Earl Godwin and Thorold, who both looked stunned at the news.

Canute pointed toward the ground. Leofric dropped to his knee.

"Your Majesty," he said.

"All of Mercia is now yours to rule, according to the laws of the Danish crown. Handle it well, Earl Leofric, so that Saxon rule may persevere in England."

Leofric slowly began reciting the words he had committed to memory so many years ago, knowing someday they would be his.

"I vow to be your man, to serve you and England as earl in Mercia until death or the king's displeasure. I shall serve the kingdom with my assets, my blade, and my life. In my service to you, I shall bear your name, with mercy or force, and be loyal and truthful for all that I am worth."

"I am quite sure you will, Earl Leofric." The king touched Leofric's shoulder, signaling him to rise. "I travel tomorrow for Copenhagen to meet with my War Council. Streona's knights and infantry shall be reassigned immediately to your authority."

"Yes, Your Majesty."

Leofric's eyes met the queen's. They were two players in a royal drama that held them inextricably bound to the court of the Danish king. Canute seemed mildly amused by their locked gaze.

"I do have but one small request, Lord Leofric," he added. "Reparations have again been demanded by my council for the great cost of settling England. I cannot delay them any further. My advisors will meet with you and set forth the details of the Danegeld tax charter. You shall announce it in Coventry immediately."

"Of course, Your Majesty," Leofric answered with no thought of the consequences.

They made their way back to the castle, the queen following quite a distance behind.

Along the way, Earl Godwin approached Leofric. "Do you know, Earl Leofric, that I have great expertise in matters of state. Should you ever falter, I am prepared to assume the lead." Leofric steadily met Godwin's gaze but didn't say a word.

By the time they were back inside the hall, the guests were acting as if they had forgotten entirely about the gruesome murders at the river. There was music, food, and dancing.

The two men's bodies floated down the cool, dark waters of the river. An owl hooted ominously in the nearby trees, and the wind blew the clouds until the moonlight shone on the water again like a spotlight.

TWENTY

T he next morning came with a wash of magnificent May sunshine and a blanket of spring flowers that seemed to have blossomed overnight. Godiva strolled through town, warmly received by all. She wore her hair partially bound up. It cascaded down her back in a mane of wild beauty.

"It's a beautiful morning," she nodded to an old woman selling fruit and nuts from a small cart.

"Indeed, my lady," the woman smiled back.

Godiva strolled across the town plaza, smiling at children and greeting the local merchants. Even though she felt strangely alone when Leofric was away, the comfort of their tender farewell the day before stayed with her. The thought that Leofric and Thorold were with Canute did bring her some worry, but she tried not to dwell on her fears. Over and over again, she told herself that everything was fine.

A nearby fountain splashed in the sunlight. Godiva continued on her way toward the small church that had been built in the center of town shortly after the siege. The children's choir she led had already gathered and anxiously awaited her arrival. As she neared the church, the Cofa Tree was on her left. She cringed as she walked across the site where the pagan fertility rite had taken place less than twenty-four hours before. There were still bits of ribbon and streamers caught in the branches and trampled into the dirt.

"Good morning, everyone!" Godiva said as she entered the church. The eight children were sitting quietly in the first two rows, well behaved for once.

"Good morning!" they answered, wiggling excitedly.

"Alright, we have no time to waste. Take your places, children," she said.

"I'm ready, but he's poking me," a cherub-faced girl named Ealsbeth piped up. She was one of Godiva's favorites.

"Olaf, that's enough," Godiva warned the little boy.

"Now, line up at the altar, and let's begin with our anthem."

The ragged yet spirited little group filed up to the front and stood in their spots singing as loudly as they could from the moment she gave them their starting pitch.

Let us praise, this day, the Maker of the heavenly kingdom,
Author of all miracles.
How He gave earth's children heaven for a roof,
And a world with lands such as these to live on.
Almighty Lord, we praise you.

Wulfstan appeared in the back, feeling his way along the aisle to a comfortable spot in the center. He slid across the bench and leaned forward, listening with mirth. The hymn the children were singing was the same one that Sister Osburga had fearlessly sung in the flames at the Viking slaughter ten years before. He remembered learning the song when he sang in the choir with Godiva. It seemed a lifetime ago.

Godiva had vowed to keep Osburga's memory alive by teaching the song to every single child in Coventry. The children knew it better than any other.

Prior Aefic, the tall, middle-aged priest, walked quietly in and sat down beside Wulfstan. Wulfstan turned his head and greeted him.

"Prior Aefic, good morning."

"How did you know it was me?" the prior asked.

"Your robes always rustle a bit loudly," Wulfstan said with a smile.

"Oh," he laughed. "You see better with your ears than some people do with their eyes." He listened for a moment and then continued in a whisper. "They sing with the love and purity of the angels, do they not?"

Wulfstan nodded. "I love to listen to them. It brightens my whole day."

"I quite agree. They do wonders for my soul."

"How have you been, Prior Aefic?" Wulfstan asked, touching his hand lightly to the prior's arm while gazing straight ahead.

"Keeping busy with the Lord's work, my friend," he answered, patting Wulfstan's hand kindly.

"She misses Leofric," Wulfstan commented.

"It's their first separation since the marriage, so even a day seems like a long time," Prior Aefic added.

"I wish her never to know a moment of sorrow, as she has always been such a dear friend to me," Wulfstan said devotedly. "I still see her as she was the day of the siege, before I lost my sight, her hair dancing about her radiant face like rays of sunlight as she ran up the hill after a ball."

Prior Aefic reached for his arm compassionately. "You would still like what you see. Although I do not know much of such things, they say she is the most beautiful woman in England."

"My sight," Wulfstan said, patting his chest, "is here, and I see something as lovely as you do, deep inside her." He smiled at the prior.

Aefic smiled back. "Now that you mention it, I see that too, my friend. I see it, too."

The children finished their song, and Godiva teased the two men from the front of the church.

"I hear something behind me. Are there mice in the rafters?" she inquired playfully. The children giggled. Godiva struck the pose of a grizzly. "Perhaps a bear or two in the back pew?"

The choir laughed again, thrilled with Godiva's jest.

"Alright then, if it's not mice and it's not a bear, then what in the world is it?" she said, spinning around dramatically.

"Wulfstan, Prior Aefic? How kind of you to come," she heartily welcomed them.

"But, my lady, they come every morning," one of the children commented.

"And so does the sun. Aren't you glad?"

The children giggled. Sometimes Godiva said the wittiest things.

Prior Aefic ambled heavily down to the front.

"Is it news you bring? Will the pope finally hear us sing?" Godiva asked hopefully.

"I'm sorry, my dear. I still haven't heard from Bishop Luze," he replied.

The children left their places and hopped down the steps, gathering around Godiva and the prior.

Edgar and Lia pushed forward.

"We want to sing more!" Lia begged.

"We want to go look at the birds," pleaded Edgar.

"Yes, please. Let's go see the birds," Olaf chimed in.

"No, we still have more to sing," Lia bossed.

"Why don't we go sing to the birds?" Ealsbeth asked.

"True agents of the Gospel," Prior Aefic laughed, shaking his head.

"Of course. That's a very good idea. Let's all go sing to the birds," Godiva said, humoring them. "Perhaps Wulfstan would like to accompany us?"

The blind minstrel beamed as Ealsbeth grabbed his hand and led him out of the church. "I would be honored."

The morning grew warm, and Leofric wiped his sweaty brow as he and Thorold rode their horses back toward Coventry along the banks of the river. The cattails were already tall and lush.

"I just can't believe everything that has happened since yesterday, Thorold," Leofric sighed as his chestnut horse plodded along the muddy trail. "This is what I have always waited for. I just didn't expect it to happen in this way."

"Did you suspect the depth of Norman's betrayal?"

"Not at all. I haven't spoken to Norman for a long time. Obviously, I knew we had our differences. I tried to resolve them for the peace of our family, but he wanted nothing to do with me," Leofric sighed, "I suppose that was a good thing." Thorold started to say something but shut his mouth. "Speak your mind, Thorold."

"The truth is that we'll all be better off without them."

"You're probably right. It's just hard for me to accept. I thought...maybe someday..."

"Leofric, look over there," Thorold interrupted. "What's that in the thicket?" He pointed to a pack of wild dogs ravenously tearing at something at the edge of the water. It wasn't a deer or a bear but appeared to be a sack filled with clothes. Curious, they moved closer and, dismounting, waved the beasts away with their swords.

"Go on! Get out of here!" Thorold yelled, flashing his blade at a large dog. Thorold chased the animals, and Leofric walked up to the soggy bundle. He looked down, trying to figure out what it was. Suddenly, he gasped and stumbled backward.

"Norman. O God, my brother!" He turned quickly away, fighting an overwhelming urge to vomit. He covered his mouth and flipped over the partially consumed body with the toe of his boot.

"Uncle Edric," he whispered when he saw the bloated white face. It was not his brother that the dogs had been feasting upon. Still, he was horrified to see a man, any man, in this state—let alone his uncle. He began to shake. Thorold walked up to Leofric and stopped suddenly, retching.

"It's my uncle," Leofric said.

"You keep the dogs away. I'm going to look for your brother," Thorold said. He followed the river, squinting and prodding at every bush and log, anticipating the next discovery. He walked down to a patch of thick brush that grew in a cover beneath some large trees.

"Leofric!" Thorold called out. "Here!"

"What is it?"

"Come," he said, his face frozen in anguish.

Leofric rushed over as Thorold pushed away the brush with his sword. There, washed up against an exposed tree root, floated Norman, his head attached by a single thread of sinew.

"Help me get him out," Leofric said.

"But Leofric, Canute's decree..."

"I'm not going to leave them to the dogs. I am going to bury them, Thorold," he said with determination.

Thorold knew it had to be done, no matter what the consequences.

"Then I'll help. Let's be quick, though."

TWENTY-ONE

The Viking ships of war filled the harbor, preparing to leave. The harbor was alive with noise and clamor. Ropes and rigging were hauled on deck as the last crewmen jumped from the dock to the ships, barely clearing the waves beneath them. Canute's fleet of thirty vessels broke for the open seas, bound for Denmark.

King Canute stood at the helm of the lead ship, his flag whipping high above him. The waves broke forcefully against the great gold dragonhead that adorned the prow of his ship. The dragon's mouth was open and seemed to drink the waves that crashed against the ship as it raced forward. Two other ships came alongside the king's, and the three glided together through the water, leading the fleet.

Canute was looking forward to returning home. He had dealt with the council delegation and the issues in England that he had previously not wanted to leave unsupervised and knew that visiting Denmark would put to rest any lingering doubts about his rule. He was confident that Leofric would exhibit the wisdom of his father and loyalty to the throne while sustaining the trust of the people of Mercia. He was relieved to be rid of Edric Streona. Since the moment of the earl's betrayal, Canute had waited for Edric to turn and betray him.

As the vessels gained speed and moved further and further from shore, Prince Harold watched with growing excitement. He would be in charge in his brother's absence. By the time the ships were out of sight, he was giddy with anticipation. He couldn't contain his energy and began to pace, rubbing his hands together.

"Huscarles, we have work to do," he exploded. "While the king is away, you will take your orders from me." Harold led the Huscarles back to the castle, beginning to explain what he would expect on the way.

As promised, Godiva led the children of the choir up to the aviary she had built to feed the birds. The walk took awhile, but it was a glorious day, and the children sang the whole way.

"We still have much work to do on the songs," she reminded them as she led them into the aviary. Although quite a bit smaller, the aviary had been modeled after the one Godiva had helped Sister Osburga with at the abbey. In the middle of it, against a large oak tree, Godiva had built a small altar and decorated it with a collection of treasures she had salvaged from the ruins of the abbey and her home. In the center was Osburga's wooden cross, hung on a stand made of a small birch branch. As she did whenever she entered the aviary and set her eyes on the cross, Godiva gave the slightest curtsy of devotion. She reached her arm up, and a white dove alighted on it.

"Before we start, you can all help me for a few minutes and fill the feed bowls," she told the children.

The children grabbed handfuls of seeds and poured them into the bowls. The birds squawked and gathered as the seeds hit with the familiar pebbly sound that signaled their breakfast. Olaf accidentally knocked over the large burlap sack of seed, sending it across the straw-covered ground. He just stood there, wide-eyed, watching the birds land at the edges and start to peck. His lower lip started to quiver.

"Lady Godiva, look!" Lia cried, pointing to the mess.

"Alright. No need to fret. Everyone knows how to grab handfuls. Let's all help clean it up, and we'll be done very quickly," she said, trying to suppress a smile as she comforted Olaf.

Wulfstan sat on a bale of hay, strumming his lute and humming softly.

"Do you want to feed some?" Ealsbeth asked him as she took his hand from the strings and shoved seeds into his palm.

"I do now," he chuckled as he set down his lute and allowed her to lead him to one of the bowls.

Just then, Godiva's handmaiden, Cresha, rushed in, breathless and bubbling over with excitement.

"My lady, they're back," she announced.

Godiva's face lit up. "Please, Cresha, help the children finish feeding the birds, then take them back into town for me. I must go now."

Not waiting for an answer, she took off running toward the castle as fast as she could. Her husband was back. The gates opened, and she stood eagerly waiting. She could see Leofric and Thorold riding up the path.

Leofric and Godiva raced toward one another. He lifted her into his arms and embraced her tightly. Godiva felt a neediness in his caress and wondered what it meant.

"I've missed you so much, Leofric," she said, trying to catch her breath as he nearly squeezed it out of her.

"I've missed you too, my sweet," he murmured in her ear.

"So, Godiva, how are you then?" Thorold asked, coming up beside them. He was leading both his horse and Leofric's.

Godiva broke from her husband and ran to give Thorold a kiss on the cheek.

"Was the journey to Winchester successful?" she asked.

Thorold paused. "It was eventful," he said, purposefully being vague. "But I must take my leave. Business awaits. I'm sure Leofric will tell you the whole story." Thorold kissed his sister's forehead. Godiva laughed. She was so grateful to have a brother who had sacrificed so much of his own life to care for her.

She tossed him a thankful glance as he left, leaving her alone with her husband.

"Thorold," she called after him, "if you don't find a wife soon I will have to find one for you!"

Thorold laughed as he mounted his horse.

"Yes, matchmaker. If only we could all be as happy as you."

"Come, Godiva. Let's go someplace where we can talk," Leofric said, taking her arm. He was walking quickly, and Godiva was sure that whatever news he wanted to share was going to greatly impact their lives. She felt excited and frightened all at once.

Leofric led her to their "secret place," as Godiva liked to call it. It really wasn't secret. Just a secluded, tree-sheltered clearing on the hill beside their home with an unparalleled view of Coventry in the valley below. They watched Cresha and the children wind their way down the path to town. Leofric stood silently, unsure where to begin.

"What is it, Leofric? What's troubling you?" Godiva asked, leaning back against a tree. "Was it an unpleasant journey, my love?"

Leofric sat beside her and gently took her hand. "My precious wife. Where do I start? Godiva, I have been made earl of Mercia—both northern and southern provinces," he said slowly.

"That's wonderful news! I can hardly believe it. How did this happen, Leofric?" Godiva's eyes sparkled. She leaned over to give Leofric a hug.

"And what does your father say about all this?" she asked.

"I stopped to see him on the way there. He seemed to have had an idea that it might happen, and I have no doubt that he's pleased."

Godiva stood up and looked down on Coventry, bathed in the golden glow of the setting sun.

Then Leofric gestured dramatically with his hand, sweeping it broadly, and announced, "May I present Lady Godiva of all Mercia."

"Oh, Leofric! This is so incredible," Godiva shrieked, throwing her arms around him. "This is everything that we've hoped for." They had often sat on this same hill, speaking of their endless dreams for the future of an ever more prosperous and peaceful England. Now they could finally make their dreams a reality.

"Think of all the good we can do for the people here!" Godiva said, flinging her arms wide. For an instant, Leofric saw her as the stunning adolescent he had first seen climbing the center pole of Osburga's aviary, all those years before.

It was a magical moment. The day's last rays of sunlight seemed to brighten like the glowing embers of a dying fire.

"Earl Leofric, we must make a vow before God never to use our power of rule against the people. We are here to make their lives better, happier, and more peaceful—to protect and to love the people and never to hurt them."

Leofric turned away, saying nothing. Godiva knew something was wrong. He had held her so tightly at the gate, so tightly that it startled her. Now he stood there, stoic and remote.

"I don't understand. Even with the wonderful news, there is clearly something that troubles you. Will you not share my vow?" she pleaded.

Leofric sighed deeply. He moved away from her and stared at the gardens below. He had never seen such a spring. And yet, for all the beauty, he wished he could be somewhere else, somewhere free from the turbulence of the world, just him and his beloved wife.

Standing at the threshold of his future, Leofric felt fearful and burdened. He didn't think it should be like this. The weight of responsibility strained upon him like the world upon Atlas' shoulders. But unlike Atlas, Leofric had the strength of a mere mortal.

"Leofric, you must tell me what's wrong," Godiva said, concerned.

Leofric faced her.

"I don't want to diminish your dreams, my love, but all the news isn't good. There's more. While we were there, in Winchester, the king had Edric and Norman killed."

"What are you saying, Leofric? He killed them? Why?" Godiva's head spun. How much pain would this one man bring to her and her family?

"Canute uncovered a plot they had devised to murder Father and me and to claim Mercia as their own." Godiva's face dropped as Leofric continued on.

"Their treason did not stop there, my love. He also found that they had been secretly conferring with one of the members of Canute's council who plotted against Canute himself."

"Are you sure of this?" she asked.

"Yes. I saw the evidence in their own writing. Norman admitted it to my face before he was killed."

Godiva could not believe what she was hearing. As Leofric continued, he could hardly meet her eyes.

"As much as I would like to share your joy, at this moment, I am still deeply distressed, not knowing even my own feelings. I hardly know how to react." He began to pace.

"If it weren't for Canute, you would now be a widow, mourning my death." He paused to look at Godiva. "The king has not only given me a great honor, but he has also saved my life. My debt to him is immense."

"If he saved your life, I'm certain that it was only for his own purposes," Godiva said forcefully. "I do not want to trivialize the gratitude I should feel for his saving you, but I will never be able to trust him. He killed my family and now he has killed yours, Leofric!" Godiva had clenched her fists and was now breathing heavily. Her eyes welled up with hot, angry tears.

"I loved Sister Osburga more than anyone in the world. I saw that man beat and burn her because she wouldn't kiss his ring and give homage to his false gods."

Godiva was lost in her memories. She could still see that day in her mind. She would never recover from it, and she would never forget that Canute had slaughtered almost everyone she held dear. Leofric put his arms around her and held her tightly.

"I too remember that terrible day," he said, weighing his words carefully. "As much as we both despise what he has done, I believe—and I say this after much thought—that he has indeed changed."

"Perhaps it is not his heart that changes but merely his tactics," she said coldly.

"Whatever his motives, he has given us our chance to rule," Leofric said, reaching for her hand again.

"Maybe. I want more than anything to believe there is a purpose here."

"There is," Leofric said, knitting his brow. "He told me that he wants me to help him build a new England, one where all men, Saxon or Dane, will be treated as equals. A new England where, with you by my side, we shall carry the king's word with dignity so that the people of Mercia thrive. Can you see it, Godiva?"

"I can see it through your eyes, Leofric. I can see it when I see the conviction and confidence of your heart," she sighed. She couldn't imagine working with Canute to bring her people peace. She had been fighting him in her heart and in reality for ten years. And now Leofric was an ally of his.

"Godiva, you make me believe that I can do anything. Think of all that is before us," he smiled broadly at her. Good would come from bad, happiness from sadness.

"We must plan a celebration!" he cried.

TWENTY-TWO

T he next morning came with a chill in the air. The warm spring days had turned unseasonably cold and frosty again, and the castle drawbridge creaked as it lowered in the morning mist. The official dispatch came galloping out, soil and mud flying behind them as they raced over the bridge toward Coventry.

Five soldiers, led by Captain Vemunder, rode up to the gates of Coventry and entered with a clamor that startled children and grabbed the attention of the merchants in the square. The pigeons that had been pecking peacefully suddenly flew off in all directions.

"Fly the banners high," the Danish captain called out. A military drummer pounded his drum and the townspeople stepped back in fear of being trampled, making a path for the soldiers.

"Make way! Make way!" Captain Vemunder cried out. "Acknowledge the crown, acknowledge the royal banner. Make way for the herald."

The official emissary rode into the middle of the square as the sun tried desperately to break through the morning gloom. One of the soldier's horses suddenly stepped backward and bumped into a cart of fruit, sending apples rolling across the road. The soldier pulled his reins and moved his horse forward a few feet, unconcerned by the mishap he had just caused.

The men and women of Coventry surrounded Captain Vemunder and his men, anxious to hear what the herald would announce. Their skeptical expressions showed the wear and tear of pain and struggle, heartache and loss.

Thurman had been standing in his blacksmith shop, his iron gates open to the gray day, when he heard the commotion. He wiped his hands and made his way out to the square, still carrying his heavy hammer. He stopped a short distance from the crowd, in the shadow of the now tattered Maypole. He put his hammer down and folded his muscular arms across his chest, waiting to hear what the racket was all about. The drum stopped. Silence filled the air.

Ross the baker and his wife, Margaret, stepped out of their shop with two loaves of thick bread, surprised to see all their neighbors assembled.

"What's this?" Ross blurted out.

Captain Vemunder looked at him sternly.

"Silence. The herald speaks," he cried out. The herald moved to the front.

"By the authority of our noble king, Canute the Great, ruler of Denmark, Scandinavia, and England, we send greetings to his loving subjects. By order of King Canute, all of Mercia is now under the rule of the new Earl of Mercia, Leofric son of Leofwine."

The crowd burst into a spontaneous uproar of approval.

"God save Earl Leofric!" a man's voice cried out.

"Here, here," yelled another.

"Earl Leofric and Lady Godiva!" someone else called, as the cheers continued.

The herald held up his hand for quiet, impatient with the boisterous crowd. He cleared his throat. The crowd quieted. Their faces glowed with exuberant smiles. The rustling of fabric and whispers made it hard for them to hear the rest.

"Shh! The herald is trying to finish," an old woman scolded a couple chattering behind her.

"Furthermore," the herald called out, "the king has ordered that the Danegeld shall now be collected by Lord Leofric. The toll will be collected in..." He raised his voice. "...ONE WEEK! With the collective sum of one thousand marks of silver."

Wulfstan felt his way through the crowd, pushing his way to the front.

"One thousand! That's fourfold of last time!"

"It's impossible," the man next to him agreed.

The crowd's whispers of excitement gave way to rumbles of outrage. An old gentleman in the back cried, "We'll just see about that."

The trumpets blasted and the herald continued reading from the scroll. He cast his eyes out over the people. "In addition, the youth of Coventry who have reached the age of fifteen shall henceforth be required to accompany the Danish forces as soldiers in the king's royal service for a period of two years. Death shall be the penalty for concealing anyone so qualified to fight."

The people of Coventry groaned and shook their heads, becoming increasingly hostile and yelling at the herald.

"You can't do that!" a man cried.

"You won't take my son," a woman screamed.

"However," the herald said loudly, trying to raise his voice above the flurry of objections. Captain Vemunder rode back and forth in front of the crowd, wearing a menacing glare. The herald waved his hands to quiet the crowd and began again. "However, if any youth be desirous of cultivating the art of peace instead of gloriously serving as a proud soldier..."

"Yes, that's better. Then what happens?" the same woman interrupted.

"An additional payment of one hundred marks will excuse him from service," the herald finished.

A mother standing between her fifteen-year-old twin sons burst into tears. "Please, not my boys. I beg of you!"

"What if I cannot pay?" another mother asked desperately.

"One hundred marks!" the herald barked back.

"But I can't pay a hundred marks. I am a poor woman. Have mercy, sire," she cried. Those around her tried to comfort her, but she broke away.

Just then, a middle-aged woman emerged from the crowd and stepped right to the front, defiantly leveling her finger at the herald. "You go right back to where you came from, you devil! No one here, not one of us, holds a single mark for your coffers."

The crowd fell silent, and the herald started toward her.

"We'll see about that." But before he could finish his thought, Thurman emerged from his corner, holding his hammer lightly in his hand, and stepped in front of the woman. He had heard enough.

"This decree is the enemy of the people," he yelled out, without a thought for his safety.

The fear on the woman's face melted at his boldness and others in the crowd soon found their quivering nerves were now forged steel because of the blacksmith's boldness.

Captain Vemunder looked out at Thurman, furious. "Does the knave not understand the proclamation?"

"The knave understands everything!" Thurman yelled, taking a bold step closer and slamming the hammer into the ground for emphasis. "This means death to our town. We have nothing. A poor widow will have to part with her son or sell all she has to pay the hundred marks to save him."

"Yes," the fearful mother of the twins yelled out passionately.

"Seize that man," Captain Vemunder commanded his guards.

Thurman ran to a nearby thick-walled fountain. He quickly leapt up on its stone rim and addressed his neighbors.

"People of Coventry, have you forgotten how these Danish wolves clawed the life from our fair city once before? Will you again cower from their threats, cradling your wounds? Or will you rally the courage to fight those who would destroy your families and pillage your farms?"

The crowd cheered in solidarity. A few men in front thrust their fists into the air, and the rest of the crowd immediately joined them, shooting their hands up and shouting in allegiance.

Egin, a shaggy-haired pagan farmer who often spoke kindly of Canute, stepped forward.

"This is wrong! You can be sure to count on us, Thurman."

As the crowd howled, Captain Vemunder finally made his way through the crowd to the well. He dismounted, furiously flung his horse's reins to another soldier, and confronted Thurman.

The two men were nearly equal in size and standing face-to-face looked like two giants.

"You think that these people can stand up against the armies of Canute? You certainly sound tough, but what will happen when you have to back up your words? Let me show you real strength!" The captain lifted his heavy Norman sword from his scabbard.

Thurman jumped down from the fountain, wielding his hammer. The townspeople quickly moved back, clearing a space for the two men. A young mother with a baby in her arms gathered her two other daughters and led them to the safety of the far edge of crowd. She knew she should go inside, but she couldn't leave and miss the outcome.

Captain Vemunder was furious. He lunged at the blacksmith, wasting no time with his gleaming sword. Thurman blocked the blow with the handle of his hammer and pushed, sending the man reeling. As the captain caught his balance, Thurman drew the captain's hip knife. The captain looked up in shock, breathing heavily.

In a rage, the captain charged Thurman, intent on plunging his sword through this troublemaker's heart. The crowd fell back at the fury erupting before them. Thurman lunged to meet him, swinging downward to meet the captain's blow. Thurman let out a yelp that could be heard across Coventry. Using all of his blacksmith's strength, all of his might, and all of his passion, Thurman hammered the oncoming sword, and it shattered like glass. The crowd erupted in a deafening cheer while the captain stood there, holding nothing but the hilt of his sword.

"Bad blade, my lord?" Thurman bellowed with laughter. He dropped the captain's knife to the ground and started to walk away, clearly having made his point.

"Thurman, look out!" someone called from the ground. Captain Vemunder had lunged for his knife and was preparing to stab at Thurman. The blacksmith turned and hit the captain's arm, sending the knife flying. The captain dropped to the ground, cradling his broken arm. He screamed in pain.

"You'll die for this, you peasant swine!" Vemunder cried, his face a mask of pain.

"Not by your blade," Thurman retorted.

The soldiers were shocked. They had thought their captain would win easily. Thurman turned toward them.

"Anyone else?" he challenged.

"Come and get your tax!" he yelled, adrenaline bursting through his veins. "You'll have to go through me first!"

The men of Coventry rushed forward to protect the women and children, and now they stood shoulder to shoulder, a firm line of defense. The line had been drawn.

The soldiers looked at each other and made a wordless decision. They loaded Vemunder onto his saddle, turned their horses, and headed out of town.

As they watched the soldiers leave, the people breathed a collective sigh of relief, but they were still fearful.

"Where will this lead? I'm frightened, Ross," said Margaret.

"Fear not," her husband comforted. "This may be our first strike for freedom, but it's not the end."

"Freedom?" his wife answered.

"The time has come to take a stand against those who would once again try to steal our very souls from us," Ross said emphatically, putting his arm around her.

Thurman suddenly noticed the trampled Danish banner on the ground. He reached for it, jumped back up on the fountain, and began waving it in wide arcs.

"If they want the tax, let them come and get it," he roared. "Let them come! Let them come!"

The crowd picked up the cheer. "Let them come! Let them come!"

The church tower struck twelve, and the noonday sun broke through the clouds and over the square where the shattered sword glistened in a thousand pieces.

"Let them come! Let them come!"

TWENTY-THREE

N ear Leofric and Godiva's castle, a short way from the road, a warm-water spring bubbled out from between the rocks and fed a small pond. A bank of soft shallow fog would rise off the water, and sometimes, when the afternoon sunlight struck just right, the fog would become illuminated, revealing an almost magical beauty.

The soothing warm water was Godiva's favorite place to bathe. She would often go there in warmer weather, gingerly drape her muslin gown and lacings across a bush, and slip into the water unnoticed and unbothered. She'd splash and kick as she dove down to where the water cooled, her long hair flowing gracefully behind her like silk, almost to her toes. Godiva would spend hours there, swimming and singing as she did that day, thinking about her future and delighting in God's creation.

"I've brought your towel," Cresha called out to her breathlessly as she hurried down the hill. "Godiva? Lady Godiva, where are you? I've brought your towel."

The maiden looked across the still water of the pond, seeing nothing, not even a ripple. She stepped to the edge and looked down into the deep, blue-green water. She leaned closer and closer. Nothing moved.

"Lady Godiva!" she yelled, starting to panic. Suddenly, Godiva's face broke the surface and with puckered lips, she sprayed a forceful stream of water right at Cresha.

"Oh, good heavens!" Cresha screamed, losing her footing. Godiva laughed and paddled away, anticipating the spill and splash of her maiden. Cresha teetered on the edge, desperately trying to steady herself. Finally, she lost her balance. The maiden plunged into the water with a squeal.

"My lady, how could you?" she scolded, blinking water from her eyes.

"I'm so sorry that you lost your balance," Godiva answered playfully.

"Lost my balance? My lady, what shall I do with you?"

Godiva splashed her playfully. "Splash back," Godiva suggested.

Cresha giggled as she pulled her clothes around her and made her way to the shore.

Suddenly, a trumpet cry was heard across the glen. The soldiers were sounding a warning cry to the castle. Filled with alarm, Godiva immediately climbed out of the water and wrapped herself in the towel, running toward the peony bush where she had hung her gown.

"Quickly, help me," she called to Cresha, who ignored her own soggy condition to help Godiva dress.

"My lady, here. Slip your arms through," Cresha said, lifting the gown over Godiva's head.

"Collect my things," Godiva said hurriedly as she hopped on one foot straightening on her gown.

"Yes, my lady."

"Thank you, Cresha," Godiva called back urgently as she ran up the hill, flipping her long hair behind while frantically tying the lacings across her bodice.

Inside Leofric's council chambers, he and three of King Canute's advisors bent over a carefully inked map of Mercia, intently studying it.

"The forest here does not interfere with the boundary, if the distinction is made clearly," Leofric said, pointing at the map. Just then, someone pounded swiftly on the wooden door.

"Yes? Who is it?" Leofric asked, looking up.

"My lord," the voice from the other side spoke up, "it is your military unit with urgent news."

"Let them in," Leofric answered, gesturing to the man closest to the door. Three soldiers rushed in, closing the door behind them.

"What is so urgent?" Leofric asked, standing up from his table and maps.

"It's Coventry, my lord. An insurrection against the throne is taking place."

"Insurrection?" Leofric asked, his voice raising. "What do you mean?"

"The tax, sir. Upon reciting the royal decree, we were faced with resistance."

Another soldier spoke up quickly. "My lord, the captain was challenged before the people. He was cut down by the blacksmith."

"Thurman," Leofric said, shaking his head sadly.

"Yes, I believe that was his name," the soldier piped up. Leofric smacked the table with the flat of his hand.

Leofric's advisors all spoke up at once.

"This is preposterous. I will send word to the king immediately," one seethed.

"No! He will demand satisfaction, and it would be best to deal with this on our own," lashed the eldest of the group.

"We should call for Prince Harold. We are, as your know, currently under his rule," said a Viking delegate.

"Wait a minute. Gentlemen, with all due respect, these are my friends, my fellow townspeople," Leofric protested. "I helped them rebuild after the siege ten years ago. This is not the time for things to escalate this way."

"Whether they are your friends or your enemies matters little. You must demonstrate to them your new authority. If you allow this rebellion to succeed, it will undermine your position and bring the wrath of the king down on us all," said the eldest.

Leofric ran his hands through his hair, not knowing whom to listen to.

"Your authority, my lord, has been sullied by the commoners," said the Viking.

"I will go myself and settle this quickly," Leofric finally said.

"Earl Leofric, you must bring your infantry and be prepared to strike," urged the warrior. "If the townspeople perceive any weakness, your authority over them will be as good as lost."

"Strike the people of Coventry?" Leofric asked, exasperated. "Are you mad?"

The huge Viking moved closer to Leofric, purposefully threatening him with his size.

"If the king hears that this revolt against his personal decree was not met with vigor, your rule here will be a brief one, to be sure, Earl Leofric."

Leofric was cornered. "Send the scouts to Coventry and alert the infantry," he finally said, looking one last time at the map table.

Suddenly, Godiva barged into the room. She had listened to the entire exchange from the hallway.

"Lady Godiva," one of the soldiers said, bowing quickly as she brushed past him.

"Announce your business here immediately!" ordered the older advisor, appalled that a woman had burst uninvited into their meeting.

"Leofric, my lord, please," she said, moving toward her husband with her hand extended. He knew exactly why she had come. Whenever matters had anything to do with Coventry, his Godiva could not be logical. She held her city in the center of her heart as a mother holds a baby to her breast. And no one, not even her husband, would be allowed to bring any harm there, Earl of Mercia or not.

"Leave us, my good wife. I must attend to these unfortunate events," he said, turning his back on her.

"But, my lord..."

"Godiva, please. These affairs are mine," he snapped. This was difficult enough for him without her meddling.

Godiva was silent. He looked over his shoulder at her. Their eyes met and Leofric recognized something in her gaze that he had not seen for a long time. It was the same mixture of determination and fear that he had noticed the first time he set eyes on her. Now, however, she was not a little girl. She possessed the fury and the ambition of a strong woman who had come into her own. There was no horse he could sweep her up on to carry her away to safety.

"Out with you, all of you," he said, ushering the soldiers and advisors out the door. He was mortified and wanted to clear not only the room but his thoughts.

The Viking refused to move. "The insurrection, Earl Leofric. Would you prefer that I deal with it for you?"

Leofric glared at him. He spent a moment trying to imagine what his father would do in this situation.

"Get me to the town square," Leofric ordered the Viking. He brushed past Godiva without a glance and raced out the door to his horse, followed by the soldiers. The wind blew through the open window and rustled the map of Mercia that lay on the table, now abandoned and ignored. Godiva ran to the window and watched the men ride off below her. She didn't know what to do, but she knew she had to find a way to reason with her husband. As the dispatch of soldiers followed Leofric across the bridge and beyond the castle grounds, Godiva raced through the house.

"Cresha," Godiva called. "Send someone to ready my horse. Quickly! And bring me my key," she added.

"Key to what?" Cresha asked.

"The key to my private chamber, of course."

"Yes, my lady. I'll meet you there immediately," Cresha said, lifting her skirts and running off.

As the sun dipped low in the sky, Godiva galloped on her favorite horse, Aethenoth, toward Coventry, where men and women alike prepared to resist the Danish demands that her husband would enforce.

⚙⚙⚙⚙⚙⚙

The townspeople of Coventry hurried here and there. The men dragged wooden tables and chairs out into the dusty streets, using anything they could find to form a makeshift blockade against the oncoming forces.

"Build up the walls," a man cried as he flipped a huge fruit cart over on its side, sending the produce rolling down the lane.

"Heave," cried four others, flipping an enormous wagon onto the pile.

"Take off the hinges and add the doors if you can," someone instructed.

Two men grabbed pitchforks and shovels and stockpiled them behind the wall.

"What are you going to do with these?" two young boys who had escaped their mother's grasps asked.

"Fight," the men answered without hesitation.

"You're going to fight the king's army with garden tools?" one said incredulously.

"I'll fight with my bare hands if I have to," replied one of the men. "Let them come. I'll fight them all. Never again will those butchers enter my town without a fight," he vowed.

Crouched behind a huge bale of hay was a boy not more than thirteen. He was clutching a stick from a butter churn and watching the mob hurrying in front of him. He was shaking with fear as he clutched his weapon and waited for the entire Viking army to descend with their huge swords. He knew from the stories that those swords could slit a man's throat as easily as if he were a rabbit and slash through a woman as though she were parchment.

TWENTY-FOUR

Godiva felt the need to make one stop before heading into town. She rode to the top of the Coventry hill where she had lived as a child and climbed off Aethenoth. Pensively, she made her way through the weeds and vines that had taken over what was left of the burned beams and charred remains of her family's home. Fragments of her past still lay strewn through the underbrush. A shred of rope from a swing, slivers of glass from a broken mirror, and scorched splinters of furniture—all pieces of the place that had once been hers. She paused before her parents' grave.

"It must never, ever happen again," she whispered.

As she looked up, a glint caught her eye. She hurried over and retrieved a small item from the mud. In all her past visits, she had never noticed it. She anxiously wiped the object clean on the corner of her gown, hardly able to believe what it was.

She sighed, struggling to hold back a flood of emotions, and closed her hand around a whalebone comb that had once been her mother's. Its spine was finely etched with a sun and moon. Godiva's eyes filled with tears as she raised the comb and placed it in her hair. She stood up straight, feeling her mother's presence. Godiva's grief turned to strength.

"I will never let them kill another one of us," she pledged, taking the comb from her hair and clutching it tightly.

"God in heaven, I ask that You protect this nation from its enemies. They must not be allowed to do this again!"

She tucked the comb into a pouch she carried, jumped back on Aethenoth and galloped toward Coventry. She rode wildly, whipping and kicking her faithful stallion to urge him to run even faster. The sun hung low in the sky and Godiva could see the fires of Coventry's commoners burning as they readied themselves for the fight.

Suddenly, a small figure appeared out of a thicket and stumbled down the road. Godiva squinted in the dusk, trying to make out who it was.

"Whoa," Godiva said, slowing her horse. Scared by the massive stallion, the little girl stumbled down the road, screaming, "No, no, leave me alone."

Godiva quickly slipped from her horse and ran to the distraught girl. "Lia, Lia, is that you?"

"Please, please, don't let them kill me," the little girl sobbed.

"No one is going to hurt you," Godiva promised, sweeping Lia into her arms.

"Mama says hell is coming again, like when she was young. I saw them coming, riding toward our farm, Lady Godiva," Lia stammered. "Mama went to find little Albert, and I was left there by myself, and I was afraid, so I ran. I ran, because they want to kill us."

"I'm here. You're safe now, Lia. I'm here," Godiva said, rocking her.

"Will you help us, Lady Godiva?" Lia asked, searching Godiva's eyes.

"Of course I will. I will do everything in my power to protect you and your mama and little Albert, too," she said, hugging her.

As Godiva held the child, for an instant she saw herself as a girl, years before, also powerless.

"I'll protect you," she promised for a second time. And as she vowed to Lia, she once more vowed to herself that she would never let Coventry again be destroyed, no matter what the cost.

"Now go back home, Lia," Godiva said, looking deeply into the little girl's eyes. "Go directly home and wait for your mother." The child nodded.

The sound of the army's drums could be heard in the distance as the infantry grew steadily closer to the line of commoners who were as ready as they would ever be, with sticks and shovels and swords, committed to defend themselves or die in the process.

⊙⊙⊙⊙⊙⊙

Thorold had arrived at the well shortly after Thurman's skirmish with Captain Vemunder. Upon seeing the mobilization of his countrymen, he was deeply shaken. An onslaught seemed inevitable. He needed to speak with Leofric, but first he rode quickly to the church to ask Prior Aefic if he might bring the oldest and youngest of their town there for safety. The good prior, of course, agreed, and Thorold rushed out to the main road to try and gather those who would need refuge.

"Please, I beg you, go seek safety in the church. The church is open as a sanctuary," he called to everyone he saw. But few seemed inclined to move in that direction. They were all working to reinforce the barricade.

Thorold passed the crackling fires on the outskirts of town, where young boys were adding sticks and logs to build them higher. He rode as fast as he could with his mind focused on his mission: he must force Leofric to listen to reason and turn back.

"Leofric! Earl Leofric," he yelled out, as he saw the men in the distance.

"Hold!" Leofric commanded.

"Leofric, wait," Thorold said as he arrived at his brother-in-law's side. "You must be reasonable. You must take the time to meet with the people."

Leofric looked at his friend, searching for an answer.

"I will give them their chance to speak, Thorold, but they must stop this rebellion," he stated.

"Have you already, on the first occasion of being tested, forgotten our pact? You and I vowed to fight, without fail, for the people and not against them," Thorold reminded him.

"What I do, I do for all the people!"

Thorold eyed him dubiously. Leofric looked into the eyes of the man he admired most, after his father, a man whose anguish showed blatantly on his face.

"I will do my best," he pledged.

The military began marching again, parading past Thorold, who stepped aside, watching them with great trepidation. The line of soldiers seemed endless.

✿✿✿✿✿✿

Only three very elderly people were brought to the church, and once they were settled in, Prior Aefic left and climbed a nearby hill. He stood watching from a distance, wondering what horror was to befall the innocent as he beseeched God to intercede on their behalf.

✿✿✿✿✿✿

A trumpet blew as the earl's first guards approached the green fields that spread out before the town of Coventry. The soldiers lined up and waited as the sun began to sink in the western sky.

"The earl comes. Leofric is on his way," the herald announced. The field in front of them was not much more than five hundred yards across, yet it was the only thing that separated the people of Coventry from the oncoming brigade.

Leofric led his men into position. "This night must set the tone of my authority," he called. "Let's make them understand it."

The king's men wore plated armor, and their Norman swords were heavier than anything the young peasant boys could possibly lift. They covered their faces with their helmets while the peasants they would be fighting stood in the firelight, dirt and sweat glowing on their unprotected skin as they gazed out on the army before them.

Leofric's battle drum began to pound. It was the only sound besides the wind rustling in the trees. Earl Leofric rode slowly into the middle of the field and addressed the men waiting behind the barricade.

"Good people of Coventry," he called out. "I stand before you tonight, most honored to be your earl. As your friend and neighbor, and one entrusted with power by King Canute, I realize that the hardship of the tax is great. I also know that this tax is more than it has been in the past. Still, I have no choice but to enforce it. No motion of rebellion shall take it away. Step forward and provide your worth."

Thurman stepped out into the open, wielding his blacksmith hammer.

"Has every one of you forgotten that Saxon England exists no more?" asked Leofric. "We are now subjects of King Canute and Denmark, and by his charity alone, we reside on the fragile boundary of his empire."

"Speak for yourself, Lord Leofric," Thurman shouted back venomously.

"You dare to insult the edict of the king?" Leofric challenged. Thurman lifted his hammer.

"What is meant for the man is meant for the master, at least in Coventry, good Saxon earl," Thurman chided.

"Citizens of Coventry," Leofric called out, "the tax must be collected. If you do not provide it, as the king has ordered, I will have no choice but to command my army to extract it."

"You'll collect nothing," Thurman yelled back, "because there's nothing here to collect."

"What say the rest of you?" Leofric asked.

No one else spoke, the silence answering his question. Leofric had no idea what to do next. He wished for Leofwine's reason and wisdom.

Thurman turned his back on the soldiers to address his townspeople.

"This is it," he cried. "This is Leofric's moment of truth. If any of you don't want to be part of this fight, you may go to the church for sanctuary."

None of the peasants moved. Their resolve was clear. Up on the hillside, Prior Aefic rubbed his head in dismay.

"Very well, if it's a fight they want, we'll give them one," Leofric said, spinning around with his eyes blazing. He raised his sword above his head.

Prior Aefic looked down in shock. "No, Leofric. Don't do this. O dear God, do something. Help these poor people!" he prayed aloud, watching Leofric's sword wave in the air. The line of soldiers prepared to charge.

Leofric waited a long moment, his sword raised. He breathed heavily, glaring at Thurman.

"Coventry, I plead with you. This is your last chance to willfully remit what is owed."

The line of peasants braced themselves.

Leofric addressed his men. "Let no one stop you from entering Coventry and collecting from each guild, shop, farm, and household. Confiscate livestock, jewelry, and any other items amounting to the value of the tax."

The drum stopped. He turned slowly and dropped his arm, signaling his troops to attack. Leofric stayed still, watching the line of horses gallop past him kicking soil and grass into the air. The soldiers shouted, heading to the barricade intent on tearing it down.

Suddenly, out of the trees, a most unlikely sight appeared. What seemed to be a vision of white gossamer flowing atop a white horse made a wide arc, directly in the path of Leofric's forces. Those who saw it were astounded, wondering if something supernatural was in their midst.

"Lady Godiva! It's Lady Godiva!" one of the townspeople cried.

It was indeed. She spurred her horse and pulled ahead of the charging line. Godiva rode directly in harm's way, her veil trailing in the wind.

Leofric saw his wife in the path of the soldiers and screamed as loud as he could, "Halt! Hold the attack! Stop! Draw back!"

The soldiers desperately tried to reign in their charging thoroughbreds.

Godiva's mount reared high. The soldiers stopped, their horses breathing heavily.

For a moment, all was quiet.

Godiva looked at the people on both sides of the line. Leofric was furious as she dismounted and walked slowly over to her husband. The king's appalled advisors moved in closer, and Thorold, who had been following behind the earl's men, moved in closer to his sister.

Godiva's heart beat wildly as she hoped that she could somehow find a way to reason with her husband. She opened her mouth, but before she could begin to speak, Leofric hissed, "Return to *my* castle at once. This is no place for a woman."

"Leofric, do you know me so little to think that merely because I am a woman I would not defend those I love from the sword?" she asked boldly.

"Do you not see that you shame me before all men by your actions?" He tried to keep the conversation quiet but could hardly contain his fury.

"My dear husband, I am long past shame, for it is the lives of the people of Coventry and the actions of the man I love that have brought me to this place."

Leofric shook his head. "Godiva, I don't know what you think you are doing, but I insist that you leave this field immediately."

Godiva spoke fearlessly. "Leofric, it is you who must consider what you are doing. This is Coventry. These are our people. Have you forgotten?"

"The stubbornness of these people is to blame. Everyone needs to pay the tax, even you and I," he barked.

"Leofric, you have the power to end this. Send away these soldiers. Let it be over. Please, let us go home before violence is once again visited upon the people we love."

Leofric was livid. "*Go home?* Your peaceful, gentle citizens are in arms against the will of our king."

"Only against the cruel tax, my lord. They are not against you or me. They cannot pay! This will destroy them. Speak to the king on their behalf. Help him to see the harshness of the taxes. Then, my lord, you will hear a shout of joy that rises up to heaven. You will hear the voices say, 'God save Leofric. God save Leofric.'"

"Do you not realize, my lady, that God *will* have to save me if you don't leave this field immediately?" he asked, gritting his teeth in anger.

"Are you going to ride tonight against this defenseless band? God forbid, Leofric. Would you do that?"

"If the tax is not remitted, I have no other choice!" he protested.

"What if they were remitted?" she asked. Leofric was confused by her question.

"Do we now speak in riddles? If the taxes are paid, then of course the king's demand will be fulfilled," he answered.

"Then so be it." Godiva lifted a small chest that was lashed to her horse, struggling with the weight. She knelt down and opened it.

"What is this?" Leofric asked.

"The tax shall be remitted. By me," she said. "Master Thurman?"

"Yes, my lady?" he said, stepping forward.

"My friend, I give of my fortune freely to the good people of Coventry."

Thurman gasped at the wealth before him. The chest was piled with priceless jewels.

"Dispense these pieces according to the demands of the decree," Godiva ordered.

"It would be one hundred marks for each of the lads, my lady, and one thousand for the city of Coventry," Thurman said with alarm.

"Let it be dispensed," she responded without hesitation. Leofric jumped off his horse and lunged to the chest before Thurman could get there. He grabbed his wife by the arm.

"Godiva, are you mad? What in God's name are you doing?"

"I do not compare the value of those whom I love to the vanity of precious stones and metal. These jewels are mine," she said, fearlessly jerking her arm free. "By the law of this country, I am free to do with them as I please."

"You are my wife!" he yelled, glaring at her.

"Yes, I am your wife, Leofric," she said passionately. "I am proudly and devotedly your wife, but I am also bound by blood and heart to these good people. I cannot forsake them."

Leofric did not reply. He stood there in the middle of the battlefield, his gaze locked to hers as hundreds of soldiers and townspeople watched. In a millisecond of time, everything that knit Godiva and Leofric together as husband and wife had unraveled, leaving them as virtual strangers.

Leofric was reeling. He didn't understand how she could willfully go against him like this. But even in conflict, he could read her eyes. He knew that she did it for love. He mounted his horse and jerked the reins angrily, riding over to his men.

Godiva solemnly lifted the chest and carried it over to Thurman. Some of the townsfolk begged to see the jewels, if only for an instant, before they were handed over to the king's emissaries.

Silently, the people paraded past the chest. Some tentatively lifted a hand to touch the wealth before them, but most drew back quickly, afraid to make contact with anything so precious.

"In all my born days, I have never seen anything so beautiful," said an old peasant woman whose hands were as lined as marble as she lifted up a necklace as carefully as if it were a fragile butterfly wing.

"Look here," an old farmer cackled, swinging a string of pearls in front of the baby boy he held against his hollow chest.

Many mothers broke down in tears of gratitude.

Everything had suddenly changed, by the kindness of a single person. Instead of despair, there was hope. Instead of fear, suddenly the people were filled with joy.

"Bring them forward now," Godiva said kindly. Thurman carried the chest over and laid it at Leofric's feet.

"There. The tax is paid. Let us rejoice, for now we can live in peace." Godiva watched for Leofric's response, then looked out on the sea of smiling faces. Her people.

Leofric couldn't meet Godiva's eyes. He glanced at the jewels and felt a pain deep inside. He looked up to the darkening sky, wishing that the day were over.

Leofric's Viking advisor carefully observed the proceedings. Leofric briefly caught his admonishing glower as he rode off toward the road to Canute's Winchester castle.

"Go home now," Godiva instructed the people. "Return to your homes and be at peace. The taxes have been paid. Let King Canute record that all of Coventry has provided its obligation."

A cheer went up as the crowd of peasants hugged each other and shrieked with joy. Leofric turned to the king's emissary.

"Take it," he said, gesturing to the chest. "The debt is now paid in full."

Godiva turned to her husband with a look of hope.

"My dear husband, hear me. For now begins a time of greatness, a time of peace for all the people. Let us use our powers for good and not evil."

Godiva's words stung his soul as he remembered her pledge the day before on the hillside. He could not understand how the gap between them had grown so incomprehensibly large, so quickly.

Godiva looked into her husband's eyes and saw that he felt deeply betrayed. "Please, Leofric, do not forget those who have been a family to us, who love and honor us in their hearts."

"Godiva, if only life were as simple as you see it to be," he said painfully. "You speak of love and honor. Do you not see that this display of yours dishonors me? By this act of kindness, you have started something that may well end in my death!"

Suddenly, all the peasants cried out, "God save Godiva! God save Godiva!" The soldiers lowered their weapons, some removed their headgear in respect.

"You have no idea what you've begun," Leofric whispered. "You may as well bid me farewell now. And bid farewell to your good people." Leofric turned his horse and left.

"Move out," he signaled his men. He looked back at Godiva. He knew that something had changed; maybe everything had changed. Leofric charged off toward the castle, away from Godiva and away from the townspeople whom he could do nothing for.

Godiva was swept into the crowd who surrounded her, proclaiming her as their hero. She pushed through her admirers, mounted Aethenoth, and turned toward her home. Someone handed her a torch, and she carried it proudly. Behind her, some walking, some riding, the entire town of Coventry escorted her home. The peasants sang as they marched jubilantly along.

A tear fell down Godiva's cheek. They reached the drawbridge of her castle and stopped. A light glowed from a single tower window above. The rest of the castle was dark. Godiva turned and faced her people.

"Let us be thankful that Coventry is at peace," she said.

"We owe you our lives, my lady," Thurman yelled out.

"Here, here!" someone added.

"Thank you, dear lady," said a woman timidly.

"I can go back now and finish cooking my stew!" a woman shouted, and the crowd burst out laughing. "That is, if I can find my pot and spoon."

"Yes," Godiva chuckled, slipping off her horse to lead him in. "We can all go home now and sleep safely."

Lia and Edgar, the children from the choir, ran to Godiva and threw their arms around her. She crouched down to their level.

Lia kissed Godiva on the cheek. "I want to learn to be brave like you, my lady."

Godiva smiled broadly. "Remember this moment, my dear ones, for He who watches over the sparrow watches over you."

All the children giggled, knowing her words were from one of the songs Godiva had taught them.

Godiva straightened. Tears filled her eyes as she looked at all the illuminated faces in the torchlight. How she wished that Sister Osburga and her parents could be there. As she turned to walk away, she looked up into the sky and whispered a sincere "Thank You." The feelings of peace and love that filled her heart had not been there since the morning before the attack on the abbey.

"Good night," she said, raising her hand.

And the people of Coventry shouted, "Good night, my lady! Good night!"

Thorold stepped out of the crowd. "I am so proud of what you have done tonight, Godiva. You are truly an embodiment of our mother's grace and our father's courage. I know that they would be proud," he said, placing his arm around her shoulder and squeezing.

Godiva reached for her mother's locket beneath her cape. She held the heart charm between her thumb and forefinger.

"It is their memory that spurs me on," she said, choking on her words and smiling to cover it up. "Good night, dear brother. Thank you."

Godiva hugged him and then turned to face the torch in the upstairs chamber and what awaited her there.

From high above, the figure of a man could be seen looking down from the window on the people of Coventry. Leofric watched his wife stand before them, jealous of their love for her.

TWENTY-FIVE

Godiva climbed the long, dark stairs to the master chamber. She entered the room and took off her outer robe, laying it on the four-poster bed. Before her stood the familiar silhouette of a man, yet the feeling in the room was anything but ordinary.

A torch threw shadows across Leofric's face, and as he turned toward her, his features seemed frighteningly elongated and angular.

"Good evening, my lord," Godiva said carefully.

"If only I could find goodness in this evening. I never imagined a greater hell than this," Leofric said, glaring at her. "I sought to do my duty and was cut down and humiliated by the woman I love. I have been made to look like a tyrant in the town I worked so hard to build!"

"Leofric, what choice did I have? I could not let the people of Coventry be harmed. Now that the taxes are paid, you can request an audience with the king and speak to him."

Leofric looked at her in absolute disbelief of her naiveté. "Did you not see the king's man ride off? By this time tomorrow, word that you have undermined me, and the Danish mandate, will have spread like wildfire through Canute's court. The only audience I'll be enjoying is the one before me as I dangle from a tree by my neck!"

Godiva recoiled as Leofric railed on. "What seems like a great deliverance to you may well be our downfall. You do not seem to understand that in your passion, you have sealed the fate of Coventry. I know the mind of Canute. He will take this as an insult and come down on us all. Unless the God of heaven intervenes, we shall most certainly perish."

He fell silent for a moment.

"Leofric, these good people are hungry and poor," she began. "We must do everything in our power to protect them. Surely your heart has not darkened so quickly, my lord, as to embrace that which you condemned in Edric and Norman!"

"Godiva, how can you possibly say that? What greater insult exists than to liken me to Edric and Norman? You see only the good in what you have done, but I cannot. I must look up to see the inevitable storm that will come down on us with all the fury of hell!" He grasped the post of the bed and shook it vigorously.

"I wish you would have just thrust a sword through my heart rather than cut me with your words. For I am hopelessly caught, and I cannot control the outcome."

Godiva did not answer.

"I hate what has happened to us," he said bitterly.

She had never seen him so upset. The pain of conflict drained them both; all kind words were gone. They were no longer able to communicate.

"Godiva," he began quietly, "everything I have done I have done on behalf of the king for the sake of these good people."

"For their sake? How can you say that?"

"Canute has every intention of ruling them judiciously," Leofric protested. "In return, he demands their respect. He will do what he must to ensure that this one town doesn't compromise the empire with rebellion. Godiva, you are kind and the ways of your heart are admirable, but you know little of the ways of kings."

"Forgive my words, my lord, but you are wrong," she said firmly. "I have learned much in my life about the ways of this king."

Leofric turned away, unable to meet her gaze.

"I had no choice. I did what I know to be right. It is worth every bit of trouble to save one life!" Godiva cried.

"And what now? I also did what I thought to be right. Is this how it will be? Is this our new life?"

Godiva moved to the bed and sunk down. She had no strength left. Leofric stormed from the room without another word. As the door closed behind him, she laid her head back on a pillow, feeling more alone than ever before.

⊘⊘⊘⊘⊘⊘

The atmosphere in Coventry was electrifying. Gloom and resignation were replaced by song, dance, and celebration. Many Christians went to the church to give thanks, and many pagans to the Cofa Tree. Some families invited neighbors to revel in their homes around a meal, although they had to scramble to reclaim their tables and utensils from the battle line. Still others, the rowdier factions, frolicked in the local pub. Musicians played while the laughter spilled out onto the streets and into the night. The entire town was united in rejoicing at Godiva's releasing them from Canute's decree.

"Leofric will have to answer for this," Ross the baker commented to his wife Margaret as he guzzled ale at the pub. "It's just a matter of time."

Overhearing his words, Thurman replied, "Well then, we better start drinking! Hey, Scop! Scop?" Thurman called out. "Where is he?"

"Somebody call my name?" A tiny man with a huge floppy hat stumbled from a bar stool and crashed to the floor near the blacksmith. Thurman helped the barely-four-foot-tall story-teller to his feet. He was a good-natured fellow, and no one had any idea how old he was or where he had come from. Nonetheless, he had turned his tiny stature into an advantage and often enjoyed acting out his stories from any convenient tabletop.

"Yes my friends?" Scop laughed, slurring his words and staggering in a wide circle, looking at the crowd. "What would you like from old Scop?"

"Tell us a tale of this fine and memorable day, Scop," Thurman shouted, lifting his glass.

Scop lunged up to the bar and licked his lips preparing an eloquent speech.

"This ought to be good," Thurman said, elbowing Ross and smiling.

Thorold entered the pub and watched intently as the room quieted to a whisper.

Scop set his mug down and waved his arms, readying himself. "I shall now weave you a tale," he said grandly. He cleared his throat and rolled his eyes around the room.

> Insurrection, the tolls have caused—
> Assessment decreed, scribes make it law,
> Coventry is saved by our lady's jewels,
> Manhood is—

Scop paused, searching for the perfect word. A mischievous smile filled his face.

"Manhood is severed in this daring duel." The crowd exploded in laughter as Scop took a swig from a nearby goblet.

"Finish, Scop! Don't leave us hanging!" Thurman yelled.

Scop swayed from side to side, then centered and picked up the pace.

> Man and wife in battle fight,
> The tale of two at war tonight.
> Canute's new earl, pushed by King's decree,
> Points his sword at Coventry!

The Scop's story of Godiva and Leofric spread throughout England like wildfire, along with the catchy tune. In no time at all, a pudgy monk in East Anglia had heard the story of the taxes in Coventry, and he added his own verse to Scop's as he dipped candles.

> More tolls they cry,
> More tax, more presents—
> More gifts they give
> From the backs of peasants!

And, far away at a washhouse in Northumberland, a group of women covered with suds shared the spreading tale with their own version.

> Soldiers defeated by nary a stone,
> Ah but, sweetest Godiva,
> Drives armies back home!

And a week later, in yet another pub in Essex, a drunk and boisterous man stood willfully before his fellow townsfolk. The legend had hit full stride as he added his own rhyming verse.

As she faced Leofric, we'll challenge each Earl—
to keep what is ours, and reclaim our world.
Anger we'll face from Canute the Great—
Prince Harold alone will trip for the bait.

Everyone in the pub laughed and clinked their glasses in agreement. From the local Coventry pub all the way to Essex, the news had traveled of what Godiva had done on the green fields of Coventry.

However, in a darkened corner of that Essex pub, several men sat hunched together, not nearly as amused as the rest of the population.

The boisterous man brazenly cackled and repeated his verse, "Prince Harold alone will trip for the bait," then he leaned forward for all the pubsters to hear.

"With brother away he will become a man, or so he will try, with blood on his hands!"

Everyone roared with laughter. The man in the back of the pub slowly lifted his head. There, in the dark corner, sat Prince Harold—drunken and dangerous.

"Bring him to me...now!" he hissed to his close friend Balthazar through clenched teeth. Before anyone could stop them, the boisterous man was shoved out of the pub, tied to the back of the Prince's horse, and dragged out of town across the rocks and ruts of the road. Harold's horse galloped at racing speed, ravaging and beating the man. A half hour later, the prince and Balthazar dismounted and approached the still breathing but bloodied man who lay there torn and bruised. Balthazar cut the rope and the man rolled over, barely able to let out a groan.

"Let's see if bad news travels back to Coventry as quickly as it found me here," he said, leaving the wounded man struggling to move.

TWENTY-SIX

T he afternoon sun streamed onto a large plaza in Copenhagen in which King Canute presided over a sea of adoring Danish subjects. The cheers were deafening as he majestically waved his hand at the crowd. This was his Denmark. These were the people of his own blood.

Canute gave one final wave to his subjects and headed for the Danish council hall. Representatives from every region lined the walls of the massive wooden rotunda. He made his grand entrance with a twelve-man entourage, parading ceremoniously to the far end of the room. With all eyes on him, he took his place on the throne.

An imposing official addressed the king and assembly. "Your Majesty, King Canute the Great, we of the governing Thing Council graciously welcome you back to Denmark." A hearty cheer echoed through the hall, and Canute nodded to him courteously.

"Greetings, council. It is with great honor that I convey to you the progress we have made in England since my last meeting with your envoy," King Canute said. "We have, at last, found undisputed favor among the Saxons."

Everyone in the room clapped their hands and stomped their feet in approval.

As the noise died down, Canute became very serious.

"By this time, you have certainly been made aware that I have removed some so-called 'heroic leaders' from our midst for crimes of treason. Elsorn foolishly thought he could undermine my authority, simply because he had gained some favor in this council. Knowing that I would soon stand before you, I thought it best to make a display of the reign of my power. Some of you were led to believe that he would be the preferable leader. I decided to put the challenge to the test the Viking way, a man-to-man contest of strength and wit. Though I gave Elsorn ample opportunity to defeat me, to which the distinguished General Gunnor can attest, he was able to triumph neither in a battle of wits nor in a battle of swords. Therefore, I can only assume that our gods still favor my rule."

The room grew silent. The message was loud and clear. No one would dare challenge Canute now.

"My loyal council," he continued. "I ask for a review of your efforts in my absence."

"There is much to inform you of, Your Majesty." The first councilman opened a huge leather ledger that held the record. "We have defeated Norway's strike against our border, but once again the army's great cost weighs upon our citizens." The councilman paused, carefully approaching the next subject. "Your Highness, we have always supported you in your heroic conquests, but we have yet to receive taxes from the territories."

King Canute smiled, ready with his answer. "You will be pleased to learn that the Danegeld has been instituted across England and is presently being collected in Mercia."

"Then it is Edric Streona who raises money for our expanding empire?" the councilman asked him forthrightly.

"Edric Streona is dead," King Canute replied. A low rumble of voices rolled through the room.

"Dead, my lord?"

"He plotted with Elsorn. He was a treasonous cad who cared only for himself," Canute said, surveying the reactions in the room. "I have instead made Leofric, son of Leofwine, earl of all Mercia, northern and southern provinces."

A murmur echoed through the hall.

"But he is a Saxon," said the councilman. "I—rather, the Thing Council—believes that a Dane whose loyalty has been proven would best be able to raise the taxes we so sorely need. Our Danish lands are nearly penniless, Your Majesty."

"Trust me, as your king, the one appointed by our gods. I can assure you that Leofric will be loyal." Canute spoke with a distinct air of certainty. He looked out upon the council members.

"There are those who think my way of settling the new lands is a mistake. Let me make it very clear that I will tolerate no rebellion. We will be a united kingdom. The wealth of the new English territories will make us a far more prosperous and influential empire." He looked sternly at the faces in front of him. "This assembly is over."

He rose abruptly and walked out. All who were present stood hastily as the king paraded past. Canute was visibly angered that his royal judgment had again been called into question.

That night, the king dined with his father's old confidant Gunnor, who advised him to prove his favor with the gods in the old ways before a select group from the court who would then dutifully circulate stories of his power and commitment.

"Show them that your heart is still that of a Viking," Gunnor urged, "and that you can encompass England without forsaking your own."

The next morning was gray and foreboding. The black waves crashed violently against the Danish shore, along a secluded beachfront. The tide was moving in and the crabs that had been stranded in the wet sand since dawn were at last lifted and carried back to the safety of deeper waters. In the distance, a lengthy procession could be seen approaching, steadily lumbering over the pebbly dunes. Robed in his finest silks, Canute was being carried over the sandy knolls by four brawny attendants. Crowned and holding his scepter, he floated like a god, high above the rest.

Queen Emma trailed behind with her maidens.

"Stay close," she said, tending to the care of the seven-year-old little boy holding her hand. Prince Hardicanute, their fair-haired son, pulled her along hurriedly.

As the procession arrived at the water, Canute solemnly called out his order.

"Put me down by the shore's edge. There, in the clearing between the rocks, right before these waves," he commanded.

Concerned, those in the procession looked back and forth at one another as the sea breeze whipped the waves and foam ahead of them. Canute's throne was gently lowered to the edge of the oncoming surf. The legs of the great chair sank into the soaked sand and several of the spectators retreated quickly to avoid the rushing tide.

"Emma," Canute called forcefully, "I want Hardicanute. Send him here."

Hardicanute looked up at his mother then broke from her grasp and ran to his father's side.

"Look at this, my son," the king said, offering a tender smile.

Canute reached deep into his cloak and pulled something out. There, in his massive hand, he cupped a tiny, perfectly scaled model of his dragon ship. The head was painted gold, just like his real ship was, and ferocious teeth carved from whalebone had been set into the dragon's mouth.

"I made this for you with my very own hands, my boy. It is the first of many ships you will take charge of," he said proudly, bending to speak into his small son's ear. He handed Hardicanute the ship, and the boy beamed.

"Thank you, Father," he said respectfully. "I will treasure it."

"Good. Now watch, son, and learn how, by my command, I shall repel these waves, so you may walk between divided oceans."

"I would like that, Father," the boy said, looking up at him in awe.

From the rear of the procession, an advisor trudged up to the rear of the crowd. He watched for a minute, observing the odd spectacle of the monarch and his son.

"By the great Odin's favor, is not everything possible for this throne? Even these wicked skies shall obey my commands!" Canute shouted, raising one hand toward heaven while holding his son's hand in the other. The gray skies cracked with thunder. Canute fixed his eyes on the turbulent seas and dark heavens. Black clouds loomed high above. Then, with such force in his voice that it made Hardicanute flinch, he shouted, "As lord of the ocean, I command these waters to recede!"

The surf instead pounded closer. King Canute and his son were slapped with sea foam as the chilly waters washed defiantly around the base of the ornate throne. They waited expectantly, faithfully, for something to happen. Nothing did.

The foam swirled around them, showing no intention of obeying the king's demand. The royal courtiers exchanged nervous glances, wondering what in the world the king would do next. His long robe was already soaked, and Hardicanute tightly clutched his father's hand so he wouldn't be pulled down by the undertow. Canute pleadingly wrapped his hand around his precious Norse ring. He studied the hammer of Thor and turned back to the heavens, pausing once again to face the turbulent seas. The gods would not let him down! Suddenly, rain began to fall from the skies. Little Hardicanute blinked and wrapped his arm over the top of his head to shelter himself.

"To all the gods that are mighty, humbly do I request your power and strength," Canute entreated, with the deepest sincerity he could muster.

A wave even larger than the others arrived, and in one powerful jolt, the king was thrown from his throne. His robes were drenched and his scepter dripped as he sat there, spitting out seawater before his royal court. Hardicanute cried out and ran back to his mother, tightly clutching his tiny ship. Canute lifted himself from the cold water and turned wildly on the procession.

"Do not think that by this ludicrous gesture I believe that the sea will obey my bidding. I alone am king, more powerful than anyone present, and I am only proving that there is one mightier than I and that the waves that wash my feet would surely drown all of you!" Canute lifted his soggy robes angrily and stomped heavily out of the water and onto the rain-dampened sand.

Suddenly, he noticed the advisor crashing through the crowd and heading straight toward him.

"What are you doing here? You are supposed to be in Mercia, collecting tolls with Earl Leofric," the king snapped, wiping the water from this face.

"Forgive me, Your Majesty," the man stuttered, "but there has been an insurrection in Coventry against the decree of the tolls." The Viking could see the fury rising in Canute's brow and slowly stepped backward into the crowd, attempting to position himself out of Canute's reach.

"Insurrection? Come here!" Canute barked. Before the Viking could react, the king's voice grew to a roar. "Come here, I said. Come here!" The advisor took a few brave steps toward the king.

"Now tell me," Canute ordered.

"The peasants, they rose up in rebellion against Leofric's armed dispatch," he explained.

"My taxes were not collected?"

"They were, Your Majesty. But paid for on behalf of the people by the wife of Lord Leofric."

"What!" Canute bellowed.

"Yes, Your Majesty, paid in full."

"By Lady Godiva?" Canute exploded. He reached for the man's neck and began squeezing it tightly. The bearer of the unwelcome and poorly timed news collapsed to his knees, gasping for air.

"Do they dare to rear the head of Saxon pride before me?" Canute seethed. "Is this how they repay me? By allowing this woman to insult the throne?"

He flung the advisor away. The man fell face first onto the sand, gasping for air and struggling to stand.

⊙⊙⊙⊙⊙⊙

Back in England, Prince Harold had taken well to his brother's absence. After a long, lazy lunch, he arrogantly strutted up to the castle map room as if he had truly become the king. His friend and advisor, Balthazar, imagined himself second in power to the supreme authority. A thought crossed his mind, and Harold laughed aloud. He plopped down in a tufted chair, straddling one leg over the arm, kicking it happily.

"Do you know, I actually feel sorry for this Lady Godiva," he chortled. "Have you seen her, Balthazar?"

"No, but I hear she's quite beautiful."

"Not only is she beautiful, but she sings and speaks with the melodious voice of an angel."

"An angel, you say? A Christian angel? Well, I've also heard she has the body of a temptress," Balthazar observed lustfully.

"How could I forget that? I only saw her once. She has this saintly air, though. Her charms are clearly only for that lucky fool, Leofric. Still, she enflames the passions like no woman I have ever met." Harold stopped for a moment, looking out the window as he pondered. "It really is a shame that she is the property of Earl Leofric. It's hard to imagine what a man wouldn't do to possess her."

"Perhaps, Prince Harold, we should see this beauty for ourselves." Balthazar's eyes shone with possibility.

"After all, as comely and clever as Godiva is, she's a fool to think there will be no repercussions," Harold chortled, imagining her punishment. "My brother must be spinning at this news. His face must be as red as a pomegranate. I can feel his rage all the way from Copenhagen." He could just imagine his brother stomping and swearing—helpless to do anything as he battled his council across the sea.

"It will be no laughing matter when he arrives back in England," Balthazar said gravely. "You do know, Harold, that this might present an opportunity for you to take power for yourself."

"What do you mean?" Harold asked, sitting up straight, suddenly attentive.

"Your brother must tend to this Saxon spirit before it undermines the throne."

"Yes?"

"But what if you tended to it first?" Balthazar asked, smiling craftily.

"How?"

"Perhaps by putting our pretty little songbird in a cage for all to see. Upon the king's return, he'll find a wise and worthy brother who has efficiently dealt with the rebellion in his kingdom. Unchallenged favor in your brother's eyes will be yours."

"And the worthy advisor who has instructed me will be at my right hand," Harold commented, grinning.

"Adversity can sometimes rear the head of opportunity, my lord."

"Indeed. Very well, then. Let's get busy."

⟐⟐⟐⟐⟐⟐

At the fortified gates of Coventry, the prince's herald stood before a crowd of commoners who had gathered at the sound of the trumpet. A guard waved the royal Danish flag. The herald unrolled a scroll and began to read. Children and women from the marketplace hustled around to hear the news.

"Prince Harold greets his loving subjects of Coventry. On behalf of King Canute, be advised that no person or persons shall have the right to pay on behalf of commoners, peasants, or serfs any ordered tolls commanded by the throne. The taxes tendered by the Lady Godiva are hereby nullified and rendered void. The Danegeld continues to be due to the throne and must be remitted immediately. Further tolls are lodged in the counties of Litchfield, York Moors, South Downs, Cotswold, and Cheshire. Payment is the direct duty of each of His Majesty's subjects. Any persons paying on behalf of another is subject to immediate arrest and prosecution by the full authority of the throne. It has been so decreed."

The herald rolled up his scroll and turned with the flag bearer to leave.

"This can't be!" a woman in the crowd yelled out.

"They got their tax money! Why should they care where it comes from?"

The whispers and comments grew into a roar of disapproving groans and shouts as the herald disappeared from sight.

⚙⚙⚙⚙⚙⚙

Saturday morning, Godiva slowly rode Aethenoth into Coventry. She was still dismayed by her row with Leofric and was in her own world, trying to figure out what to do as she neared the church and came across two women talking.

"Lady Godiva, have you heard? Prince Harold has disallowed your payment of the taxes and Coventry is once again in jeopardy!"

"How can this be? I have heard nothing of it! I will talk to my husband and see what can be done," said Godiva, horrified by the news. She started to go into the church but decided instead to visit her friend Wulfstan, who lived nearby, before she went back to Leofric.

She was soon walking down a rock-lined path that led past a small grove of low-hanging trees and up to a quaint stone cottage with a narrow arched oak door.

She could hear shuffling noises coming from the garden in the back of the tiny house. She approached quietly so she wouldn't startle him. There, in the dappled sunlight, she saw Wulfstan making his way to a seat in the garden.

"Hello, Wulfstan," she said.

Upon hearing her voice, Wulfstan turned and welcomed her.

"Godiva! What a pleasant surprise. What brings you to my home this morning?"

"I just needed a friendly ear," she said, trying to hold back tears.

"Well, I have two just for you," Wulfstan said with a laugh. "Follow me to the parlor, my lady. I'll make you a cup of tea."

"I would appreciate it."

As they entered, Godiva took in the barrenness of the one-room house.

"Wulfstan, would you please reconsider and let me provide you with some furniture? Or at least a better bed?"

Wulfstan chuckled and invited her to sit down. "What do I need of such things? I can't see them and would probably only trip over them. I have absolutely everything around me that makes me happy. I am rich in the things that matter, Godiva. What more could I ask for? Now, the tea...I have some fresh mint that I cut this morning."

"Thank you. That sounds perfect," she quietly replied.

"Godiva, my old friend, I hear the sadness in your voice. When you are ready to share with me, I will gladly listen and help however I can."

"As I said, I just need someone to talk to—someone who might help me to understand my husband."

"Is Leofric still upset about your paying the Danegeld?"

"I've never seen him like this. He can hardly look me in the eye. I really don't know what to do. My marriage is in turmoil. We have never spoken such harsh words to one another. I'm afraid to think what will become of us."

"Oh, Godiva. I'm so sorry."

"Leofric feels that I have humiliated him and is fearful of what the king will do to punish us when he returns." Godiva's voice began to shake.

"I love my husband, Wulfstan. I have no desire to go against him, but I didn't know what else to do. I had to protect Coventry, and now it seems to all have been in vain. Prince Harold has decreed that the tolls are to be collected again—and that each person must pay for themselves."

"That is horrible news, Godiva. I don't know how, but someway we'll find a solution. And as for your marriage, you and Leofric love each other so much that I know this will soon be a memory."

Godiva watched him carefully pour the tea, amazed how he didn't spill a drop. "I'm sorry to trouble you, Wulfstan. I have hardly anyone else to confide in like this. Dear Sister Agnes is so loving and kind to me, but spending so much time alone, I'm afraid she understands little of relationships."

"We have known each other all our lives, Godiva. You are my dearest friend. It makes me happy to know that you trust me enough to unburden your heart here."

"I am worried most of all by what this position of earl will do to my husband. If this decree is to be enforced, he will once again be forced to ride against the people of Coventry."

"Leofric is still the man you married. The goodness that you saw in him has not changed."

"He won't listen to me. He can hardly even speak in a courteous tone."

"You may find this difficult to believe, but he probably feels quite the same way about you."

"Do you think so?"

"You must remember that men and women are very different in the way they look at things. In an ideal situation they would be able to work together and learn to blend the best of their different perspectives. Too often, though, women and men seem to think that the other side has little of value to offer. Together, they would be able to solve problems much more quickly. I suppose that is the reason that the world is best understood when we can count on both our eyes and our ears. Believe me; I ought to know."

"O Wulfstan, what would I do without you?"

"Godiva, I want to let you in on a secret. I pay close attention to those around me, and I have learned that love, especially to a man, is very much about respect. A man's pride is his foundation. When you damage it, you damage his ability to function. His reaction is anger. But it is usually only temporary. He will find a way back. Leofric is a proud man. It might not make sense to you, but it's in his nature. That is how he is made."

"It is rather confusing."

"To succeed in marriage, you must learn to work around his manly pride, not ignore it, for it is an integral part of his makeup. Leofric may never want to admit this, but he thinks you have chosen Coventry over him."

"But I haven't. I could never do that. Leofric is my husband. I know we both want to protect Coventry."

"Love is hard, Godiva, for all of us. Just let him know that you respect him, even if you totally disagree, and you will be amazed by what happens."

"I hope you're right."

"Please, trust me. I know what I'm talking about," Wulfstan assured her.

Godiva got up and leaned over to give him a hug.

"I knew I needed to come here today," she told him.

Godiva rode Aethenoth homeward on the path along the Sherbourne River. She was thinking about Wulfstan's advice and was readying herself to reconcile with Leofric when she noticed a woman with two children down near the river's edge. She looked closer and gasped at the nightmare in front of her. The woman wailed and sobbed while the small children kicked and screamed.

"She's shoving them under the water," Godiva said to herself. "My God! She's going to drown them." She kicked Aethenoth, frantically urging him to the river's edge. As she drew near, the woman tried to shove the girl's head under the water. The child screamed and fought to the surface as her brother tried to push their mother away. The girl slipped through her fingers, and the mother reached out again in another attempt to keep her beneath the surface. Godiva was horrified.

She jumped off her horse, screaming, "Stop! Stop! What are you doing?"

The struggling and thrashing continued.

"Stop this immediately," Godiva yelled again, reaching toward the woman.

The mother let go of her screaming daughter, and the girl thrashed into the shallower waters, crying and gagging.

"My lady, I have nowhere else to turn. More tolls have been ordered in Litchfield. I can't feed them. We've no more food! These children are going to starve if we pay. I won't let my children starve to death. This is the merciful way," the woman cried as she stepped into the shallower water, weeping.

"Merciful? You think drowning your children is merciful?"

"O my lady, will you help me? You are Lady Godiva. You saved Coventry. You could save me. Please help me, my lady. Please!" The woman sobbed as she clung to the bottom of Godiva's now soaking gown.

"No, I cannot. The prince has made a decree. It has been strictly forbidden. Please come up out of the water."

"With the failure of this year's crops in Litchfield, many people are left with nothing. Do you know what it is to watch a child starve to death? I cannot give them sticks to eat." The woman moved back into the murky depths.

Godiva nervously scanned the surrounding shoreline. No one was around. She looked at the shivering, terrified children and quickly slipped off her ring.

"Come out of the water. Please. Take this. Pay the tolls, and go away from here," she whispered desperately. As the woman grew close enough, Godiva shoved the gold and ruby ring into her wet hand and closed her fist over it for good measure.

"O good lady," the woman cried, "how can I ever thank you? O my lady, my children and I thank you. You have saved my children." The woman waded to the shore with her children. They shook from the cold, but no longer fearing what their mother might do to them, they reached for her hands.

"Thank you, my lady. Thank you," the woman said as she turned to leave.

"Hurry. You must get the children warmed," Godiva said as she climbed back onto her horse.

"I will, my lady. Thank you."

Suddenly, the king's Huscarles, under the command of Prince Harold, broke from the tree line. The guards descended on the riverbank and encircled the two women.

"Lady Godiva, you are under arrest for defying the decree of the throne. Seize her!" the captain ordered.

"No, wait! What are you doing?" Godiva screamed as two men grabbed her arms.

"You are under arrest," the captain repeated. "Get her horse," he yelled to one of the soldiers, who immediately grabbed Aethenoth's reins and held them tightly.

The Huscarle roughly pulled Godiva from the horse's back. She struggled to get free, and the horse writhed and stomped his hooves in protest, but it was no use. One of the soldiers pinned her arms behind her back and swiftly bound a thick rope around her hands. He tied it so tightly that she cried out in pain as the dry, rough bonds rubbed against her soft skin.

"I'll get her legs," one of the soldiers said with a snigger.

"No! Don't touch me!"

Ignoring her pleas, he and another soldier bent to the ground and began lifting her wet skirts to get to her ankles. They exchanged a leer, acknowledging the good fortune of their assignment.

"Leave me alone," Godiva screamed, kicking her feet. Another soldier brought over a pair of shackles and fastened the cold metal chains to her feet, with no regard for the pain he was inflicting. Godiva stood on the shore, bound and trembling. The Huscarles threw the dripping wet mother a pouch of silver. She smiled gleefully, revealing her broken yellow teeth. Her eyes locked with Godiva's.

"How could you do this?" Godiva asked, horrified that the woman would be so devious. The woman shrugged and held up the pouch. She shuffled off, greedily clutching her bounty, with her wet children trailing behind.

"Get her on the horse," said one of the soldiers. Godiva was hoisted up and laid across Aethenoth's back like a bundle of straw. She could feel her gown bunching up and was mortified that her legs would be displayed to anyone they might pass. The bouncing of the horse felt as though she was being punched in the stomach. Godiva could only lay there helpless and humiliated before the boisterous, vile soldiers.

Prince Harold rode up to the men from where he had been watching from the tree line.

"Enjoying your ride, my sweet lady?" Prince Harold wore a sick smile of amusement.

Everything in Godiva wanted to break down and cry, but as she strained to look up at Harold, she refused to give him the satisfaction. Instead she reached down deep inside and grabbed hold of the strength she had found as a child.

"I will not let Harold triumph over me," she said to herself as she bounced along with her hands bound behind her.

"Leofric," she whispered, closing her eyes. "Oh, my husband, I'm sorry."

As they reached the town of Coventry, the Huscarles yanked her off the horse and forced her to walk. Struggling to pull the heavy chain between her legs, she had no choice but to shuffle clumsily along. The Huscarles paraded her down the main street as an angry throng of townspeople fell in behind, heartbroken by the sight of their fair Lady Godiva in such dire straits. She looked up and caught sight of some of her beloved friends.

"Come on, keep moving now," a soldier came up behind and yelled at her.

She had never felt so humiliated before. She was led through the entire village of Coventry but refused to shed a single tear.

None of the townspeople knew what to do. They followed her silently, as demoralized and downcast as Godiva herself. She tried to close herself off to all that was going on around her and do the only thing she could—surrender her fate to God.

TWENTY-SEVEN

T he light from the torches that surrounded the Winchester castle of King Canute filtered through the ornate stained-glass windows and dappled Prince Harold's face. The king's younger brother had smugly taken over the throne room. He wiggled about wildly in the king's high throne, fitting the king's chair to his taste like an oversized shoe. He cackled like a hyena.

"You were right, Balthazar! Adversity does rear the head of opportunity."

"Just like crushing a flea," Balthazar observed.

Pleased with himself, Harold continued, "Did you see her, Balthazar? Did you see her remorse? Did you see her legs? This kingly business is really rather...simple," he laughed while far below, in the king's dungeon, the light did not glimmer so brightly.

Godiva stood isolated behind bars. Water dripped down the walls in the dank darkness, and cries of pain and hunger filled the heavy dungeon air. Something scurried across the floor. She thought back to another time when she was cold and hungry, hiding in the water with Sister Agnes.

The groans of those around her in the cells never stopped, and the smell of human stench penetrated every breath she took. A guard approached indifferently and slid forward a bowl of rotten mush. She inspected it in the dim light and saw it move. She kicked the bowl aside in horror and it slid across the wet stone floor, landing against the wall.

She peered out across the corridor, straining to see the other prisoners. Devices of torture and those who had suffered severely by them occupied the surrounding cells. Prince Harold's guards patrolled the dungeon corridor, and Godiva heard their laughter approaching. Suddenly, in the dim light, slopping through the puddles, Prince Harold arrived at her cell. He paused to look at her. She stiffened.

"Enjoying the hospitality?" he asked.

"The food leaves something to be desired."

"Amazing. I thought you would have lost some of your spunk by now. Perhaps we shall find a way to remedy that."

"I promise to change my ways as soon as you shrivel up and die like the slug that you are," Godiva spat at him.

"You should be nicer to me, Godiva. At this moment, I am the voice of the king, and I can do with you what I please," Harold scolded mockingly.

"Not for long, Harold. The real king will be here shortly, and you'll have to find someplace else to play mighty ruler."

"Feisty, aren't you? Perhaps more than Leofric deserves. Actually, Lady Godiva, I generously came here to offer you release. That is, if you will publicly renounce your—how shall I put this?" he hedged. "Your transgressions."

"Which transgressions might those be, Prince Harold?" she fumed.

"Those that incite the people to rebellion, of course."

"I will not renounce something that I would, without a doubt, do again," she said vehemently.

"I underestimated you, my dear. You've had your chance. Drop her in the pit," he ordered the guard as he stormed out.

Godiva blanched. She had heard that the pit was a hole in the floor that ended in a rock pile nearly fifteen feet beneath the dungeon. Most people who were thrown in the hole would break their legs or back, and all would be left to starve at the bottom. It was a gruesome fate, and one Godiva shuddered to think of. The guard looked as shocked as she.

Weak hands reached out to Prince Harold through the bars of the other cells as he passed the tortured and wounded victims, some who had been there for years. He ignored them all, and the hands dropped lifelessly back into the darkness.

Thorold led Leofric through the long, wet corridor past dozens of hungry, tortured prisoners and into the inner dungeon. It was a scene out of a terrifying dream—though never, even in his worst nightmares, could Leofric have imagined Godiva imprisoned in such a gallery of horrors. A prisoner reached his hand through the bars, calling out in agony as they passed by. Leofric and Thorold moved away quickly, troubled by their own helplessness.

"I have spoken to the guards. They have strict orders that she is to be held until further notice," Thorold said.

"This is madness!" Leofric said. "We have to get her out." Godiva's cell was at the end of the corridor. She sat alone in a shadowed corner, her head down and her long hair covering her face and flowing down to the floor. It was matted with all kinds of filth. She absentmindedly rubbed the spot on her wrists where the ropes had cut into her.

"Godiva!"

She lifted her head, and her eyes filled with tears. "Oh, Leofric!"

"Godiva, what happened?" he demanded.

"I saw a woman about to drown her children, so I gave her my ring, but it was all a trap of Prince Harold's."

"He will pay for this!" Leofric was furious. "I'm going to get you out of here. You will not be here long, I promise."

"Have they mistreated you?" Thorold asked, squeezing her hand through the bars.

"I was to be dropped in the pit, but the guard has defied Prince Harold. Now I worry for his life. Leofric, I'm so sorry. I had to help. The woman was going to drown her children!"

"You have no need to defend yourself, Godiva. That putrid scab tricked you. How could you know that she wasn't really going to kill them?"

"The news of your imprisonment has traveled everywhere. The people will take up arms if you aren't released soon," Thorold added.

"The king will be back shortly. You must stay here until then. I won't leave your side," pledged Leofric, holding her through the bars.

"Leofric, let me stay instead," Thorold interjected. "The king will return soon. You should go prepare your petition for her release. You can help Godiva most by reasoning with him. I'll stay the night here with her."

"I can't go, seeing her here like this!" Leofric argued.

"It's alright, Leofric," Godiva said bravely, hoping her voice wouldn't break. "I'll be okay with my brother. Please, find out what I must do for Canute to let me go."

Leofric kissed his wife through the cell bars, loath to leave her. She held on to him, feeling the same.

"Godiva, look at me," he said, taking her face in his hands. "You are and always have been the bravest woman I know. I will get you out of here. I swear I'll get you out! I love you so much." Leofric tenderly kissed her brow. In spite of all that had happened, Leofric's words set her heart at ease.

"I love you, too," she whispered. After a moment, Leofric placed Godiva's hand gently in Thorold's protective grasp.

"I'll see you in the morning," he said.

Thorold and Godiva sat on the damp floor, holding each other's hands through the bars.

Deftly slicing through the northern seas, Canute's thirty-ship armada sailed southward, drawing closer to the English shores under the light of a soft full moon. On the bow of the lead vessel, as silent as the stars, stood the mighty King Canute. Beside him stood Queen Emma. She was tense as she held on with one hand to the side of the ship and with the other to her son, Hardicanute. She analyzed the king's muteness, waiting for him to speak. Canute's eyes followed the rolling sea, and like the crashing white caps, he seethed and crashed inside with anger, silent because he knew he could not control himself if he spoke. The wind whipped around the trio as Queen Emma tried, one more time, to reason with him.

"My king," she said cautiously, "perhaps you should wait to..."

"Wait for what?" he hissed with a withering glare. "I offer them a future. They repay me in insolence!" he roared.

Queen Emma fell silent and looked out at the approaching harbor. The sun was just beginning to rise. Hardicanute was exhausted and wrapped himself in the folds of her cloak. King Canute's great armada drew closer to the English shore. Soldiers and workers scurried about in preparation for the arrival of the king's vessels.

As Canute's ship docked, the king could see Earl Godwin waiting on the shore, poised to grovel to him as usual. Queen

Emma followed her husband as they made their way down the long gangplank. She held Hardicanute's hand and helped the sleepy child maneuver his way off the ship. No sooner had the king's feet touched solid ground than the earl rushed up to him.

"Not favorable, Your Majesty. Not favorable at all, I'm afraid."

The king sighed heavily, and Queen Emma cast her eyes to the ground.

"Lead on," Canute said, listening to the earl as they walked.

❧❧❧❧❧❧

Prince Harold was oblivious to the arrival of the king's great fleet. He gallivanted around Canute's throne room, dressed in his brother's red, flowing robe, swinging his royal jeweled goblet in the air and laughing heartily. In drunken exhaustion, he collapsed onto the throne. At that moment, Balthazar, who had been drinking with him, suddenly spotted King Canute coming down the hallway. He quickly stepped to the window, as far as possible from the preoccupied prince.

"Hello, Harold. Taking advantage of my absence to play king for a day?" the king lashed.

"Brother?" Harold asked weakly.

"I am your *king*," Canute yelled, letting his anger explode.

"You were not supposed to be back..."

"You stupid fool. Look at you! You're disgraceful. Earl Godwin has informed me that you placed Lady Godiva under arrest. Is this true?"

"To quell the uprising. To break the spirit of these rebellious commoners," Prince Harold explained, shaking with fear.

"To break their spirit? In the name of my authority? How dare you!"

He ferociously pulled his younger brother from the throne and pitched him to the ground. Then he yanked him back up and cuffed him in his right temple. The inebriated prince sat on the floor, dazed and holding the side of his head.

"I thought it would please you, brother," Harold protested.

"Why? Why would you meddle in these affairs, you inept fool?" Canute towered over him, screaming. "More sound advice from your maggot-hearted little friend, Balthazar?" he asked, glaring at the man to show him that he had not gone unnoticed.

"I thought..."

"You thought? You don't know how to think! You get your advice from this droning, pockmarked, ill-bred ferret! Godiva's imprisonment has now raised all of England against me! Rather than break the commoners' spirit, it gave them a martyr! They rally in her name!"

Canute pulled his brother to his feet and flung him into the wall as easily as he would a rabbit, then pummeled him into a bloody pile. Balthazar stepped back in horror. He could hardly imagine what fate awaited him.

Canute kicked his brother one last time then turned to face Balthazar.

"I will never have to be concerned with another ill-begotten utterance from you." He grabbed the young man, pulled his head back, stretched out his tongue and sliced it off with his dagger. Balthazar stumbled around the room, gagging and bleeding.

"Kill him," Canute calmly said to his guards.

Nearly unconscious, Balthazar was dragged by the neck to the cutting block. With badly bruised eyes, Harold was forced to witness his advisor's execution.

Godiva sat on the floor of her cell, resting her head against the dank, cold wall. Her hands folded limply in front of her as she drifted in and out of sleep—her only escape from the horror that surrounded her. A prisoner would scream, and she would be suddenly awakened, only to find her eyes wet with tears she had cried unknowingly in her sleep. She awakened from a fitful rest when the cell door opened slowly with a squeak. She squinted through the darkness, terrified to see who it was.

"Godiva, are you awake?"

"Who's there?" she asked.

"It's Thorold."

"Oh, Thorold," she cried, struggling wearily to her feet and then falling into his embrace.

"It's okay," he said, patting her back. "I'm sorry, I had to leave for just a moment to talk to the guard. I didn't know if you were awake to notice. I have good news."

She pulled back to look at him. "Good news?"

"Yes, the king has ordered your release. Now let's get you out and into the sunlight," he said, putting an arm around her and half carrying her through the cell door. "I was able to get your horse back, too."

"Oh, thank God," she breathed. "Where is Leofric?" she asked, looking around.

"He's been summoned by the king."

"What is Canute going to do to him?" Godiva asked.

"It's hard to say. We must hope that the king's regard for Leofwine will temper his response." Thorold answered, leading her through the damp corridor. "You have been commanded to remain within your castle walls. I'll take you there now. Come, let's go!"

TWENTY-EIGHT

P rince Harold, in the king's conditional favor, had been ordered to keep a close watch on Earl Leofric. Harold was still smarting from the beating and the reprimand. In spite of his attempts to save face and act authoritatively in his task, few in the castle regarded him as anything more than a buffoon.

Leofric's mind raced. Outrage, anxiety, uncertainty, and distrust tightly collided within his chest. An icy silence chilled the air between him and Harold as they made their way through the castle to the king's private chamber. Upon entering, Leofric took in Canute's looming form, standing over a partially played game of chess on his table. The king looked as cold and unmoving as the marble knight on the chessboard. The only sound was the crackling fire, which lent the room some dim light.

"Lord Leofric, Your Majesty," Harold announced.

"Your Majesty," Leofric bowed respectfully.

"Well, well, well," Canute mused. "Leofric. Leofric the Saxon? Leofric the Incompetent? Leofric the Traitor?" Canute turned and faced him. "Which do you prefer?"

Harold skulked into the background, intent on avoiding notice so he could linger and watch Leofric get what he deserved.

Leofric stood silently before Canute. The king began to circle him.

"Well, Leofric, have you decided?" he challenged.

"Simply your servant, Your Majesty," he replied, staring straight ahead.

"Perhaps you mean my *humble* servant? I put you in power to uphold my laws and collect my taxes, not to encourage your wife to lead a rebellion against me."

"If I may speak in her defense, Your Majesty, by paying the tolls, Lady Godiva thought only to fulfill the king's decree," he explained, keeping his face blank.

"Do you have any idea of the trouble that this *thought* of hers has caused me? The entire council wants me to install a Dane to rule in Mercia. I stood before them with great confidence. I put my honor, my word, on the line. I persuaded them that Leofric was the right man, that he would efficiently execute my laws and collect the Danegeld, which is now long overdue."

Leofric's hope spiraled down deeper and deeper with each word Canute uttered.

"Men who previously trembled when they spoke my name are now plotting boldly against me. Before I left Denmark, word of this had reached the Thing Council. At this very moment, there are those who conspire against me, and the fuel that ignites them is the perception of weakness brought about by your wife!"

Leofric absorbed Canute's words. He appreciated the fact that, in spite of his tirade, Canute remained rational instead of threatening. But Leofric still dreaded what might be ahead for him.

"I understand what you're saying, my king. I sincerely regret that these events have brought you such trouble. It is my most earnest desire to be a help to you and not a hindrance."

"A help to me? The king? Save me your trite apologies. Do you realize that new revolts have already broken out in seven other towns, and they grow worse by the day? The story of the heroic Godiva—the one who defies both husband and king for the sake of the English people—has spread like a plague through this land. Though she has broken no specific law, she has, without a doubt, ignited a fireball of sedition against me.

"You see, Leofric," the king lectured, pacing in front of him. "Left unchecked, this wave of rebellion will fundamentally undermine my rule. It will leave this fledgling nation of ours without the ability to survive. We will fall because of weakness!"

Prince Harold perched in the corner, grinning like a Cheshire cat, thrilled to watch someone else bear his brother's wrath.

Canute continued to rant. "According to my advisors, there is a very simple answer to this problem. In order to squelch this rebellion, they say I should massacre everyone in Coventry as an example, starting with your wife!"

Leofric's heart pounded in his chest. He swallowed hard, looking for the words that might deflect the horrific threat.

"By her death," he ventured, "you would only fuel this revolt."

"I see that you summon your wit against me as readily as you once summoned your blade," Canute sneered.

Harold couldn't keep still any longer. He had an idea that would most certainly get him back into his brother's good graces.

"Your Godiva is the fairest in all of England, isn't she?" Harold asked.

"Certainly to me," Leofric answered quietly, looking over at Harold, whose presence he had nearly forgotten.

Harold emerged from his chair in the corner.

"Brother," he said, smiling wickedly at Canute, "I myself have seen this rare dove. I must say that if it weren't for her vile manipulation of men's minds she might be better suited to rule Mercia than Leofric."

Leofric struggled to contain his fury. He clenched his fists, nails digging into his palms. His breath grew ragged.

"Perhaps you lack the will to fight, Leofric? Perhaps the skill of your blade isn't what it should be?" the prince gibed.

"My king, please forgive me, but your brother intends to provoke a fight. I don't wish to raise my sword against the prince, Your Majesty. What good can be found in this demonstration?"

"Afraid, Lord Leofric?" Harold taunted.

"Of you? No, I'm not afraid. I am willing to defend my honor, and that of my wife."

"You have no honor," Harold challenged. "I defy you to prove otherwise."

Leofric looked to the king.

"Your Majesty?"

"Defend yourself, Leofric," Canute said wearily.

Leofric reached for his sword. He gripped the hilt with confidence and the two began to circle, sizing each other up. Harold lunged wildly toward Leofric and missed, revealing his impetuous nature. He recovered his balance and spouted, "Don't worry about your lovely wife, Leofric. After I finish with you, I'll make sure she's well taken care of."

Leofric refused to let Harold's taunts incite him into making a rash move. He remained calm, skilled, and calculated. He countered and drove Harold backward with a furious assault, his momentum carrying them both across the room.

"Have I angered you?" Harold mocked him.

Leofric was cautious at first, concerned that his opponent was the king's brother. The king, however, had given his consent. Leofric freed his mind of concern. He drove Harold back to the wall, his sword flashing faster and faster. Harold edged his way along the length of the room, trying to keep Leofric at bay. Leofric whipped his blade closer and closer to Harold's face.

"Perhaps I should cut out your tongue, as I heard was done to your friend. Maybe that will silence you," Leofric threatened.

Canute, who was aware of Leofric's skill with the sword, was amused. Harold, on the other hand, had not suspected that Leofric was this good.

"I am your prince, you fool!" Harold screamed, fearing for his life. "Brother, help me!" Harold tripped and stumbled onto the wooden floor while Canute watched. Leofric brought his sword down, stopping it within an inch of Harold's neck.

"Is this the fight you were seeking?"

"You never did have the sword to back your big mouth." Canute's disgust was evident.

"She deserves more respect, you insolent scum," Leofric shouted. It was taking all his willpower not to bring his sword slashing into Harold's neck—as it was, the blade was nearly touching.

"Enough!" Canute cried out. Leofric lingered a few seconds before he sheathed his blade.

"Come with me, Leofric," the king commanded, leading him into the War Council chambers. It was much like the one in Denmark. The stone walls were covered with tapestries, while weapons of every shape and size were lined up between the flags of conquered enemies. A large table sat in the center of the room, and some of Canute's handcarved Viking ships rested on its corner. King Canute leaned across it and looked directly into Leofric's eyes. His tone suddenly became decidedly different.

"Do you know, Leofric, that when I selected you to be earl, against the will of my council, I believed that you were truly the key to unifying my provinces? I had spent months mulling over my options until I came to the conclusion that the intelligent son of Leofwine was my best hope."

"I was unaware of that, sire," Leofric answered, stunned by the revelation.

"The world is on a course of change. The old Viking ways will have to give way to a new system of rule. My primary problem is that far too many members of the Thing Council are incapable of understanding this. They want to continue the 'way of their fathers,' 'the Viking way.' They are threatened by change and distrustful of it. They expect me to dominate with brutality and fear. They lust for the good old days, when England provided them with abundant Danegeld. They want nothing more than to eat, drink, and fight. Many believe that subjugation by the sword is the only means of ruling a conquered nation."

Leofric nodded, waiting to see what Canute's revelation would mean to him.

"This king wants to build a new world, one that isn't constrained by the old rules. If I'm going to succeed, I need to find men who will be the pillars of my new edifice. I believe that you are one of those pillars, Leofric."

Canute was caught up in his vision and continued to paint Leofric a detailed portrait of his new world. He had designed every detail of an enlightened Northern European empire that would grow and thrive for hundreds of years, etching its place in the annals of history beside the Romans and the Greeks.

"The sword is mighty still, but wisdom...that is our greatest ally, wisdom and the rule of law." Canute paused. Leofric could almost hear his father's voice speaking through Canute.

"Would it surprise you to know that I have spent many long hours pouring over the laws of King Alfred and the other eminent leaders of this great isle? Their words have provided me with a different view of this land and of the world. Yes, I desperately need taxes to satisfy my aged, brutish Viking lords, but that is not my primary concern. The England I seek is a much greater prize than the plunder we can reap." Canute stopped to see that Leofric understood.

"I was unaware that you had studied the writings of Alfred," Leofric said. "We have this in common. He left a strong legacy for my family to follow. My father insisted that I too be knowledgeable of his writings."

"Like Alfred, I am not content merely to read history; I intend to engrave my name upon it. I want nothing less than to create the greatest nation on earth. Our future is in uniting the people of England into a new, powerful kingdom, one that can survive and even lead the new world. But how, Lord Leofric, can I do this when my subjects mistrust me and rebel at my every pronouncement?" Canute searched Leofric's face, appealing to him for an answer.

"I myself have longed for an England as great as you say; both Godiva and I have. I am thrilled by your passion for a great country. I long to see this England born, Your Majesty."

"Oh, how I wish I could find in you a true ally. Together we could create precisely the great nation we speak of," Canute said.

"With your leadership, I can see that it is possible, Your Majesty," Leofric said.

"Now you sound like that imbecile brother of yours, Norman. Don't patronize me, Leofric. As a fellow scholar, I want to know what you honestly think."

Leofric stepped back, startled by Canute's rebuke.

Canute continued, his voice growing louder with each phrase. "Do you see that all eyes are turned to you and me, watching our every move for even the slightest sign of weakness? There are those, English and Dane, who want to exploit the current tax problems to their own end, and we must not let them. I have ruled my kingdom with an iron hand, and it has made me feared. Feared and respected! Up until now, I have been regarded by some in my homeland as Canute the Great. But do you know what some misguided members of my War Council have secretly taken to calling me? Canute the Weak! I loathe that name. I loathe weakness. It disgusts me beyond all faults. This title, I cannot tolerate."

Canute took a few deep breaths and visibly composed himself.

"The situation with your wife has led these detractors to further question my authority." His voice again became forceful. "I cannot tolerate my subjects viewing me as weak. Can I, Earl Leofric?"

Leofric wasn't sure what to answer. He had the distinct feeling that he was backed into a corner. He knew he had to move with caution or be trapped.

Canute paced around the long room, studying the tapestries left to him by those who had previously held the scepter of power. He gazed upon one that displayed an ancient battle and became reflective.

"I understand the iron first, but a truly great leader must not only rule by force but by finding a way into the hearts of the people. If he is in their hearts, he will always have their loyalties," Canute said, turning to Leofric.

"Do you know who taught me this?"

"No, Your Majesty."

"You should. It was your father. He is a very wise man, don't you agree?"

Leofric was stunned. "Yes, I do, Your Highness."

Canute's face brightened. He took Leofric by the arm and led him to the table to be seated.

"I used to worship my own father and believe everything he said. But during these past ten years, I have come to see things quite differently than he did. It has taken me that long to recognize the foolhardiness of his barbaric Viking ways. Yet his approach so deeply penetrated my soul that I struggle within my own being. Like a sickness, I seek to cut his ways out.

"When I made you earl, it was with the highest motives. I have no intention of leaving the same foul legacy as my father. The reason that you are here today is not only to hear my anger or my philosophical waxing but also to understand my plight.

"I am determined to be a great king, Leofric, one who is loved and honored by his subjects. Unfortunately, with the course of events that has taken place in Coventry, it seems that the hearts of my subjects have already been won."

Leofric didn't answer. Canute never once broke his penetrating gaze.

"By a single heroic act, your wife has become the rallying point against me; not only for Coventry but for the greater part of England.

"What am I to do? I am now faced with an incredible paradox. While you are potentially my most important ally, this rebellious act has positioned your wife as my greatest obstacle."

Leofric's thoughts raced. *What could he possibly be planning to do to Godiva?* he asked himself fearfully. As he looked in the direction of the room's arched entrance, he noticed someone quickly pull back from the side of the doorway. Harold had been lurking in the hallway, eavesdropping on their conversation.

"I imagine, Leofric, that you must love Godiva a great deal," Canute commented.

"Yes, Your Majesty, I do."

The king leaned in close across the table.

"Then one could presume that you would do everything in your power to keep her from being executed as a traitor?"

Leofric stiffened. "Anything, sire. Please."

"I believe, Leofric, that I have devised a plan that may allow us to save her life. Shall I share it with you?" he smiled, but Leofric was not put at ease by Canute's bared teeth.

"I would be most grateful." Sweat beaded on Leofric's forehead as he waited.

"Your wife has won the hearts of the people because of her sacrifice in paying the taxes. In doing so, she has turned both you and me into villains. I ordered the taxes, and you attempted to collect them.

"When I was in Denmark, the council gave me an ultimatum. They have given me only a short time to collect the Danegeld and deliver it to them.

"You do know that I hate ultimatums, but I am also aware that we cannot afford a war with the council. If the people are allowed to refuse to pay their taxes, we will soon have no country. Without money, we would have no soldiers; without soldiers, we would not be able to defend ourselves against those who would destroy us. Do you see my problem, Leofric? We have no choice but to make an example of Coventry."

Leofric clearly understood Canute's logic although he was afraid of what it would mean for his beloved town, and even more, his beloved wife.

The king continued, "But Coventry has the support of the people. As easy as it is to settle this with the sword, we must find another way. We must find a way to separate your wife from the people—to drive a wedge between them.

"This is my plan: I have concluded that the answer to our problem lies not in what Godiva will do for the sake of the people of Coventry but in what she will *not* do for their sake.

"Your wife is known to be a woman of faith. Is that true, Leofric?"

"With all her heart."

"Interesting." Canute smiled. "And the pagan festival of the summer solstice is next month, is it not?"

"Yes, that's right."

"Coventry is the sacred site of the Cofa Tree. Perhaps there is a way to exploit this to our own use." Canute drummed his fingers on the table; pleased with the way he had manipulated the conversation.

"What do you suppose would happen if, at the height of the noon hour on the summer solstice, instead of a pagan...what if your wife was to fulfill the traditional fertility rite?"

Leofric eyes grew wide at what Canute was suggesting.

"What if," the king proposed matter-of-factly, "Godiva was to ride on a white stallion, completely unclothed, through the streets of Coventry to the Cofa Tree? And if she completed the ride, the people of Coventry would be released from all taxes owed to me, past and future. Do you think we would win favor from the people? Would they love their king?"

"Of course, King Canute. To be free of taxes forever? The people would love you, but to ask this of Godiva is impossible. No matter how much she would want to do this, she would not be able to. The church would excommunicate her. The state of her soul itself would be in question."

"Really? Her eternal soul hanging in the balance?" the king mused. "Now you are beginning to understand my strategy.

"In a game of chess, you must allow for your opponent to surprise you. You must be prepared with your reaction, regardless of their choice of move."

"I'm not sure that I follow you," Leofric said.

"I'm going to offer your wife a way out of her troubles, a way to save the people she loves. At the same time, this will give me influence with my father's pagan supporters in the council. They would see this ride of Godiva's as a moral victory. They would much rather have your wife defame her Christian faith and take the pagan ride than have her dead."

"Your Majesty, my wife's love for Coventry is great, but to ride through the middle of Coventry, naked, dishonoring God in the most pagan of all ceremonies? Godiva would rather die than do that." Leofric hung his head dejectedly.

"That is good news, precisely what I was hoping for," the king said, rubbing his hands together as he thought of Godiva's powerlessness against him. "When she refuses to do it, then *she* will be blamed for the suffering of the people, not me. They will soon forget the paltry jewels she offered for their taxes when they have no food."

"I can't believe what I'm hearing, sire."

Canute shrugged. He had Leofric exactly where he wanted him.

"Then again, we could go back to the plan of simply killing her."

Leofric began to wring his hands.

"Don't be afraid, Leofric. I have no intention of harming her. No, my friend, we have no need, for this is a worthy plan." Canute's face glowed with his victory.

"You, Leofric, shall be my spokesman. You will make it perfectly clear that the king has made a generous peace offering to the people, to free them from taxation, and that it is your wife who is unwilling to meet the requirements. Simple, isn't it?"

The king waited a moment, allowing Leofric time to wrestle with the outrageous proposition.

"If my plan works, I will be able to give the council the taxes they demand and still find my way into the hearts of the people."

"I understand," Leofric answered solemnly as Canute continued.

"The common people have hope because Godiva has helped them in the past. When she refuses them, their faith in a savior will fade. Instead, through my generous offer, perhaps I will become their hope. Be of good cheer, Leofric. By putting this ride before her, we can save Godiva's life and turn Coventry from their rebellion.

"The taxes will still be collected and your fair, but meddlesome, wife will no longer have any influence in these matters. She can go home to your castle and find her womanly place supporting you as you help me to build a better England."

Canute finally stopped talking and smiled calmly, waiting for Leofric's response. Leofric stood there silently for a long time.

"I will go and discuss these matters with her."

"Yes, go to your wife."

"My king," Leofric paused to take a deep breath. He bowed. "Thank you for releasing her to me."

"Yes, Leofric, do remind her that it was I who released her," Canute said, peering right into him.

Without guard or companion, Leofric rode home, aghast at the snare that he had wandered into.

❀❀❀❀❀❀

It was late, but Godiva couldn't sleep. Since she had been released from the dungeon, she hadn't stopped worrying about Leofric and his audience with the king.

She wrapped her red brocade cape around her shoulders, lit a torch, and walked mournfully out to the aviary to find a moment's peace. She set the torch in its bracket, got down on her knees in front of her small altar and Osburga's wooden cross. Surrounded by birds and lush plants, she prayed to God for her husband's safe return and for renewed peace in their lives. Then she sat in silent mediation for several minutes, trying to hear the Lord's answer. She folded her elbows against her body and cradled her head in her hands, closing herself off from the world that loomed around her, threatening to destroy her.

"What else could I have done? What else should I have said?" she turned the question over and over again in her mind, searching for answers. She cloistered herself there in the aviary for hours, worrying, weeping, and praying for mercy.

❀❀❀❀❀❀

Leofric silently slipped through the netted door, careful not to let any of the birds escape. He walked to the back of the aviary where the torch shone and for a moment watched Godiva as she prayed. Godiva heard him shift and turned to see her husband standing behind her with a weary expression on his face. She stood up quickly and looked him over for any signs of injury but saw none.

"Oh, Leofric, you're safe. You're here. I was so afraid that you might be...." She couldn't bring herself to say the word *dead* and instead broke down crying into his shirt.

"No," he sighed as he closed his eyes and held her tightly.

"After what happened to Norman, I feared that I would be the reason you were slain," she whispered.

"My love, my dear Godiva," he crooned into her hair as he held her.

Godiva looked up into his face. "Leofric, I was so hopeful that peace had finally come to this land."

Leofric moved away from her.

"So was I," he sighed, "but news of the revolt in Coventry has spread to other towns and villages. The king feels that he needs to make an example of us. He has been advised by his council to attack immediately."

"What will become of us?"

"Though the king faces many difficulties, I have learned that he intends to override them and seek a peaceful way out of this," he said. "The king has given you back to me, for now."

"Then he has shown mercy!" Godiva cried.

Mercy? Leofric thought to himself.

"Canute is under tremendous pressure from the Danish War Council to collect the Danegeld. They are so enraged that some are plotting to overthrow him. He is a cunning strategist, though, and determined to do things his way. He has taken the council's ultimatum as an insult and has no intention of capitulating to them."

"What are you trying to say?" Godiva interrupted.

"Some appeasement will be necessary. He must collect the taxes to hold them at bay."

"What is he going to do? March against Coventry again?"

"The king spent many hours seeking to explain his thoughts to me."

"What thoughts?" she pressed.

"At first I didn't trust him, but I realized that something has changed in him these last years. He now sees his entire legacy tied to the success of England. If England is strong, it will mean that he is also strong. His dream for this nation is not so far from our own, Godiva. The Danish Council wants England kept as a source of plunder. Canute sees England as a great nation that could lead the world into the future.

"He still wants me to help him build this nation. In fact, he told me that I was his most important ally," Leofric continued.

"He said that?"

"Yes, and that he needs my help."

"Then this is good news," Godiva said, smiling tentatively. Leofric held up his hand for her to wait.

"But Coventry's revolt has become a thorn in his side. The king is making the first move to resolve the problem in Coventry. He has devised a plan in which the taxes would be forgiven if certain conditions were met. If not, Coventry will have to pay the taxes like any other town."

"What is the plan?"

"He has decided to extend to Coventry a special peace offering. But at a staggering cost." Leofric paused as he nervously picked up a fallen rose petal and rubbed it between his fingers.

"Tell me, Leofric," Godiva demanded.

"Coventry is to pay the taxes, unless..."

"Unless what?" Godiva said, placing her hand on Leofric's cheek and gently turning his face to look at her.

"Unless," he began again, letting out a deep sigh, "you consent to take the pagan ride, the fertility rite, at the time of the summer solstice."

"What?"

"Fully unclothed, on horseback, at the height of the festival."

"Ride naked through Coventry?" She paled.

"Then all tolls owed by Coventry to the throne, past and future, will be rescinded," Leofric said finally.

Godiva glared at him. "I can't believe what you're saying. How could he even suggest such a vile thing?"

"Godiva, I told him you would never do this."

"I have lived my whole life to honor God. What kind of perverse pleasure could this possibly give this so-called 'changed' barbarian? He truly seeks to destroy me, doesn't he?" she asked, recognizing his motive. She wrapped her arms around herself and, turning her back on Leofric, walked to the far side of the aviary.

"He is quite certain that you will refuse. This is his way of regaining control and giving you back your life."

"Giving me back my life?" she stopped in her tracks and whirled around. "Giving me back my life? What sickness lives in the heart of this man? Does he think that he is a god who dispenses life and death so easily?" she screamed, sending the birds flapping around the aviary. "What good is my life if it causes more suffering for the people of Coventry? What is this charade of a peace offering? How will this help the people of Coventry at all? We are right back where we started. Nothing has changed, Leofric!"

"Godiva, he is under tremendous pressure to hold you up as an example and execute you for treason. The fact that he resists shows how he has changed. You have to understand..."

"I do understand, Leofric. I understand that the cost is unreasonable. He took away Sister Osburga. He took away my parents. And now he wants to destroy me!"

"He has given you back to me, alive."

"Alive for what? To be shamed and silenced? To watch my people die a slow, unjust death? He is killing me, Leofric. I hate him. I hate him with every bone in my body." She picked up a potted ivy and hurled it to the ground.

Leofric stared in shock at the broken pieces of pottery and plant scattered across the ground.

"Canute is filled with as much evil as ever. He offers me the salvation of my people but only if I will damn my soul to hell!"

TWENTY-NINE

As a cool, delicate fog rolled over the countryside the next morning, soft white light crept through the window, awakening Leofric. He rolled over, reaching out an arm to caress his wife, but felt only the bed sheet. Sleepily, he reached again, his eyes cracking open. The bed beside him was empty. Godiva was gone.

Godiva hadn't been able to fall asleep all night, Canute's proposition churning over and over again in her mind. She could hardly wait for day to break so she could seek the counsel of the only person to whom she could confide her desperate situation.

She rode Aethenoth down a familiar narrow path. The fog was dense as she made her way through the thick, dark timber. Wet branches drooped down in front of her, and she had to push them away before they could slap into her. A flock of birds darted out of the trees as she approached the tiny, isolated hermitage that had been her sanctuary and place of answers for so many years. She tossed Aethenoth's reins over the gatepost.

"I won't be too long," she promised him, patting his neck.

She walked past the robust herb and vegetable gardens and knocked softly on the small door. It hadn't been closed completely and swung open when she touched it. Agnes was sitting at the table eating breakfast. She seemed thin and frail. But when she saw her dear friend, she smiled brightly.

"Godiva, I'm so pleased to see you," she said, rising and crossing the room with her arms outstretched.

Upon seeing Agnes, all of Godiva's emotions came flooding out. She fell into her friend's embrace.

"My child, why are you so upset? Tell me, why is there so much pain in your eyes?" Sister Agnes led Godiva to a chair and sat down opposite her.

"Where to begin? Sister Agnes, the king has nullified my payment of Coventry's taxes and has ordered Leofric to ride against the town if each person does not submit his due. It's an impossible request! And if that weren't enough, the king has turned his wrath against me. He holds me responsible for the growing rebellion across the country. He intends to make an example of Coventry!"

"How dreadful," Agnes said, taking Godiva's hands.

"I don't know what to do, Sister Agnes. I can't understand how my actions, intended to save lives, now threaten so many more."

"Godiva, I'm sorry that you suffer so much over these things, but this burden isn't yours alone. You have done so much for the people, for many years. Like your parents, you have always been a vessel of goodness."

"I have done nothing but turn the king's outrage against them. I have to find a solution," Godiva said.

"You cannot blame yourself. You have bought the people of Coventry time and have inspired them with your courage."

"But now they are as helpless as ever." Godiva paused, readying herself to tell Sister Agnes the rest. "Even now, the king lays out hope for them. He pretends to offer them a way out. But it can never be."

"What hope does he offer them?"

"Do you know of the ride to the Cofa Tree?"

"If you mean the licentious display of flesh that some call a fertility rite, yes. I know that it is an appalling sacrilege to God. Why do you ask?"

"For some reason, the king has offered to forever forgive Coventry's taxes if I, a Christian woman, will deny my faith and take the ride...fully naked."

"Is this true, Godiva?" Agnes shuddered.

"It is possible that he says it merely to torment me. How could he be so wicked as to offer Coventry freedom, the very thing I want most in the world, for the price of my soul? Have I not done everything in my power for these people? Have I not already given of my fortune for them? But nothing I do is ever enough. Must I also go to hell to redeem them?"

"No, of course not, Godiva!"

"Sometimes I wonder why God would allow such an evil man to exist upon the earth." Godiva closed her eyes and sobbed as Agnes anguished over trying to find a solution for her friend's difficulties.

"The king has asked for my humiliation. How could the church not condemn me?" she asked Agnes desperately.

"Godiva, I'm not sure that I understand your question. I hope you aren't considering the king's offer."

"Sister Agnes, I'm so confused. I don't know what to do. My worry is so great that I can't sleep. My dreams are haunted by the slack jaws and blue lips of dead Coventry children. I have nightmares about them every night.

"Every morning at choir, I see their faces filled with fear. They ask me over and over to protect them. They're just children! And I am only one woman. What can I do to protect them against Canute?" she wailed.

"I want so much for this to end, but it never does! I cannot watch another child be slaughtered. Not one more!"

"Godiva, you are so angry."

"Of course, I'm angry. What else could I be?"

Sister Agnes put her thin arms around Godiva and held her tight. She looked Godiva squarely in the face.

"To lay down your earthly life for a friend can be a godly thing. But to damn your eternal soul is not." Agnes paused to make sure that Godiva was really listening.

"If you are the only hope of Coventry, then where is God? Are you more caring than He?"

Godiva was shocked by the question. Was she playing God?

"Godiva, I am your friend, and the pain of your soul deeply moves my heart. I feel for everything you say, but I also hear the words that you do not say." Agnes took a long breath. She was about to say something that she had never said aloud.

"When Sister Osburga was killed, my world was shattered. I loved and respected her so much that I had built my entire world around hers. Then, suddenly, she was gone and I had lost everything." Her eyes filled with tears as the memories flooded her mind.

"For a time I may—I can hardly say this aloud—I may have lost my faith. Oh, I didn't admit it to myself, but I held God responsible for allowing her to die and taking her from me." Agnes began to cry, the grief welling up from deep within her. She struggled to control herself as she said, "But that is not all. We all face grief.... There is one more thing that I need to tell you. When you were young, I couldn't say the words. In fact, I have never told anyone.

"At the time of the slaughter at the abbey, a Viking soldier raped me."

Godiva's face filled with horror as she reached out to Agnes. Agnes put her hand up.

"No, let me finish. The vile creature took away from me the precious state that I had given to Jesus. I was so angry, and I masked my fury with hatred for Canute and the others. I lived in that rage every moment of every day for many, many years. It was so overwhelming that it kept me from going into town and being with the people of Coventry as they rebuilt. It pounded endlessly in my head, until one day, I thought I could no longer go on.

"Then, very early one cold, winter morning, I thought I heard the smallest whisper of something soft and kind in the midst of all the rage. I now know that it was the inner voice of God's love. He was showing me the bitterness I held not just toward Canute and the Viking who defiled me, but also toward Himself. I was shocked. I never thought that I could hate God."

"You, Agnes?"

"Yes. But then, deep down in my soul, I heard Osburga's words entreating me to forgive these evil men for their crimes, to forgive myself for the crimes that had been committed against me, and for the fact that I had lived when so many others had died. Most of all, I could hear Osburga begging me to listen to God. To trust Him."

Godiva could sense the purity of Agnes' heart and suddenly remembered Osburga's parting words to her.

"And remember that all things work together for the good of those who love God. You must trust Him above all else." Wasn't that what she had said?

"I was stubborn," Agnes confessed. "For a long time, even after I knew I should, I didn't forgive. I couldn't forgive. I held on to my hatred. I made it my ally. I justified it, using it as vengeance against Canute. All the while, it ate me up inside, destroying every good thing in me little by little. My spirit and body ached beneath the weight of it."

Godiva looked at her in amazement. "Sister, how can this be true?"

"My sweet child," Agnes laughed. "Remember all those years when I was in hiding. The years I hardly spoke?"

"Yes, of course. You barely gave me a word, but I assumed that you were mourning for Osburga. I thought you were always in prayer."

"You have always been so dear, and I was afraid I would infect you with the venom that flowed through me."

Suddenly, the room filled with the sweet sound of a bird chirping. Agnes led Godiva to the window, opened the shutters, and pointed to the feeder she had hung outside.

"Do you see my lovely friends? This is my choir, sent from heaven."

"Yes, Sister. They are wonderful," Godiva smiled, thinking of the aviary.

"Let me tell you a story. One day, as I looked out at my precious birds, I saw them acting very unusual. They were anxiously moving their heads back and forth, nervously darting about, pecking and scratching at their seed. But they wouldn't sing. None of them, not even one. I was so worried. I couldn't figure out what was wrong. As I stood there watching, a hawk suddenly flew down and attacked one of them. I realized that the flock would not sing because they were afraid.

"In that moment, it came to me that Canute was like that hawk. Before the attack, we were like the birds, delighting in the peace of our garden. The abbey was filled with song. But after the attack, I didn't sing for a very long time.

"Then, watching the hawk's assault, I understood the silencing of my faith. I knew, as strange as it might sound, that God missed my singing as much as I missed the singing of the birds. So I tried to sing for God. I opened my mouth, but nothing came out. My soul was resisting. I couldn't sing. I had nothing to sing about. As I looked deep inside myself, I didn't like what I saw. I was fearful, angry, and bitter. I couldn't help but weep. I finally came to see that I was hindered, not only by my fear, but also by my inability to forgive. You see, my dear child, I had to release the burden of hatred in order to regain my own being."

Godiva dropped her head and stared sadly at the ground.

"I had to choose between love and hate. And only one could guide my life. I knew that I couldn't have them both. In all of this, I learned that God extends His mercy to all. He makes the sun and the rain fall on the righteous and the unrighteous alike. Though my journey has been long and painful, I have found my peace. I have been set free." Agnes beamed, and Godiva could see the love in her soul shining from her eyes.

"Agnes, I don't understand how you could forgive Canute for what he did. I don't see how I could ever find the strength to do that."

"Godiva, listen to me. The things that seem impossible with us are possible with God. He gives us both the grace and the strength to do His will."

"I wish I knew His will."

"God's will is found in love, for God is love. That is the truth I have come to know. I almost lost it through unforgiveness, but now I cling to it as life, and no one will ever take it from me again. Not even myself. I will not let hatred take away this love. God will tell you, in your heart of hearts, what He wants you to do. But before you can complete His purpose, you must know for certain that your heart is pure."

"Pure? How?" Godiva asked.

Agnes smiled knowingly. She took Godiva's hands and looked into her eyes.

"Don't you understand? You must forgive the man who killed your family."

"Canute? You want me to forgive that tyrant? Sister Agnes, as much as I want to honor Osburga, as much as I believe the words you say, how can I even begin to forgive this man? He is a wicked murderer. I could never forgive him for what he has done to me!"

"The act of forgiveness is more for the one who gives it than for the one who receives."

"Since I was a child, he has made my life miserable," Godiva protested.

Agnes looked firmly at Godiva. "If you do not forgive him, he will make the rest of your life miserable, as well.

"If you are to free those in Coventry, you must first free yourself from the hatred you have for the king, from the hatred that torments you. Unforgiveness is a bitter root that springs up inside you and poisons your soul. It will make you—even you—old and ugly before your time.

"It took me too long to realize this truth." Agnes said, gesturing to her face with a self-depreciating smile.

"Oh, Agnes. You are the most beautiful person I know."

"Only in your eyes, Godiva," Agnes countered.

"I have not forgotten what Osburga taught me," Godiva said. "I just don't know how to use it all. My heart refuses to listen to my head."

"It's not impossible," Agnes urged. "Do you think it was easy for our Lord to hang upon the cross? How horrible it must have been to submit to those who tormented Him so. But He chose love, and in His dying, whispered, 'Father, forgive them.'"

Sister Agnes' words were working their way into Godiva's heart.

"You must overcome evil with good, Godiva. Perfect love, that which embraces forgiveness, has compassion and is never fearful—this is what we must embrace."

"Perfect love." The words sank in, and Godiva bowed her head.

THIRTY

Leofric was relieved to hear that his wife had gone to visit Sister Agnes. He knew that she needed a trusted friend to talk to and that Agnes would guide her well. The night before, he and Godiva had started to heal the rift between them. There were still problems, but they were a team again, and together they would somehow find their way through their problems.

He called his private council to his chambers. He leaned over the large table and addressed the group somberly. The group sat very still, and no one interrupted as they usually did.

"Today our heralds will be making the new conditions of the tax known to the citizens of Coventry," Leofric began. "If Coventry will not pay the tolls, our forces must be ready to ride with the king. King Canute intends to make an example of Coventry in order to quell the rebellion in other towns that have heard of the revolt."

"My lord, has it truly come to this?" asked a Saxon advisor. "Must we ride against our own people again?"

"What choice do we have?" Leofric asked. "We've seen this coming for quite some time. I dread it, but we must do our duty." He looked around the table at each face. The men all nodded in agreement.

"I suppose I must inform you that Canute has proffered an alternative proposal," Leofric said. "He has offered Coventry a reprieve, but the conditions are impossible to fulfill. Therefore, in spite of the celebration, Canute plans to attack on the Summer Solstice. We have many preparations to make and not much time. You all know what must be done." Leofric stepped back from the table, closing the meeting as quickly as it had begun.

Each of his commanders left to tend their duties. Leofric was alone. He walked to the window and looked out at the beautiful day. The sun was high in the blue sky, the grass was green, and the birds were singing, but he could feel the darkness encroaching.

The peasants swarmed around the herald and his four guards as they stood at attention in the middle of Coventry's square.

"Not again. All I want to do is get some work done," the cobbler said, holding a broken leather boot he had been repairing. "But with Canute on the throne, it seems the wife and I, or even these boots, may not live to see tomorrow." He laughed sadly.

"What is it now?" a frightened woman asked, trying to push her way to the front so she could see.

"One can only guess," Thurman said, stepping into the group.

The herald stood with his chest out a little further and his voice a little louder than on other days, as if he were trying to assert his strength. He nervously glanced around, as though he were plotting possible escape routes. He cleared his throat, unrolled the scroll, and began to read.

"Earl Leofric has announced that, once again, His Majesty King Canute and the Danish Council have demanded the payment of the taxes that are owed to the royal throne by this conquered nation."

Murmurs and groans rose from the crowd.

"Good people of Coventry, King Canute the Great has taken note of your sufferings and is aware of the many hardships that the tax would mean for the people of this town. His Majesty seeks peace and extends a unique offer to his subjects in Coventry. Because Coventry is the home to the sacred Cofa Tree, the king, in his mercy, has established certain conditions. Upon their fulfillment, Coventry will be declared free of all taxes—past, present, and future."

A roar of delight rose among the people. They began to cheer and dance in the streets. When they calmed down, someone asked, "What are the conditions you speak of, herald?"

❦❦❦❦❦❦

Leofric stood alone, contemplating his large arsenal. He didn't notice as Godiva walked in. She stood at the door, watching silently as he reached for a Spanish sword. He checked the grip, tilted his head to inspect the angle of the blade, then set it down.

"Good morning," she said, stepping forward.

"You were up early," Leofric said without looking at her. He closed one eye, held out another sword, and examined the sharpness of the blade.

"I couldn't sleep."

Leofric knew that Godiva wasn't going to like what he had to tell her. He spoke quickly so she wouldn't have a chance to interrupt.

"On the morning before the solstice, Thorold will escort you and your handmaid to my family's hunting lodge. Thorold will need to be in Coventry the next day, but you will be safe there. No one will find you.

"When the conditions of the ride were read, the king's decree was not received well. Coventry again readies herself for battle. This time, they have rallied support from other towns. The rebellion grows."

"What do you intend to do?" Godiva asked, suspicious of his manner.

"I have thought it over carefully and have decided to ride with the king. I cannot let this nation be torn apart by the stubbornness of its people—even those I call friends," he said firmly, setting down his sword.

"Leofric, you can't. Think of what this means," she cried, grabbing his arm.

Leofric broke away from her grasp.

"I have no other choice. I've come to realize that this is not just about us and not just about the people of Coventry. This is about something much bigger." He opened a massive wooden armoire that housed more swords.

"King Canute is poised to become the greatest ruler England has ever known. While some are bound to suffer, many more will thrive in the years to come. I will stand behind him."

"'Some are bound to suffer?' How can you say such a thing?" Godiva exclaimed. "Let it be someone else, not the people of Coventry. They have already suffered enough!"

"I have no power to stop it, Godiva. What would you have me do? Defy the king? He would not only destroy Coventry but us as well. Is that what you prefer?"

Godiva stared at him, silently fuming.

"I have always dreamed of being a great earl," Leofric explained. "Of being loved and revered by my subjects like my father. However, I see no path to such favor in these times. I'm being logical. You are being emotional. Your reasoning has become clouded by fear and sympathy." He still would not look at her. Godiva was quiet as he moved about, cleaning the sword he had chosen. Leofric finally looked over at her.

Sadness filled her voice. "These people's lives are left to us. They must not die the way my parents and the Sisters of the abbey were killed. Ten years ago, you saw me try to release the birds to freedom and decided to not only save my life, but to help the birds to safety, as well. Are these people today not as deserving of life as the birds and I were then?"

Leofric lowered his head, stung by her words.

"To serve the people of Coventry, you must persuade them to pay the tax, or least make some motion of it," he said.

"They have nothing, Leofric!" she argued. "You know that Canute has ordered the impossible."

"Then let them offer what they can!" he bellowed back.

Cresha entered the room, and they both fell silent.

"Earl Leofric, your father has arrived. Shall I inform him that you're unavailable?" she asked uncomfortably.

"My father, here? No, Cresha. Thank you. I'll be right there."

The handmaid quickly scurried out, and Leofric tried once more to get his wife to see his reasoning.

"There is nothing I would rather do than find an answer that appeases everyone," he said. "But I am the earl, and I must serve my king first or he'll find someone else who will. What you refuse to understand, Godiva, is that he is the only one with a say in these matters, and he will proceed as he pleases whether you and I like it or not."

When she didn't answer, Leofric stormed out, knowing that his father would only add another voice to the mix, albeit more temperate. The door crashed shut behind him. Godiva slammed her fist down on the table in utter frustration.

THIRTY-ONE

Prince Harold arrived alone at the Wessex castle of Earl Godwin just after daybreak. He had purposely come without an escort.

"Who goes there?" a sentry called down from one of the towers.

"Tell Godwin that Prince Harold is here with urgent business."

"Yes, Your Highness."

The prince looked around nervously, checking the surrounding trees for possible spies.

The sentry appeared again. "Right this way, my lord."

The drawbridge slowly creaked open, and he quickly made his way inside.

"My lord, if you'll follow me," the sentry motioned.

Harold was led through the grand court of Earl Godwin's castle. He attempted to nod his head regally as he greeted those who walked by.

"Prince Harold," the page announced as they stepped inside Godwin's chambers. Godwin bowed respectfully to him.

"It is good to see you, Prince Harold. I received word that you were coming, and I'm glad to see that you have arrived safely."

"Thank you, Earl Godwin." Harold glanced around at the other men, surprised to see them convened so early in the day. He raised his eyebrows.

"Please, take your leave," requested the earl. His counselors quickly left the room. Godwin turned to Harold.

"What brings you all this way, my prince?" he asked.

"I have come to discuss something that affects both of us. But first, let me be rude and ask you for a drink."

"Of course, Prince Harold. Where are my manners?"

"Some ale," Godwin yelled out the door to a servant in the hall. He motioned to a seat at the table, and the prince sat down.

"How is my fair sister doing, Godwin?" the prince asked.

"The beautiful Lady Gethna is quite well."

"Give her my fond regards and make sure that she understands my desire for her to come to the banquet honoring the king in Winchester."

"I most certainly will."

The servant entered and placed a foaming goblet in front of each of them. The man quickly bowed several times as he rushed out, closing the door behind him.

Harold gazed intently at Godwin. A devilish grin spread across his face.

"I will waste no more of your time, Godwin. I would like to take you into my confidence. I suppose that I can count on your discretion. You are, after all, my brother-in-law."

"Of course. My loyalties to the king, and to you, Prince Harold, are unwavering. I am here to be of service any way that I can."

"Good. I will come straight to the point. I am still most dissatisfied with my brother's selection of Leofric as the earl of Mercia. As far as I'm concerned, he has become far too powerful too quickly and too easily. I resent the undue influence he seems to have on the king."

"I couldn't agree with you more," said Godwin.

"From the beginning, I was opposed to giving such a vast territory to someone so pathetically inexperienced. Now, even after he has shown such incompetence with the affair in Coventry, my brother still caters to him. When I seek to bring this to Canute's attention, it seems to fall on deaf ears. In fact, he acts irritated at my mentioning it.

"My brother spends long hours studying the writings of the old English kings. His fascination with them seems to strengthen his relationship to Leofric. He no longer listens to my council as he once did. I fear that those of us who have his interest at heart are soon to lose our influence in his court."

"Frankly, I have never understood the king's appointment of Leofric," Godwin agreed quickly. "But as I am loyal to the king, I withheld my opinion. Like you, I have always felt that there were better men to rule Mercia than Leofric. Men like you, Prince Harold," he groveled, never having been particularly fond of the man but seeing a potential opportunity for himself.

"You are very generous, Godwin. And I also believe you to be one of those 'better men.'"

"Perhaps Mercia should once again be divided. What would you think of that, Harold?"

"I think we should keep it in the family. Close family."

Both men laughed. Godwin leaned in closer to the prince.

"Perhaps you have already devised a plan by which we can sway our king's decision," Earl Godwin said with a smirk. "Do you, by chance, have a solution to this mutual problem of ours? Could I be of service in any way?"

Harold smiled. "I am confident that we can find a way to assist our good king in rethinking his reliance on Earl Leofric."

"Yes, Harold, I suppose we can."

Back in Coventry, shifts of peasants took turns guarding the town's gates, watching the distant hills and the road from Canute's castle for any sign of his men. Their faces were filled with apprehension as they grasped their weapons. They had seen no movement, no soldiers. It had been quiet so far. Too quiet, some felt.

THIRTY-TWO

E arly the next morning, Godiva gathered her things,
once again being very careful not to wake her husband.
As the first small glow of light appeared in the east-
ern sky, she quickly buttoned her cape. She had been troubled
all night, unable to free her mind from worry over Coventry
and the secrets that Sister Agnes had confided. She knew she
needed to do something. She headed out the door, turning
to look at Leofric once more. He slept peacefully in the bed
without her.

She crept across the yard to the stables, trying to tiptoe and
run at the same time. It was chilly in the barn, colder than it
was outside.

"Lady Godiva, what brings you here to the stable this early
in the morning?" a voice blurted out of the darkness.

"Elbic, you startled me!"

"I'm sorry, my lady. I'm nearly always up at this hour. These
horses can tell it's breakfast time even before I can!"

Godiva had hoped to be off on her journey before anyone
found out she had gone, especially Leofric.

"An early visit into town, my lady?" Elbic asked.

"Not exactly," she hedged. Elbic gave her a strange look, and she felt she had to tell him more. "I need some time alone to think my troubles through. A lovely ride in the countryside is sure to do me some good. Don't you agree?"

"My lady, I couldn't agree with you more. A nice ride on an animal as fine as Aethenoth would lift anyone's spirits. Let me ready him for you," Elbic offered.

"Oh, thank you. I'm sorry to be a bother to you this early in the morning."

"Never a bother," Elbic said, taking the saddle and tightening the straps around Aethenoth.

Godiva rode away from her home as quickly as she could. She didn't want Leofric to wake up and see her through the window. As she rode, mile by mile, along the lengthy path, she formulated what she would say, momentarily talking herself out of her fears and attempting to control her anger and hate.

Many hours had gone by when Godiva finally saw her destination ahead of her. She tried not to cower at the sight of the intimidating stone walls. Gathering all her courage, she steadily rode up to the outer gate of Canute's castle. A guard stepped in her path.

"Stop," he ordered. "Where do you think you're going?" he asked, looking her over. It was rare for a woman to appear alone at the gates. He didn't recognize her.

"I need to see the king."

The guard smirked. "The question is, does the king need to see you?"

"Sir, please," she pleaded.

"I can't let you pass, my lady. Unless you have a summons, you have no right to be here."

Godiva was incensed. "I have every right to be here, and I must see the king."

"Who are you that you come to these walls and make such demands?" the guard asked, a flinty tone coming into his voice.

"I am Lady Godiva, wife of Earl Leofric, and you had best move out of my way and let me pass."

"Really? I'd 'best.' Imagine that. Aren't you a peppery little thing?

"Sir, you have to let me in these gates. This is important."

"I 'have' to let you in?" he mocked. "I don't have to do anything of the sort."

"You don't understand. I have come a long way and need to see King Canute!"

"Does he know that?"

"Why don't you go and ask him?" she snipped.

He glared at her and finally hollered her request up to another guard, stationed at a tower above.

"You stay there and don't let her make a move," the second guard ordered.

"We'll just see about all of this," the first guard told her, trying to sound important.

Godiva's face showed her determination. She would not accept no as an answer. No guard of Canute's would keep her from her mission.

"Send her ahead," came the faint cry from the top of the wall.

"So, it appears that you get to go in after all," the guard said. "Go on. And don't forget to pass by my station on the way out. I'd hate to miss my chance to bid you farewell," he chuckled.

Godiva went through the outer gates and proceeded through the large courtyard, making her way to the castle's front entrance. She looked up at the imposing stone structure rising toward the sky. Soldiers busily moved about the top of the walls. People on every side of her were busy building stages and raising banners for the upcoming solstice festivities. Her stomach quaked, and her palms began to sweat. She tried to take a deep breath but realized she was hyperventilating. The shiver in her stomach turned into a knot as she thought how she would soon be face-to-face with the man who had killed her parents.

"Forgive, forgive," she whispered.

"This way," a guard said, snapping her out of her thoughts. The guard motioned that she should leave her horse with a stable boy, and she followed him on foot through the castle. She could no longer think of a single argument that might penetrate Canute's icy heart. Where had all her courage gone? Where was the logic that had seemed so clear that morning?

Even with the fear in her heart, she refused to turn back. Soon she was standing before the massive door to the king's chambers.

"Who's this fair maiden?" the soldier standing guard asked her escort. "A fancy present for the king?"

"Quiet! The queen's about the castle, you know," her escort said.

"Where is your summons?" the guard asked acidly.

"I'm afraid I don't have one," she said. "But my business is urgent. I must speak to the king."

"As much as I'd like to help you, I don't feel much like losing my head today. And that is exactly what will happen to me if I allow you to enter without having been invited."

Godiva glared at him, then looked up to her escort for direction.

"I must see the king," she informed him. "Let it be on my head."

Queen Emma watched and listened from the shadows, amazed by the young woman's bold demands. She turned and whispered to her lady-in-waiting. The lady walked over and relayed the message to the soldier. Godiva glanced back and forth between them, waiting to see what would happen next.

"I apologize, my lady. I have been informed that you are to pass after all."

"This way," the lady-in-waiting said. She led Godiva into a sitting room and left her alone. Godiva gazed out the window and again tried to rehearse what she would say to the king.

Queen Emma strode into the room and spent a long moment observing Earl Leofric's wife. For all she had heard of her in the last few days, Godiva looked neither devious nor heroic. She was pretty but seemed nervous and weary. The queen approached her regally. Godiva heard the swish of skirts and turned.

"Lady Godiva, your visit is most unexpected. What brings you here to Winchester?"

"Your Majesty." Godiva curtsied before her. "I didn't imagine that I would have the honor of meeting you today," she said clumsily.

"I am the one who gave permission for you to enter," the queen explained. "Now, you must tell me, why have you come?"

"Your Highness, I need to speak to the king on behalf of the good people of Coventry."

Queen Emma was taken back by her straightforward manner. She smiled. "As you might imagine, the king is busy, occupied with the many demands of his kingdom. It is impossible to see him without going through the proper channels."

"Please, help me, my queen. He would certainly listen to you if you chose to intercede on my behalf. I would not have come if my plight were not so critical."

Queen Emma looked at her intently, recognizing her strength and determination. *Rare in a woman,* she thought.

"You have to understand, my dear, that to interrupt the king would be a foolish thing to do, even for me. It could result in a sentence of death."

"I realize that what I ask is not according to convention, but you must understand that even if it means endangering my life, I must try to see him," Godiva said.

"I see that you feel your situation is desperate. But quite honestly, I don't know if even I can help you. Let me hear what you have to say, and I will consider your request."

"Thank you, Your Majesty. The problem is this..."

"Let us retreat to a more private place," the queen interrupted. "There are those who may be listening and would work against us." Emma led Godiva through the castle's massive kitchen and out the servant's door. They quickly made their way through the royal gardens to a shaded path.

The queen led her into the woods. Godiva felt shiver of fear as they entered the trees, but she obediently followed Emma through the maze of branches until they reached a clearing. There, lit by the sun, stood a small stone building.

"A chapel? Here, Your Highness? What is this place?" Godiva asked.

"Come, I'll show you, Lady Godiva," the queen said.

Although the chapel appeared abandoned from the outside, the door opened easily. Inside, there were fresh flowers on the altar. It became evident to Godiva that, although the chapel was hidden, it was well cared for and used often.

"I had no idea that a place like this could have existed at your castle. I wouldn't think that the king would allow it. He has always displayed such disdain for Christianity."

"Sadly, what you say is true," the queen agreed. "That is why I must worship here, so far into the woods. Even as queen, I cannot change Canute. I am, however, a devout woman and, though few know it, that is what sustains me," she revealed to Godiva.

The queen's sincerity touched Godiva.

"The king and I have come to an understanding," Emma continued. "I don't interfere with his decisions as king, and he doesn't hinder the practice of my faith."

The queen looked at Godiva, fearful that perhaps she had divulged too much. All of her life, Emma had been trained never to reveal anything that was private or personal. But as she stood there in the chapel, it became evident that she wanted to share with Godiva. She wondered if she could trust her, but after a moment's consideration, she decided to risk it. It had been many years since the queen had had someone in whom she could confide. She continued.

"Being a queen, Canute's queen, is a lonely life. My child and my faith are the only things that make my life tolerable."

Godiva became quiet. The sparkle left her eyes.

"What's wrong?" Emma asked, reaching out to take Godiva's hand.

"It's just that this place reminds me of the chapel that was at the Coventry abbey a long time ago. Before it was destroyed... Forgive me, but before it was destroyed by your husband," she said shyly. The queen squeezed her hand, and Godiva felt that she could also share with her.

"In a single day, the king took away everything good in my life. I lost my mother, father, and my dearest friend, Sister

Osburga. They were murdered for no reason. And now, he seeks to slaughter again. I am so sorry to say this to you, my queen." Godiva trembled.

The queen was silent but patted Godiva's hand. She considered standing up for her husband but couldn't find it in her heart. Godiva looked into the queen's sad face.

"I have made a vow to protect the people of Coventry, and I have made a vow to honor the Lord. Yet the only option that the king has given me to save my people is to shamefully ride naked in a blasphemous pagan ceremony. He has asked me to betray and dishonor all that I am and all that I hold dear. I just don't understand his reasoning."

Emma was shocked. As Godiva opened up to the queen, all that she was holding inside came spilling out with a flood of tears.

"He has already captured the loyalty of my husband, so now I have little left to lose. Even though he may kill me, I must try to speak with him. At least then I will know that I did all I could and will be able to find my place in heaven with those I love."

Godiva looked at the floor, unable to meet the queen's gaze. "I have tried so hard to forgive your husband, just as Sister Osburga taught me," she said. "But I cannot." Godiva lifted her head passionately, her eyes ablaze. "I'm sorry, but I have hated your husband. I have hated him with a perfect hatred!"

Emma gently touched Godiva's cheek.

"My dear child, so have I," she said softly, her eyes filling with tears.

"But he's your husband!"

"He is my husband in name only. This marriage is nothing more than a political charade. Just as his offer to you is a charade. He knows full well that you could never take the ride."

"I don't understand."

"Yes, I have hated him," Emma slowly continued. "But now some of my feelings of hatred have given way to pity.

"Believe it or not, he is trying to become a better, more enlightened person. I have tried to reach out to him because I understand what has made him the way he is.

"On the one hand, he wants to be a great king. He wants his followers to love and admire him. But he is a tormented man. What he wants to be, he cannot. To sympathize with the weaknesses and needs of others, one must allow for weakness in oneself. This he could never do. Admitting weakness is not a luxury that Canute's upbringing allows. He was trained to be hard and strong, no matter what. The very things that could help him—empathy, compassion, and understanding—have been twisted in his life so they appear evil to him.

"Believe it or not, he does carry a glimmer of goodness inside him. I see it when he is with our son, Hardicanute. When he is unaware that I am watching, he is tender and kind in a way that he never experienced as a child.

"What I have hated most of all about Canute," the queen continued, "is that he denies the glimmer of goodness inside him, a good which could bring light and hope to his whole kingdom. I know that you cannot see it now, but more than anything, he does want to make England great."

Godiva fidgeted, playing with the hem of her cape. She had trouble picturing Canute as anything but an evil Viking warrior, but Leofric had recognized Canute in the same way the queen had described.

"I wish I could see more than a brutal murderer," she said, shaking her head.

"I understand that it's hard for you. For the most part, the image you have is real. But my husband wasn't born that way.

When he was a young boy, he was kind and open to the world around him. But his father ruined him. Have you ever heard the tale?" Godiva shook her head. "No, I don't supposed you would have.

"When he was small, Canute had a dream about Jesus Christ. It was vivid and real, and he excitedly ran in to tell his father, Swein Forkbeard, about it. His father was furious. He dragged him to a bench in front of a crucifix, laid him down, and whipped him until he bled and denounced Jesus Christ and everything Christian."

Godiva's eyes grew wide. "How could anyone do such an atrocious thing to a child?" she cried.

"His father was a wretched, evil man. He was intent on killing all Christians, anyone who didn't follow the old Viking ways."

"Why did he hate Christians so?"

"When Swein's father, Harold Bluetooth, was king, he became fascinated by a certain village priest, named Father Poppo. Bluetooth loved to debate with the old priest about whose God was the strongest. One day, King Harold challenged the priest. Father Poppo had told him that his God gave him the strength to walk through the fires of life. King Harold laughed and asked him if he would be willing to prove that. 'Of course,' Poppo replied, not realizing what the king was asking of him. Harold Bluetooth took his fiercest warrior and pitted him against the priest.

"He told each one to pray to his own God for the strength to withstand the flames and put their bare hand into the fire. The warrior was a Viking, a worshiper of Odin and Thor. Father Poppo, of course, prayed to Jesus Christ. King Harold Bluetooth reasoned that whichever man gave up and removed his hand first must have the weaker God.

"King Harold's strapping Viking is said to have immediately screamed out in pain and withdrawn his hand from the fire. Father Poppo stood quietly for several moments, and, when he took his hand out, it was as if it had been in water. It was a miracle, Lady Godiva. There were a dozen witnesses. The priest was not burned in the slightest.

"Seeing the power of Poppo's God, King Harold made the decision to embrace the One who prevented the priest's skin from burning. He became a most generous Christian, a man of love, forgiveness, and kindness.

"Canute's grandfather would have been far better suited to raise him than his father, Swein Forkbeard. His grandfather was the noblest man I have ever known." Emma's voice trailed off, and she seemed to grow distant for a moment.

"The son of the warrior who burned his hand in the fire went off to form an avenging group of pagans, devoted to finding a power greater than that of Jesus Christ. They claimed they found the secret to controlling the weather. Their legend and numbers grew and, in time, they ingratiated themselves to Swein Forkbeard and convinced him to join them and denigrate the Christian God. Canute's father, Swein, finally murdered his own father, Harold Bluetooth, in order to become king."

"Canute has told you all of this?" Godiva asked in shock.

"He has told me nothing," Emma answered. "I know because my mother was Swein's sister. King Harold Bluetooth was also my grandfather. For the sake of the people, I was forced to marry my cousin, a man that I hate," she finished. "A man who could have been great but chose power over faith."

"Dear God, I had no idea," Godiva said, hugging the queen.

"If, after all this, you still want to see King Canute, I will make arrangements for it to happen as soon as possible. I have an appointment set for tomorrow but will gladly give you my time. You can come back and see him then."

"Thank you, Queen Emma. Thank you so very much," Godiva said, hugging her again.

Early the next morning, the people of Coventry were roused from their beds with the noise of drums and shouting. The townsfolk emptied out into the streets, wondering what the racket was for. Thurman and Ross stood before the crowd, and Thurman stepped forward to address them.

"If we pay, we starve. If we give up the youth of our town, the widows of Coventry will be defenseless against the winter," he began, reiterating the facts that everyone had already gone over a million times in his or her mind.

"What of Godiva? Does she still speak for us?" a woman yelled out.

The people waited for his response, fearful and feeling abandoned.

"The price the king has asked her to pay is blasphemy, my friends," Thurman explained.

"What kind of blasphemy?" a peasant asked.

Thurman raised his voice. "To ride through these very streets fully unclothed to the Cofa Tree would go against everything she believes."

"The king wants her to ride naked like a pagan maiden," a woman said. "What's wrong with that?"

"We will not tolerate such blasphemy," a man answered her.

"Blasphemous to whom? Not to us," a man wearing a fertility symbol on a necklace shouted out.

Wulfstan waved his arm in the air. "Quiet, pagan. This ride is impossible. She would never do it."

"Let the choice be hers," a woman yelled out desperately. "Perhaps she could see her way clear to do it for us."

"No, she has risked enough. How dare you suggest it," the first man answered.

"There is nothing wrong with it! It means nothing, and it would save us all. How could you not urge her to help, for all our sakes!" yelled one of the pagans. Suddenly, Coventry erupted; the pagans and Christians were no longer united in a common fight.

Thurman noticed Godiva's brother, Thorold, riding down the street.

"Sheriff, what say you of Godiva's ride?" he called.

Thorold rode up to the crowd, dismounted and stepped up to the platform. The crowd grew quiet, awaiting his response.

"It wouldn't be worth the dust her horse would kick upon you," he spat. "King Canute has no intention of lifting the tax. Hear this: As her brother, I will protect Godiva from harm. Like my father, as sheriff, I shall stay true to Coventry until I die!" Thurman slapped him on the back, and the crowd seemed appeased for the time being.

The next morning, escorted only by Aethenoth and one of the falcons from her aviary, Godiva once again made the long ride to King Canute's castle. She was encouraged by Queen Emma's generosity and strength. As she rode, the falcon stayed perched on her left arm, which was protected by a thick leather sleeve. Godiva glanced at the bird. His blinking eyes seemed intelligent, reassuring her that there was nothing to fear.

The summer solstice was growing closer, and the festivities in Winchester were officially starting. Godiva could hear the music echo over the hills. She took a deep breath, dreading her return to the king's gates.

King Canute sat at his large desk, trying to write. He couldn't concentrate. The festive sounds of the celebration's inauguration forced their way into his study. He labored over his words. Dissatisfied, he frowned, crumpled the parchment, flung it into the fire and began again.

"How dare they," he thought, knowing he could not realistically demand the people to stop. Suddenly, there was a huge cheer. Canute scraped his chair back, put down his writing plume, and stomped out to the balcony to look over the noisy courtyard. He used to love events such as these. But life had changed, and now the festivities seemed silly, overdone, and childish.

As few storm clouds had begun to collect. Canute eyed them carefully, watching for a sign from the gods as his father had taught him. He looked out over the many dancers and celebrants, not noticing Lady Godiva making her way through them. His gaze was drawn to a large bonfire just below his balcony.

Suddenly, a strong gust of wind swept across the blaze, blowing hundreds of hot embers into the air. They danced on the breeze, up to the balcony where Canute stood. They landed on his robes and blew in his face and around his hair, engulfing him in a shower of large sparks. He panicked and, for a moment, felt as though he was being set aflame.

There was no one to help him as he flailed his arms wildly about, trying to beat the embers off his robes. Finally, he fell back onto a chaise against the wall, swatting his clothes and snuffing out the last of them. He brushed off the soot and took a breath. He lay down, strangely drained of strength. He couldn't move a muscle. He closed his eyes and surrendered to a sudden deep sleep.

The sounds of the festival grew distant, and in seconds, he was dreaming. The images that flew before his eyes seemed impossible but were as vivid and tangible as reality. He saw before him, rising up from the burning blaze of the solstice festival, none other than the charred body of Sister Osburga, the Coventry nun he had put to death all those years before. He shuddered in horror. Ice seemed to flow through his veins in spite of the heat that was burning his brow.

Then, out of the ashes, rose the voice of Osburga singing her hymn:

Let us praise, this day, the Maker of the heavenly kingdom,
Author of all miracles.
How He gave earth's children heaven for a roof,
And a world with lands such as these to live on.
Almighty Lord, we praise You.
We praise You, we praise You, we praise You.

The sound grew louder and louder while the charred flesh of Osburga's face and hands slowly turned pink and smooth. The burnt remains of her habit started to restore themselves as she transformed into the rosy-cheeked nun he had first laid eyes on. Her body solidified as she rose from the pyre to meet his gaze. She smiled at him.

Canute screamed out in his sleep. "No! Keep away from me. What do you want? Keep away, witch!"

Her face remained peaceful. Kindness filled her eyes, just as it had on the day of the siege. She continued to sing.

Let us praise, this day, the Maker of the heavenly kingdom,
Author of all miracles....

In the dream, Canute stood up, unsheathed his sword, and swung through her image. Nothing happened. He sliced right through, into thin air.

> How He gave earth's children heaven for a roof,
> And a world with lands such as these to live on.
> Almighty Lord, we praise You....

Nothing he tried would make her go away. Osburga continued to sing, but the words slowly seemed to change. They began to repeat a simple phrase to the same melody:

> Do not harm her, do not harm her, do not harm her.

She sang the lilting chorus over and over again.

Canute had no idea what the nun meant. Was it she herself that she sang of? Even in his dream, it made no sense. Canute finally dropped his sword to the ground and looked up to the sky. A light drizzle began to fall, and Sister Osburga and the pyre had vanished. Canute bolted awake.

"What?" he said, rubbing his face groggily. "I was dreaming. How did I fall asleep?" He got up slowly and walked back out to the balcony, noticing the tiny burns from the embers on his clothes. He looked down on the festival. The people were running for shelter because of the rain that had actually begun to fall.

❀❀❀❀❀❀

Godiva made her way through the wet courtyard. She had to forge through the crowds of loud, bawdy revelers. The festival in Coventry was tame compared to this. She forced herself to block out the chaos around her and to focus on her goal. She finally reached the massive door. A Huscarle blocked her path.

"I am Lady Godiva of Coventry," she announced. He looked at her face and long mane of hair and smirked. He knew exactly who she was. The soldier who had seen her the day before had made sure everyone was aware of her.

"Would you please inform the king that I have come to see him and have brought him a gift?" she said as sweetly as she could. She extended the falcon to him. He admired the bird approvingly and then turned to lead her in.

"Come with me," he said.

The guard left Godiva standing alone in the long room of Canute's outer chamber. She let the bird perch on a chair and looked around at her surroundings. The tapestries on the walls were ornate. Some were of warriors in Viking garb; others portrayed mythological beasts and gods. The gods gripped lightning bolts in their huge hands and looked wrathful, ready to strike at any moment. She walked over to the falcon. His bright yellow eyes blinked.

"What are we doing here, my old friend?" she asked.

The door was suddenly thrown open and Canute strode in, his heavy boots making ominous thuds as he walked and a massive robe billowing behind him.

Godiva curtseyed deeply.

"Ah, the beautiful Lady Godiva," he said smoothly, motioning for her to rise.

"Your Majesty, I am grateful for this audience," she said.

"To what do I owe the honor of this visit, Lady Godiva?"

Godiva shifted nervously.

"Please, sit down," he invited, motioning to a bench.

"Thank you, Your Majesty." She breathed deeply, searching for the words to start.

"As I already asked," Canute prodded, "what was so urgent that you had to entreat the queen to persuade me to see you, Lady Godiva?"

Godiva placed her hands in her lap and sat up straight. Her gown fit perfectly, but at the moment, it felt tight at her bodice and loose at her back. She crossed her legs at the ankle, putting forth the most demure image possible.

"Your Highness," she began, "my husband has told me of your dream of a greater England, where every man would be equal."

"Yes?" Canute prompted.

"I have come to suggest that Coventry be held up as an illustration of this most remarkable ideal. I have come to request mercy on behalf of those who suffer because of my impulsiveness. Perhaps, with this gesture, we could demonstrate a new way to the world."

The king looked at her closely. Without replying, he moved over to where the falcon perched. He inspected the fine lines of the bird.

"A well-bred falcon. Is it trained?"

"Yes, Your Majesty. I raised him myself."

"Another of your many talents, Lady Godiva," he complimented her. "I do, indeed, look forward to the day when all of my subjects shall live in peace—a day when my subjects prosper. But as your husband must have told you, I also face many problems. The Danish Council places many demands upon me. After much consideration, I have found the only way that I could save your Coventry from the taxes they are unwilling to pay. Because your husband is important to me, I have made you a merciful offer to save your beloved Coventry. Unless you take the ride, Coventry will be held responsible for its debt like every other town in my kingdom. I have brought you a copy of the charter that describes the conditions of my offer. It has been signed and sealed."

Canute handed it to her.

"This is all I can do."

"Your Majesty, I would do anything for these people, but I cannot bring shame on my Lord with this ride."

Canute was amused. "Lady Godiva, your husband made it clear that you would not be willing to take this ride. I wonder though, what shame could there be for a woman as beautiful as you to display her body in our festival?"

Godiva courageously stood as she answered.

"Please, Your Majesty, I have come to plead for the people's salvation, not to discuss the differences in our religions. Hear me, king, as I beg for your mercy. They have struggled for so long and suffered so much."

"Lady Godiva, as a woman of such position and stature, why do you care so much about these people? You are not a peasant, a commoner. You are a woman of reputable lineage—of power and privilege." His voice rose in frustration. "Why do you concern yourself with issues that are not your own?"

"You may see otherwise, but I am one of them. Since the death of my parents and my teacher, Sister Osburga, they have been a family to me."

The king's faced turned ashen as his dream came flooding back to him.

"You knew the nun Osburga?" he asked forcefully.

"She was my teacher and my closest friend. She meant the world to me," Godiva exclaimed sadly.

"What do you know of her death?"

"I was there, watching from the woods. I was a child, and I saw you give the order to have her burned at the stake."

Canute erupted in fury. He grabbed Godiva by the shoulders and shook her.

"How dare you come here to accuse me! Are you out of your mind?"

"No, I only..." she pleaded.

"I should have you executed tomorrow in Coventry's square. Perhaps that would clarify my message to those insubordinates you call family," he bellowed.

"No! Please I didn't mean to..."

"Mean to what?" he roared. "Invoke the name of that enchantress-nun who sang as she burned?" He released her so forcefully that she fell back, banging her arm against the table with all her weight. She collapsed to the ground in a daze, clutching her arm. Canute stepped back from her, fuming and breathless, trying to restrain himself from grabbing her by the neck.

"I didn't come here for my sake," she said, crying.

"Leave my chamber," he screamed. "Go tell your peasant friends that if they don't pay, they will get exactly what they deserve." He stood over her as she lay on the floor. Godiva dropped her head, trying to hide her tears.

"They cannot pay," she said quietly.

"Then they will die!" Canute exploded.

"Then kill me now, as you threaten, good king! Keep me from that which I cannot bear to witness," Godiva said, knowing there was nothing she could do.

"You want me to kill you? Is that what you want? To be a martyr, like your Osburga?" Canute gritted his teeth and roughly pulled her up by her injured arm.

"Get out of here! Leave. You have caused me enough trouble. I am through with you." He flung her away.

Godiva backed away from him and bumped into the table. A small golden Viking ship fell to the stone floor and rolled across it. Godiva and Canute both watched it. The king took a breath and glared at her venomously. He let out his breath in a slow hiss. His hands were shaking with anger.

"If I wasn't so sure that your adoring followers would turn you into a martyr to weep over, I would have your head at once. Maybe I should just get it over with."

Godiva drew back in fear. Just then, the king grew faint. He lifted his hand to his forehead as the room spun around him. He fell to one knee. Through the haze, the words of his eerie dream echoed through his mind. "Do not harm her..." Godiva stared at him, wondering what was wrong. He pulled himself up and leaned on the table.

He refused to look at her again, but said, "I have made you my offer. Now get out." He stumbled out of the room dizzily, still holding his head, as Godiva picked up the little ship and placed it carefully on the table. She looked at the falcon, which had turned his head to watch the whole interplay.

"Now what?" Godiva whispered to the bird. Her shoulders ached from the king squeezing them as he shook her, and her arm throbbed from her fall. She bit her lip to stop the tears that continued to flow. She stood there a moment, then picked up the charter.

❦❦❦❦❦❦❦

Leofric and Thorold rode along, stopping at the remains of the manor house of Thorold's parents.

"So, Thorold, this is where you were taking me. A journey of the heart, eh?" Leofric asked.

"One might say. Look, Leofric. Look down carefully at the town of Coventry. Do you realize that if you ride with Canute, you will never again see this sight? He will destroy everything this time.

"Look over there, Leofric. That is where I buried my parents—your wife's parents. The same parents who were killed by this king you so nobly believe in."

"He's not that same man, Thorold," Leofric protested. "He is trying to change things. It's no longer a personal issue to me. I do not believe in the man, but I believe in the vision that he has for this nation."

"But what good is a great nation if all those you love are dead?"

"I know what you are saying, but there are no other choices. You must understand that I don't *want* to ride against Coventry."

"Then it's very simple. Just don't do it," Thorold said frankly. "I want to you know, Leofric, as a friend and a brother, that if you fight alongside Canute, I shall be in battle against you. I will be fighting on the side of Coventry—on the side of the just and the innocent. I am not the only one. There are others, Leofric. They will come. Their memories are not so vague as to let this happen again. Not without a fight."

"What you say may be right, Thorold, but it's not as simple as you make it out to be. I want to do what's right for England forever, not just what's right for one small town today."

THIRTY-THREE

L eofric decided not to return home that night. Wanting to be alone, he spent the night at the ruins, searching for answers. He had been moved by the words Thorold had spoken, but he still struggled to find the right thing to do.

He rose early in the morning to head for home and snuck quietly into the bedroom. He sat on the edge of the bed as he took a moment to watch Godiva sleeping. He didn't know about her restless night's sleep or about her visits to Winchester in the days before. He bent over her, giving her a light kiss, and whispered in her ear, "Shh, rest, my love."

As he stood up, he patted Godiva's arm gently. She unconsciously pulled away with a quiet whimper. As he looked down in the morning light, he noticed something on her arm. He inspected it more closely, pulling back the sleeve of her nightgown. As he exposed the large purple bruise, Godiva awoke. She pulled her arm away.

"Good morning," she said, sleepily.

"Godiva, what is that bruise on your arm?"

"What?" she asked drowsily, rolling away from him and trying to go back to sleep.

"Godiva, what is that on your arm?" he asked again, turning her over.

She turned her head away and didn't answer.

He asked again, more forcefully. "Tell me how you hurt your arm."

Godiva covered the bruise with her hand. Her eyes filled with tears. She knew she couldn't lie to him.

"Don't be angry. I went to see the king, hoping to intercede on behalf of the people."

Leofric jumped up angrily. "You what! Godiva, I can't believe you would go to see King Canute and not tell me."

"Would you have let me go if I first asked?"

"Of course not."

"I had no choice, Leofric. I told you, I have to do everything in my power to save these people."

"Did you save them, Godiva? Did you accomplish your goal?"

They both knew the answer to his question. They stared at each other, both stubbornly clinging to their position.

"Let me see your arm again," Leofric said, changing the subject.

Godiva painfully extended her arm. Leofric gently touched it and she jumped. Godiva bit her lip as he examined the bruise.

"Who did this to you? Was is Canute, or one of his soldiers? Tell me."

"I, I just went there to help. I..." Godiva exhaled shakily. "Canute got angry. He pushed me, and I fell and hit the table."

Leofric's feelings of mistrust for Canute began to return as he thought of the king raising his hand against his wife.

"Canute pushed you? Intending to hurt you?" He paced up and down and then stopped to look at her. "Canute promised me that he wouldn't hurt you."

Leofric teetered on the edge between his loyalty to England and his anger at Canute. All at once, the years of Canute's violence crashed upon his mind. He could no longer rationalize his support of the man.

Godiva watched the transformation in her husband's face. She had not seen that look in his eyes since the day of the siege when he saved her from the Viking warrior. There was murder in his eyes.

"Please, Leofric, don't do anything rash," she pleaded.

"How could I have been such a fool? I'm going to put a stop to this right now. I'm sorry, Godiva. You have seen everything more clearly than I. Tell Thorold to gather as many people as possible in Coventry."

"No, wait!"

Leofric fended off her reaching hands. Stepping away from the bed, he looked down at her.

"I wanted so much to give you a world of peace where we could raise our children without the horrors of war."

"Leofric, no. Please. You can't go!"

"I love you, Godiva. I love you with all my heart. I'm sorry I wasn't able to hear what you were saying earlier." He checked the sword in his scabbard and bolted from the room.

"Leofric. Please don't," Godiva screamed after him. She ran to the window and, moments later, watched him gallop furiously away toward Winchester.

She fell upon the bed, weeping. Suddenly, a thought popped into her mind. She jumped up and raced downstairs, tearing through the kitchen to the back of their castle-like home. She called to the first person she saw, one of the kitchen servants, Francis, a hefty woman about her own age.

"Francis, Francis! Come quickly," she yelled.

"Yes, my lady?" Francis said breathlessly, peering in the doorway. "You scream as if the house were on fire."

"It might as well be. Quickly, we have to hurry."

"What is it, my lady?"

"Hurry to the stable. Tell them to ready my horse. Send someone to find my brother Thorold and have him meet me there."

"But, my lady, all the pots are boiling, I shouldn't be leaving. Where is Lord Leofric?"

"Please, Francis, just do it!" Godiva rushed out the door.

Thorold was on the castle grounds and raced to the stables where he found Godiva already mounting Aethenoth.

"What's wrong? What has happened, dear sister?"

"Leofric has gone to kill King Canute."

"What do you mean? Just yesterday Leofric reaffirmed that he has pledged himself to serve the king."

"Thorold, I went to see the king to plead with him for Coventry's sake. When Canute found out that I had witnessed him burning Osburga, he went into a rage and threw me to the ground. When Leofric heard about it and saw the bruise, he was furious and stormed out."

Thorold's anger also began to rage. "Leofric once talked me out of killing Canute myself. Perhaps it's time for me to finish the job."

"We must stop him, Thorold. Please ride with me to Winchester."

"We may be able to catch him. We must leave immediately."

"Yes, let's hurry," she said, dashing off on the road she now knew all too well.

Leofric raced furiously toward Winchester. Along the way, he reached the small village of Orkshire and stopped at a tavern on the edge of town to give his horse a badly needed rest and find some food and drink for himself.

As he sat down at the bar and ordered some ale, two men in the corner abruptly stopped their loud conversation. They both wore dark Danish leather and had heavy accents.

One of them jabbed his companion in the side.

"Will you look at that? Earl Leofric himself."

"Saves us a lot of time riding to his castle. Can you believe our luck?"

"Come on, we need to get out of here."

They went outside and questioned the stable boy about which way Leofric had been heading.

"What's it worth to you?" asked the boy.

The men exchanged glances and one handed him a coin.

"Thank you, good sirs. That way," the boy pointed.

"Winchester," they said together. Within moments, they were on horseback, riding as fast as they could.

A few miles up the road, one gestured to his companion. "In here," he yelled.

They led their horses off the road and into a thick cover of trees to lie in wait.

"Look. We can see the bend in the road from here. It's perfect."

It didn't take long for Leofric to reach them. He slowed his horse as he rounded the bend in the road.

"That's him! Look at the markings on his horse's tack. Do it!"

One of the men reached for his bow, took aim, and pulled back. Leofric never saw the arrow as it flew into his chest under his right shoulder. He tumbled from his horse, landing hard on the road. The men raced toward him. Blood poured from the earl's chest onto the ground.

The two men approached him carefully. Leofric waited until they were almost on top of him, then drew his knife and stabbed it upward into the closest man's leg. The attacker screamed in pain and fell to the ground. The second man jumped back, drawing his sword.

Although wounded, Leofric was able to stagger to his feet. He couldn't move his right arm, so he leaned over and took the sword from the man he had stabbed. Leofric was barely able to hold the man at bay. He was at a huge disadvantage—wounded, dizzy, and fighting with his left hand. He was afraid he would pass out.

Godiva and Thorold, who had been riding hard and hadn't stopped to rest, came racing around the corner.

"Leofric, Leofric!" Thorold yelled at the top of his lungs. In one wild motion, he leapt from his horse and dragged Leofric's assailant to the ground. The two men rolled around on the ground.

"Be careful, Thorold!" Godiva yelled, terrified that after all that had happened, she would lose her brother, too. She rushed to Leofric, whose knees had buckled, bringing him to the ground.

Thorold and the man had both managed to draw their knives. Thorold twisted to the right, exposing his side. The assailant's knife slashed across Thorold's side, grazing him, but Thorold used his momentum to swing up and drive his knife straight into the man's belly.

"Danish pig," Thorold growled as the man fell to the ground, dead. Thorold stood up, wincing as he touched the bloody scratch on his side.

"Oh, Thorold. You're hurt!" Godiva cried as she left Leofric and ran up to her brother.

"It's nothing. How's Leofric?"

"I pulled out the arrow, and the bleeding seems to be stopping, but he's weak." She wrapped Thorold's arm over her shoulder, helping him to walk.

"Here, sit down."

"No, I'm fine."

"Be quiet, and let me look at this." Thorold winced as she pulled off his shirt and ripped off a strip from the bottom to make a bandage. She wrapped it tightly around him. Leofric moaned, and Godiva turned to him quickly. Thorold stood up.

"What are you doing?"

"We can't just lie here bleeding. We have to get out of here. There may be others."

"I'll go get help in the town we just passed," said Godiva.

"No, Godiva. I will. Stay with Leofric." With no further argument, Thorold mustered his strength and took off down the road.

Godiva was relieved when he returned with a cart a short time later.

"Oh, thank God," she sighed.

"I borrowed this from a farmer," Thorold explained. "We'll load him up in here. We have to get him home." Leofric was drifting in and out of consciousness as they lifted him into the wagon and turned back toward Coventry. Godiva rode Aethenoth beside the wagon, watching Leofric's limp form bounce over every rut in the road. She softy whispered the words, "I love you."

❦❦❦❦❦❦

King Canute was reading in his study when his brother arrogantly pushed through the door.

"What do you want, Harold?"

"Don't you ever tire of reading the words of dead men?"

"The hour is late, and I have business to attend to."

"I think, brother, that we both have business to attend to. I have just been visited by two members of our War Council, who told me that, after they came all the way from Copenhagen, you sent them away, refusing to see them. Do you think it wise to snub the council at this critical point when there are already rumors of war?"

"I have better things to do than listen to them make demands on me for the Danegeld."

"You wouldn't have had a problem with the Danegeld if Earl Leofric had done his job correctly," Harold reminded him.

"Still smarting from the beating he gave you, eh? Is this your attempt to strike back?"

"You might appreciate knowing that our champion is not as strong as you think, given that he is on his deathbed with a large wound in his chest. Well, at least, that's what I have heard."

Canute had already lost patience. He stood up and glared at his brother. "Perhaps, with all that you have heard, you can tell me what you know about two soldiers who came all the way from Denmark and just happened to ambush Lord Leofric as he passed by. I'm also curious to know how you knew of the attack long before anyone else."

"Purely by chance, brother." Harold was shocked that Canute had already received the news but did his best to cover it up.

"By the way, now that Leofric is even more unlikely to be able to perform his duties in regard to our tax problem," he began slyly, "don't you think that perhaps someone else should stifle this revolt? It grows larger every day.

"Maybe you are unaware of the fact that the English are rising in rebellion and the Danes threaten to invade, all because of Leofric's incompetence. Don't you see? If we don't act, we may well be fighting a battle on two fronts."

"So who would you recommend to handle my problem?" Canute asked, floored by his brother's audacity.

"Perhaps someone with a strong hand who is unquestionably loyal to the king," Harold suggested.

"Dare I say someone who longs for more authority as well as more lands, Harold?"

"Your generosity is legendary. Why wouldn't a loyal servant capable of putting a stop to this uprising expect to receive a just reward?"

Canute was backed into a corner. With Leofric ailing, he had to find someone else.

"Harold, sometimes I think you may be as rotten as Edric Streona. But right now, I have no one else to send. Go. Take care of this problem. I want to end this now."

"Yes, Your Majesty. Consider it done." Prince Harold was feeling quite smug as he turned to leave. A thought popped into his head, and he turned back to Canute.

"If I should need a little assistance from Earl Godwin, I suppose that would be acceptable to you? After all, he is family."

"Between the two of you, I don't think there is any room in England for more ambition," Canute observed.

"I thought ambition was a good thing," Harold laughed.

"You weary me, Harold. Do whatever you have to do to quell the revolt and collect the tax. But I'm warning you not to escalate this into a bigger problem like you did before. Now do me a favor and leave."

Harold nearly skipped out the door.

꧁꧂꧁꧂꧁꧂

Godiva and Thorold laid Leofric down on his bed and glumly sat watch over him. Servants scurried in and out, bringing water and fresh bandages.

"Godiva, please don't let worry overwhelm you. He has lost a lot of blood, but the wound isn't deep, and it didn't damage anything vital," Thorold comforted.

"I have already lost too much in my life. I couldn't stand to lose Leofric."

"Godiva, he's going to be alright. Now about Canute..."

"Please, Thorold, don't do anything foolish. You know that even if Canute were dead, it wouldn't be over. Surely Prince Harold would unleash further vengeance upon us." Godiva walked over to the fireplace and stirred the logs with a poker.

"Canute hurt you. I can't blame Leofric for reacting as he did. What else could he do?"

"It's doesn't matter. It's trivial in light of everything that is at risk."

"It does matter. Leofric is supposed to protect you. He was shamed. Not to mention that Canute broke his word."

"Canute would have killed him," Godiva said.

"Your husband put his relationship with you at risk because he thought he could trust Canute. Now he has been betrayed. He feels foolish. Any good man would have done the same."

"If you hadn't been there, he would be dead." Godiva paused. "Thank you, Thorold."

"It's far from over. We now face something bigger than just vengeance."

ༀༀༀༀༀༀ

Canute sat in the dark, looking up into the night sky from the balcony outside his bedchamber. He meditated on the stars. The news of the growing rebellion filled his thoughts. Any hope of a united England was beginning to fade.

The night was still except for the sound of the breeze rustling the trees. He had not had a moment this quiet in months—though it felt like years. He was deep in thought when Queen Emma stepped out onto the balcony and cleared her throat. Canute turned around, startled.

"How are you this evening?" she asked with a smile.

"I suppose it depends on who is asking."

"It is the best of me, the part of me who sees the best in you."

"Emma, sometimes you say the most enigmatic things. From where do you get these words?"

"These are the words of my heart. Only one who is brave enough to go there can understand. Though they seem strange to your ears, they are spoken in truth."

"I wish I could believe that your words are true. But years of your cold anger makes me doubt what you say."

"If you only doubt, maybe there is hope."

Canute turned away from her and looked back up into the sky. Emma moved closer to him, unwilling to give up her mood of determined benevolence and concern.

"Canute, have you ever understood what it's like to have a friend—a person who could love and respect you for who you are rather than merely fearing you for what you might do to them?" she asked.

"Emma, you speak like a woman. You talk of love, of feelings. What use does a king have for these things? As you should know, feelings come from weakness. Weakness and vulnerability lead to the grave."

Emma pulled a chair up next to him and sat down.

"I see that your father's words still have a hold on you. He certainly had no place for feelings in his icy heart."

"Of all people, you should know what happens to a great king when he gets muddled by feelings, when he starts to care about people and situations in sentimental ways."

Emma was silent for a moment. "Why should I, of all people, know?"

"Because of our grandfather."

"You always go back to that. It's too easy, my king. You are clearly your own man and not merely a shadow of your past."

"You and I will always see Harold Bluetooth differently. He was killed because of his weakness. He was a fool...soft and distracted from the ways of our people."

"I really don't think he was a fool."

"I know you don't, because you are foolish, as well. He let himself be seduced by that magician who claimed to possess supernatural powers, and he died for it in the end."

"You may have my head for saying so, but how do you really know that grandfather's way was wrong? Do you still believe that when your father killed him, he was right in doing so? Because he tortured you as a child, will you someday treat our child in such a way?"

"Emma, are you trying to enrage me? Of course you know that I would never treat our son so."

"Then why can't you allow yourself to say that what your father did was wrong?"

"How is it that you have suddenly found the courage to talk to me this way? Why do you not fear that I will kill you for speaking so impertinently? Questioning my father is an insult to me and to my throne."

"I'm sure it is, my lord, for almost everything is an insult to you." Undaunted, Emma got up, walked over to Canute, and started rubbing his shoulders.

"What are you doing?"

"I'm merely expressing my devotion to a man who needs someone to care for him, a man I have grown to care for."

"How can you say you care for me now? I forced you into this marriage. We both know it was only political. You have provided me with an heir who will not have to battle the Normans. Nothing more, nothing less."

"Maybe you're right," she said, resting her hands on his shoulders. "Maybe you are as cruel as you think you must be. But I, for one, do not believe it. Do you think that I am blind to the moments of tenderness that you show our child? I have seen the way you laugh with him and spin him in the air so lovingly. Do you think it doesn't catch my notice when you anguish over these books, trying to find a better way to rule, pouring over them day and night looking for the secret to becoming a better king? No, Canute, I do not believe that you are a monster. I believe that deep inside, you know something better.

"Have you ever asked yourself why you had the dream for which your father beat you? Perhaps it was a sign to show you a higher path. Maybe that innocent child is still inside you, crying to get out. This is what I believe. Through all the hatred and violence, through every evil that you have inflicted on me, I have learned to rise above it all. You may not want to hear this, but I have actually grown to love you. I cry for you, I hurt for you, and you don't even know that I exist as anything beyond a political alliance."

Canute suddenly stood up and turned to look at her. Emma couldn't decipher the look on his face. She stepped back quickly, never having seen him like that before.

"Canute, please," she whispered.

Canute reached out and grabbed her by the arm. She grimaced, expecting him to squeeze it painfully. But he didn't. He just held it firmly, but without aggression or hostility. They stood there like that for several minutes. Emma's heart pounded. Her husband's brow furrowed and he pulled her a few inches closer to him.

"Please, Emma, say no more," he said, bringing his face close to hers. "I can't hear these words of yours anymore. Leave me, woman, before I come to my senses and strangle you," he cried, suddenly dropping her arm.

Emma looked at him in shock and backed away, trying to control her tears.

Canute was left in the dark, agonizing over the emotions that his wife had conjured up.

Godiva, Thorold, and Leofwine waited beside Leofric's bed. He had been sleeping for several days and was just beginning to awaken. Still very groggy, he tried to speak.

"Godiva, what's happening? Why am I bandaged so?"

"Don't you remember? You were ambushed on the road by two men."

"It's all very vague. I have dreamed so many things that I'm not sure what's real. How did you find me?"

"When you left, Thorold and I followed. We found you on the road, fighting with one of the men."

"There is an awful pain in my chest."

"They had to remove an arrow, son, " Leofwine said gently. "You must be careful not to move about too much and open the wound. You've lost a lot of blood."

Leofric took his father's hand. "What about Canute?"

"Fortunately," he replied, "he knows nothing of your anger and deadly intentions and has been very anxious to learn of your condition. He seems genuinely upset that something has happened to you."

"I am lucky not to have revealed my heart to others," Leofric winced.

Thorold leaned in close to Leofric. "You once kept me from killing Canute, and over the course of time, I came to see that you were right. Now it's my turn to tell you that my sister needs you now as much as she needed me then. Please swear to me that, when you're well, you won't try to go after Canute again."

"I vow to you all, here and now, that I will not do anything so impetuous again."

Thorold reached for a package that was resting on a nearby table. "Canute sent a messenger with a gift and a letter for you. It is sealed with a penalty of death to anyone who wrongly opens it. What would you have us do?"

"Please, you can open it and read it to me, Thorold."

Thorold carefully broke the wax seal and began to read aloud.

"Earl Leofric, I am most grieved to hear of the attack on your life. This certainly was not the work of thieves as some people attempt to say. I believe it was part of a greater plot to thwart the establishment and unification of our hopes for a new England. You and I must not let them pull us apart. We must band together, all the more, to fight for our great dream. To that end, there is something I must do.

"Though I am king, and by right have no need to apologize for any of my actions, I have also come to see that even a king, if he seeks to build true allies, must admit when he is wrong. Therefore, as sovereign king, I choose to apologize for my outbursts of irrational behavior. I have been a violent man far too long. I was wrong to lash out at your wife. I have sent a gift to prove the sincerity of my apology."

Leofwine smiled as Godiva opened the wax-sealed wooden box and pulled out a finely made jeweled necklace. All that he had counseled Canute through the years was evident in the king's words.

"Goodness. I have never seen anything like it," she gasped.

"It is beautiful," Leofric said. "Will you accept it?"

"I have no intention of being bought by his gifts, though they may be exquisite."

Thorold continued to read.

"Leofric, I need you to recover and join me in our battle to save this nation. The Danes want me to rescind my appeasement of the English and return to my Viking roots. They have sent me an ultimatum to either collect the taxes or face war. The Danish Council is now prepared to invade our land. As you know, many of our towns are in rebellion against the Danegeld. I am caught in the middle. If you still have any desire to salvage what we have started, you must join me as soon as you are well. I only hope that it is not too late. With your absence, I have no other choice but to appoint someone else to collect the taxes. I have reluctantly decided to turn over the responsibility to Prince Harold. I will continue to offer Coventry its reprieve, but I can only do so on the original terms."

"It's signed by Canute," Thorold finished.

Leofric, Leofwine, Godiva, and Thorold looked at each other in disbelief.

Thorold was the first to break the silence. "How can anyone know the mind of this man?"

Godiva's thoughts were of her beloved town. "If Harold now collects the taxes, Coventry will be worse off than ever. He will not hold back his forces. He will have no qualms about killing them all."

"Leofric," Leofwine began, "you are faced with perhaps the greatest decision of your life. Canute obviously has incredible respect for you and will not take kindly to betrayal, yet he has not assumed that you will support him. Do you intend to ride with him?"

He looked at Thorold and Godiva, "I know I have spoken otherwise," Leofric flinched in pain, "but I was mistaken and will not abandon the people again. I now see no other way out. I will take my forces and fight on the side of Coventry.

"Father, I hope this pleases you, for you are the greatest teacher I have ever had. Thorold, you must make the people aware of my intentions." Leofric grimaced and pulled himself up. "Rally all England, if you can, Thorold. We will not give up without a fight. We have a few days. Harold's forces will not attack until Earl Godwin's army arrives from Wessex. Go now, and I will do my best to meet up with you at Coventry."

"Leofric, you must rest. This is no time to be making plans for battle. There must be another way," Godiva pleaded.

"There is no other way," he replied, locking eyes with his father.

In the small Coventry church, Prior Aefic knelt before the altar. Godiva's handmaiden Cresha stepped into the sanctuary and silently approached him as he prayed. Aefic looked up from his prayers to see who it was.

"Prior Aefic," she murmured, with dread in her voice, "it's my lady. She needs to speak with you."

Cresha led the prior outside to where Godiva was waiting.

"Godiva, you shouldn't be out. The army is on its way. You should be at home," the prior said. "We don't know at what hour they might attack."

"Prior, I desperately need to talk with you. It will only take a minute." Both of them looked at Cresha.

She bowed and silently moved a distance away so they could have some privacy.

Prior Aefic began, "The townspeople are now divided. Some pray for miracles, while others are incensed that you will not take the pagan ride on their behalf. Most, however, are just thankful for what you have already done." Aefic stepped closer to Godiva and touched her arm supportively.

"What will become of our people, prior? I have so many questions running through my mind. Will God let them be slaughtered? Does He still care?"

"Godiva, I understand how you feel. Most of the time, I love being a priest. It is my greatest joy to bring hope and love to the needy of this world. I must be honest with you, though. Sometimes I abhor being a priest. There are times when I have such love and such passion to bring goodness to the people, yet I have no power to do so. In these moments I also wonder why God seems so far away."

Godiva looked to Aefic with sympathy and saw a kindred spirit. She knew the goodness of the man's heart.

"Godiva, we have known each other far too long for me to give you a trite answer. I have no idea what will become of this town. I have thought and prayed for an answer until I had no more strength. All I can say is that the people have decided to face the army rather than pay the tax."

"Prior, they will be slaughtered. Prince Harold is a maniac. He will show them no mercy. Leofric has decided to take his soldiers to fight alongside Coventry, but that will only mean more killing and bloodshed. It may well be that all I know and love will be gone in hours. How can I let that happen?"

Godiva stared off into the distance, picturing the people of Coventry.

"Listen for a moment," she said slowly. "If I were to take this ride..."

"Blasphemy, Godiva! This pagan rite is tantamount to sorcery. Don't you see? It is treason against God Himself."

"My heart is given to God. What I would do, I would do only to save the lives of the people," she said quietly. "God knows that. He knows what is in my heart."

"I understand what you are saying, but that doesn't change the fact that the pagan beliefs would be confirmed by your actions. It would validate and condone their ungodly, wicked practices. It would be a stumbling block to the weak in faith. It may well lead them away from God. You cannot do this! Do you realize that the king has informed the bishops of his deal with you? The pope himself is aware of this and the church has readied its response against you. You are facing the weight of the entire church now, my dear. I beg you, tread cautiously. I don't mean to use excommunication as a threat, but you must understand. You don't want the church against you."

"Against me? Aefic, do you really believe that God would condemn me? Saving innocent lives that are His?"

"We are talking about blasphemy. Eternal hell awaits those who would be led by these false ceremonies. You personally will be regarded as a blot against the laws of the Vatican, as a stone of stumbling to the church," he pleaded.

"I love the church, but I love these people with the heart that God gave me. I have no choice but to trust that heart. I can do nothing else but give my life, even my soul, to save these people," she replied with conviction. "Coventry looks to me for salvation. I am sworn to them. To let them die would be the gravest sin."

"Godiva, your concern for them is great. But do not let it confuse you. If you ride to their pagan symbol, you will be considered a heretic. A heretic, Godiva!"

"If history is to remember me as a heretic," she said passionately, "then, Prior, hear my confession!" She suddenly dropped to her knees and bowed her head before him. The prior closed his eyes and shook his head sadly. He hesitated, then reached out his hand and placed it lovingly on her head as he prayed.

"O God of heaven, please give Your child the wisdom to do what is right."

❀❀❀❀❀❀

The prior returned home that evening, tormented and driven to prayer. He did not eat his usual small dinner of bread and water but instead lit several candles and prayed. He tightly clenched his hands, calling out to heaven with his eyes shut.

"Father, Father. What can I do to understand this mystifying will of Yours?"

He buried his face in his hands desperately. The candlelight glimmered as he sank deeper and deeper into his soul, searching to pull from it an answer from God. He opened his eyes for a moment and noticed a shadow cast by his small silver cross on the wall. As he shifted slightly, his own shadow eclipsed the lower extension of the cross. A light went on in his head.

"Oh, yes, my God! That's it! Thank You. Thank You, Lord!" The joy in his heart bubbled up in a hearty laugh.

THIRTY-FOUR

Leofric was still very much in pain as he braced himself upon his horse, prepared to ride to Coventry along with his men. His knights and infantry filed in. Weapons were checked, swords sheathed, and the royal banners were raised high. Leofric and Thorold were both grave. They knew that the peasants were outnumbered and, even with their army, were no match for the great militias of Canute, Harold, and Godwin.

At the gates of Coventry, fortifications had once again been set up as the whole town prepared the best they could for the attack. The terrified citizens looked out to the hillsides beyond. All was quiet. Thurman kept his eyes forward. Margaret held on to Ross while tears flooded her eyes.

"This waiting is terrible," she cried.

"Margaret," said Ross tenderly, "I want you to know that if this is the last day of my life, I will die a rich man, for you have always been and always will be my treasure. Today, my dear, we take a stand to claim our lives as our own."

Down the lane, Prior Aefic approached with a hay wagon.

"I need some help here," he called, jumping down.

"As we all do, Prior," Ross called back.

"Come, Ross, bring some of the men," he requested.

The prior, Ross, and a small group feverishly loaded heavy timbers onto the hay wagon where there were already thick, coiled ropes and heavy pulleys.

"What is all this?" Ross asked, as he lifted the end of a log.

"The Lord's inspiration," the prior answered breathlessly as he helped lift the timber onto the back of the wagon. "Hurry!" he urged the men. "Load it all. And quickly."

The men finished, and Prior Aefic gave Ross a hearty hug.

"Pray that God will make this work," he said, leaping into the wagon.

"I will, prior, although I don't know what I'm praying for!"

"You will," he said, tapping the horses with the reins. "Follow me." Ross and the men trailed after the wagon, wondering what they were about to do.

As soon as the prior was out of sight, the enemy armies became visible far in the distance. Canute and his infantry approached from the north. In the east, Earl Godwin's legion lined the hillside. Harold's army stretched out even further, snaking over the countryside. All three divisions appeared on the horizon, poised to strike.

Two heralds were dispatched from Canute's infantry and approached Leofric's army with the white flag flying.

"Earl Leofric, the king has sent this message to you," one announced.

Leofric opened the dispatch.

"Leofric," it read, "although I am quite sure you will not, know that it is not too late for you to come and join me. I hope you realize that regardless of what happens here today, I will always keep the dream of the Northern Empire of which we have spoken. Your father has told me that you feel you must stand with your people. I too must do my duty to history. My hand is still graciously extended to you. Let us see where the day will lead. Your friend immutably, Canute, King of England and Scandinavia."

It was hard for Leofric to imagine that he could feel so conflicted. He knew that Canute was striving for a greater vision, a greater England, and wondered if, in the long run, his way could possibly succeed. Leofric wished that he could go and consult once more with his father, tap into his ability to recognize the essence of any matter and to act strategically with that knowledge. But his father had returned home, and Leofric knew that it was his time to commit to his own reasoning, to summon his own intellect.

Leofric felt a tug of regret, but he would not abandon those he was sworn to—the people of Coventry.

⚬⚬⚬⚬⚬⚬⚬

There was no dazzling sunlight as Godiva quickly rose for the day and saw her bath already drawn. Heavy clouds had darkened the sky, and a storm seemed to be brewing over Coventry. Godiva stepped into the water, her long hair wrapped on top of her head. She sat down slowly in the water and began sponging the back of her neck with her eyes closed, praying. Her fingers trembled in fear. Her composure was slipping. Once again, she was alone.

If she could have, Godiva would have stayed in the bath forever. But she knew it was time to go. She reached for her long crimson cloak and placed it on her shoulders. From her bureau, she produced a case. Inside was the comb she had found in the ashes of her family's home. She looked at the sun and moon engraved on it; how beautiful they were. Clearly remembering how lovely it looked in her mother's tresses, Godiva swept her hair up and secured it with the comb.

She walked slowly to the aviary and listened to the birds singing, even though the sunlight was dim. She knelt before the altar with Osburga's cross, for perhaps the last time. She covered her face.

"Dear Lord," she started to pray weakly, "I come to You, humbled and more fearful than ever before. I am truly lost, Lord—lost between my heart and my soul, between heaven and hell. I beg of You for strength and for guidance."

Francis had come from the kitchen to pick some mint and heard Godiva's voice. She stood obscured from Godiva's sight, riveted by what she was hearing. Godiva continued her prayer.

"How can I ride naked through those who would see me dead and those I would die to save? But how can I not? For my heart tells me that I must give of myself as I saw my sweet Osburga give her life for me. By enduring the pagan ride, I would save those whom You love. Through this I would hope to honor and not deny You, Lord, yet I fear You shall forsake me," she said, her voice breaking as she burst into tears.

"In Your grace, I ask You, Lord, to sanctify this ghastly act. In this heart of mine, which You alone have made and molded, I believe there is no other way. I must trust that this is the answer You have put before me, the way to serve Your kingdom. I beg of You to lift my doubt. Lord, please send me a sign of Your approval."

Godiva paused, consumed by fear. The doves in a nearby tree cooed lovingly and a hummingbird fluttered past her to suck nectar from a blossom. Godiva looked up at the small crucifix as she had so many times before. She looked at the little figure of Christ carved there, in the center of it. As she looked closely, she saw something she had never noticed before. There were the hands and feet she recognized, the beard and the face looking heavenward in agony. But something was different. For the first time in her life, she looked at the tiny carving and was conscious of the fact that Christ was hanging on the cross naked. In that moment, she understood the agony and yet the ecstasy of His sacrifice. She remembered His words, "Greater love than this has no man, than to lay down his life for his friends."

She stopped crying and stood up.

"If You could be naked in front of the whole world to save the people You loved," she said out loud, "then I too can give of myself to save the people that I love." Once again, she remembered Osburga's words: "You must trust Him above all else." Her crying stopped. Osburga had trusted and so must she.

Peace suddenly penetrated the room, and she noticed the overwhelming scent of jasmine for the first time that year. She felt as if someone was standing behind her, placing a hand on her shoulder. She quickly turned, but no one was there.

She sensed something else as well. Her trembling hand glided nervously to her stomach. She closed her eyes and sighed deeply. She kept her hand on her stomach and broke into a smile. She was sure she must be with child.

"This day is not so dire, as to still the newest of life," she said serenely.

She was no longer afraid. Faith filled her heart and girded her with strength. She embraced the task before her, believing that the Lord was with her.

Thunder rumbled in the distance as Godiva hurried out to the stables. The rain had not come yet, but the clouds swirled ominously above.

As Godiva walked to the stable, Francis surreptitiously followed her. Godiva opened the large doors and penetrated the darkness, blinking to adjust her vision. The smell of cool, moist hay surrounded her. She readied her horse, convinced that the ride was her destiny. Francis suddenly dashed across the courtyard. She peered into the dark stables, unnoticed by Godiva.

❦❦❦❦❦❦

The three armies at the disposal of King Canute waited, with the town of Coventry helpless in the middle. Prince Harold paraded outside Coventry's fortified gates. The peasants, who stood as sentries, held their position and banded together at the front, defying Harold's men as they approached.

"We fly the royal banner. His lordship, Prince Harold, wishes to speak to the people of Coventry," the commander announced to the guards at Coventry's gate. The sentries looked at one another and then let them pass. Harold and his commander rode into the plaza. All eyes were upon them. The townspeople gripped their homemade weapons, bracing themselves. Thurman and Ross waited for Harold at the center of the square.

❦❦❦❦❦❦

Godiva heard the thunder crash from inside the stable but shrugged it off. It didn't matter if it stormed. Her resolve was set. There would be no turning back. She gathered her long cloak tightly around her, the length of it covering her entire body.

She stepped back to survey her work. Aethenoth's white coat glistened. He was fully outfitted in red tack and saddle. A rich crimson blanket covered him, and he held his head up proudly, seeming to understand that he too had a place in destiny.

❦❦❦❦❦❦

Harold waited on horseback before Coventry's people. The townsfolk quieted themselves as he trotted forward to address them.

"I am Prince Harold of Denmark, and under the specific jurisdiction of King Canute, I have come to collect the taxes that have been ordered," he said directly.

There was nothing—no response. No one moved or spoke. Prince Harold looked out at the sea of faces, growing nervous at their silence.

Thurman finally spoke up. "There is nothing here for you." He folded his arms strongly in front of him and spit into the gutter.

Harold smirked, confident that the blacksmith would soon be dead.

"As far as I'm concerned, the time for asking nicely is over. But my brother, the king, extends a final chance. He pleads with you that you pay these taxes."

Thurman uncrossed his arms and took a step forward angrily. "Tell the king that we will no longer be slaves, compelled to feed the fat bellies of Danish Lords."

"Perhaps I should cut you down to size right this moment, blacksmith?" threatened Harold, leaping from his horse with his sword drawn.

"We are ready for you."

The commander rushed over. "Prince Harold, the king has ordered that no action be taken before the noon hour. He has given his word."

Harold glared at Thurman but nodded to his commander and got back on his horse. They made their way back through the town. The people cheered as they passed through the gate and out of Coventry.

✦✦✦✦✦✦✦

Lady Godiva swung her leg up and mounted her horse. She arranged her cloak around her nervously.

"My lady."

Godiva looked down to see Francis standing tentatively behind her.

"Francis, what are you doing here?" she asked, surprised.

"I've come to beg of your common sense," the woman said, tugging at the side of her apron as she spoke. "Forgive me, my lady, but I heard you in the aviary. You are a Christian like me. I beg of you, you mustn't take this ride."

"I don't want to do it, but there is no other choice," Godiva said.

"But you will be condemned to hell!" Francis cried.

"If God measures the hearts of men, He will know mine well enough."

"But, my lady, please..."

"Your concern for me is great, but I must..."

Just then, Francis bolted for the stable door. Aethenoth moved back skittishly at the sudden noise.

"Francis, what are you doing?" Godiva spurred her horse and rushed through the long stables. Francis was steps ahead of her and ran out into the yard, slamming the stable doors shut in front of Godiva. She flung the bar across them, trapping Godiva and Aethenoth inside.

"Francis! Open this door!" Godiva yelled.

Francis didn't stop to listen to her. She ran frantically across the yard to the drawbridge gatehouse, racing through puddles at full speed, not caring about the mud that was being flung on her dress and apron.

Godiva leapt from the horse and pounded against the doors. It was no use.

"Francis! I command you to let me out! Please!"

Her eyes drifted from the wide frame of the stable door then over to Aethenoth. She took a breath and climbed back on him.

"Alright Aethenoth," she said. "We can do it!" She spurred him toward the doors.

"Come on, boy, come on," she commanded. He reared. His powerful front legs pounded against the door over and over.

He screeched and whinnied with each kick, fighting his way out for Godiva. Suddenly the doors swung wide, and they escaped. They bolted out of the stable and across the yard, racing as fast as they could toward the drawbridge.

Francis had beaten them there. She had grabbed hold of the large wooden crank and was pulling with all of her might. She leaned heavily on it, struggling to get it to move and groaning painfully with each heavy push. The weighty gate slowly began to rise as the chains grinded on pulleys and screeched with movement. The wide planks lifted, exposing the first inches of gap.

"No," Godiva yelled from the courtyard as the saw the bridge starting to rise. She urged Aethenoth faster and faster. He galloped furiously toward the lifting bridge, accepting the challenge like a champion. Godiva shifted her weight and rose up in the saddle, leaning over the horse's shoulders. Francis watched in disbelief as Godiva raced headlong toward her and the rising planks. She renewed her efforts on the grinding levers and pulled them as hard and fast as she could. Sweat dripped off her forehead.

Godiva did not let up. She just kept urging the horse on.

"No, my lady. No!" Francis screamed out in terror as Godiva approached the bridge that was lifting in front of her. The separation between the bridge and the land widened and the water in the moat below could be seen lapping underneath. The horse and rider were now at full speed, headed for the lifting bridge before them.

Aethenoth's hooves hit the lifting wood with a crack. The angle of lift loomed more severe by the second. Aethenoth reached the end of the bridge and fearlessly leapt. Godiva held her breath as they sailed over the divide.

Aethenoth landed effortlessly across the trench and continued his breakneck pace without missing a step. Godiva said a prayer of thanks and set her eyes toward Coventry, not looking back.

As soon as Prince Harold left, Thurman and his army of townsfolk returned to their positions. The resistance had grown into a long stretch of over five hundred men who braved the front line.

Prior Aefic, Ross, and the group of men led the wagon carrying the long timber, pulleys, and rope.

"Hurry, men. Careful," the prior commanded them.

King Canute was on the hillside due north of Coventry. Prince Harold and Earl Godwin approached to talk with him.

"Your Majesty," Prince Harold said.

The king wasted no time with small talk. "Did they remit?" he asked anxiously.

"No, Your Majesty."

"Ready the attack for the noon hour," Canute ordered, turning to his aide beside him. The entire countryside was now filled with soldiers. The peasants had always been aware that the king had a huge army at his disposal, but they had never realized how many men that would mean. Harold and Earl Godwin rode off together, returning to their brigades.

"Finally, we will be rid of this Leofric once and for all," Harold commented.

"Your plan has proven to be more brilliant that I expected. How could this have worked out any better?" Godwin asked.

"Flattery aside, are you ready?"

"Yes, ready and anxious."

"The gods are with us. We shall have to celebrate our victory at Leofric's castle. The fair Godiva will need someone to look after her, don't you think? Perhaps the king will reward me with the spoils of war."

"Harold, you think like a true Viking. You are your father's son."

※※※※※※

Godiva led Aethenoth down the hillside path to Coventry. He ran with spirit and drive, as if he understood the importance of the ride.

Prince Harold looked down at the town, meagerly fortified with barrels of wood, bales of hay, and hearts of courage. The familiar battle lust rushed through his veins. He could almost smell the blood in the air as he poised to strike.

Leofric examined the faces of his men. Some were stern and bloodthirsty. Others were mere boys, engaging in their first real battle. He looked out at the brave faces of Coventry. People he knew, people who were willing to die today. How had things ever come to this?

※※※※※※

Godiva spurred the horse to ride faster. She blotted out everything, everything but the thought of reaching Coventry in time.

※※※※※※

Outside the city gates, three figures approached Thurman—a woman with a wild look in her eyes accompanied by two men.

"You're wandering a bit off course, aren't you?" Thurman asked as they drew near. "I don't think you want to be here right now."

The woman cackled, revealing a toothless grin. "This is Coventry, isn't it?" she asked in a thick country accent.

"This is the town resisting the tolls, is it not?" one of the men, who looked like he hadn't bathed in years, asked at the same time.

"Indeed, it is," answered Thurman.

"Well, then we're in the right place," said the third. "We're here to fight."

"All three of you?" Thurman asked. They nodded.

"Coventry thanks you. We're grateful. But go back home and save yourselves. We're outnumbered more than fifty to one. We won't ask you to lay down your lives for us."

"You're outnumbered?" the woman laughed. The men looked at each other and shook their heads. Thurman wondered what madness they were suffering from.

"We've brought friends," the woman explained, pointing to the west. Thurman followed her finger to see an endless stream of England's peasants, serfs, and commoners appearing over the horizon. They began to yell as Coventry came into sight. They poured in, cheering and shouting, armed with an eclectic collection of weapons.

"You see," the toothless woman continued, "your Lady Godiva not only spoke for Coventry but for all of England."

"Her brother, the sheriff, made sure we heard," the man said.

Thurman threw his arms around the old woman, nearly knocking her down.

"Open the walls and let them in," he shouted. "Help has come! Help has come!"

No sooner had he said it than the first wave of serfs and peasants barreled through Coventry's gates into the town square, cheering.

From up on the hill, Leofric looked down, amazed by the flow of supporters pouring into Coventry. He called out to Thorold, who could not suppress an expansive grin.

"I've never seen so many people together," he said, moved by the display in front of him.

"Canute never bargained for this," Thorold replied.

"Who are they?" Leofric asked.

"Apparently many still believe freedom is worth dying for."

Leofric clucked to his horse. "Come, let's have a closer look," he said.

❧❧❧❧❧❧

Across the fields, Canute cantered forward. He gazed upon the swelling masses, civilians bearing axes and knives. The noon deadline was fast approaching, and with these new arrivals, it looked like an actual battle might ensue. He signaled to Earl Godwin.

"What do you know of these meddlers?" the king asked irritably.

"Moths to the fire, I presume," Godwin answered.

Canute looked out at his armies and back down at the peasant masses growing in front of him. "So very many."

"You see, sire, this is why I insisted on offering my troops. Though they are many, I guarantee they'll pose no match for you," Godwin cajoled.

"Even more come," Canute said, pondering. "Something must be done."

❧❧❧❧❧❧

The people—serfs and peasants; men, women, and children—prepared to fight while Prior Aefic and his helpers were busily at work at the Cofa Tree. The timbers from the hay wagon were lashed together and hoisted up by the spinning pulleys. The men strained and labored to raise the weighty logs.

"Heave...heave...heave," the prior yelled.

The timbers rose higher and higher. Soon, everyone could see what the prior had been up to. The timbers had been made into a giant cross, and the prior was desperately trying to raise it in the center of the square, right in front of the Cofa Tree.

The pagans of Coventry saw it and stopped what they were doing. They rushed over to Aefic and his men.

"You mock our beliefs, prior! This belittles what we hold sacred," one man protested.

"Please understand, my friend, that it is not you I mock. It is my wish to save the one who rides to save us. Let Godiva ride to the cross, so that the church can find no condemnation," the prior beseeched him.

Elfwick, a Druid priest, broke into the conversation. "How do you know she will even come?"

Aefic looked over at some children who were fearfully huddled together. "In case she does," he replied.

Many of the pagans were torn. They wanted to help but could not go against Elfwick. They moved away from the Christians whose hands they had just clasped so joyfully. The noon hour was approaching. Frozen in a standoff, Aefic knew they would soon hear Canute's trumpets, signaling his attack.

THIRTY-FIVE

A t first, no one noticed her. Her face was like a rock. She leaned forward in the saddle, galloping at full speed. Aethenoth's hooves thundered beneath her as the battlefield came into view. She gripped her saddle and fearlessly emerged from the woods, riding parallel to the armies.

Then Leofric noticed something moving out of the corner of his eye. As he peered beyond the vast cloud of fighters, he could hardly believe what he saw. Once again, his wife was taking a stand on the field of battle.

"Godiva, no!" he yelled, though he knew that she could not hear him. He helplessly watched her speed to the center of the field, like an arrow to its target.

"She's going to take the ride," Thorold exclaimed, shocked. He and Leofric tore off for the Coventry gates.

It was nearly noon. Canute was poised with his sword held high, ready to release the order to attack. He would show these peasants that his word was not to be taken lightly. Suddenly, Godiva appeared, arcing directly in front of Canute. He froze.

In his wildest dreams, he hadn't imagined that Godiva would actually take the ride. His mind raced as he quickly tried to devise his next move.

Godiva stopped the horse in the center between Canute and the Coventry defense line. She caught her breath as she looked out on the people in front of her. She patted the saddlebag holding the king's decree. Godiva pulled her mother's comb out of her hair and slipped it between her saddle and the blanket. She shook loose her wild tresses, and they fell long enough to reach the line of Aethenoth's saddle, protectively draping her body. She took a deep breath, reminding herself why she had come.

With her heart pounding, she slowly untied her cape. For a moment, she held it closed around her. Then she raised her head and released it. The cape dropped ceremoniously to the ground. The townspeople gasped, and silence fell on the crowd.

Godiva sat there, not moving, and for a moment, the clouds parted and sunlight shone brightly on her bare shoulders.

Above her, King Canute agonized over what he saw. Harold approached him cautiously.

"I thought you said she would never take this ride. Do we send the soldiers to stop her?"

"Wait, Harold. I must think." Canute considered every possible course of action. "Harold, I have given my word. I have set my seal upon it. I must let this play itself out. If she completes the ride, I will stand by it."

Harold smirked, remembering another promise Canute had made long ago.

"I see, my king. Just as you kept your promise to bring Princess Élan back to England."

Canute glared at his brother.

"If our father's way has become distasteful to you, then I would be happy to do it for you," Harold offered.

The king continued to look at his brother, recognizing his uncanny resemblance to their father. He understood for the first time what he himself had become.

"There is no need, Harold. Let her punishment come from the church. Their wrath upon her shall last forever."

"I hope you know what you're doing."

Canute had had enough. "Harold, get out of my sight."

"Remember what our father taught us about weakness," Harold sneered as he moved away.

Canute suppressed his anger then looked over to Godwin.

"Surround Coventry and hold your arms," he growled.

"Yes, Your Majesty," Godwin said as he headed off.

Aethenoth's head bobbed up and down as he stomped his front hoof in the dust. Godiva sat on her mount, feeling the smooth blanket against her bare legs. She patted the horse's neck. Her faithful steed was a comfort to her—her only friend in the world at that moment. She was surprised how difficult it was for her to speak with all the eyes on her.

"Will you permit me through your streets?" she asked the townspeople. The sun was high in the noon sky.

The people answered by parting before her, making a path for her to ride. Their sincere and earnest faces gazed up at her uncertainly. She nudged Aethenoth and started her journey toward the Cofa Tree on the opposite side of town. The silent townsfolk followed behind her. All that could be heard was the sound of Aethenoth's hooves.

The skies above grew dark.

"This betrayal of her faith serves my purposes precisely. Thor and Odin's favor are ours," King Canute yelled out.

"What about the tax, Your Majesty?" Godwin asked.

"I am after something much more valuable, Lord Godwin—her disgrace," Canute said, charging toward the square.

Godiva approached the washhouse, a long shed at the entrance of the High Street. She continued toward the market square, passing the baker's, the blacksmith's, and the cobbler's.

"She frees us," an old man said, holding back tears as he reached his arthritic hand toward her.

"This is not for a Christian," a woman spat. "Hell awaits her."

Canute's forces moved in to secure Coventry's gates. Leofric and Thorold arrived at the rear of the crowd and tried to push their way through.

"Where is she?" Leofric asked, starting to panic as he tried to see over the tops of people's heads. "I've got to get to her!"

"There! On the way to the Cofa Tree," Thorold pointed. He and Leofric pushed madly through the street toward the plaza.

Godiva suddenly grew frightened. Everyone was shoving around her, moving in too tightly and bumping against her bare legs. Her thick, lustrous hair concealed her body, but she stiffly pulled her arms close to her sides and hunched her shoulders, trying to protect her modesty. The peace that she had felt earlier was rapidly evaporating.

"They're too close. They're nearly on top of me. What if they knock me from my horse," she panicked. "Help me, God!"

"Godiva, Godiva," a man yelled, touching her foot.

"My lady," a woman cried, reaching up and pulling a lock of her hair.

Alarm overcame her as she tried to hold on to the reins and finish her ride to the tree. She became fearful that she wouldn't be able to make it that far. If only everyone would step back and stop looking at her. But she couldn't find the words to ask them. Her face was flushed, and she felt as if she were going to faint. She lowered her head, and the people engulfed her all the more tightly.

She didn't know what to do. Where was God? She didn't feel His presence anymore. Had this all been a mistake? Had God abandoned her because of her pagan ride?

The crowd moved in front and began leading her onward. Godiva closed her eyes. She was dizzy, and her hands fell from the reins. Someone else picked them up and began leading Aethenoth. The horse whinnied in protest. Godiva felt the crowd swallowing her up. She feared that she might disappear.

Osburga's words again echoed back to her. "You must trust Him above all else." But trying as hard as she could, trust was so difficult to find in her heart just then.

Beside the Cofa Tree, Prior Aefic and the others strained at the ropes with all their might, but they were unable to pull the cross up without the help of the pagans. The weight was too great. A look of anguish hardened Aefic's face as he prayed and pulled. He knew Godiva was heading in his direction. He had to help her. He looked at the largely pagan crowd nearby, wondering if all his work had been in vain.

Suddenly, a man appeared from the top of the Cofa Tree, hurling a rope over one of the branches to help lift the cross and move it into place.

"Grab this rope. Let's help him. Pagan or Christian, life must be chosen above death," he cried. It was Elfwick. The Druid priest had changed his mind when he saw the armies approaching. The others immediately pitched in to help.

Together, they struggled to hoist the massive cross.

"Yes!" Prior Aefic shouted as the cross stood high above the Cofa Tree. The crowd took a collective breath as the cross wavered and then settled into place.

Prior Aefic could hardly contain his relief. "Well done, my brothers. Well done," he said, climbing down and heartily patting his comrades on the back.

〰〰〰〰〰〰

When Godiva momentarily opened her eyes, she was stunned by what she saw. A cross, a huge cross, bigger than any she had ever seen, was towering over the Cofa Tree's loftiest branch. She gasped at the sight of it, realizing the effort that had been made to sanctify her ride. The townsfolk stared in astonishment. The man who was leading Aethenoth stopped in his tracks. A rush of peace overtook Godiva and gave her the strength to carry on.

She leaned to the man in front of her.

"Please give me the reins," she said kindly but firmly. He obliged without question. She took the reins, sat up straight in the saddle, focused her eyes on the cross and continued onward. God had not forgotten her.

〰〰〰〰〰〰

King Canute was stunned by the sight of the cross suddenly towering over the revered pagan symbol.

"A Christian cross at the Cofa Tree? Why don't the pagans stop them?" Godwin barked.

Prince Harold taunted his brother angrily. "The disgrace is yours, brother. She has mocked you and the throne yet again!"

Canute looked at the skies above. They were growing black with gathering thunderclouds. Lightning flashed across the sky.

"I saw this once before with Father. He told me that the powers of heaven were at war," Canute said to himself.

Harold had grown impatient. Now, not wanting to hear any more, he became incensed.

"We have no time for this." Without waiting for the king's command, Earl Godwin raced off.

"Let's go," he yelled. The prince gave Canute a foul look as he followed after Godwin. Six Huscarles fell in behind them and they forced their way through the crowd to get to the Cofa Tree. Several people screamed out as the party arrived, fearful that a slaughter was about to begin. Prince Harold muscled his way up to the cross. He glared at Prior Aefic.

"Your strategy is laughable," he said loathsomely. Harold stretched his hands around the timbers and grabbed the corner where the ropes were secured. He slid a foot-long knife out of its sheath and wasted no time starting to cut the ropes. The prior lunged forward.

"No!"

Prince Harold was furious. He swung around, waving his sharp blade at the prior.

"Stand back, or you'll be next," he threatened. He had managed to saw halfway through the rope, and then he severed the rest in one fluid motion. Pulleys spun. The heavy ropes swung down and dropped from the beams. The cross lost its supports. Prior Aefic jumped out of the way.

"Look out," he yelled.

The townspeople scattered.

First the heavy crossbar, then the base logs crashed to the earth, breaking in pieces. Dust and debris spread in a cloud toward the crowd.

Godiva stopped the horse. Her heart seemed to break with each crash of the cross.

Earl Godwin watched with glee as her expression fell. He raced back to the king.

One of the prior's helpers looked tearfully at her leader. "What now, Father?"

Terror engulfed the crowd as they looked to Prince Harold. He scowled at them. Turning his head toward Godiva, his face broke out in a smug grin.

Canute stood at a distance, watching. Black clouds cracked louder as lightning lit the sky.

"It's the fury of God," a Christian woman from the crowd called out. "He shows His anger."

"No, no. Be quiet," the prior begged.

Godwin returned to Canute's side.

"Your honor is restored, Your Majesty," he smirked.

Canute looked into the sky as the dark clouds rolled overhead. The wind began to blow harder. Suddenly, a large bolt of lightning hit the Cofa Tree, splitting off a large branch. The tree began to smolder. Blue and white smoke filled the air.

Canute's face filled with awe and confusion. He looked up into the sky, wondering what would happen next.

"It's her! Run! The wrath of God is upon us," a peasant yelled, stirring up the crowd.

Godiva didn't know what to do. She glanced at the faces around her. She was torn. She couldn't keep going, and she couldn't go back. Her whole ride, her humiliation had been in vain. She couldn't believe she had come so far to fail.

"Father, forgive me. I don't know what to do. Do You abandon me in my time of need?"

Suddenly, a sound emerged from the crowd. It was the voice of perfect innocence. There, standing on the pile of broken timber and ropes, stood Lia from the choir, singing. All alone in front of the huge crowd, she sang without fear or hesitation, lifting her small voice in total confidence.

Let us praise, this day, the Maker of the heavenly kingdom,
Author of all miracles.
How He gave earth's children heaven for a roof,
And a world with lands such as these to live on.
Almighty Lord, we praise You.
We praise You, we praise You, we praise You.

She sang the anthem that Godiva had taught all the children of Coventry. It was the song of Sister Osburga, the song she had sung years earlier as the flames engulfed her.

Little Lia sang out with all her heart. Another voice joined in, this one deep—Wulfstan. He felt his way through the dense crowd and awkwardly emerged into the open. He steadied himself by leaning on a stranger's shoulder, then moved slowly toward Lia, carefully stepping on top of the timbers, following the sound of her voice to find his way.

Over and over they sang Sister Osburga's song. Godiva's heart swelled. She knew then that she was not alone. She slowly urged Aethenoth forward, toward the broken cross. Tears filled her eyes. She pictured Osburga singing through the flames.

Canute's face was unmoving, but his heart was thumping in his chest. He rode slowly forward.

"Shall I make them stop?" Prince Harold asked, gesturing with his sword in the direction of the little girl. Canute held his hand up. He listened intently. It had been many years, yet he knew the song as well as he knew his own name. Then he remembered that it had been in his terrifying dream of Osburga. He looked up into the sky as the light broke through the clouds.

He looked back at the girl and could not take his eyes off of her. He could hear nothing but the sound of their song.

Other children stepped forward, joining in the song that they all knew. Prior Aefic walked over and added his voice to the hymn. Gradually, fear was replaced by courage. Soon, the entire town joined in the singing.

Godiva looked up from the crowd and cast her eyes to the heavens. The dark clouds were rapidly receding. A warm light streamed in from above as if on cue, lining the path before her. In that moment, Godiva understood Osburga's faith like never before. The crowd began to move back to the edges of the path as the light shone down.

Prince Harold could take it no longer. "You must stop them," he urged Canute.

"No, Harold. I will not," King Canute answered forcefully. Once more, his gods had betrayed him.

"Can't you see that she has power over these skies?" he asked.

A gust of wind blew from behind Godiva, urging her on. As the chorus of voices grew, she found the strength to finish what she had begun. She gently nudged Aethenoth. Sitting high in the saddle, she moved steadily forward.

Leofric and Thorold watched as Godiva rode the last few feet to the fallen cross and the Cofa Tree.

Wulfstan, the children, and the crowd smiled lovingly at her. Their voices trailed off. Slowly and carefully, Godiva dismounted, placing her bare feet on the ground, her hair tumbling around her. Leofric raced through the crowd to meet her.

"Godiva!" Leofric was overwhelmed by her bravery. He removed his cloak and wrapped it around her. Godiva was no longer fearful. She stood boldly in front of the man she loved, in front of the king, in front of the world.

Canute approached her and the crowd backed away. Godiva turned to face him.

"Do I meet your conditions, Your Majesty? Will you keep your word?" She held her gaze steady. Nothing could make her afraid ever again.

"Like the nun, you have power over these skies," he said.

"It is not my power, my lord."

"Yet they open for you. From where do you summon this power?"

She paused. In that moment, Godiva realized that she had finally found the power to forgive. The man before her was no longer a monster; he was just a man, a man with great human frailties.

"Not from rings, Your Majesty," she said boldly.

"I have heard those words before," Canute said, thinking back on the nun, Osburga. "My grandfather was a great warrior. He believed in your God, and my father murdered him for it. My father was wrong." Canute struggled to say the words. "How could I ever be forgiven for all I have done?"

Godiva was moved with compassion. King Canute looked deeply into her eyes and saw his answer.

After a moment, Canute gazed out at the people with new eyes. For the first time, he saw his subjects for the people that they were; he saw their hunger, their needs, and their fears.

The weight of all the injustices he had perpetrated against innocents such as those before him now pressed heavily upon his back. Humbled, and no longer afraid of weakness, Canute then did the unthinkable. Slowly, the king lowered himself onto one knee and bowed before Godiva, before the people of England, before his own soldiers, and before God.

"It is *I* who is now naked before Him," he whispered softly.

Canute looked around and, reaching for a small splinter of Prior Aefic's fallen cross, pledged to serve the Christian

God that Godiva had revealed to him for the rest of his days.

Prince Harold was horrified. He sputtered, for once at a loss for words.

Godiva looked down on the king and saw a new man.

Canute stood up slowly. His eyes met Leofric's.

"Earl Leofric, your duty was to uphold the word of your king."

"Yes, Your Majesty."

Canute gave him a long look. "You have served me well, Leofric. Your wife is honored."

"Thank you, Your Majesty," Leofric said, bowing.

Prince Harold grabbed his brother's arm.

"Have you gone mad? Let us attack at once and end this treason. It is the power the people understand."

"You understand nothing. Leave me!" Canute said, pulling his arm angrily away.

"But, brother, you have to act!"

"I said leave me, Harold!" Canute bellowed.

"You are a fool," Harold said. "This is not the end. The council will not take this lightly. There will be war." Prince Harold pushed his way back through the crowd, shoving people out of his way.

"Godwin," the king ordered, "release your troops at once. Send them home."

Godwin stared blankly.

"Your heard me. Release them. It is finished."

The king turned to Leofric. "Set the people free."

Godiva pulled the cloak more tightly around her, finding comfort in her husband's covering. She looked up at Leofric.

"By your word, Leofric, set them free, that your heir might live in peace."

"My heir?" Leofric blinked. "What? We are going to have a child, Godiva?"

"We are, my dear," she smiled.

He stepped forward and raised his arms to those before him, grinning widely.

"As the Earl of Mercia, by the grace of King Canute, I am pleased to announced that the citizens of Coventry are hereby relieved of all taxes and tolls."

The townsfolk let up a deafening roar. Leofric leaned over to his wife.

"Kiss me." He moved his lips to meet hers.

Canute retreated and watched from a distance. He could still hear the deafening cheer as the crowd chanted, "God save Godiva! God save Leofric! God save Canute!"

Canute's face broke into an ear-to-ear smile. The people loved him. He thought of someone else who loved him—his wife, Emma. He would have a lot to tell her, a lot to make up to her. He could hardly wait to see her.

Down below, Leofric kissed Godiva again and gazed into her eyes. "Godiva, God's gift...a son?" he asked.

"Or a daughter," she smiled.

Out of the massive crowd, Godiva's eyes landed on one person. It was Sister Agnes. Her eyes were bright, and she held her head high. After years of isolation, she had finally found a reason to return to Coventry. She came over and wrapped her arms around Godiva.

"Perfect love," Godiva said into her ear as they hugged. "That which embraces forgiveness, has compassion, and is never fearful. Your words, Sister Agnes, are here, alive, today."

And so, in the year of our Lord 1027, a brave and beautiful English woman took a ride and freed the town of Coventry. In the

months to come, King Canute came to see and understand the faith of his grandfather, King Harold Bluetooth. He and Emma found a love neither had ever imagined.

Leofwine lived long enough to see his dream come true. England was at peace and King Canute, along with Godiva and Leofric, rebuilt the abbey of Godiva's youth, naming it after the great nun, Osburga. Canute turned his heart to the God of heaven and, to the end of his reign, ruled his people with justice, mercy, and love.

About the Author

David Rose

D avid Rose, former CEO of Santa Monica Studios, has been an innovator for more than 30 years. He has produced two theatrical films and developed more than 40 screenplays. VisionArt, his special effects company, created scenes for *Star Trek: The Next Generation* and *Star Trek: Voyager* and won multiple Emmys for its work on *Star Trek: Deep Space Nine*. VisionArt also created visual effects for the Academy-Award-winning movie *Independence Day*.

Rose started his career in Jerusalem, Israel, designing products for the American market. After returning to the United States, he launched a successful development business that built American castles. Later on, as he expanded into the oil and gasoline industries, he began exploring the use of computers, which led to his career as a special effects innovator and expert.

Rose's broad experience encompasses his two greatest passions in life: caring for others and creating stories. *Godiva* is his first novel.

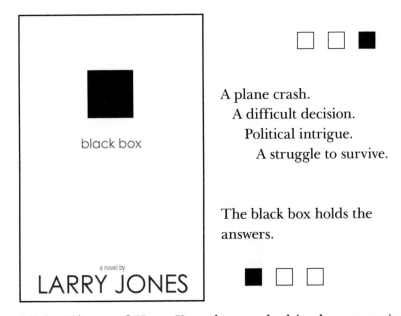

black box

a novel by
LARRY JONES

A plane crash.
A difficult decision.
Political intrigue.
A struggle to survive.

The black box holds the
answers.

Flight 027 out of Hong Kong has crashed in the mountains of central Asia. Four men and three women who, moments before, had been on a routine airplane trip suddenly find themselves stranded in a snow-covered wasteland, fighting for their lives. As the group struggles to endure, intrigue and mystery arise as some of the survivors seem bent on carrying out a hidden agenda—an agenda that centers on finding the plane's black box. Caught up in a web of deceit, the survivors must look within to find the deliverance they so desperately desire.

Black Box
a novel by
Larry Jones
ISBN: 0-88368-872-7 • Hardcover • 304 pages

W
WHITAKER
HOUSE
www.whitakerhouse.com

Nightbringer
a novel by
James Byron Huggins

An ancient evil has darkened the halls of Saint Gregory's Abbey in the Italian Alps. The once-peaceful monastery becomes a murderous battleground as a group of monks and tourists find themselves locked in combat with an unstoppable force. Cut off from the outside world by a sinister snowstorm, the abbey's defenders must fight for their survival—and for their souls. From among the defenders arises an ageless holy warrior who alone has the skill and power to stem the bloody tide of evil. In the epic battle that will decide the fate of all involved, the warrior must not only struggle against a familiar foe of mythic might, but also rediscover the faith and love that have carried him through a thousand battles.

ISBN: 0-88368-876-X • Hardcover • 304 pages

www.whitakerhouse.com